BLACK MOON

Book of the Traveler
Volume I

A Novel by
HOWARD
SCARROW

BLACK MOON

BOOK OF THE TRAVELER:
VOLUME I

A Novel
By Howard Scarrow

Courtney, Colin, and the Street Team
This one's for you

ISBN: 978-0-359-57249-6

Howard Scarrow
Sarnia, Ontario, Canada

HowardScarrow.com
Twitter.com/howardscarrow/
Facebook.com/hsauth/
Intstagram.com/howardscarrow/
Twitch.tv/PixelPerfectPlaythrough/

Edited by:
Howard Scarrow
Colin Anderson
Alex Brambilla

BLACK MOON
Book One:
The Long Night

Book Two:
The Lord of Dragons

Book Three:
Where Dragons Dwell

Book Four:
Black Moon

BOOK ONE:
THE LONG NIGHT

Black Sun

When the Moon hung in the sky, a beacon in the night for us weary travelers who didn't have a place to call home, I was only a boy. I have vague memories of that great, silver-colored coin, that broke through the otherwise black night as if to keep the sky from wanting for the Sun to return, as it did every morning, to banish the Darkness and bring back its warm and soothing Light. The Sun and the Moon were two of the only things that someone could count on to not change.

Until they did.

No one was quite sure why it had come, but a shadow crept over the lands from somewhere far off. Many of us spoke of temples being opened, or ancient words being said, that doomed us and the world into an eternity of darkness. There were legends of times before, when Darkness ruled the world. The fact of the matter was, however: none of us *truly* knew. Even those that claimed to be present for some 'event' that brought about the end of the Sunrise as we knew it were only grasping at straws, tangentially referencing events that, while common knowledge, many could not parse from the state of the world as we knew it. These people rose quickly in fame—more like infamy—until their stories were proven untrue, and they fell just as fast and hard.

That skepticism and doubt—that's just another part of the world that we can count on to never change. It will one day help keep us honest.

I was eight years old when the first sunrise was missed. That night, which we looked back on as the beginning of the Long Night, went on for twelve days before the Sun finally breached the Darkness on the Eastern horizon, bringing with it a burning light that our eyes had already begun to forget. After that, in a matter of months, the dawn only came a handful of times, the nights being longer or shorter seemingly at random, despite the best attempts of our scholars to the North to determine the cause.

By the time winter had rolled around that year—this all started in early spring—the Sun had seemingly given up on rising. The Moon had already disappeared behind the mountains to the west of my home—a small village named Littlehollow, north of Dewpond—and we truly entered the Long Night. It was during that time that some began to wonder if the Sun and Moon were not still up there, still encircling us and rising and falling as they once did, only a thick veil of Dark had been pulled over our eyes.

The absence of light brought with it a certain madness, though it remained unclear whether the people were succumbing to the Darkness, or simply driven mad to not see the Sun as they had each day since they could remember. Riots began and entire settlements were burned to the ground. People started killing one another—crimes of passion and fear more than anything else—and were shocked to find that the dead were no longer staying buried.

One of our elders, Oran, wise as he may have been in the Light, was one that had succumbed to the Dark. He grew paranoid that the people were conspiring against him. His grip on our community tightened, and we began to live in fear of who may appear at his feet, begging for forgiveness for some trite act next. Since there was no morning—and no dawn or dusk, no noon or night—there was no time where people could be considered safe. People stopped sleeping properly, as their bodies just didn't know when it was they were supposed to rest. Some people never woke up. Others never slept again.

The innocence of being a child was stripped away from me after the first onslaught by the dead. It was the same innocence that kept my internal clock somewhat attuned to the old times. I still slept for what felt like long enough and was still active during what felt like the day. I had gotten good at getting what I needed, as quickly as I needed, in order to be at my fullest.

The hardest part was for our eyes to adjust. There were only so many torches, and too many houses burned down by people that were far too reliant on the celestial light, desperately burning whatever they could in order to keep some light going. Others still doused themselves in flames, though that was one of the more uncommon ways for people to meet their ends. By the time we could begin to see our new world, it was already too late.

To the east of my home was the Necropolis, sprawling out as far as the eye could see on even the brightest days. It was situated in the center of the four points of the great cities, one for each cardinal direction on a compass. My home was just north of the Western point, Dew-pond. It was customary for all settlements—Alduin in the North, Brakas in the East, Castleford in the South, Dewpond in the West, and all the little towns and villages, names I've long since forgotten, in be-tween—to bring their dead to the center of the compass. Our collected history was buried with the bodies, without thought for the ever-ex-panding grounds needed. When I was still young, they had begun to stack the graves, instead of building them side by side. Even now I wonder if there are any still left in their caskets, and shudder at the thought.

The centralized location also spelled our downfall when the dead began to rise. They had some force driving them, of that much we were sure; they carried weapons and attacked with some sense of tac-tics. What we couldn't sure of were their motives. People saw loved ones return, though nothing seemed to remain of the person they had used to be. They were collected in their intents; united in their cause to add to their ranks. Who—or what—was guiding them to do so was the subject of much debate, until the question of why didn't seem to matter anymore. Had it just been the rising dead that we were dealing with, I'm sure things would not have fallen to chaos the way that they did. The dead, while greater in numbers than those living—and even that balance was being shifted the wrong way as the attacks came—were finite. The living were much more resilient in battle, and even as I was forced to take up a sword before I was even ten, mastering it by the time I hit puberty, I knew that it was a matter of outlasting them. If we held them back for long enough, chipping away at their numbers, we would eventually stand alone.

Then fire rained from the sky.

Our eyes had only just begun to adjust to our new world, dark as it was, when the rains came. They illuminated the horizon with an amber glow before setting aflame what structures were unfortunate enough to stand in the way of the seemingly random path of their de-struction. Many of us hid underground, in the ancient Catacombs that had long since been sitting beneath us, and waited for the storm to pass before we learned that it wasn't a storm at all.

It wasn't me that heard them first, but one of the more paranoid members of our little survivor's camp. A roar, animalistic yet still be-yond anything we had ever heard before, echoed through the tunnels that we had—thankfully—constructed years earlier, first as a run-off for the necropolis before it was repurposed for transport of bodies as well. We did not believe it at first until we all heard the cacophony from above.

Three volunteered to go topside to check. One of the women tried to hand us a torch, and Desmond, tall as he was muscular, stepped in her way. "No," he said. "We don't want to go up there carrying a beacon." In my mind, I knew he was right. Even at that age, I knew that calling attention to themselves would spell certain doom. The creature sounded large—too large—to notice three amidst the darkness.

"Won't you be blind?"

One of the surface party agreed with her sentiment, nodding enthusiastically and reaching for the torch. "Our eyes will adjust," Desmond said, putting a hand on the man's chest to push him away.

Not one of the men returned to the tunnels.

Out of fear, we remained there for what felt like weeks before we were brave enough to move our encampment just south to join the main network of tunnels beneath Dewpond. There were hollows constructed just off the four main cities that connected with several of the villages located around them, Littlehollow being one of the emergence points the served as both a remote entrance and exit to the tunnels below. Though we weren't sure of the full origin of the Catacombs—many had studied them, and found that they were in fact quite old—man had gone to work early to repurpose them for our survival. Rooms that were used only for storage over the years were quickly converted into armories and medical rooms and anything that we thought we would need.

Time began to fly as we engaged in a cyclical regimen of training, stockpiling from the isolated stores in the hollows surrounding, and otherwise just trying to make do with what we had. People began to grow weary of our situation, with several losing their minds and threatening to return to the surface. The exit to the north, Littlehollow, was the one used for those that couldn't be talked out of leaving, as many did not want to attract any unwanted attention to Dewpond, or any of the major cities—while none were talking to one another after some time. No one that left ever came back, and we thought that for the best. It only served to extend our supplies.

People did try to steal more than their fair share. Because of this, an order of guards was elected. I was chosen to protect the medical stores, though at what age I was I could not tell you. Without the passing of days into nights, and nights into days, it became incredibly difficult to measure time. Ages became something that no one ever really spoke of again. If you were ready, you were ready. I was handed a sword and some armor and was stationed outside of the door to the medical supplies. We worked on three rotating shifts.

My watch came to an abrupt end when I was disturbed from my

sleep by a sound within the storeroom. There was a small crash, followed by the distinct sound of someone cursing. I rose groggily to my feet, rubbing the sleep from my eyes. I grasped my sword and stepped to the door of the medical stores. There was one other, Penn, still asleep on the ground next to the door—at least, I thought he was asleep until I saw the puddle of blood beneath his head. I didn't know where Kat, the third guard, and whom I was meant to relieve when I was able, had run off to. I had hoped that she had left to get helped, but feared that she may have met a similar fate to Penn, and stood by the door with bated breath.

I pushed open the door slowly and peered inside. There was a small fire on the far side of the large square room that made the shadows of the boxes dance on the stone walls opposite. I quickly slid along the western wall, trying to hide amongst the shadows to cover my movement and get a better look at who was raiding our supplies, wondering if that would be the first time that I bloodied my sword; I couldn't—and still can't—help but shake my head at the notion that even in the times we were becoming accustomed to living in, it would be another person that felt my steel first.

Huddled over a broken jar on the ground, trying to pick pickled plants out from amidst the shards of glass, were two people. There was a woman there that sparked recognition in me immediately, and a man I had never seen before. I recognized the woman as Kat, the third guard assigned to the medical stores. She kept her hair shoulder-length, and she was lithe and strong. She was wearing leathers, not unlike the ones I was wearing, though they did not seem to fit her as well as they did the men. It was a point of contention for her that she had shared with me many times during our shift changes—the only time we had to talk to anyone else—so it was difficult to not take notice.

I tried to move closer, to get a better look at the man's face, but I stopped when they began to whisper to one another.

"He is probably awake," Kat said. She cursed in a language I wasn't familiar with—I could tell it was a curse based on her tone—and then stood.

"We should have killed him, too," the man said, coldly. I swallowed, thankful that they hadn't.

Kat threw her arms out, catching herself before she raised her voice. "I didn't want to kill anyone," she whispered to him. "Penn was a good man."

"He was an idiot." The man never looked up from what he was doing. "Both of us told him, did we not? 'Go back to sleep, you see nothing'? It is not our fault he refused to listen; his nobility to nothing cost him. We have reason to be here." His tone remained unchanged, and I felt myself growing angry that he drew blood down here, where we were supposed to be surviving together. I didn't know what for, and I didn't care. And while I agreed that Penn was not the brightest, or the greatest to talk to; he didn't deserve to die.

"We're going to get killed for this," Kat said. She leaned against a wall and looked across the room, where her eyes found mine. She quickly looked down at the man, and then back to me. He had not looked up from the broken jar. She mouthed something to me, I'm not sure what, and then gestured to her right (my left) before looking down at the man again. "I'm sorry I dropped it," she said to him. "Do you think it woke him up?"

She almost seemed confused as to which side she was on.

The man looked up at Kat, and I slipped behind another stack of boxes to my left. I tucked my sword against the bottom of my forearm, so the blade would be off the ground, and if I was discovered I would be able to make a quick slash before resetting my stance. In my training, I had tried to focus on silence and speed, as they seemed to be the deadliest in the dark, and I learned just how true that was. I had taken my eyes off Kat and her friend for just a second to vault over a low box when I heard him. "What are you looking at?" he asked.

I jumped out from behind the box and heard Kat yell something, though I didn't realize until later that she was pleading with me to not kill the man. It was too late—one had already died by his hands that night, and I couldn't risk becoming a casualty myself. It didn't appear that Kat was armed, and at most, the man had a dagger—it was lying on the ground next to his foot, where he could quickly grab it as he rose. I did not make a sound, or at least tried not to. I crossed the room in a flash, and as the man rose to his feet, I saw he had the dagger in his hands. He turned to where I was coming from, unawares at what was truly happening, more turning to see where Kat was looking and yelling to than anything. When he had fully turned around, I wasted no time, and quickly brought my blade across. I felt the warm splash of fresh blood hitting my face as I strode past, and the man fell forward, slamming lifelessly into the ground and creating a pool of his own blood, not unlike the scene outside the door.

"No!" she screamed, looking at him, and then screamed it again to me.

"Be happy you got to share his final moments," I said, trying to imitate the cold tone of the man even though my nerves were all but shot. "I only wish Penn's daughter was afforded the same luxury."

"You didn't have to—"

"This is not who we are," I said, wiping the man's blood from my blade. Kat had ran to him, and rolled him over to check if there was any saving him. I could see his face more clearly, and although I thought I had known everyone down in the tunnels, I did not recognize him. "We cannot afford to steal and kill from within when we don't know what's out there."

"He wasn't one of us!" she said through tears. She explained to me that he had come from the North City, Alduin, as they had run short on supplies. Kat told me that his name was Ian and that when they were children they had played together, when her family took her to Alduin on business. Through letters, they had stayed close and even spoke of marriage before the Long Night began, and Darkness descended on the world. When Ian's mother fell ill, he had come to Kat in the hopes of getting what she needed to survive. "Now, thanks to you, she will die."

"A pity that not only will she die, but two others had to die this night for nothing," I said, looking down at Ian's still bleeding throat, and then towards the door where Penn rested just on the other side.

There was a long silence as Kat quietly wept. She finally looked up at me, furrowing her brow. "Are you going to kill me now?"

I looked down at my sword, and then up at her. I shook my head and walked towards the door. I pulled it open, and poked my head outside, shouting to get someone's attention. As I did, Kat tried to push me out of the way, but her small size compared to me did not afford her the opportunity to escape. I was able to grab her shoulder and throw her to the ground behind me. I saw the flames of torches dancing on the walls of the tunnels leading to the storeroom I turned to Kat and took a breath. "You will have to put your trust in fate, now."

EMERGENCE

Kat, the woman who helped the young man, Ian, kill one of us, and try to rob our medical supplies, was the first to be so publicly banished to the surface. No one that lived below the ground wanted to become executioners, choosing to stay their hands that they might get bloody. They chose the blissful ignorance of letting the world outside do their work for them, telling themselves that she would at least have a chance at life—though we all knew deep in our hearts that it was likely untrue. She was not the last person to be sent above, and by the time I too emerged from our home, there were few who remained and even fewer who survived the subterranean war that I had unknowingly begun.

After it was discovered that someone from Alduin, the great and wise city to the North, had come to steal our supplies, and once they had learned that their man had been killed—my doing, I will admit—conflict began to stir. They sent the first group of infiltrators, sneaking out food when they could. There seemed to be a measure of spite there, as they would often try to poke holes in our security; taking what they could while avoiding conflict, damaging only our stocks. We couldn't be sure how long the Night was going to last, so the dwindling supplies sparked in us a great desperation that made us strike back.

The conflict that came from it—the "haves" versus the "have-nots"—only exasperated the situation. In corridors beneath the surface, man and woman engaged in open battle with one another, and the bodies began to pile up. Those that made it back were treated, so that they might go out and fight again. But the short-sighted nature of those that took charge during this time began to backfire almost immediately. The medical supplies quickly dissipated, and we began to look elsewhere,—Brakas to the East and Castleford to the South—for replenishments. The South was blocked from us, much as the North became. There were no guards at the heavy iron doors barring entry to the South, and our requests for communication were met with only silence. The East, on the other hand, was as wealthy in the Dark times as they were when the sun still hung in the sky. Their coffers were full to the brim, but they were not fighters; only priests and drunkards. Our people—I was not with them when it happened—did not like to be turned away, and the taste of the fight had already infected them; they began an attack on the peaceful survivors of Brakas, east of the Necropolis.

It was shortly after I learned about the massacre that took place that I made my decision to leave—though it was in a roundabout way. There was a madness that was spreading amongst my peers that I had only seen during the early days of the Darkness. Years on, I had learned to fear that kind of madness. Many of the people I knew changed right before my eyes, and while they claimed they only had the greater good in mind, I knew that it was their survival instinct kicking in. They didn't see the people on the other end of their blades as people; they saw them as faceless enemies, standing between them and the rest of their lives. Like a cat, thrown into desperate fits when he can see the bottom of his food bowl, the people I had thought I was protecting became paranoid and desperate; a dangerous combination to say the least.

When the party that headed east returned, all smiles, and told us what they had done, I had to see it for myself. I had been taken off guard duty shortly after the encounter with Kat and her friend from the Northern City of Alduin. I was given something more of a patrol, and the autonomy to do what was necessary to keep the peace. I was not the first to spill blood underground, but I was the first to do it in order to stop an outsider—although I was beginning to silently question the term 'outsider' as it felt as though such separation was ill afforded by man in those times. I tried to keep my thoughts about the growing conflict underground to myself, but it was becoming more and more difficult to keep from feeling as though I was in more danger underground than I was above. It was only a matter of time before we began to turn on each other, and I was beginning to fear that any words warning as such would only fall on deaf ears.

I took up my sword, and while the guards to the Eastern passage were asleep, I snuck past them. The tunnels ran through the Necropolis, and I had made sure to speak to a member of the returning party—the least excited one, who we called Rat—to calm my fears that the dead would have broken through the walls and infested the passageways. He assured me that, although they did encounter a few "deadheads" as he called them, the trip was mostly without resistance. It took all I had to speak to him with an even keel, still before seeing the damage that he and his friends had caused. Even still, considering I was making the journey alone, I took the necessary precautions. My hopes were that there were no survivors left, as I didn't want to have to defend myself. If there were, I had hoped my tongue would save me from having to use my sword.

The path through the Necropolis was winding, weaving between the deep graves that had been dug there. The sounds of water dripping somewhere in the distance never seemed to get louder or quieter as I walked, and the stone walls had a sheen to them from that made them look as slimy as they felt to the touch. The sense of dread I felt was expected, which made it easier to compartmentalize; but that didn't mean my mind was at ease. I was quickly learning to filter the paranoia, condense it into a waking resolve that kept me alert and ready for anything. For all I knew, the Undead could have been waiting around any corner, ready to pounce. Not to mention the people of Brakas, to the East—if Rat and his friends had done what they claimed, any survivors would likely be mobilizing to strike. Being one man, I would be able to hide from them, but I wouldn't be able to warn those at home. Then again, I wasn't sure that I would want to, after seeing what they were becoming.

I hadn't seen any since the final days on the surface, but I had heard stories from some of our search parties that encountered them. They told us that the decaying corpses of our ancestors, loved ones, and acquaintances, while frail, were highly skilled and carried weapons. Many were also attired in armor, bearing the symbol of the four cities: a diamond with a cross through it. Others still rose in the clothes that they were buried in, now only rags, carrying daggers and knives that they found as they wandered towards their prey. They seemed as though they were being controlled; guided by an unseen force that told them how to swing most effectively. Many had died in open combat with them, though one-on-one they were easily dispatched. The problem with the dead is that, as time rolls on, there are more of them than there are living people left. It became a unified hope that, should you find yourself surrounded by them, that you lose your head—you can't come back if you don't have a head.

That journey, heading towards Brakas, was absent of any of the Undead. I breathed a sigh of relief when I reached the manufactured end of the Necropolis, staring down the heavy iron door that lead to the Eastern Catacombs. I took a deep breath, and grabbed the handle of the door. I was unable to see what was on the other side, and could only quietly hope that there was nobody waiting to attack me. I tapped on the door, and pressed my ear against the metal, listening for anyone to react to the noise, but there was nothing. It didn't mean there wasn't anybody there; just that if there was, they were smarter than that. I pictured a line of them, wielding spears, ready to make me a pincushion as soon as I stepped through the doorway.

I pushed the thought from my mind, and pulled the door open. It gave with a screech, as the moisture in the air had caused the whole area to swell, and the iron scraped across the stone floor. I had to grit my teeth, and tried my best to lift the heavy door to eliminate the sound, but there was nothing I could do. I tried to avoid wincing—it was truly an awful sound—and kept my eyes on the darkness beyond the precipice. To my relief, I saw nothing. There was no movement of pikes, no whispering of orders, and more importantly, there was not a single soul waiting to take my life.

Instead, I was greeted with a smell. I couldn't quite place it, but it smelled hot, fresh, and almost made me gag. Once I stepped through, and began to explore the catacombs, I saw what it was.

Bodies littered the winding tunnels, scattered about with twisted and pained expressions on their faces. Many bore slashes and stab wounds, and some had limbs severed. Blood splattered up and down the walls, and I knew that the smell was the collective of fresh death that I stood amongst. I examined my surroundings, and once again almost became sick to my stomach. Not because of the macabre and viscera that almost seemed to be collecting at my feet; rather it was the realization the few, if any, of these people were armed. In fact, most of them were facing the door that I had entered through, and I knew almost at once that they weren't fighting. They were trying to flee.

I cursed Rat and his friends for the sickening sight, and that disdain only rose as I ventured deeper into the dark tunnels. I saw the fruits of their labor, and although I didn't find any at the time, I knew in my heart that few would have remained if they did survive the assault. Even more, I found that Rat and his friends must have located the Brakas stash, and raided it, as the stores were empty. Only they didn't return with anything, which meant they were hoarding it for themselves.

I began to teem with anger. They began to represent everything I hated about humans and their selfish desires, and I wondered quietly if I would have allowed it if I was with them. From their perspective, it was a way to guarantee their survival long beyond ours. At the same time, was it not condemning us to continue down this desperate path? Would that not eventually fall back on them, especially when someone else decided to do as I did, and head to Brakas? And what's to say someone wouldn't seek them out, and their hidden stash, when our own supplies began to dwindle, as they already had? I tried to consider the possibility that someone from Alduin had made it here, but I dismissed it. Their focus seemed to have been on us, and they fought like a people that were on the brink of starvation; if they had secured the Brakas supplies, I doubt they would have nearly wiped themselves out coming after us.

I saw red. The collected weight on my soul and mind of the sight of the bodies lining the floor, like a morbid carpet of flesh, thicker in some parts than other, was almost too much for me to bear. I didn't know if I wanted to get sick or get vengeance for these people; these people that I did not and could not know, as they were no longer there. Just their shells; their vessels remained. And in my rage, I saw only the face of the men who had returned from Brakas.

Upon my return, I made a decision that would ultimately lead to me living amongst the ruins, and the things that inhabited them now, above ground. While they slept, I plunged the blade of a dagger that I had found in Brakas, next to one of the bodies, into the necks of each and every man that ventured east, and then promptly turned myself in. I did not try to plead innocence—I knew what I did was a crime—but I did provide an impassioned plea to those that were left to let the bloodshed end there. The human race could not survive against what was above if they continued to kill each other below. I was met with silence and downturned eyes, and was sentenced to walk the surface of the Earth until my dying days.

When I returned to the catacombs, much later, I found that I had outlived each and every one of them.

The Weight of the World

When I first breathed the surface air, after so many years underground, it was thick and almost stifling. There were few trees still around, at least to the West where I was, having been burned by the fires all those years ago. Still, there was a purity to the air, unburdened and undrawn by the whole of the human race for two decades, at least. It was the first, and possibly only comfort that I was able to find upon my emergence.

It wasn't completely dark above ground, especially once your eyes could naturally adjust to the changes. There was ambient light—not much, but still some—that seemed to come from various corners. Fires were burning far off, though the thought of survivors above ground seemed strange to me, it wasn't unreasonable—I had to hope that, otherwise I would just be resolved to death upon emerging. I couldn't see any directly at first, but the possibility of finding other people was mildly exciting to me. Although, after what I had seen people do down below, the excitement didn't last long, dissipating into distrust almost as quickly as it came; distrust for people I hadn't met, and couldn't even be sure were still alive.

There were also the Wisps.

When I first saw them, they were at a distance. I had only heard vague stories of them, restless spirits of the dead stuck here for one reason or another. It was alarming at first, to see the dancing blue lights in the distance, darting between the ruins of the city I used to call home. Some of them moved quickly, as if yanked by invisible strings, jerking this way and that unpredictably while others barely moved at all, lazing around listlessly as I watched with a furrowed brow, amazed and confused at the same time. There was a sentience to them that made me think they could have been insects, the likes of which I had never seen before, evolving to live in this new dark world; which to me seemed far more believable than the stories.

In the years before the dark, the children told almost as many stories as the adults did. One that seemed to run between them was the weight of purpose on one's soul. We are all driven by a desire to do, we're just not sure what it is that we are supposed to be doing. The assault from the Undead, and the fires raining down from the sky, and who knows what else had happened since my people and I had retreated to the underground: it ended a lot of lives very abruptly. When lives are taken that quickly, I had heard growing up, they can stick to this world; cursed to wander searching for the purpose that had eluded them in their life. The notion that they simply hoped that it may present itself in death was, in my eyes, almost as sad as the death itself.

Because of the Wisps, and their ambient glow, my eyes began to adjust easier to the brighter corners. It wasn't long before I could see what was left of my home. The embers had all gone out, and the smoke had cleared, and all that was left was the stone monuments to buildings that once stood, devastated by percussive blasts and flame. It was more than an army of the dead could do, and far more coordinated than an eruption of the Volcano to the far north, which had been dormant for as long as we had been around; those things which had driven us beneath the ground in the first place. There were a few bodies, decomposing to the point of almost being nothing but skeletons, with skulls cleft and hewed to the point that there was little chance of them returning, littering the main road that ran north to south through the entirety of Littlehollow, encased by the husks of homes that once stood, proud of their imperfections. Now, they were shells of their former selves, and I couldn't even be sure that any of the people who had lived in them were still among the living.

I gripped my sword tightly. I didn't trust all of the bodies on the ground, especially those with weapons next to them. Some of the men that trained me to fight had joked with me that the undead were the absolute best at playing dead. It was funny in that humbling way that reminds you that laughter is sometimes the only way you have to deal with some things, especially those beyond your reason or comprehension. When it came to the dead, we had neither. Wit was our only armor against the things we couldn't see—both in the dark, and in the mysterious fog that surrounded all that had led to our fleeing the surface—and even then, the cracks were beginning to show long before I had finished learning to take up arms.

I cursed to myself, feeling the grip of the sword in my hand. I had not seen the Undead up close since the attack, when I was but a child. Now that I had grown considerably, I was not afraid to fight.

No, I cursed to myself because of my choice of weapon.

In the darkness ahead, I could just make out the corner of a taller two-story home. Its frame mostly stood, although the roof had collapsed on the side closest to where I stood. The heavy stone walls, however, made for a perfect hiding spot. As I walked towards it, I couldn't help but imagine the ambush coming from around the side. One or two of them, taking me by surprise, would be the end of me. My eyes, while finding their way, were still not quite adjusted to the dark. My sword was still very much sheathed, and depending on how quickly they descended on me, it could very well have stayed that way. It was not an outside possibility that the dead could come in many forms—I vaguely recalled seeing more skeletal forms as I was fleeing, all those years ago—and a sword would only be good so long as flesh was exposed. The Undead that were more skeletal and more armored would ill be affected by anything but a true and well-aimed sword strike. A blunt weapon, I thought, would prove much more useful against an armored foe.

I began to search the corpses on the road for something better. I wasn't sure what all I would encounter here—the world was quite different from the one that I left, though I was having trouble remembering much of it as I had spent more time under the ground than above it—and I wanted to be prepared. Prepared, at least, for the things that I could be.

After nearly half an hour of kneeling next to corpses, almost blindly patting around until my hand found something of interest, I saw the glow of a Wisp just a few yards away, drawing a beautiful blue halo above one of the fresher corpses I had seen. Next to the right arm of the woman, who was lying on her side in a pool of her own blood, her face locked in a twisted expression of pain and anger beneath a crushed dome, a crimson mess exploding out from the top of her head as though it were stepped on, was a heavy iron mace. The blue light of the Wisp danced off the iron in a way that made it seem like a beacon, calling out to me. I quickly rose to my feet and dashed over to the corpse, and dropped to my knees. I picked up the mace, appreciating the weight of the weapon in my hands, and the light began to dim. I turned to see the Wisp dissolve into the air like dust, and my confusion returned again—though I was happy that I could see less of the gruesome death that had befallen the woman before me.

The mace felt perfect. Its handle was wrapped in leather, just enough for me to get both hands around it comfortably, though the weight of the weapon was such that I could easily use it with one hand, freeing up the other for a shield. The iron shaft ran up from the handle into a thick club, carefully forged with short but sharp fins of metal protruding from the heavy concentration of metal at the end. It was heavy enough to break bones on its own, I could feel that just by holding it; the blades just added insult to injury, allowing the wielder to rend flesh as well, and even possibly pierce through lighter armors.

I turned back and thanked the air where the Wisp had been. I wasn't sure that there was any truth to the stories I had been told, but I couldn't help but feel like I had been aided by something more than coincidence. It had been formless, just blue light concentrating into something resembling an orb, though it seemed to shift organically as it moved as though someone were waving a bright blue torch.

That calm did not last long.

Rustling; I heard it, just up the street. The sound of feet dragging in the dirt, loose armor trying to find a stable home on weak shoulders, and a weapon scraping along the stone path all came to me at once. I opened my eyes wide, to try and see as far as I could. At the edge of my vision, I saw it: an undead soldier. He was wearing armor that, I was sure, must have fit him in life—though he was but a gaunt and sickly version of what he must have looked when he was alive. He looked to be a soldier, or at least a guard from the looks of things— they were often buried in their armors, especially if they had fallen in battle—but I couldn't tell. What remained of his skin was grey, and clinging to the bone as if by nothing but a few points. The muscles had all gone. His arms were hanging at his sides, one bony hand holding a short sword, whose blade was drawing a line on the stone the Undead walked on. Both arms were thin as sticks, though not quite as brittle. It shuffled, almost shambling towards me, and I hoped there was no one else to hear the sound of the sword tip dragging along the ground. Had he just been standing there the whole time, waiting for someone to arrive?

When I knew it had seen me, there was a sound the likes of which I don't think I will ever be able to accurately describe. It sent a chill through my entire body, causing me to freeze as soon as it hit my ears, my blood growing still in my veins. I was stuck in that trance for just long enough to be hit by a second one when the soldier's body began to emit an orange glow, growing in intensity to much the same as his scream did. The light given off by this new glow revealed more of the ruined city behind it, and the three additional Undead soldiers that were lying in wait.

And as soon as the new soldiers took notice of me, they began to give off that knowing glow as well, and the streets were lit as if by many fires.

Instinctually, I felt my right hand tighten around the mace. I gripped it with my left hand as well, and rose to my feet, holding it out in front of me. The dead man was coming for me, and picking up speed. I tried to shake off the piercing of the noise it was making—the others had begun to make a similar noise, though it was weaker at a distance—and I realized that there was only one way to truly quiet it. I broke into a dash to meet my foe, holding the mace down by my side. Using momentum, I swung the mace across, putting enough force behind the swing that a strained grunt escaped from behind my clenched teeth, and I felt the vibration run through the club, up both of my arms, before finally dissipating when it reached my shoulders. I followed through on the unfamiliar weight of the mace until the mace head rung off the stone below and I picked it up and readied myself once more.

I had cleaved the monster clean in half with my strike, the mace tearing through the midsection just below where the steel curais had stopped. I noticed, as the upper half crawled towards me that most, if not all, of the man's abdomen had wasted away during his years buried in the Necropolis. I had swung through his spine, the only thing still keeping him whole. I watched in awe as the half-man tried just as hard to attack me, driven to purpose even in the disassembled state he was in. I brought my boot down on his head, and he ceased to move, scream, and glow.

I looked up the street at the others, the one closest to me moving quickly in my direction. I once again tested the weight of the mace in my hands, getting a feel for it and how it swung, and began to feel almost immediately comfortable with the new weapon—I just needed to practice.

So I did.

When the fight was over, and darkness had returned in the absence of the sentries' glow, I felt winded. I looked for a place to sit down, and saw an old fire pit that had been erected on one of the paths leading east, out of the town. I thought about lighting it, but knew that fire would only serve as a beacon for whatever else may be lurking in the darkness. I had wandered from where I fought the four Undead, hoping that even their light would not have attracted anything more. Instead, I sat, and imagined a fire. I imagined the warmth that it would bring. I looked up, and pictured the stars in the sky, and the faded glow of the moon. I imagined the world as it used to look, and for the first time felt wistful. We had taken the Sun—taken light—for granted. I never did appreciate the way things were, before the Darkness came; I didn't have time! I was only a boy, with no realization of just what the world could have been. Robbed from me was more than just my youth, but also possibility. No one knew prosperity in the new world; I had seen what attempts at prosperity earn you below. We had returned to our basest form: survivors. It was up to instinct to guide us through now, more than ever.

Worse still, as I sat by that phantom fire, reflecting on my life to that point, I realized something: I was alone. I had returned to a world that no longer wanted me, and I had done it alone, and I would continue to walk it alone until my dying day. I began to wonder how long I would be waiting. I began to wonder if maybe I should allow myself to join the legions of the dead. Or perhaps I would become a Wisp, helping a lost traveler like myself?

"Traveler"—I liked that word. Maybe that's what I would be in this new world; I could make my way east, and see for myself what hell had become of the surface in the absence of the light. Or I could head south, to see the Castle and cliffs I had heard so much about— such legends—or perhaps the Academy to the north, where all of the elders learned the lore of Alghast but none of the lessons that the stories carried with them.

But my thoughts, just as they had begun to turn pleasant or even slightly optimistic, were answered by some sort of divine justice. In the distance, I heard the familiar roar of a beast.

The same roar we heard when the fires rained down.

I peered behind me, a chill running up and down my spine. I gripped the mace tightly in my left hand, though the club was still resting on the ground. With my right, I grabbed for my sword. Something in me told me I would be needing both of them to face whatever it was that made that sound.

Over the center of the village, along the main road where I had fought the dead, I watched as a large black shadow swooped overhead. It brought with it a wind that made a percussive slap as it hit what still stood of the buildings lining either side of the road, dust and dirt sent flying in quick clouds, disturbed from where they had rested for so very long. At least one house collapsed under the weight of the gust and even at my distance, I could have sworn that I felt it, passing through me and threatening, even so far away, to knock me off balance.

I followed the shape as it soared back up into the sky, where it was lost amidst the darkness; but only for a second before I heard the sound again. It was the roar of the beast, I was sure. Whatever we had heard before, I knew then without a shadow of a doubt that the beast I saw had made the sound. In the darkness, I heard another noise: two great wings, flapping with great strength. The thing was hovering above the town somewhere in the dark, scanning for whatever had disturbed the otherwise silent night—or was it day? I couldn't be sure.

Suddenly, and brilliantly, there was light again, vibrant and blossoming out from the end of the monster's snout, as it drew in air and began to churn it into fire. I watched in awe as the jet black scales lining the long, horse-like head of the beast reflected the light of the fire back at me, and I began to see more of its massive shape. Its neck was long, with spines running along the back of it, jutting out like small black daggers. The wings spread out wide, thin but powerful looking. Its haunches were thick and muscular, and its tail, much like the rest of it, was long and lithe, but almost looked bladed like an axe at the end. It was a shocking sight that I will never forget, even though it only lasted for a moment. And for the quickest second in that even quicker moment, I thought I saw a man, or some facsimile, riding on the back of the dragon.

And just like that, the light was on the move, leaving the dragon's mouth and traveling down to the main road of my former home, the last remnants of the village of Littlehollow. I watched in horror as the fireball came in on an angle, and connected with the ground with a liquid-like splash. I thought it would stop, but the flames danced down the road for what seemed like fifty yards before it finally ceased. Everything burned, and our last day above ground suddenly made more sense.

All at once, I knew why the dragon had come. In a world so dark, any light could be seen as a beacon, calling out to the things that have likely grown weary of the silence that the Long Night brought. While the wisps might not have been anything new, I was sure that my encounters with the dead, and their strange orange-red glow, might have drawn the attention of the beast.

Where was it hiding? I thought to myself, suddenly grateful to myself for not lighting the fire I sat at. *And how long was it waiting there?*

Beast of Legend

I should say here and now that, as I write this, I am burdened by knowledge. Knowledge that I could not have known or even thought possible at the time of which I write.

You see, I have learned a great many things on my travels. I have improved as a swordsman and warrior. I have been afforded the gift to see in the dark as though the light had never left, and even further to see the world as it truly was. I have even learned to use some of the arcane arts that were only whispered about where I grew up. And all of these things I have learned I took at face value and individually, choosing not to look at how each and every step I took set forth a path —a quest that I did not, and would not realize I had undertaken for quite some time. I learned a great many things, but none of which were more important than the why.

I needed to know why the light went out from our world.

It is the sole reason why this reflection is even necessary, as the knowledge has been more of a curse than a blessing. I know now where the light had gone, and I would soon—but not soon enough—know how to restore it; though I would also be sure that there was a cost, as with most things, for restoring the world as we once knew it.

Enough time has passed that those of us who remember the world as it was are largely outnumbered by those that have known nothing different—whether they were too young, or just not born until after darkness became the standard—or by those that thrived in the new world, whether it be the army of the dead or the dragons or any of the other beasts I had yet to encounter on my journey. Our history was buried in the Necropolis, and stored in the libraries to North and the West—Alduin and Dewpond, respectively—though, one served more as a home for legend, the other for proper lore.

After I saw the dragon, I decided to head south from Littlehollow to Dewpond, the Westernmost of the four great cities, and where I had descended first into the Catacombs. Most, if not all, of my young life was spent below the streets of Dewpond. Although I had never thought too much about my time there. When I was exiled, they sent me out the same way that we always used, to the north of the city, and the dragon only helped me to understand that choice. After making the trek to the city on the surface, however; I very quickly wished that they had let me out there.

The journey there, while short in theory, was set upon by the Undead. They seemed to travel mostly in small groupings, never more than three or four at a time. Most of them were soldiers of the four cities, wearing the four-pointed crest on the chest of their armor, still visible through the years of dirty and soil that had built up on them. I was able to strike them down with ease, thanks to the mace; though I had tried my best to avoid them at all costs. I was worried that the glowing aura, a reaction for when they saw me as far as I could tell, had alerted the dragon I had seen rain fire earlier, and didn't want to chance it still being around.

When I reached the top of the hill that separated Dewpond from the villages north, I was able to discern why it may have been worse to emerge there than the small village of Littlehollow where I hailed from. Dewpond was, being one of the Pillar Cities of Alghast, very large, both outwards and upwards. I had memories of buildings reaching up high to the skies, so high that if you stood at the base of them, you couldn't quite see the top without hurting your neck. And in the center of town stood the Library—complete with the massive black Spire that reached to the sky, and possibly beyond, it was so hard to see the end of it the way it tapered into a point; it seemed like it could go on forever. It was a beautiful landscape that I took in many a times on the very hill where I stood, and I was always happy that fate and fortune had birthed me there, instead of one of the other cities that made up Alghast, although in my short time above ground I had scarcely known of them, save for stories I heard *after* the Long Night began.

But now, in the world of darkness, Dewpond was figuratively and literally a shadow of its former self. The impressive buildings, the ones that still somewhat stood, were hollow and disheveled; it was a marvel they were even still standing with how little foundation remained beneath them. Even in the dark I could see the scorch marks of the fire and explosions that had rained down—the very same ones that drove us underground in the first place. I could see, from a distance, the familiar and increasingly comforting glow of the Wisps, and shadows cast by the glow. The city wasn't infested with the Undead that I could see—which wasn't much—but I knew that there would be resistance once I entered the city proper.

It was then that I truly realized that the fiery rains that had taken the surface from us were not acts of vengeful Gods or some prophecy or anything like that; it had been dragons, hidden from us for how long, that returned with one singular purpose: nothing would live but them. Did that mean that Undead were in league with the dragons? I couldn't know, and it was just one of the questions that would begin to pile up, driving me and my quest to its bitter end.

Somewhere deep in the city, another light caught my eye. After staring for some time, I was able to make out the glow of a fire. At first I thought maybe it was one of the Undead soldiers, alarmed by something and giving off that eerie glow that they had in Littlehollow when I emerged; but it was too big, and it wasn't moving, save for the dancing shadows of the flickering flame. I watched it for a moment just to make sure, and then turned my eyes to the blackened sky, straining to see if it had attracted anything.

I saw nothing and I heard nothing above.

I wondered how long the fire had been burning without drawing attention, and started to wonder if it *would* even draw attention. I could see it from where I stood on the hill, but it looked like the glow was aimed mostly upwards, through the gutted shell of a building. It was possible that it dissipated nicely before breaching the upper sides of the walls, so those on the grounds wouldn't be able to see it. And unless the Dragon Rider, whoever it may have been, was flying overhead, I doubt it would be seen by anything but chance for miles. Or, worse still, I thought that maybe the fire was the Dragon Rider himself, taking a break from burning what had already been burnt, and killing what had already been killed.

I pictured him, sitting in front of the fire. His armor was black and sheen, reflecting the light in such a way that should the sun ever return to its former glory, it would be blinding just to stand in his presence. It reminded me of the dragon's scales, as I had seen them illuminated by the fire brewing in its maw. I saw him with a mask shaped to honor the form of the dragons, sharp teeth and protruding jaws encircling a hardened face, complete with scars and a default brood. And then I saw myself sneaking up on him with my blade ready to take vengeance for driving us underground—and for all I knew, stealing our light—before he spun, piercing my abdomen with his spear.

Then I snapped out of it.

I realized that even though I had seen a silhouette, I had not been able to make out any details. I couldn't even be sure that the rider was wearing armor—or even a man. It was just a picture I was piecing to-gether from storybooks I had read as a child, images of some fantasti-cal character that the hero must strike down, and I knew it wasn't helping. The weight of the situation was starting to descend upon me, and in my loneliness, I found that it was difficult to keep my mind from wandering. I had to focus on something. I needed a task and I reminded myself that procuring supplies for the long journey ahead—which is what I referred to my newfound quest for survival as—would be that goal for the time being.

But first, I wanted to check out that fire.

I moved down the hill, and through the edge of the city. There were some houses scattered about, a light residential district with some rural flairs; the outermost homes were complete with what used to be limited farmland. People tended to favor locally grown crops, even though the limited space had caused them to catch a fair bit more gold at market than stuff grown just to the North and South. Now, very little of the houses still stood, and the fields were forever scarred by fire. Though I did follow a Wisp into what remained of one of the homes, and found a footlocker containing some gauntlets that ap-peared to be used for smithing. I had not been sent above with much, just a worn brown leather tunic over a grey cotton shirt, some stan-dard trousers, as well as the boots and gloves that I had been wearing for years. I put the smithing gauntlets on, and started to feel a little better. They were worn, but they would be able to offer more protec-tion than nothing. I was about to search the rest of the house when I noticed the Wisp was gone. I searched anyway, but found nothing. It was curious to me, how they had been and would continue to help me find items useful in my quest, whether it was pieces of armor or food and medical supplies; they seemed invested in me staying alive—though if they were the lost spirits of people, they were probably just to know that anyone survived. There's a purity to the soul, after death, that I began to respect. Without a body to protect, suddenly these spir-its could look outwards.

As I ventured deeper into the city, trying to keep the direction of the fire in mind, I did my best to remain hidden in shadows. There were quite a few of the dead that I was able to sneak up behind, strik-ing hard and fast with my mace to try and put them down before they spotted me. They reacted to sound, but slowly; if any where in earshot when I struck with my mace, I was able to get to them before they dis-covered me, difficult as that was. I was hiding in shadows behind what was left of a shop—a bakery, I gathered—getting ready to strike, when one of them turned to face me. I had thought I was concealed, but the familiar glow began to emerge, and I saw its jaw beginning to drop to emit that awful noise that would only serve to alert others— and possibly something worse—to my presence. I moved quickly to silence it, but it was too close for my comfort. I began to wonder if they were gifted with perfect night-vision, and realized the disadvantage that put me at. I would have to be careful, somehow, to avoid being seen at all.

The fire had been in the foyer of the Library, situated in the center square of the town. I knew this before even entering the building because, much to my amazement, there were signs of it visible from behind the great stained-glass windows that stood nearly fifteen feet high on either side of the heavy double doors, marking the entrance. It almost filled the small courtyard in front of the building with light, and as I reached the edge on the other side, I stopped. I sat deep on my haunches, burying myself as much as I could in the darkness while I surveyed the area. The roof of the tall front section of the building had been torn away, though the rear of the building which housed that massive Spire seemed to be intact. The visibility of the fire, even from the ground, was beyond concerning; I opened my ears and listened for the flapping of wings as I looked on.

The courtyard was wide, but the buildings surrounding it closed in on it, making it feel contained and claustrophobic. There was a fountain in the middle, largely untouched by the destruction, though it had ceased to work long ago. There was still some murky water in the basin. I was able to spot at least one corpse floating face down in the shallow pool, bloated and sickly, something from it was dirtying the water around it, though the filth had spread a fair distance, like a nasty halo around the body. There was a stone path circling the fountain, stretching out ten or so feet all around for ample foot traffic, with stone benches littering the circumference of the circle. Behind them was a small circular garden, bushes and the like, though they had all withered and died. It was amazing to me how little of the courtyard seemed to be hit by the dragon's breath or even the battles before, but it filled me with a comfort to know that not all of the old world had died completely. I recalled the throngs of people that would spend summer days in that courtyard, watching the fountain or reading a book.

Did I remember that? Had I even *seen* that? It seemed like another lifetime ago; a different person and a different story, lighter than the only one I knew—the only *world* I knew.

That comfort quickly vanished when I returned my gaze to the ever-present glow coming from the library windows. I scanned the edge of the courtyard for movement, but saw nothing. I was perplexed how the sight and sound of the dead was able draw the Rider to me before, but this beacon seemed to draw no one. Suddenly, my vision of it being the Rider himself seemed all too possible, and I thought about turning back.

Unfortunate as it may have been at the time, curiosity got the better of me, and I took a step from my hiding spot and into the courtyard proper. In both hands, I held the mace tightly, but I was ready to grab for my sword if I needed it. Something about it felt like an ambush waiting to happen, so I tried to stick to the outside of the yard, sneaking amongst the skeletons of bushes and shrubbery. I began to attempt to balance my attention, shifting my eyes from the truly dark spots to my right, to the brightly lit and open area to my left.

The doors were almost within reach—just a few strides to go—when I heard a sound inside the library, just behind the large doors, adorned with Four Points of Alghast. There was a hushed voice, dripping with urgency but also mindful to not be heard. I tilted my head to the side as I pulled out one detail I had not been expecting: it sounded like a woman's voice. If it was the Rider, I could only surmise that she was issuing orders to the dragon—though it would be hard to imagine the beast being able to fit comfortably into the foyer. I was about to make one final rush to the doors when a loud bang erupted from within the library, and the sound of something heavy scaling the interior wall drew my attention upwards.

The open ceiling, blown away by collateral damage more than anything—considering the pristine nature of the lower two-thirds of the Library—had torn away some of the upper wall when it was destroyed. Some twenty-five feet up, the glow of the fire was briefly interrupted by the shape of something large as it breached one of the sections of wall that had been torn away. Before I could fully piece together what it might look like, the shape dropped down the front of the building, landing before the doors with a loud crash, cracking and concaving the stones beneath it.

It stood from the landing, and I could finally see it, backlit by the windows of the library: it stood about as tall as the windows, fifteen feet if it was standing upright, with broad shoulders, about as wide as I was tall. It was muscular, with two long arms that almost scraped the ground as it stood, though its knees were slightly bent as well as its back, the thing hunching forward as though the impressive upper body was too much for the rest of it to handle. Its skin seemed to be covered with scales that were a deep blue in color, though tightly weaved to the point that one might be forgiven for not noticing that they were scales; worse, they seemed to jut out at the shoulders, like spiked shoulder guards. Its face was human-like, with two eyes and a wide mouth; though it seemed to be missing a nose. Its ears were pointed at the tops and bottoms, like sharp butterfly wings, but were pulled tight against its skull. Four fangs—two on top, two on bottom—stuck out from behind thick, dark blue lips a few inches in either direction. Its jaw was square and strong, and when it finally saw me, I watched in horror as it almost seemed to detach from the joints as it opened its mouth to scream. The skin on its cheeks separated with a disgusting wet sound as the mouth tripled in size to facilitate the coming battle cry, and I began to worry that it might be able to swallow a smaller man whole.

I tightened my grip on the mace, and looked up to face the beast. I was sure that it was a Dawnflayer, though until that point I had always been skeptical that they existed. Growing up beneath the surface, there were many stories about the monsters that roamed our world once the light had gone; beasts and demons of the old times suddenly became popular again, and legends were given new life as our imaginations had no choice but to run wild. And now, one of those fabled creatures was standing before me, in all its apparent glory, ready to gobble me up.

I thought about running but I knew I wouldn't get far. I stood, unmoving—though the shakes were hard to subdue—and faced the Dawnflayer, meeting its eyes. It held its arms out to the side, as they were its primary weapons, and I saw its muscles tense, rippling out from chest to wrist like a wave through the scales. There was a brief moment of silence between us before it started to come towards me, taking huge, lumbering steps. He swiped at me with a right, and in my surprise and shock, I was just shy of being too late to dodge the swing, rolling under the massive arm. I felt the air break above me as I dodged and thought about what would have happened if it had connected. I was sure that there was enough force to crush every bone in my body, and possibly even send me soaring back to Littlehollow.

When I found my footing, I saw that the momentum of the swing had not quite run its course, and the Dawnflayer was turned away from me, albeit slightly. I ran up to it and swung, connecting hard with the inside of its right thigh, just above the knee. The leg gave slightly as mere drops of blood seemed to shoot out from where I hit, and the Dawnflayer let out a yelp more of surprise than pain. It swung its arm back, with a fraction of the force of the attack before, but it was still enough to send me flying.

I landed hard on my back, some ways away, and pushed myself to my feet, ignoring the pain that rippled throughout my entire body, willing it to the level of a throbbing that seemed to make the world around me contract and expand with every breath. I held the mace in front of me once more, and watched as the Dawnflayer came at me. I dropped my right hand from the mace and reached for my sword— but I couldn't quite draw it before the next attack came.

He pulled back both hands, a low roar escaping his lips as he thrust his palms out towards me and down, trying to flatten me into the ground. I barely had time to look around and consider my options but I allowed instinct to take control, and I jumped back to avoid the attack. I was sent tumbling over the stone bench that I had not seen behind me, and crashed into the ground, my entire body screaming in pain, while both of the Dawnflayer's massive hands seemed to pierce the ground with impressive force, and I saw that, if only for a moment, the beast was stuck.

I rose to my feet and ran forward, screaming a battle cry of my own through grit teeth. I stepped onto the seat of the stone bench, and then vaulted off the back, swinging across. I felt the impact in my shoulders as the mace connected with the side of the Dawnflayer's head, and it whimpered in pain as it stumbled to the side, almost falling over. The impact of my attack had sent it toppling, and it filled me with a strength and resolve that I had not felt to that point—for the first time I felt like I actually had a chance.

In falling, the Dawnflayer was able to pull his hands free of the ground. He took a step back, and shook off my attack. We made eye contact, and there was a pregnant pause between us. It was breathing almost as heavily as I was, and he turned his palms out, facing me. Once again, he raised his arms to his side, and let out that beastly scream, the muscles rippling beneath the scales once more. Only this time, the scales lifted, jutting outwards like they were on his shoulders. Suddenly the Dawnflayer was covered in small spikes, including his head. I thought about drawing my sword, but worried that if I did not strike a killing blow, the network of scales would make it difficult to retrieve the sword without leaving myself too vulnerable and too close for comfort. He stood upright, straightening his legs, and was taller than ever before. He pointed at me with his left hand, and I watched with cautious anticipation. I wasn't sure what to expect, but then the attack came. Out of his forearms, the Dawnflayer shot a string of scales at me, like a quilled animal does when frightened.

I sidestepped without thinking, though I was a second too late. A handful of the scales sliced at my leg. None of the wounds were too deep, but I could already feel the fabric of my trousers clinging to my skin, wet with my own blood. There was a sting, I was sure of it, but I didn't have time to feel it. Adrenaline had taken over, and I dropped my right hand from the mace, drawing my sword. I, too, held my arms out to side and screamed at the Dawnflayer.

He almost seemed to smile at me.

There was an eerie silence between us—a calm before the storm—that only lasted a few seconds. It felt like longer than that. I pushed off first, springing into a run towards the creature as it was doing the same, and my mind began to run all the possibilities. I thought about swinging with the mace to knock away an arm before trying to plant my sword in his throat, but there was a swath of spiny scales there as well, and although I hoped such a strike would kill the beast, I was scared to take the chance that it wouldn't, or that I wouldn't strike true. I thought about dropping and sliding between his legs, hopefully rising quick enough on the other side to get on his back and maybe do some damage there. I thought about leaping left or right to dodge his attack before going for the legs; I had already made him bleed once, if only a little, by an attack to the legs.

It's amazing how much you can process in a matter of seconds when your life depends on it.

I ended up doing none of them. Before we met for what may have been our final exchange of blows, there was an enormous bloom of light that blinded me to the point of agony. I dropped to ground, scratching at my eyes and waiting for the end when I heard a voice ring out.

"Brok, enough," the voice had said. It was a louder and stronger version of the woman's voice I had heard before.

I tried to force open one eye, and saw her standing at the open library doors, the light of the fire spilling out from behind her into the courtyard, brighter than any firelight I had ever seen before. It reminded me of what it felt like to stare directly into the Sun on a clear morning, and I remembered how my head would be throbbing for hours afterwards. It was such a small thing, but began such a yearning that I could not ignore for long.

"Bring him inside," she said, and I felt a massive hand close around my ankle. Then, I was being dragged. My head hit the lip of the stone path when I was dragged from the soft ground, and I lifted it as best I could, the sting for some reason hitting me harder than any of Brok's attacks prior. The searing pain in my leg left by the scales was starting to increase, and I wasn't sure if the heat I felt was from the blood pooling, or from the wounds being tugged on, as Brok was pulling the injured leg. "Watch his head," the voice said again. "Might be something useful in there."

FIRESIDE

After Brok had pulled me inside the library, I was propped up against a wall. My strength had left me, more from fatigue than anything, and I was allowed to sleep. When I awoke, the fire was still very much burning in the center of the room, only it wasn't any fire that I had seen before. There was no wood nor pit; the flames were hovering above the ground, never changing size or intensity. There was no sound, either; no wood to crack, no embers to launch. It couldn't have been real, I remember thinking to myself. I was sure that I had hit my head hard enough to knock something loose, and all I was seeing was an illusion—if only I had carried that doubt with me. Then I remembered the dead, the dragon—and its Rider—and the Dawnflayer I had faced, which sat across the room from me, docile as could be.

Perhaps things were a tad different now.

Next to Brok, on the other side of the floating flame, sat the woman I had heard before. She had a hardened look to her, like that of a warrior. Her face was locked into a scowl, and her hair was kept short, cut to her ears at the longest. She wore leather armor over chainmail, and I could see a broadsword resting next to her against the bench she was seated on. She stared at me, and for a moment I thought I could feel her staring *through* me, the fire reflecting in her eyes as both to enhance the fury that no doubt lived behind them; but it also indicated to me that the fire was hers to cast—was it magic?

I felt my eyes adjusting to the new light and sighed. Surely that could only mean I would need to once again train myself to see in the dark once I left the library, if I was to leave it at all.

"Where are you from?" She asked as she was pulling some sort of bread from the satchel on his hip. She broke a piece off and offered it to me, but I declined. I was not feeling hungry.

I cleared my throat, as it had been some time since I had to speak out loud and I wasn't sure I still had a voice. "Littlehollow, originally,"

I said weakly, my voice breaking somewhere in 'Little'. "Though I lived most of my life under Dewpond, in the Catacombs." Part of me did not want to reveal that there were people in the catacombs, but I remembered what those people were descending to, and thought better of protecting them. Either way, it was my turn for a question. "Aren't you afraid of the Rider?" I nodded towards the fire and looked around at the brightly lit Library.

Even from the outside, it did not seem as bright. The foyer was large and open. And though there were symbols on the ground and banners hanging on the walls, none of them spoke to me or interested me. The stacks, which took up all of the back half of the building, were still a ways away, and I couldn't be bothered to examine them at the time. I would have other opportunities to investigate the rest of the great building—though I had already seen it, plenty of times, before disappearing beneath the surface.

She turned to Brok, and they shared a confused look. The Dawn-flayer looked smaller than he had outside, much smaller, and I wondered if it was just an illusion put forth by him being seated. "Rider?" she finally said incredulously.

I told her what had happened in Littlehollow when I emerged—I left out the part about being exiled—and she and Brok hung on every word. When I was done my story, they once again exchanged a look before both shaking their head.

"I don't know about that," she said. "We have been here for quite some time now—at least three sleeps—and you are the first living visitor we've received."

"First 'living'?"

"When we came here, in search of supplies, we were set upon by the dead. Between Brok and myself, however," she started with a smile, "let's just say we are more than proficient by this point."

"How long have you been up here?"

"We were never down *there*," she said, nodding to the ground. "When the light went out, I was north of Alduin, hunting wood hogs for my father and camping in the woods. When the sun stopped rising in the morning, I had tried to return home, but was descended on by creatures the likes of which I had never seen before. They were horrible beasts, composed of the bodies of the dead. Amidst the attacks I found a Dawnflayer that was smaller than the ones we'd heard about in stories, taking his licks, and I saved him." She nodded towards Brok, who turned his eyes to the ground in embarrassment. The woman got quiet. "And then he saved me more times than I can count. When we finally returned home, I watched as the dragons rained fire on everything."

"So you saw the dragons?"

"But no Rider," she said quickly. "No man, woman, or beast has ever tamed a dragon, by legend or otherwise. I highly doubt your 'Rider' exists."

I trusted my eyes more than I trusted her, but she *had* stopped Brok from pummeling me into the ground, so I decided to forego an argument, and instead took a deep breath. I looked at the flame, and my face must have been displaying the difficulties I was having piecing everything together. "I've never seen fire like that," I finally said.

"I can tell," she said with a snicker. "It's Faerie fire. Invisible to dragons, but not to people. Something I learned north of Alduin, in the Quiet Wood. A nymph there taught me a great many things about Faerie magic, in the short time I was able to stay with her. She was very wise, and knew much more about this world than you or I could ever possibly know."

I pointed my chin at Brok. "And him?"

She looked at her companion, and then back to me. "The death of light did a lot more than wake the dead and the dragons," she said as she rose to her feet. "Through some scar of the world, the monsters deep below are beginning to stir. Though, as you can see, some were friendlier than others. Brok is the only Dawnflayer I have seen thus far."

"Monsters?" I asked with disbelief. Surely she was joking, but once again I ran down the list of all the things I had seen.

She simply nodded, and walked over to one of the windows, peering out into the courtyard. "I only hope you and Brok didn't attract any more attention with your fighting."

"Do you know what happened to the Sun? To the light?"

She turned to look at me, and I saw her face fall somber. She shook her head slowly, and returned to looking out the window.

"Someone stole it," Brok said, his voice deep and raspy, but sounding almost simple; as if speaking was still new to him. The woman shot her companion a look that shifted to a weak smile. Brok never looked up from the ground.

"I think he was looking forward to seeing it, too. It didn't sound very bright in his home, wherever that was," she said, staring at him. "He didn't come to our realm willingly. But I will help him find his way."

"And return the light to the sky?" I asked.

"If we can."

"I want to help." I stood, clenching my fists tightly.

"I wish you could," she said, turning her smile on me, the gently upturned corner of her mouth just dripping with pity. "But we've both heard those words before, haven't we Brok?"

Brok nodded sadly.

"Then what would you have me do?" I asked, watching her walk back over to the bench and taking a seat.

She sighed a deep sigh and stretched her legs out. She looked off to one side, at nothing in particular, searching for the words. "Survive?" she finally said, hoping it would satisfy me.

"You've seen that I can fight," I protested. "I almost beat your brute!" Brok took issue with that, looking up at me with angry eyes, and I saw the familiar ripple of his muscles beneath the now softened scales. I backed down out of respect more than fear. "Sorry, sorry," I said, holding out my palms to him before turning back to her. "I think I have proven my usefulness."

"True," she said after thinking for a moment, "but let me tell you a little more about how Brok and I have survived to this point: alone." She pulled her legs in, and leaned forward in her seat, resting her arms on her knees and clasping her hands together. "We have tried to let wayward travelers like yourself—yes, you are not the only one that wanders the dark, just the first we've seen in some time—we have tried to let them join our cause before. We have learned some valuable lessons. One: other people only serve to split your concern. Brok and I have a generally uniform task at hand. The others came with their own motives, such as your desire to see light returned to the world, or perhaps there was someone they aimed to save or a title they wished to have bestowed upon them—hero of the humans! our savior! We can't afford to dilute our goals with the goals of others. Two: the larger the group, the more likely you are to be discovered. Sure, you don't seem the type to charge headlong into a fight—hell, you got too close to *us* before we noticed you—but that doesn't mean you won't slip up. I don't want someone else that I can blame for giving away our position. And finally: you can't trust anyone but yourself in those all-to-common life-and-death situations that arise in this new world."

"What about him?" I asked, nodding to Brok again.

"Brok can still hear you," Brok said, looking down at the ground again.

"He knows me—the truth of me," she said. "And he has saved mine more times than I care to count. Brok is the exception to the rules, and he has earned his place at my side. He was put in my path by fate, of that I am sure. And helping him find where he belongs, and where he came from…that has become the guiding light in this world of darkness, illuminating a path for me when I had none."

I had run out of arguments. She seemed steadfast in her resolve to continue traveling with just the Dawnflayer, and I could not think of any way to convince her otherwise. "Where will you go, then?"

"So you might follow us?"

"No," I said curtly. "It is merely so I can make sure I head in a different direction, so that I might not have to come to blows with your brute again."

She tried to stifle a laugh, and then looked wistfully at Brok. "I can only hope he learned a few things from your encounter," she said. She turned to me and feigned a whisper. "I think you almost had him, after all." Brok scoffed and she let out a bigger laugh. "But if you must know, we will be heading to the East, towards Brakas."

I nodded. I was lost, and knew not what to do. "I suppose I might head farther to the West, see if I can cross the mountains, out of Alghast."

"You could," the woman said. "Though I can't speak for what, if anything, you might find out there. Plus, the mountains and forests surrounding Alghast, while already treacherous, have oft been spoken of as infested with strange and hostile creatures. It is quite dangerous, especially in the dark. Could I offer a suggestion?"

I cocked my head to the side. "Why?"

"Just because I don't want you traveling with us does not mean I wish you dead," she said. "Castleford, the Southernmost City of Alghast, is said to be returning to the surface. How they are surviving is beyond me—perhaps these Catacombs you spoke of—but it may be worth checking out for you. Safety might await you there, and live out the rest of your days without worrying about any more scars." She nodded towards my leg, my pants cemented to my flesh with dried blood.

"Scars don't scare me," I said. "But you have peaked my curiosity." I collected my weapons, and headed for the door.

"You'll leave now?" she asked, standing quickly. "You are welcome to remain here. We have food and you might get some more rest," she said while gesturing towards a bench opposite hers. "I won't send you to your death tired and hungry." She smiled at me, and I couldn't help but smile back.

I rested comfortably for some time. I am not sure how long she allowed me to sleep, but when I awoke, I felt refreshed. I saw that I had shifted closer to the flame that danced in the center of the library foyer, and quickly shuffled away, though I did not feel any heat—only warmth, if that makes any sense. I reached a hand out, and placed it close enough to the fire that I expected to be burned at any moment, but nothing happened. And while I had grown up hearing tales of Faerie magic, it was always placed somewhere in my mind with the other legends; I was aware of them, but thought them as nothing more than fables. They were stories that I listened to for their entertainment, though now I wished more than ever that I had listened to the ramblings of my elders and my peers. And for the first time since my banishment, I missed being able to pass the time listening to them talk.

There could be something useful in those stories, as well.

"It's special, isn't it?" I heard her say, and then I felt a soft hand on my shoulder. I looked up to see her, bathed in the light of the flames, and her touch sent a shiver through me. Her touch was cold and made me yearn for yet more warmth from the fire that caught my attention once more. She sat down next to me, and looked into my eyes, pulling her hand back. "And so are you," she finally said, somber, just as I was beginning to grow concerned.

"I am no one," I said, turning my gaze to the floor.

She scoffed. "We are all someone," she said with a smile. "And it's not for you to decide that truth." She pulled her knees into her chest, resting her head on them and looking at me. It was the most she'd let her guard down since I arrived, and it was alarming to say the least. "I was nothing more than a hunter's daughter before... Well, before all this started, and now look at me. I have my very own Dawnflayer bodyguard, and have even learned a spot of magic. The world makes us who we are."

I nodded slowly, taking in what she was saying. There was a softness to her that I had not seen before, and it was helping the words go down easier. At the very least, it was enough to renew my desire to survive, and Castleford seemed like the best option. "Thank you," I said, looking to her as she nodded.

There was a brief pause, contemplative for her and confusing for me, before she finally spoke: "I promise this won't hurt for long," she said quietly, and her expression changed. Before I had a chance to ask what, she was thrusting the palms of her hands into my eyes. There was a terrible burning, and a bright light pierced through my closed lids as I screamed out in agony. Hot fire replaced my blood in my veins, and I felt like I was going to explode any second. I felt a great scaled hand cover my mouth to mute my screams, but saw nothing. I was being held from behind by Brok to keep from squirming. When she finally pulled her hands away, and the burning pain subsided.

I saw everything.

THE ROAD SOUTH

Rayna, that's what she had told me her name was as we were leaving the library, standing just outside the precipice before we parted ways. I asked her what she had done to me as I stood on the stoop and took in my surroundings. Gone was the darkness I was growing accustomed to. In its place I saw details that I hadn't seen since the Sun hung in the sky on the clearest of days, and I had to fight the urge to weep as the memories of sunny days came rushing back.

"You can see the world for what it is, now," she told me, placing a hand on my shoulder. For the first time, I saw her age in her face; years of hardening from survival on the surface. It was still and stoic. I doubted highly that she was only a hunter's daughter—it looked more like she had been in many battles, even before the Long Night began. "You just have to let go of what used to be, and look forward. Find your path."

My path was leading me to the South. Rayna had told me of Castleford, and the emergence that had begun there. If nothing else, I was curious how they were keeping the dead at bay, let alone the Dragon Rider and his flock—if there was one, I couldn't be sure—and had to see for myself what it would take for humankind's hold on the surface to be restored.

I had been given what Rayna called the Sunsight; another of the Faerie spells she had learned in the wake of the world ending. It had allowed me to see far better than I ever thought possible, illuminating most things as though it were daytime.

When Rayna and I parted ways, I looked to the sky for the first time since I saw the dragon, on the day I emerged from the catacombs. Gone was the sheet of black I had seen back then, replaced by a sea of sparse clouds, backlit purple by the pure aura coming from the far distance. Purple was just one of the colors I saw as I stared into the sky, others joining in as my eyes slowly shifted, trying to take it all in.

It was like nothing I had never seen before. I scanned the sky, left to right, until my eyes had found a new shape up above: a black orb, sitting just in front of the brilliant colors. There was something about it that caught my attention about it immediately, and I was able to picture it as I truly remembered it; a glowing silver disc in the night sky.

It was the Moon, black as pitch and hanging ominously in the sky, as though waiting.

I had thought the celestial orb gone completely, as did everyone I had spoken to before I came above ground. It was accepted as truth that the Moon, and the Sun were both disappeared. But what I saw before me could not be mistaken.

Unless, of course, Rayna's 'sight' was nothing but an illusion, brought on by some sort of poison, administered while I slept—or my understanding of Faerie magic was woefully incomplete. It would have been so easy to do *something* to me, I slept so heavily after the battle with Brok. It was the thing that made the most sense, though I was learning to reject the thought of 'sense', as it, itself, no longer made sense in the world.

That was the Moon, staring back at me, and I thought I could hear it calling out to me. There was a whisper that hung in the icy silence as we seemed to look at *each other*, instead of me just gazing upon *it*— what it was saying, I couldn't have possibly known or understood. I could feel it in my bones as I looked upon it, as though the tendrils of silver light were reaching out to me before being suddenly stopped by an ethereal darkness beyond comprehension.

My mind was reeling, trying to make sense of it all. I felt like I was going mad! My thoughts, scattered as they may have been, once again began to focus on a new thought, in light of my rediscovery of the Moon:

If the Moon was there, then surely the Sun was under the same affliction?

I thought about waiting, to see if my theory was correct. There was an instinct that I just couldn't ignore, and when I had made it to the Southern end of Dewpond, easily spotting and dispatching any of the undead that still remained in the city, I sat upon a hill that ran down into a river. On the other side, a small village had been sacked, and I saw no movement there. The bridge to cross the small river was much further down, and I knew that it was deep enough that the Undead would likely be unable to cross. So I sat and I waited for the Moon to set in the West, and the Sun to rise in the East; all the while waiting for the brilliant colors in the sky to take hold, if only for a moment, so I could see what art they could make with an entire canvas to themselves.

I had never watched a sunrise before, at least not with the same anticipation that I felt then. Any time before had simply been coincidental, or at least not memorable. It occurred to me that the context surrounding watching the morning Sun crest on the Eastern horizon was often more important than the Sun, itself. Moments like those we take for granted; the things we stumble on without even realizing what things would be like if they were gone.

So there I sat, cross-legged on a hill overlooking the deep plains before the sudden rise of the mountains to the West at one end of the river—the same range that encircled the entirety of Alghast save for the far East—waiting for the Moon to set, and the Sun to rise. I told myself with some certainty that I was waiting for something real, and not just fantasy.

It was as I had feared.

The Sun never *did* rise.

Instead, the Moon remained. It hung in the Sky like an unmoving black hole sucking in all of the colors around it. It was draining to look at, and I absent-mindedly wondered why I had never noticed the pure Dark that was hanging above, so unnaturally.

Rayna had shown me the world.

We had thought the surface dead; a distant dream that we would never achieve, scorched by fires from above and left to die. Yet, here it was; perfectly fine and just as we had left it. Fires had raged through the lands, yes; but everything leaves a mark. Everything leaves a memory.

Villages and cities along the path that used to prosper still stood, in essence. Their graves were marked with what remained of foundations and corners too stubborn to fall, burned and melted but not destroyed. Their memories were carved into the ground in the forms of scorch marks, left when the physical forms were torn away by fire.

It was all so difficult for me to swallow. I just couldn't quite comprehend the 'why' as I walked the final leg of my journey to Castleford. My legs had grown weary of the trek, and I was now acutely aware that I had not slept in what must have been days, though I had long forgotten how long a day truly feels.

When I reached the hill leading up to Watta, a small farming village known for corn and cattle, I paused to catch my breath. It was not a steep hill, but any incline made my legs scream in pain, and I knew that I would not be ready for an ambush at the top.

I found my strength, and began to scale the hill. As I did, something in the distance caught my eye: a black point, piercing the sky on just the other side of Castleford. The higher I got, the more I could see of the tower, and what it was attached to.

On a cliff overlooking the town, I saw the Castle the town was named for, standing in all its glory; a black sentinel watching over its namesake. The tower I had seen was only the tallest of five, standing tall at the cross-section of the other four wings of the great castle.

The same castle that had famously disappeared nearly a century earlier.

AZAZEL

Castleford, the Southernmost City of Alghast, used to be one of wonderful advancements. Most of the weaponry and armor used by the realm was designed there, with instructions sent out to smiths and armorers the world over, scattering apprentices to the four points, and taking in new ones to train in their stead. It was a near constant cycle of learning and teaching, until darkness fell. The architecture of Castleford could be seen the world over—only now it is merely the remnants that stood.

It was said that Castleford was largely unassailed during the first volley. The attacks came from the South with the fires burning up the realm to the North until all was ash. Even as I stood on the outside, looking at the city I could see that it had not felt the fires as bad as other places I had seen.

And then there was the Castle.

It was in that castle, the one that sat upon that cliff overlooking the great city of armor, where it is said that one dragon, with a heart as black as her scales, sat the throne, commanding all others—dragons and monsters alike. A wonderful story, to say the least; far more terrifying when you begin to see the signs that it may have been true.

Some legends are better left on the pages of storybooks.

As I approached the outer gates of the city, I took notice of the gaps left in the wall by the attacks. Rocks had been piled up in a makeshift attempt to block the holes. It was crude work, at best, and I doubted very highly that it would keep anything out for longer than it would take to shamble over the pile of heavy stone.

The gate stood closed, though at first glance I couldn't see anything keeping it so. I reached out, grabbing for the cold rusted metal, the white paint mostly chipped away, and felt a chill run up my arm. I shuddered quietly to myself, and started to pull on the gate before being stopped abruptly as someone spoke from the dark corners of wall.

"We don't get many visitors 'round 'ere," a voice spoke from behind me. I spun to see the man sitting on the stones to the right of the gates. I was shocked I hadn't seen him before. He was dressed in armor, plated steel over a leather curais. His face was covered by a similarly plain helmet. His sword was resting on the stone next to him. He was fiddling with a flask. "Where did you come up from?"

"Littlehollow," I told him with some hesitation, taken aback by the sudden interaction. "It is north of Dewpond."

The man chortled. "Dewpond? Been to Dewpond; almost broke my bloody neck trying to see how far the library Spire flew. Pierced the heavens, they all said; just like the one here." He nodded to the city square, though it sat empty. I could not see a Spire. "They say there's one in each of the four cities, but it looks like the one here's gone missing, wouldn't you say? I'd sure love to see them all someday."

I listened to the man's ramblings. I'd thought to interrupt him, but there was a growing wistfulness in his voice that was captivating. If the library Spire had been that impressive, I couldn't recall; I had set eyes upon it enough in my youth that I thought nothing of it. I had heard that they were present in the other cities as well, though that being a product of Castleford's designs spreading across the world was easier to believe than anything else.

"I returned here when I heard the Castle had reappeared." He reached for his helmet, lifting the face mask. Even with my sight, his face was shrouded by something. "Had to see it for myself, after all the stories mum told me when I was growing up." He took a healthy drink from the flask, knocking his face mask back down when he was done. "And it was something to behold, just look at it. They say that *he* returned as well. It was just before the world was set aflame." He trailed off, looking to the castle.

"I know you are waiting for me to ask," I said, crossing my arms across my chest. "He is the master of the castle?"

The knight nodded. "He is the master of more than just the castle, I fear. They say he is also the master of the fire; the Master of Dragons. But in truth," the Knight laughed quietly to himself. "In truth, I believe he is nothing more than an old Wizard. No master, he is."

I couldn't help but smile. Part of me wanted to believe him, but something about his speech made me question his mind.

"Before they sent me here, they told me we were no longer needed. I was a guard in the Necropolis, y'see? I wasn't one of the peasant guards, either; I was stationed at the Cathedral of Woe, deep in the center. That was a special post, only awarded to the most trusted of knights. I had earned that post, and they just cast us out. Said something about the Long Night and dragons. Next thing I knew, I was being sent home, for 'protection'. Then the dark came."

"The Long Night?" I took a step towards him, my interest piqued.

"Yes, you've heard the stories?"

"Stories," I laughed. "No, I, like you, lived through the start of the Long Night."

"They won't let you into the Cathedral," he said, quieting his tone. "They won't let anyone into the Cathedral. You can't even get close."

"What is there?"

"You can't even get close," he repeated. He pointed past me, and I turned to see what he meant.

The Cathedral, while sometimes visible at great distances when the sun still shone, was never much to look at. It was a large square building with a flat roof. There were ornate statues standing at each of the corners, facing outwards, and ornate pillars ran along the sides. The roof was flat, and had little to speak of. It had no bell tower, for no one within distance was alive to hear a bell. Its walls were dark, which is why it could only be seen on clear days, accented with a deep grey that was also the color of the roof.

I wasn't sure if it was because of the Sunsight, or perhaps something else; but as I looked where the knight was pointing, where I knew the cathedral would be, I saw something more spectacular. The Cathedral was still there; but surrounding it was a dome that glowed a deep green. It seemed to pulsate as I watched it, framed nicely by the purple in the sky. The inner third of the Necropolis was encased in the dome, and I knew at once that even if I wanted to, I couldn't get into the Cathedral. Something inside me felt the strength of whatever magic had created the barrier, and I shunned the thought of even trying to get to the Cathedral—though why I was tempted, I had no idea.

I couldn't even get close.

I tried to press the knight for more information, but he had ceased to be helpful—if he was ever truly helpful to begin with. I turned my attention back to the gate, and slowly pulled it open.

I crossed over to the other side into a small meadow—at least, what used to be a meadow. Even still, I could see signs of life in the soil. There were a few bits of green breaking through the black earth beneath my feet as I walked through the once and future garden, trying to remember the smell of flowers and failing, as I had been a child when last I smelled the sweet combination of the flora and the air.

We had tried to keep flowers in the catacombs. The elders, who had decided we would be better off underground, saw to it that we did not forego all surface pleasures. Somewhere between the mess hall and the medical rooms they had brought down what they could salvage from the witch's garden—there was a woman that lived just outside Dewpond that many thought was a witch, as her crops never seemed to cease growing even when others could grow nothing. It had lasted until I began to grow stubble on my face, but there was something stifling about it being confined underground. Something smelled off about it. And without the sun, I wondered how those flowers lived as long as they did.

Damned witches.

When I reached the other side of the small meadow, I was greeted by a young man and a young woman, standing shoulder to shoulder, smiling from ear to ear. It was irritating, and I wondered how many more interruptions there would be, even if I was unsure what I would even do once I finally reached the city.

"Can you see us?" the young man asked.

"Can you hear us?" said the woman, almost an echo if not for the different word.

I furrowed my brow and they laughed. Clearly they could see me as well as I could see them, and I started to wonder if the Sunsight was more common that I had originally thought. Or perhaps the master of whatever magic was at work down South was able to lift the veil of darkness as well. "I can see you," I said while coming to a stop a few cautious feet from them. "I can hear you, too."

They seemed to smile wider and the man stepped forward. "Good," he said with an unnerving tone. He was young, younger than me by more than a little bit; hardly old enough to even grow a proper beard, and it showed. There was a youthful enthusiasm painted across his pale white face. Dark hair matted to his forehead and he wore a black leather vest over a white undershirt, a crest baring a dragon embroidered onto his chest. "What business have you with Azazel, master of magic?"

I was taken slightly off guard. I wasn't even sure who Azazel *was*; especially not enough to have any sort of business with him. "None, I've just heard—"

"We appreciate your visit, and ask that you be on your way." They seemed to speak in unison, though they made no signal to one another. It sent another chill running down my spine. Just what was happening to the world?

"Why have you begun to surface here? How do you keep the dead at bay? Or the dragons?"

The pair exchanged a look with one another, their smiles never faltering, before returning their attention to me. "There is work to be done," the man finally said.

"Much work to be done," the woman seemed to echo.

I was trying not to grow frustrated with their little game, but I felt a sense of urgency after seeing the Cathedral. Things were more amiss than I ever truly thought while living underground. I thought back to the fables of my youth, specifically the stories about dragons and Dawnflayers and distinctly remembered the hearty laugh that came at the end of any one of those stories. Magic wasn't real, as far as I and many others were concerned where I had come from. Though I was beginning to accept that we might have been wrong.

But just what kind of spell were these two under? They were both too young to have seen the light of day. There was an ominous tone to their voice, and an almost sing-song cadence to the way they spoke; each time one finished speaking, the other seemed to carry the tune for a few bars more.

"What work do you speak of?" I asked them, expecting no answer.

"The end of the Long Night," the Twins stated in unison.

"And the start of a new life," a new voice continued, sounding as though it was coming from the air itself.

I nearly snapped my neck trying to find the source of the voice, scared witless by its sudden appearance. Something about it seemed otherworldly; as though it managed to worm its way into my mind, rather than being heard as I was used to. The Twins just seemed to smile more as I surveyed the area, my eyes crossing them over as I searched left to right. On the return, there was a third figure, standing just behind them, dressed in dark robes. I almost didn't see him, even with the Sight.

His hair was long and flat, sticking to his skull like a cap and draping over his shoulders as though it were fastened to his cloak. Even in the mess of colors I now viewed the world, I could see that the strands were of vibrant silver, framing a soft but menacing face. His eyes were piercing, and his nose was pointed yet small on his face. There were signs of a beard, or at the very least stubble; but it was just as lightly colored as his hair, and I couldn't tell if it were merely shadows playing tricks. His hands were clasped together in front of him, large rings adorning his fingers. His skin was pale, his lips were thin, and I was immediately put on edge by the way he approached me.

He smiled a knowing smile in my direction. "You remember the start of the Long Night well, don't you?"

I did, but something about him made me hesitant to begin a conversation.

"You know my name, don't you?"

I only had to think for a second, taking in the glazed over eyes of the twins standing behind him. "Azazel."

He just smiled and nodded at me.

"Do you have something to do with all this?"

"I do," he said softly. "I will. So will you."

I paused for a moment. Something in his tone sent some of those worries away. There was a determination I detected that rang true with something deep inside of me. To that point, I had not considered the possibility of ending the Long Night, though I had felt set on a path. It was a path that would lead me to more questions than answers, but the questions only served to burn my resolve brighter. It all began to build in that moment as though it had been there all along, a fire waiting to be stoked. It was a longer moment than I had intended.

"How do we stop it?" I finally asked.

THE NECROPOLIS

The necropolis sat in the center of all we knew, tucked into the mountains as we were, sprawling outwards like water. Whether or not it was so, I remembered the ground turning grey and the skies darkening overhead as it expanded, as though its touch was enough to spread the death it carried. It was the only thing that could afford to expand. When it needed more room, it usually meant that the cities and villages surrounding it needed a little bit less.

That didn't stop it from reaching capacity more than once, requiring some graves to be dug twice as deep, so that it could be used for two caskets, stacked, instead of one. Others still, in cases of illness or battle, were deposited into mass graves—wide holes dug in the soil, where the bagged bodies would be tossed in, mere vessels for the souls they once carried.

The more pious of us were never fond of the burial methods when the number of deaths began to outnumber the space allotted. It was a nice gesture, at first; but it had grown to such a size that the notion had become almost ignorant—as though the ones who built it were unaware of the fragile nature of human life. So many lay dead and buried for so long. Until the Long Night began, that number only increased in favor of the buried.

Now only those lucky enough to lose their heads remain in the ground.

As I looked around, I saw more of *them* walking our world than *us*. The dead always outnumber the living; that much is fact. And never will that balance be thrown into question. It's because of that fact that I have so many scars, after all.

And while Azazel wasn't clear on what would be needed to return light to the Sun, he had been very pointed in his suggestions. "Find a way into the Cathedral," he had said.

I had told him of what the Knight outside had spoken and he acted as though he knew of no such Knight. Instead, he turned my attention to the deep green glow of the dome surrounding the Cathedral.

The Cathedral of Woe housed the Sept of the Sun; a group of priests tasked with keeping the spirits of the dead. It is from them that stories of wisps came from. They were essentially telling of their own ineptitude, but it made the children feel hopeful that their parents might return should one of the priests sleep on the job.

They usually wore black robes, with a long white line running down the middle before branching out and tapering off. Around their necks they all wore a chain bearing the symbol that adorned the walls of the Cathedral—as well as so many other places in Alghast, I would learn.

Very few were permitted to be inside of the sacred building—it was reserved for funerals and other matters of the dead, and for a scarce few other things. It was not an attraction that many sought out, as it required passage through miles of graves to reach.

I vaguely remember being there once, when my mother died. I was so young that the memory remains blurry.

The tombs of the old Mothers and Fathers immediately surround the cathedral. Large in their own right, they housed the bodies of the elder families that settled the great cities, sending their children out in an unspoken game to see who could settle the most land. Villages such as Littlehollow were founded by the children, and when they died, they were laid to rest with their family, until there was no more room for the children, and the children's children.

Out from those were the military fields. Each city had its own guard, all bearing the same basic insignia of the compass of Alghast. The city they hailed from would be the point that shone bright with the cities gemstone: Onyx for Alduin; Emerald for Brakas; Ruby for Castleford; and Sapphire for Dewpond. When they swore their life to the guard, they swore their names. Their graves were marked by their swords; plots of grass with bouquets of rusting blades sticking out from them.

From the soldiers' graves, the necropolis begins to lose any semblance of order or organization. The fields had, at some point, been kept as clean and tidy as the keepers could have kept them. At some point, before I was born, there was even fields of grass still covering parts of the necropolis; though by the time I drew my first breath, a thick air of despair clung to the soil like a parasite, killing any color that tried to shine through.

Stone caskets were left piled on the ground in some areas, from foolhardy people thinking there was space for them in the inner circles

of the necropolis and being too put off to try and carry the heavy boxes back. It became less about respecting the dead, and more of an in-
convenience any time someone had their breath escape them with
enough coin in pocket for a traditional burial.

As time went on, the costs began to grow. The Sept began to ask
more and more of the families of the dead in order to hold them a spot
—even if they weren't sure that a spot still existed—and the families
thought their coin better with the dead than themselves, so they
would pay it. And each time they paid, someone would have to find a
spot for a new body, while someone else got rich.

Over time it had become a city in and of itself; beggars began to
nest amongst the stacked caskets, finding recluse amongst the haphaz-
ard piling of grave-keepers that felt they had better things to do. The
farther in a grave was, the less likely it would be for a family to make
the journey to visit it, making it even more frustrating that they insist
on proper burials; but those without a place to call their own were
among those that still believed in burials. It gave them a rudimentary—if not macabre—shelter. The grounds were scarcely patrolled for
vandals and grave-robbers when I was young, so it was more of a
haven for vagabonds than any of the cities, which seemed to insist on
outward appearance, choosing to *hide* its less-fortunate instead of *help*
them.

Still, a life among the dead was something that would drive anyone insane, and it was with some mercy that these people ended up
the first slain when those piled caskets began to open, and when the
swords that had marked the graves of soldiers began to disappear,
reclaimed by the very bodies those swords had failed to protect in life.

None are quite sure where the armies of the dead began to rise
first, but news did not travel fast out of the Necropolis. When the first
corpse of a vagrant was found and reported, we had already been set
upon twice by the dead. And when we did finally receive news, it was
from three separate locations, and was afforded the same level of concern that the vagrants were when they still lived.

As I had stated before, these creatures were nothing more than
husks. They were the bodies of people that had lived before, yes; but
anything beneath the surface had been replaced by something else.
They were driven by a force that we couldn't quite understand; a uni-
versal desire to add to their ranks was the best that any of us could
guess, though to this day I would argue that the death itself was all
they strived for, if they strived for anything at all.

It wasn't something transferrable, either. We didn't know at first if
it was something in the air, or the matter at which you fell that dictat-

ed whether or not you would return. We grew cautious of bites and scrapes, as we had heard of the Brackish Hounds to the East—snarling beasts that carried with them a toxin that was known to destroy the human mind, if only for a time.

I had learned the truth when my uncle, Thomas, met an unfortunate fate. He was an apprentice armorer—unafraid to learn a new trait so deep into his thirties, even amidst the jawing from his peers—though he had been quickly promoted when it became clear that the attacks weren't going to stop. He had not been proficient at weaponry at all, but as we began to lose people, others had to fill certain roles.

I wasn't there for the accident, but I was at the shelter—families began to collect as houses were burned, turning homes that housed four into madhouses of much more than that—when he was brought home. His skin had been charred up his right side, kissed by flames. His tunic, dark and grey, was black and melted into his side. I remember thinking that he had an arm off, only to see that while it was still there, it had been pulverized by a percussive blast, and was hanging useless amongst the tattered shreds of his clothing. He was trying to cry out in pain, but even I could see that his throat had collapsed. It was a wonder he was still breathing at all.

Through no effort on our part, Thomas managed to live into the night. We had little in the way of medical supplies—and a decision was made in quiet that they would not be of much use here. Someone stayed up to watch him, and in the early morning, Holm—my uncle's new apprentice—was waking me up by shaking my shoulder gently and whispering my name. "Tomas is dead," they said as I opened my eyes.

I was unsure if I was still asleep and dreaming, so I took a moment to process the information. I looked over to the table where Thomas had been lying, and then back to Holm in disbelief. "No, he is not," I said while pointing to the table. Holm followed my gaze and we both witnessed Thomas sitting up, and scanning the room.

There was something different about his eyes, and it was someone sleeping closer to the table, woken up by Holm's gasp, that drew the connection before we could. "He rises!"

The sudden cry caused Thomas to shriek that inhuman shriek, and he leaped from the table, staring down a collection of scared people. Desmond, young but strong of will and body, took care of the situation quickly. He ran Thomas into a wall with a halberd that had been resting next to where he slept. When it was clear that it wouldn't be enough, he didn't hesitate to pick up a sword, lopping off the head of my the husk that had been my uncle.

There was nothing left of my uncle in there. I was sure of it, and so was everyone else that had come to know him. It was then that we learned the truth of the dead: husks, piloted by some unseen force, using the likeness of the people we loved or hated or whatever the case may be. Some necromancer had set them upon us, and we had no idea who or why.

The overcrowded Necropolis was one of the reasons why the fight against them was so difficult. Those closest to the surface were able to free themselves and attack us without issue. And when we thought we were making progress, new waves would emerge, as it took them longer to crawl out of their graves.

It also turned the Necropolis into a mess that was almost impossible to traverse from all of the cave-ins and open graves. It would make for a perilous hike, and although Azazel's words made it sound like such a journey would be necessary to undo whatever had been done to our world, as I stood on that hill and looked over the great city of the dead I had not fully given myself to such a quest.

If only saying "no" was an easy task.

Eastern Promises

"Brakas," Azazel had said, placing a hand on my shoulder and gripping tightly. His fingertips were sharp, almost pointed, and I could feel them digging in to my flesh through my shirt. "You must go to Brakas, and find the Stone."

"The Emerald?"

He nodded. Something about the way he spoke, the smooth cadence of his voice and the feigned desperation that soaked each and every word; I couldn't help but hang on to his instructions.

"Where is the Emerald?"

"The high priest of Brakas was a proud man," Azazel said. "He keeps the gemstone of the great city seated at the end of his staff, instead of where it belonged. Find the staff, and you will find the stone."

It seemed simple enough, though after nodding my approval, clarity returned. "Where it belonged?" I took a step forward. "And of what purpose do these Stones hold? I've heard many stories, but none that would drive me to risk life and limb for them."

Azazel looked up to the sky. "Do you wish to see the Sun rise again? Do you remember the days, so long ago; when there were still days?" He spoke wistfully, lazing about. "And the nights! Oh what fun could the nights be! Can you truly appreciate the smaller things in life if you cannot see them under the light—and the absence, of course—for which they were made? We did everything in service of the Sun and the Moon, and they have left us."

Something inside my mind resonated with his words, rippling out like water droplets in a pond as the morning rains began, and I felt as though there was a fire blooming from the depths that I had forgotten was there; buried by years of doubt.

"We are not creatures of just the night, or just the day," he continued. "We never were. Even now I watch in horror as people return to the surface here, sworn to my protection as they always have been, even in my own absence. But these are not people anymore. Whoever did this sought to eliminate people and they succeeded. The world of men has fallen, and as far as I can see there were no survivors." He paused for a second, affording me a side-eyed look. "Well, *one* survivor."

I looked down to the necropolis once more, the green light of the dome shining back at me, muted enough that I wondered if someone without Sunsight would even be able to see it at this distance. It wasn't duty that ran through me, or a sense of purpose; curiosity, more than anything, drove me to take my leave of Castleford and head east. I had forgotten why I had even ventured south in the first place— to find out why people had begun to return to the surface—and began to think of what the future might hold for me.

Just outside the dome, I saw familiar blue lights dancing amongst the distant graves and stacks of caskets. The Wisps were in force down in the necropolis, and it almost seemed as though they were calling out to me, begging for help to be set free. I thought about the ones I had encountered along the way, that had ushered me to discover the items I had found, and the way that they seemed dissipate after helping me. It was true to the stories: they were the lost souls of the dead, searching for that feeling that they had nothing left to offer the world of the living. There was something warming about the notion that helping me allowed them to pass on, but I wondered if they even knew who I was outside of a traveler. Perhaps they knew better than I did what my destiny held, through some connection to the spirit world that I couldn't possibly understand?

"When I return with the Emerald, then what?" I asked, staring out at the distant souls mingling amongst the graves.

Azazel just smiled. "Then there will be only three Stones remaining."

"Then we can stop this?"

"The Stones will afford us the power necessary to breach the dome and so much more," he explained, with a tone that made me believe he had explained before, when I was lost in thought. "We can return the world as it should be then," he said.

"And then," he continued, holding up an index finger. "Then, I will use the Stones to rid us of that pesky dragon problem." He pointed the finger to the mountain behind me, and I turned to follow. "Up there, there is a door. Behind that door lies a prison, built by the ones who came before us to hold the dragons. It appears a few escaped and with the Stones, well..."

I asked about the gems for the other cities, including Castleford.

Azazel explained that while those would be needed, the Emerald of Brakas was the first to be seen in the hands of a man in countless years.

There was a curved smile that always seemed to be tugging at the corner of his mouth, and I couldn't quite place why he was fighting it so much. The tone of his voice gave much away, and I could tell that there was a joy at the prospect of collecting the Stones that was bubbling just beneath the surface.

"Will you come with me?" I asked, unsure of myself for the first time. I could hear the pleading hidden beneath the words; I only hoped that no one else did.

He shook his head. "*They* need me here." He turned to look at Castleford, and then back to me. "I promised them safety if they returned above, and I cannot provide that if I am not here."

"Is that why you have returned?"

He nodded.

"How are you keeping the dragons, the dead, at bay?"

"They call me a Wizard, do they not? I *am* an old Wizard, you see," Azazel said, beginning to pace around me. "And as such, I know a trick or two. I have placed a spell of protection around this fair city; my home for many years, even when it seemed as though I had left. I have welcomed the people back. I have given them the ability to see, much like you have now." He stopped his pacing, and looked into my eyes. "Though I can already tell that yours is fading."

I blinked quickly, and looked skyward. I could not see much of a difference, though I was still unaccustomed to the colors of the new sky. I heard Azazel begin to chuckle, and looked back down to him.

"You will not notice a difference here," he said through his laughter. "The spell I have cast is not unlike the dome you see over the necropolis, only mine provides the people within with all the light they need; not at all useful to you on your quest, however." He paused for a second, bringing a finger to his lips. "Yours still seems to require more energy than you have to spare; without it, it will fail you."

I had not fully considered the magic failing altogether. Rayna mentioned nothing of what she was doing to me when she gave me the Sight, so I could only hope that it would remain. Though I was remembering some times where it had seemed to dim on me, much the same way that day turns to dusk. Without the Sun or the Moon providing any sort of light, there shouldn't have been a change in my vision, but I did not consider that I knew of the failing that he was speaking of. But the sight had come back to me, returning as vibrant as ever not long after it faded, so how could it be failing?

"Though the journey from Dewpond to here should have surely left you blind," he said, as if reading my mind. "So how is it—Ah!" He pointed with excitement. "How many did you slay?"

"What?" I asked him, perplexed.

"The Undead?" he clarified.

I shook my head, trying to count. They had thickened on the road from the Vale to Roughshod, just north of here; I had bloodied the mace I carried on my back many times there. I had encountered some fresher corpses further north, by Lowynn; between there, it seemed to me for the first time—and not the last—that the ones in between were almost inconsequential to me. "I'm not sure," I finally said with some weight.

"You've seen them glow?" Azazel said, ignoring my moment of guilt. "When they see you, they glow? You see, these are not corpses raised by a simple curse or spell. There is no way there could be one to raise them *all*. No, this is something else. These ghouls are being powered by something far greater than a curse. I believe that whatever magic is in you is fueled by this same light. It could be," he tapped his foot pensively, stroking his chin. "It could be that when you kill one of them, you replenish your own light."

Though it sounded absurd; the more I thought about it, the more it seemed to fit. After each encounter I felt I was able to see a little clearer, the road ahead less mired by encroaching darkness.

"Just remember, traveler; these creatures are no more people than ant. They serve one master, and hold no will of their own. There is no soul there, only a shell," I felt his hand on my shoulder, and I spun, unsure how he was able to get behind me. "You need not feel pity for them."

The Twins had, at some point during our conversation, vanished. I was not sure where they had gone, or when they had left; I was so entranced by Azazel. The way he moved was so fluid and quick, it felt like you had to be alert in order to keep your eyes on him. It filled me with a sense of distrust almost immediately, but I could see the evidence of his promise right behind me: Castleford seemed to be bustling beneath whatever protection Azazel was offering.

So I agreed to head east to Brakas, opting to take a path that skirted the outside of the Necropolis. I thought not of shelter, or of quitting. I thought not to ask of staying there in Castleford, under his protection. I only thought about the promise of morning.

HELCAT

The air grew cold as I approached the outer edge of the Necropolis. I pulled at the collar of the heavy cloak that one of the Twins—the male one—had given me as I departed from Castleford, heading northeast to the great city of Brakas.

It was the chill I had half-expected when I crawled out of the catacombs, what seemed like an eternity before. There had been many stories in the years we spent down there about what the surface would be like. Almost all of them claimed it would be barren and desolate; though one that always interested me painted a picture more true to life: one of fires from the sky, continuing long past the days that drove us to find shelter in the first place.

When we went underground, we did not think dragons. We thought the heavens grew tired of us, and rained their judgement. We thought the sky had begun to fall. We thought all manner of things to keep ourselves underground. Stories were told of the dangers of above, and each time a party was sent out, they failed to return. All any of it did was solidify the grasp on us that fear had taken. We would rather succumb to madness beneath the soil than dare stand up and face whatever it was we were afraid of.

To think of it—even now, as I give this account—gives me a headache. How could we have been such cowards? As I left Castleford I thought of it, again and again. I had only seen one dragon as I left. There were likely far more of us than there were of them. Why had we not fought for our homes? Why had we fled so quickly?

I was distracted by these thoughts when I had the wind knocked out of me.

Something hit me from behind, sending a wave of pain from my spine through my chest. And just as quickly as it hit me, it had sprung off, sending me falling forward into the soft grey dirt below me.

I spun quickly onto my back to see the rapid, water-like movements of the creature before me. It was covered with long grey fur that stood upright, making it look like it had quills. Its ears were long and pointed, the fur darkening to black at the tip of them, much the same as the tail did. It stared at me with black and beady eyes, its long jaw opening. I knew what it was as soon as I saw the saliva drip from the creature's fangs and freeze instantly, adding to the already impressive teeth an extra inch or so of solid 'ice fangs'.

It was a Helcat.

Another myth spread amongst the youth, far before we even had gone underground. They were said to be the watchers of the dead. Not protectors—not by any stretch. No, the helcats were in place to make sure the souls of the dead remained away from our world. They were said to have love for chasing wisps, but that was just them trying to return a lost soul to the beyond.

How many more stories crossed over like that? I'd no time to hold the thought then, and it escaped me in the moments that followed; but it was one that would have been good to spend some time on.

Helcats were also fiercely territorial. Their job went both ways, and anyone that came too close found out just how quick they could be.

I rolled to my side, just as the cat lunged at me, digging its claws into the dirt. I rose to a knee and grabbed for my sword, unsheathing it but at the cost of my balance. While I stumbled, the cat leaped at me, and I felt the full weight of it across my chest, sending me tumbling to the ground. I still grasped my sword, quickly swinging the blade around to protect myself from the long snout of the Helcat.

I was able to get the blade sideways into the cat's mouth, wincing each time I heard the crunching sound of the sword cutting into the ice-fangs it had grown.

Then the crunching sound became more of a squish.

I almost wretched when I heard the sound, followed quickly by the whimper of the beast, low at first as though it simply surprised itself. I felt it tugging up and down as it tried to free itself from the blade. I wanted to let go; but I also knew that I didn't want to face a helcat on its own, let alone a helcat armed with a sword. I had to shift my body left and right try and avoid the frantic slashes of its claws, feeling it tugging at my coat as we shifted as one in the dirt.

I felt the sword give from the bottom jaw, and planted my feet in the dirt. With all of my strength, I pushed the blade upward, into the upper jaw of the beast, where it was still stuck, and I pinned it to the ground below me. I felt its back claws paw at me, several slashes making it through my clothing and finding flesh. I pushed down on the blade as hard as I could, planting my boot on the end of the blade. With one hard step, the thrashing of the beast fell quiet, and I stood wearily.

It took me a moment to free the sole of my boot from the blade of my sword, and I was impressed that it held such an edge—happier it wasn't *more* of an edge. It took a little longer than that to get it free from the beast, and I looked down at the limp body of the creature. Its wounds had frozen over. I wondered if I had dealt a less fatal blow to it if the ice might serve as some sort of temporary healing or shield, an impressive advantage that I needed to be mindful of in the future.

Everything also got a little brighter. It seemed as though it was more than just the Undead that were fueled by whatever magic Azazel was speaking of.

I continued my trek, wary of what I may encounter on my path. I had to sneak through a section of the Necropolis that was one of the main throughways for bringing in the caskets from just south of Brakas. Coffins were stacked four or five high, though many stacks had fallen when their occupants broke free. Amidst the stacks I saw at least two more Helcats that I was able to narrowly avoid.

I was far from Azazel's protection. There was no telling how much it would take to bring a dragon down upon me. There was little in the way of activity on the surface, with mankind mostly being beneath the ground. If there were only a few dragons, it would take them time to be drawn to me.

If there were more than a few...

I stopped myself—had I really bought into the notion of it all?

That was the first time that doubt began to tug away at me. I knew that there would be an end—I had seen daylight in my life so I could believe in that, and it would one day disappear into legend much as the dragons did; just like the Helcats and Dawnflayer and the giant insects that once roamed the forests, long thought to be extinct.

That's when it struck me. Rayna was heading to Brakas as well. Perhaps I would find her and Brok—though it had been some time since Dewpond, as she had a head start and a more direct path. They might be able to help me make sense of all of this and at the very least, I could make a convincing argument for banding together. Many blades trump one, after all; though I was sure her skills could undoubtedly match or exceed mine. Neither of us had survived for so long for no reason—if they *were* still alive. I had hoped that they stayed, but when I laid eyes on Brakas I realized that there wasn't much reason to.

BRAKAS

Brakas was, at its peak, the most boisterous of the four cities. Its streets were lined with buildings four or more stories high, and almost every other one had a tavern or smokehouse on the first floor. There were legendary festivities thrown there, once upon a time.

But those times are long gone.

Most of the buildings had been reduced to one, maybe half a story, if that. Others were nothing but piles of rubble, with signs and glasses strewn about as if to mark what they once were; miraculously surviving the fires to serve as a standing memory of what used to be.

It was also the spiritual capital of Alghast, strange enough. It was as if the debauchery needed the appropriate balance close at hand. The church stood tall in the center of the city, amidst the largest buildings. Even there, nestled amongst them, the Spire of the chapel rose high above all else around it, tapering off to a narrow, needle-like point, so that all of the lost souls could find the place of forgiveness after a night where questionable morals reigned.

I had not been there before we were driven underground, but I had heard plenty of stories. A lot of our elders in those catacombs would spin yarns about nights in Brakas: how they couldn't wait to get back there. Only, as I crossed over the horizon and looked down upon the great city of Brakas, the image in my head, constructed from years of those stories, shattered like glass.

The city I looked upon was far worse than the others I had seen. Dewpond had been ruined, yes; but there was still some semblance of the city that I knew there. And Castleford had seemed virtually untouched by the fires—though I wondered how much the magic of Azazel had to do with that, given his sudden yet timely arrival.

Brakas was rubble. The only structure that still stood was the church, tall with its impressive and unharmed Spire. The buildings around it had been reduced to piles of rocks and stone and ash. It looked less like fire had rained from above, and more as though the buildings had been destroyed by some kind of explosion. There was very little evidence of roadways left, and almost nothing living; I saw no trees or bushes for as far as I could see. The city looked like the rocky encampments along riverbanks, only stretched farther and wider than one could even want to risk passing.

I wondered where Rayna and Brok could be hiding amidst all of the wreckage, if they were still around. There weren't many places that a Dawnflayer could hide, and Brakas was devoid of any cover for someone his size. It was possible that I had missed them entirely, but there was a part of me that hoped I had not. There was still a sour taste in my mouth from speaking to Azazel and the Twins, and I wished for nothing more than to be in the company of someone more level-headed.

I stood atop a hill overlooking the city and tried to map my route. I would head to the chapel, I was sure about that much. If the high priest was hiding anywhere in the city, it would likely be in the one structure still standing. It was clear to me—as it no doubt would have been clear to him—that the building was too important to fall victim to dragon's fire.

That's if he was in the city at all, I told myself. There was still the possibility that he had ventured into the Catacombs with the rest of Brakas. He could be lying dead or worse, roaming among the dead down there. I shuddered at the thought of all the bodies I had seen, and if they had begun to rise. I didn't want to go back down there, and wished that I had thought to take care of them—even if that was unlikely to be possible for me and me alone.

In the distance I saw a familiar orange glow that caught my eye. It was just east of the church, towards the waterfront. Beyond the beaches—another hot spot in Brakas, long before the Night—I saw the Great Wall that had been constructed, stretching across the gap in the mountains and protecting us from the Sea. In the early days, it is said that mankind tried to venture out on the water, only to find there were horrific things living beneath the glassy surface. To protect us, where the mountains failed to, we built a wall; first of wood and mud, then of stone and metal.

As I looked at the water, I saw it as something else. I didn't see it as a glass surface with things I couldn't imagine living below; rather, it was a mirror for the sky, reflecting the colors I had seen surrounding the black void where the Moon still sat. That, too, was reflected on the surface of the water and acted as a reminder, setting me back on task. I returned my attention to the glow I had seen.

And then more orange glows, here and there, began to pop up. The undead had seen something or someone that spooked them. I had grown accustomed to that trait in my travels, and felt a tugging in my arm, wanting to reach for my sword and head for where they were. Something in me was beginning to *enjoy* the fight; but I calmed myself.

I strained my eyes to see, wondering if the Sunsight was beginning to fail me, or if the distance was just too great; it seemed to me there was another light, darting between the orange glows. The other light was the same blue I had seen when encountering the wisps, only growing much brighter each time it came close to one of the other lights, fading again as it got away.

I had not seen wisps reacting to the dead before, or the other away around, so it struck me as odd. There was no pattern to the wisp's darting from one spot to the next, either. It didn't seem as though it had a destination in mind, it was just trying to get away from the shambling corpses. The bright blue light had been far brighter than even the ones I saw before I was able to *see* again. And it moved with much more haste than any I had encountered before. Perhaps that was only because it was fleeing, but something about it didn't feel that way.

I turned my attention upwards, feeling the chill rising up my spine before I was even able to see the dragon from Dewpond appear overhead. It was quite a ways off, but I could still feel the wind from each flap of its impressive wings, as if it were pushing me away from the city. I thought about returning to Castleford, and asking Azazel to blind me again, and let me stay there. I thought about how easy it would be to even return to Dewpond, and take up residence in the library. Hell, I even thought about heading north to Alduin, and continuing farther into the woods farther north. There was a volcano past there that I had always wanted to see.

I wanted to be anywhere the dragon *wasn't*.

Instead, I stood and watched as the great beast hovered over the city, watching the lights dance on the ground beneath it. I waited for the flame, but it never came. The dragon didn't even so much as begin to churn the great fires within its maw. It just watched, and waited; just like I was doing. The brow of the dragon was different from the one I had seen before; more narrow and long than wide. There was something else that was missing...

I saw no Rider.

It was difficult, but I was able to pull my attention away from the riderless dragon to look down at the dance of the lights in the city. The blue light had finally pulled away from the growing cluster of orange lights behind it, and while it still shone bright—fear had overtaken it completely—I suddenly lost sight of it. Somewhere amidst the skeletons of some buildings, the light had vanished.

I craned my neck to try and look around any obstacles, as though I would be able to find a magical perspective from where I stood, seemingly a world away from what was happening in the city below me, to no avail. If the Wisp was still lit, I would be able to see it, plain and simple. If I could not see the source itself, the surrounding glow would be hard to miss, even with the artificial light that burned in my eyes.

Then, one by one, the dead's glow began to vanish as well; all around the same spot. It was then that I discerned where they were going: They had found their way into the Catacombs.

I was overwhelmed with curiosity over the nature of the wisp, if that's even what it was. It seemed different from the rest, and the rest had proven most helpful over the course of my journey thus far. I had at least three lead me to food stores after I left the necropolis, and one that had found a portable whetstone that I was able to use to hone my blade, and it even worked on the mace.

I began to rationalize with myself. I could check the chapel, see if the priest was still there, and then investigate the chase I had seen. Or I could investigate the wisp, and then head to the church. I worried what might happen if the wisp was caught. If it was truly just a spirit, a soul looking for one last purpose on this gods-forsaken world before passing on; could it even fall victim to violence? It had been running scared, so clearly it believed it was at risk of harm; but why? What made it so different?

The questions began to eat at me, and I looked back up to the sky. At some point while lost in my thoughts, the dragon had left. I marveled at the silent quickness it seemed to possess, and how it seemed to come and go without much alarm. There was still a lot I didn't know about the dragons, and the legends were so plentiful that they were less than helpful.

But I took its absence as my moment. I quickly descended the hill, and began to move through the rubble of Brakas, not towards the church, but towards where the lights had vanished.

I was going back underground.

A Fine Mess

The catacombs were as I remembered them. The walls were still sweating with moisture and there was a stale smell that hung in the air. The sound of water dripping somewhere in the distance had yet to cease, and I felt a chill when I descended the narrow stone steps that were once tucked away in the backroom of what may have been a bakery, evidenced by some of the cookware and signs that remained among the rubble above.

It was then that I learned that the Sunsight proved just as useful underground as it had above; illuminating the otherwise dark tunnels as I tried to navigate the maze that sprawled out beneath the ground. The Catacombs were large and winding and stretched from west to east—Dewpond to Brakas—and south to north—Castleford to Alduin—with tunnels that were more like mazes than anything. It was possible it was a design decision; any intruders would be easily lost down there; but it took me and mine many years to get used to navigating them, as we were largely unaware of them until the Night began.

There were parts of the Catacombs that also ran beneath the Necropolis. I had taken one such path when investigating Rat's massacre, what felt like a lifetime before. I had briefly considered trying to navigate the area beneath the Necropolis, to see if I might find my way to the Cathedral underground, rather than above. I saw images of undead still lingering, and the winding mazes that I had never quite figured out as a child. I decided to try getting the Emerald first, before venturing into the unknown below once more.

The Catacombs also stretched north past Alduin, stopping just shy of the Misty Woods, which is said to be where the Faeries still lived, hidden in a grove said to be beset by whispers, somewhere within the Woods. It was where Rayna had learned of the magic that she used; the magic that now ran through my eyes. Faeries were not exempt from the stories of my youth, though they were talked about much more openly, having been seen up until a few decades before the Night began. They were said to offer supplementary teachings to the students of the Academy in Alduin, to teach them about magic—but something happened that closed the grove to man, and allowed the mists to descend on what *were* the Whispering Woods, before they became the Misty Woods.

Where the Catacombs ended in the North was also the end of the surface supply route. Not everything that we needed was available in the great chasm of Alghast—some of the lands have proven most barren, and unable to sustain even the most basic of crop—but the land is virtually inaccessible. Mountain ranges run from north to south down the western side of Alghast, encroaching on Dewpond and Castleford. To the East was the harbor, and while it once served as a great supply route, the waters had, as far as I had been told, become too dangerous for regular travel, the wall having been constructed. The forests to the North were set with magic that made it too easy to get lost in, and the mountains to the West and south were not easier to traverse one way than the other—Alghast was on her own, isolated and dependent only on herself; which means *we* needed to supply her.

The more I learned about the subterranean labyrinth that I had spent my formative years in, the more the little things began to make sense.

What eluded me still was where the chase had gone after breaching the surface. I could not find any signs of the Wisp or whatever I had seen, not to mention the Undead that followed it down. I couldn't find signs of anything, save for dark markings on the wall; splashes and arterial sprays that I knew, almost at once, the origins of.

I tried to map out the area the best I could, based on what I had seen above ground, and my brief journey into the Brakas catacombs all that time before. It was different, coming at it from the side that I was; but I was sure that I would have seen more signs of Rat's attack before long. Instead, after what felt like hours of exploring the dark tunnels and several chambers that I felt I recognized, I found nothing.

There were some blood stains on the walls, and some marks on the floors and walls from wayward blades, frantically searching the air for enemies. If I hadn't been able to see in the dark, I don't even think I would have been able to see those. Armaments and shreds of fabric were still littering the ground, though it seemed as though a path had been cleared—things were kicked to the side and the things that weren't had been trampled down by many feet. And even still, as I searched the rooms, I didn't take in fully what I was seeing. I already

had one question on my mind that didn't have an immediate answer,
which brought immediate anxiety to me:

Where were all the bodies?

My heart sank. In my haste to discover the fate of Brakas and the
stores beneath the ground at the hands of that dastardly crew, the nature of the world had slipped my mind. I had seen one, maybe two
raise from the dead in my lifetime; but that happened when I was a
child. And in the first years of the Long Night, there were many warnings; but our means of dealing with it were sound enough that it
wasn't something I thought about regularly, and had only sprung to
mind as I stood in the empty halls, wondering where the corpses had
gone. I drew my weapons, both of them, taking no care to be silent. I
suddenly felt a thousand eyes on me, and knew that they would be
lurking somewhere, surprised they hadn't heard me or come searching yet. The tunnels were tight and winding, but the chambers were
open enough that I knew I would be able to defend myself.

I had to find that Wisp!

I ducked through a doorway and found myself in a large chamber
that looked like it had been used as a cafeteria, with rows of tables
running lengthwise across the room made of heavy oak, complete
with benches that just looked like lower, thinner versions of the tables.
I closed my eyes and listened for any signs, living or otherwise. I
could hear the sound of the water droplets, all around me—it's a
wonder the tunnels weren't flooded yet just based on the consistency
of the sound—and of the breeze from above trying to find its way in.
And most of all, amidst the ambient sounds of the Catacombs, I heard
nothing. It was oppressive and staggering. It felt like a physical force
pushing down on me, and I had to open my eyes.

I couldn't tell if her eyes were that vibrant a blue, or if it was the
ethereal glow that surrounded her; but I found myself staring into the
eyes of what looked to me to be a woman. And although her face was
a little familiar, a little fair; it was also suddenly right *there*.

I nearly jumped out of my skin, though I tried my best not to show
it. I tightened my hold on my weapons—both of them, despite the
fragile nature of the woman's look—and took a step back. I felt sweat
break on my brow immediately, with droplets rolling down my face as
the shock of her sudden appearance tried to force its way out of me.

She was unmoving, and as I stepped back I was able to see all of
her. The blue glow subsided slightly, and it was calming to see. She
still glowed—about the same as most of the wisps I had encountered—but I was able to see more of her as the light dimmed. She was
tall and slender. She wore robes, bordering on rags, that hung off her

shoulders. Her face was soft and comforting. I wasn't sure how much was the calming blue light they seemed to emanate, but looking into her eyes helped put me at ease. They seemed to shine brighter than anything else, though I could tell the more I looked at them that there was sadness and fear hiding just behind them, growing as she looked into my eyes as though searching for something.

I snapped out of my trance, and as she opened her mouth to speak, I was looking around frantically for her pursuers.

"I lost them," she said. Her voice was like a singer's.

I swallowed what fears I had and returned my attention to her. "I don't mean to be rude," I said, proud of myself for not just blurting the question out. "But what are you?" I could not afford to chance a trap. I kept my weapons ready, just in case, but was met with the same sort of wandering doubt that had plagued me for so long, leaving me feeling more at ease.

She turned her eyes downwards, and I wondered if the question offended her. She looked back up at me, and forced a smile. "I don't know." Her voice gave her away as it shook, uncertainty and worry laced throughout the three simple words.

"What is your name?" Silence. I looked around again, making sure the coast was clear but also knowingly and irrationally growing impatient with her.

"Are you the one?" she finally asked, after a moment. There was a look of recognition in her face as she studied mine. "I have seen you before, in my endless dreams—before they ended, and I woke up."

I tilted my head to the side while looking back at her, confused. "Which one is that?"

"Maybe the one to return the world as it was?" she asked, unsure of herself. There was a look of hope, while brief, flash across her face. "Maybe fate is still working on a path for you," she said while trailing off. She wasn't talking to me anymore, but someone or something else that wasn't in the room.

I took a step towards her, and she flinched. My face had grown sour, as I felt a pressure to keep moving, weighing down on me. "We don't have time to discuss such things," I said sternly, my eyes darting from one door to the next and I realized two things: One, it had been some time since I encountered an Undead; and two, the darkness was starting to encroach on my vision.

The sight was fading from me.

I grabbed her by the arm looked into her frightened eyes. "Have you seen the High Priest?" She stared at me, dumbfounded. "Have you seen the Emerald? The stone he has on his staff? Have you seen it?" It was clear to me she knew nothing of what I was talking about. My voice had begun to raise in a panic—I did *not* want to be blind once more—but I didn't care.

It was my touch, more than my tone, that sent her into a frenzy as she tried to break free from my grasp. It was clear to me, watching her face twist, that she was trying to quiet me; to keep me from my exasperated questions, for fear of what might be drawn by the commotion. The thought had crossed my mind as well, but instead of deterring me from speaking up, it only encouraged me. I needed to replenish my eyes.

She saw them first, screaming out and then pointing behind me. The chamber had four doors, two each on the walls opposite myself and the Wisp. The other walls, bare stone brickwork, were adorned with torches that had long since been extinguished with no one to care for them. We stood in the center, about twenty long strides from any of the walls. Behind me, in one of the arched doorways, I saw the orange light creeping over the shadows on the wall, perfectly framed by the open door. Out of the corner of my eye, I saw her perplexed expression as she noticed the small smile lifting the corner of my mouth as I tested my grip on the sword.

I wish I could say the battle was over quick; as I approached the door, hoping that it would be, I heard a screech from behind. I spun, and saw the Wisp do the same, turning to face the source of the awful sound. The farthest door from where I stood was beginning to glow as well, and the closest on the opposite wall was shining bright, an undead soldier standing in plain view, with more funneling in behind him.

I very quickly lost count, and slid over the surface of a table to get back to where the Wisp stood, more towards the center of the room. I pushed her behind me, and began to strafe around her, trying to get a sense for who would strike first. I had hoped to draw *some* but it was clear to me that there were quite a few more than just *some*, filtering into the room. My foolishness be damned! It didn't take long for their numbers to topple even what I had seen when watching the pursuit from a distance, and it became clear to me where at least some of the bodies that littered the catacombs had gone—there were many in robes similar to the ones the members of the clergy wore in Brakas, and they were mostly unarmed saved for scavenged dirks and notched short swords.

As the collective encircled us, I saw that they had left the biggest of their ranks to guard the doors. I couldn't recall seeing them before; big and burly, about as tall as I was but much wider. Whether it was the heavy armor they wore, or their build beneath, I couldn't be sure; I just knew they were big. Their aura burned red, not orange, but was somewhat muted in comparison. Their armor was plate, and looked fairly new, as if it was provided to them rather than scavenged. From behind face guards on heavy iron helmets, I saw their unmoving eyes set into dark grey skin, focused on me and glowing with the same red as their aura. In their hands, they held heavy weapons: three had morning stars with spiked balls the size of my abdomen on the ends of them, the other held a battle axe that I feared could cleave the world in two, it was so large.

The Sentinels—as I took to calling them—watched as I began the defense, bringing the mace down on the head of the undead that had shambled in front of me. I felt the fire returning to my eyes and I opened them wide. It felt like I was seeing the room for the first time, and a surge took over me as I stepped away from the Wisp, and began to push back against the walking corpses. I dodged under and around swings, taking every opportunity I could to do as much damage as I could with the mace. I quickly switched to the sword as I slid over a table to get away from a group that was too close, and cut down a group that was just far enough away. I continued using the tables to my advantage, funneling groups into laneways before sliding over to deal with any stragglers. I was able to strike down fifteen or twenty, before my arms grew weary—though, fortunately their numbers dwindled to match the effort I had left.

Sweat began to soak through my clothing as I fought. I rolled out of the way of a downward strike from an undead wielding a mace not dissimilar to the one I held in my hand, and rose to one knee. My shirt clung to me, and I wiped the matted hair and sweat from my face with my forearm. They had thinned, coming at me three at a time, at most, but there still seemed to be no end to them. I continued fighting until I had to let loose screams of effort and anguish with each strike; although those would feel the most powerful of all of the attacks I had made that day. I kept fighting until there was nothing left to swing my sword or the mace at, and I stood and tried to catch my breath.

When *they* saw I finally had a moment to breathe, the Sentinels began to move. I heard the sound of the armor clattering about as they took their big, lumbering steps forward into the cafeteria. They moved in unison, as though controlled by the same strings, and held their weapons out in front of them. Without conferring with one another, one of the morning star Sentinels took an independent step towards me, and I understood at once that my fight was not over, even though I knew I wasn't ready to fight *it*, let alone the other *three*. The other three that would no doubt join the fray should I even start to get the upper hand. But I didn't know what else I could do; three of the doors were still blocked and there was a large suit of armor moving towards me, ready to cave my chest in and leave me in a pile of my own viscera.

Still on one knee, and feeling the full weight of the weapons in my hand, I watched as the Sentinel moved towards me, picking up its pace. It drew its morning star to the side, telegraphing the attack. I dove forward, and rolled under the swing; the sound of the heavy iron spike ball colliding into the ground with enough force to crack the stone. I rose to my feet and spun on my heels to face the Sentinel. Its weapon had also hit with enough force to become lodged into the stone, so I sprang towards it, holding the mace above my head. I swung the mace down with as much force as I could muster, slamming it home against the Sentinel's back, leaving a crater-like dent in his armor and sending him stumbling forward. I prepared a sword strike, raising it as I had raised the mace and looking for a spot of clearance between the helm and shoulders where the neck might be exposed.

It spun quickly, bringing the morning star around. I just barely managed to dive backwards, kicking my feet up as my back hit the ground so I could try and roll through. I wasn't as nimble as I had hoped, and landed hard on my knee, small pieces of stone sent up by the morning star digging into me like small daggers. The pain shot through my leg, and I clenched my teeth, trying not to yelp. I swung with my sword as I tried to stand, and felt the blade fruitlessly clang off a wrist guard before stumbling backwards and finding my footing—tenuous as it was.

I stood there breathing heavily, and stole a glance at the Wisp. She had closed her eyes, and buried her face in her hands. The blue aura surrounding her seemed to ripple and intensify with each passing second as it looked like she was sucking in air. Why were they no longer attacking her?

The Sentinel took a few more lumbering steps towards me and I heard the screech of a wooden chair leg being pushed along the dry stone floor. I looked to my right and dove, sliding halfway under a table, turning my head just in time to see the battle axe of one of the other sentinels collide with the stone, sending fragments flying upwards. I skittered forward along the ground until I was fully concealed by the table. I peered out, and saw the other two sentinels had begun to close in as well.

I nodded to the Wisp, who looked at me with worried eyes, and then nodded to one of the vacant doorways. She seemed to under-stand what I was saying right away, and dashed towards one the door. As soon as she was on the other side, I heard a scream rise and then sudden silence; even though I didn't have time to consider what error I had made, it was enough to distract me from the approaching Sen-tinels.

I tried to watch the doorway the Wisp had gone through, looking for any sign of her light, but I could hear the Sentinels drawing closer, and I realized that I could not worry about a Spirit I had just met. She was already dead—probably. I was not. I had not *planned* on dying underground, even when that seemed to be the only option available to us; but as I began to realize my own carelessness in putting the Wisp before myself, I had allowed the Sentinels to draw too close. It would take strategy for me to even be able to topple one—there were *four* that had descended on me, surrounding the table that I was hid-ing under.

There was a roar from the direction of where the Wisp had van-ished from my sight—familiar and fierce and full of hope instead of fear, despite what the Wisp's scream had first indicated to me. Time seemed to slow as the Axe Sentinel, towering over the table I was un-der, raised its weapon. It meant to cut through the table—and me, if it could—and all I could see around me where thick, armored legs. It was the sound of stones crumbling, that had come from behind me followed by a quick growl that brought about a change in fortunes. There was a large blur, flying over the table I was under, back and forth to the Sentinels. I could hear the swings and the grunts of effort and the impact of the attacks. One by one, the Sentinel's weapons fell to the ground, ringing off the stone. I could not see what was happen-ing fully, but I wasn't sure that I wanted to. My instincts were telling me to close my eyes, and wait for it to end.

So I did.

When I heard nothing but breathing, heavy and labored, I opened my eyes. Before me there was the headless body of one of the Sen-tinels—the axe on the ground next to it had hinted at which one—with the now exposed neck facing me. There was no blood, but I still stared in horror as I watched the legs of the brute walk around the table to where one Sentinel still stirred. The others were long dead, but this one still clung to something until a large foot came down on its head, unprotected after its helm had fallen off in the scuffle.

Suddenly, the table was ripped away from me, and I was exposed to the room. I had to stifle a surprised yelp, but the hope that I had felt earlier was rewarded. I knew the brute.

"Up?" Brok asked, extending his impressive mitt to help me up.

I shook my head, waving off the outstretched hand and nodding at my knee. "I think I will wait down here for a few moments."

"Certainly wasn't expecting to see you again." Rayna's voice echoed through the mess hall, and I turned my head to try and find her. My vision was beginning to darken, but not from failing sight—I felt like I was on the verge of passing out. "You look tired, how about we talk in the morning?" She spoke with some sarcasm, though I wasn't able to appreciate it in the moment.

It was the last thing I heard before drifting off to sleep.

The Door

When I awoke, the Wisp was sitting across from me on the floor, legs crossed. The blue aura had subsided to nothing more than a faint glow, and she seemed calmer than she had been before. She watched me with some concern and more than a little curiosity, which only served to spark my own.

I sat up in a hurry, feeling as though I was still in great danger—a carry-over from a dream I couldn't remember, or the sudden end of my fight before—and rested back on my elbows when I saw Brok and Rayna sitting together in one of the corners. Rayna was tearing pieces off a loaf of bread, alternating between shoving them hungrily in her own mouth, and handing them to Brok.

I looked at the Wisp. "What's your name?" I kept my voice quiet, not wanting to draw any more attention—though I was sure that we had taken care of most of what we would find.

She shook her head. "I don't remember," she said. "I don't remember anything." She looked down at her hands, and flipped them a few times. It was as though she were still getting used to her body—perhaps she hadn't occupied one in a while?—and I watched her brow furrow as her mind was racing. I only wished I could know what she was thinking.

Rayna had looked over and discovered that I was awake. We locked eyes and although I tried to look away, I couldn't. There was a telling fire in her eyes, angry with me for even *being* in Brakas, I was sure; but there was something else there. I had not known her for long, but we very quickly learned to have entire conversations just from looking at one another. I saw her eyes finally leave mine and dart to the blue woman sitting next to me.

Rayna was scared of the Wisp.

I returned my attention to the spirit, and began to stand. As soon as I was on my feet, she eagerly followed suit. I stood almost two heads taller than her, but she looked up at me with bright eyes, filled with hope. It wasn't as though she idolized me, or looked up to me; she was counting on me for something—I just wasn't sure yet what that could be.

"Lissa," I said, looking down into her eyes, chuckling at myself for the thought. She seemed perplexed—I was, too—but the name popped into my head as I looked at her, as though it came from her eyes and her gaze, not from my mind. "That's what we shall call you." I put my hand on her shoulder. She was cold. "At least, until we find out your true name."

My moment with Lissa was over quickly, as Rayna called out, still staring down at the loaf of bread. "I thought you were heading to Castleford?" Brok reached out with a large hand and gestured for her to lower her volume. She scoffed at him defiantly.

I turned to face her, drawing a breath. "I was," I stammered. "I did. There was a man there who told me that there may be a way to return the world as it once was."

Rayna laughed to herself, looking up at Brok. His back was to me, but I could almost see his incredulous smile anyway. "What has Brakas got to do with saving your world, then?"

I began to explain to her the story of the Stones and while she did not seem to *believe* me, she did not interrupt me. While I was speaking, I kept glancing to Brok and Lissa, and saw their expressions change as I spoke, listening more intently as the story went on. Rayna must have noticed them, too; the smile had faded completely from her face by the time I was finished.

"I read a lot of books when I was young," Rayna said after a moment of heavy, pensive silence. "Many legends about times passed, as it seems you've heard. According to most of them, the world was once overrun by monsters. We were a nothing species to them, food at best and something to be toyed with at worst, until they found four crystals, deep in the heart of the mountain to the North," she turned away from me, bringing a hand to her chin, stroking it in thought. "From each crystal, they took but a small fragment. Even those small pieces, those Stones, were powerful enough that the four souls that had ventured into the volcano were able to banish the monsters and demons from our world, and bring about the dawn of the human race."

A part of me that I had thought still remained in the Catacombs under Dewpond resurface: the skeptic that would always laugh off the stories the younger kids would tell me, passed down from their older brothers. I didn't want to believe them, and I hadn't had any bothers of my own growing up to tell me stories, or for me to tell stories to; I had always been on my own to craft my view of the world, and it was becoming more apparent to me that I had done so incorrectly.

"And on that, the first morning of *our* time, the four brought the rest of us back to the surface where they told us we belonged. They founded Alduin, the great city to the North, where they began to teach people everything that they knew, so that they might prevent history from repeating itself. But as time went on, the lessons turned to stories, and the stories then turned to legend. Man ill learns from legends," she said. She smiled, shaking her head. "It was supposed to be a cautionary tale—a warning to stop *this* from happening. Is it irony that we turned to a deaf ear to the *one* 'fable' we weren't supposed to?"

"It's funny how those stories always have such a heavy dose of it," I mused. It was still difficult for me to believe the story. While I had seen many things on my travels, believing that four were able to banish monsters and Darkness itself with Stones seemed beyond what even I could accept.

"Thank you," I said to Brok after a pause, not knowing how to respond to Rayna's legend, "for saving my life." I turned back to Rayna. "I thought you two would have been long gone by the time I arrived."

Her eyes seemed to watch mine, searching. "We were exploring the catacombs," she said. "We were trying to find any supplies that might be able to help us, but it seems like someone else already claimed everything."

I sighed, the anger returning. "They did," I said as I saw flashes of the bloody—but silent—revenge I had taken on Rat. "They paid for it in full."

Rayna looked at me knowingly and leaned forward, resting her elbows on the table. She pointed to the door her and Brok had entered through—or at least what was left of it after Brok's larger form had forced his way through. "There is a lot of blood left on the walls through that door," she said. I followed her gaze and thought correctly that she was pointing west, towards Dewpond. "There are no bodies. Since you know the fate of the supplies, and those that took them; maybe it is *your* turn to tell us a story. What happened down here?"

And so I told her about Rat and his crew, and the slaughter that had taken place. I had expected her to baulk at the notion that a small group of thieves was able to get the jump on the entirety of the Brakas survivors, but she confirmed to me that the people of Brakas were not fighters. If they were not part of the clergy, they were drunkards. In many cases, they were both.

They were not ready for the new world.

"I had expected many more of the dead to be walking these tunnels," I said with quiet confusion. "But they seem to have gone elsewhere. Perhaps above?"

Rayna shook her head. Brok turned to face me. "West," he grumbled.

I furrowed my brow, looking to him and then Rayna. "West?"

"We found a large iron door, leading to the Necropolis tunnels, where it seems most of the killing took place," Rayna said. "It was open when we found it."

Father Paxton

I was beginning to understand the task put before me, though I wondered at length as we left the Catacombs whether it was a quest that, given the choice, I would have still taken on. Had it been a choice? Had I missed that opportunity? I toyed with the idea of returning to the Dewpond Catacombs, to see what had transpired there—secretly hoping all the while that if I did, I would be redeemed and seen as a hero and welcomed into the warm embrace of complacency that we had started to fall into before tensions began to rise.

Instead, we were marching above the ground, towards the Church. I was in the front with Rayna, with Brok in the rear; Lissa was in the middle, looking all around in her sheepish way, new to the world once more. Most of the activity in the city had found its way underground earlier, but there were some stragglers that needed to be taken care of.

As we approached the building I stood in awe of how pristine it looked amongst the rubble surrounding it. The air still smelled of sulphur, a burning and rotten flesh that stung the nostrils, and there was a smog that hung over everything in the surrounding area—but the church stood tall among it, unfazed by the world around it. It was breaking through the fog like a light in the darkness; one last chance at hope and respite and calm.

The walls of the Church were white and I was sure looking at it that even something without the gift of Sunsight would be able to see it standing there amidst the dark. It was like a beacon, filling me with a warmth I hadn't felt in quite some time; it would combat a coldness that no amount of cloaks and coats could help with. The roof, slanting deep to a point, had smaller stone spires jutting upwards in pairs down the length. The main Spire, sprouting from the tip of the bell tower like a vine reaching up towards the heavens. Even as we approached I had difficulty finding the tip of it, as it just seemed to become part of the sky above.

Both Rayna and myself looked at the double doors of the Church, then back to Brok. He nodded dutifully, and moved towards them. He pushed hard and they creaked open slowly. I noticed that they seemed to be on some sort of pulley system, operated from the inside, kicking into gear once force was applied to the doors and helping to pull them open. They were so quiet that I thought the gasp I heard was the mechanism finally making some sort of noise, and not one of our traveling companions seeing the horrific sight contained within the Brakas Church that we found ourselves in.

The inside of the Church was as big as one could imagine—possibly bigger, somehow, inside than out—but it was *littered* with bones. Piles of disassembled skeletons were strewn about the floor. The wide, red carpet bisecting the room from the entrance to the massive podium where the High Priest gave his sermons was the only spot *not* hidden by the bones. The piles were of varying heights, with some being only a foot or so tall, while others still were as tall as I, maybe even taller. It was a dreadful sight, made worse by the brilliant light that seemed to fill the building as if it were a bright summer day.

The four of us entered, Brok and Rayna first, myself and Lissa close behind. The Wisp looked scared, and I couldn't blame her. She clasped her hands together in front of her, and looked around worriedly. "We're not supposed to be here," she said.

I looked back at her, and then ahead to the podium. I tried to keep my mind off the skeletons that surrounded us, convincing myself that I wasn't seeing movement in my peripheral vision.

It seemed that someone had been collecting bodies—why, I could not know. But it must have taken years to accumulate so many. And all of the bones were so clean that part of me wondered if the owner of the macabre set had extracted and cleaned them himself. The very thought of it made me sick, but I couldn't keep my mind from wandering back to it, like a moth to flame.

What had happened in Brakas?

Even the bodies I had seen below, so long ago—there weren't as many as I would have expected of a city the size of Brakas. Many died on the surface when the fires came, and it was hard to know which places were hit the worst. Of the cities I visited on my journey, Brakas was by far the most devastated by the dragon's attack. Aside from the Church, there had been little standing; but there were still too few bodies; too few Undead. Even when I had come to Brakas beneath the ground before, there had been fewer bodies than I had expected—hadn't there?

We cautiously moved deeper into the Church, weapons drawn. Brok had quickly and quietly shifted to his larger, more powerful form, and was taking point.

Click!

Behind us, a sudden mechanical sound, followed shortly after by the humming of a winch. The large double doors leading into the church were closing on their own. We spun to take notice of the door, and I could tell there was a quick decision being made by all of us whether to stay or leave. While we were distracted, the decision was made for us—we were hit hard by a concussive blast from behind, as though someone had swung a large tree trunk at us.

I landed on my stomach, a few strides inward from the door, and slid hard into the wall. I pushed myself up on my hands, the shoulder that had hit the wall seizing at once before releasing, and looked out through the closing doors. Rayna, Brok, and Lissa had all been blown through them. The trio had landed outside of the church, and were stirring, trying to figure out where the attack had come from. Rayna and I locked eyes through the closing doors just as they slammed home, and I rose to my feet. Without turning, I felt a presence behind me—the question of who it was that closed the doors and struck us was not so much a question; I *knew* that when I turned I would see him. I *knew* that when I turned I would see what it was that I had journeyed all that way for.

Standing at the base of the podium, there was a man. He stood nearly a head taller than I, and wore impressive white robes adorned with gold trim. His headpiece, tall and narrow, was similarly white and ornate. In his right hand, he held a gold staff. Nestled into the metal at the head of the staff I saw the brilliant green gemstone that had brought me here: The Emerald of Brakas, glowing beautifully in its nest as if aflame.

Anticipating chaos from the emerald, I drew my weapons. I could see a wicked smile on the face of the priest. His skin, dark and grey, seemed to hang off his bones until his toothy grin pulled it all back. His eyes were deep and sunken into his face, almost entirely covered by the shadow of his brow. His robe slid down his right arm to reveal his bony hands gripping the staff. The priest lifted the staff, and begin to twirl the head of it, drawing a circle in the air above his head. There was a trail of green energy that hung in the air following the movements, and I looked around quickly before surmising that the attack that had knocked us from our feet may not have been a physical strike. The priest looked to be muttering something as he swung the staff, and there was a loud, metallic *clink* as the priest brought the staff back down, that wicked smile returning once more.

I thought to speak and call out to the father in the hopes that some shred of his humanity had remained. I could feel more than I could see that there was no hope of peaceful resolution, though he looked as though he were far beyond what he once was, descending somewhere beneath human to the carnal and the pure animal that we all were. The priest had gone mad long ago, the collection we were amidst was a clear indicator of that; I knew he would not offer the staff—or the Stone—to me willingly.

I began my approach, taking three massive strides before I felt a hand grabbing at my leg. I stumbled and just managed to stop myself from tumbling face-first to the ground. I turned my attention to the new assailant, wondering where they would have emerged from and if they were hiding in the bones, when I saw that it *was* one the bones. It was the hand of one of the skeletons, reaching out from the pile closest to me. It had pulled itself out to the shoulders, pulled together by some unseen magic and held to form despite being nothing but bone. The jaw of the skull hung open and the skeleton shrieked— though it was more likely that it was a sound made by whatever magic was keeping the bones together.

Pulling my leg free, I heard rustling coming from all around me. The movement in my peripheral vision just couldn't be ignored any- more. Bones were tumbling down, collecting on the floor, and reorga- nizing themselves right before my eyes. I was watching them form in stunned silence, not ready to believe what I was seeing. I turned to look at the Priest, but he was gone. There was an ominous cackling ringing off the walls of the Church, dashing from corner to corner, side to side, and wall to wall so quickly that I couldn't keep track. The Priest was everywhere, all at once—what were these Stones *capable* of?

I snapped out of my trance when I felt a skeletal hand on my shoulder. I spun, and brought my sword across. The blade cut through the spine with ease, the skeleton crumpling to the ground. Whatever magic was holding them together wasn't strong enough to *keep* them together, it seemed. I still had to be careful; there were so many of them that if I let them envelope me I would not be able to escape. And while they were largely unarmed—some small swords and dirks were scattered amongst the piles, notched and broken—I would be swarmed with ease if the magic were allowed anymore time to work.

I felt a gust of wind blow past me, and turned to see the smoke dissipating as the priest was suddenly standing just a few steps away from me. The Emerald continued to glow brilliantly in the staff, dis- tracting almost in its beauty. He swung the staff in an arc in front of him, leaving a trail of captivating green light. It hung in the air like a mist before shooting out towards me, a curved blade not unlike a scimitar only made of pure energy. It spread out like a wave, thinning but widening until it stretched across the whole of the Church. It cut through two skeletons on its way to me, and I realized that it was more than just a pretty light. I dove under the wave, and quickly rose to my feet and pivoting to bring the mace around, swinging it down at the Priest with all of my might...

...And my weapon rang uselessly off the ground, slamming into the carpet. The vibration it sent up my arm radiated through me like fire, and I couldn't help but wince with pain. The priest was gone—only smoke remained where he once stood before me.

I scanned the room with haste, trying to determine where he had gone to. I was pulled from my search by the outstretched arms of yet more skeletons approaching. I caught myself thinking that there could be no end to them before reminding myself that the piles, while altered by the raising skeletons, did not look like they had decreased in size since I entered the Church. I took swings at them with my weapons, sending the bones clattering to the ground. The skeletons were serving more as a distraction than anything else, and I nearly didn't see the energy wave coming towards me as I dealt with them.

I dropped to my belly, letting the wave fly over me. I could feel the heat of it, slicing through the air above me and burning out. There was a strength to his magic that, with the benefit of hindsight, tells me that he had been using the Emerald for quite some time. He had become quite adept at focusing its magic—though I saw that no skeletons seemed to raise when he was charging these attacks. Still, the waves of energy had been enough that they seemed to steal the breath from the air as they ripped through, and I struggled to find any as I climbed back to my feet and back into the fight.

Instinct drove my strike as I swung my sword around behind me. It connected with something and stopped. It took me a moment to register what was holding my attack back, but the Priest had used the Emerald to create some sort of shield, protecting his side from my blade. I was only hairs away from connecting, and it seemed to me that if I could just catch him off-guard—as I almost had there—I would be able to strike him down and claim the Emerald.

I was taken off my feet by another concussive blast, though weaker than before. I was too close to the priest for him to be able to fully charge or launch any sort of offensive, his attack one of desperation more than for the kill. As soon as he was able to create some distance, he vanished once more.

Quickly rising from the blow, before more skeletons were on me, I scanned left and right to find the tallest pile of bones. Inspiration struck me as I looked at the pile, and I began to scale it. The bones beneath me almost seemed to *squirm* as I climbed, though I felt safe in my ascent—I couldn't see him raising all of these bodies at once. I just needed a higher vantage point, so I could track him. At the very least, I thought I might be able to draw him out.

Another blast, and scores of fragmented bones flew out of the pile beneath me. I felt the shift under my feet, and knew that I wouldn't be able to stay there for long; I just had to see where the attack was coming from. He seemed to be warping from place to place, sending energy waves at me, chipping away at my footing. I waited patiently until I was sure the pile couldn't survive another blast, and I dropped down behind it and out of his sight for just a moment.

There was a puff of smoke, just a few quick strides from me around the side of what was left of the pile of bones, and I smiled at the opportunity. I dropped the mace on the ground, and slowly started making my way around the other side of the pile. As I rounded it, I saw the priest was drawn to the mace, and the sound it made as I dropped it to the floor. When I saw my moment, I struck. I plunged my sword into his back, just to the left of the spine, and pulled him as far down on the blade as I could, grabbing and holding him from behind, my elbow hooking under his chin.

"Try your disappearing act on me now," I said, holding him as he squirmed and screamed, thrashing wildly for a few brief seconds before the life drained from him.

I removed my sword, and let the body drop before me. I looked down at the staff, containing the Emerald, lying on the ground next to where we had stood in the Priest's final moments, and felt accomplishment wash over me. Whatever skeletons had been raised started to stumble and fall apart, returning to the mass of bones that they had been when we first entered. I looked back to the large doors of the church, and moved to the mechanism to open them.

Once I figured out how, I was able to let Rayna, Brok, and Lissa back in. They looked on in horror at the bones strewn about the church in much more disarray than they had been before. They also took notice of the bloodied corpse of the Priest, and even I saw for the first time that his blood was running black. Whatever twisted evil had overtaken him had poisoned him to the very core. I walked over to where he lay, and retrieved the staff. Rayna approached, her eyes glassy, never taking them off the green gemstone nestled into the head of the staff.

"Is that it?" she asked. "Hopefully it gives us less trouble than the other one."

I looked down at the stone, and then back to her. "Other one?" There was something dawning on me, but I couldn't quite place. I held the staff in my hands, feeling the weight but not appreciating that it was there. Something about what Rayna was saying and the way she was looking at the staff took me out of the room. It was just her and I in the white space we occupied as we carried on once more, just by looking at each other.

You mean to take this, I said to her. *Why?*

She did not answer me, but instead cast her eyes on the Stone once more, ending our unspoken conversation and leaving me to answer my own question.

"Can I see it?"

I took a step back from her. There was a desperation in her voice that I was just beginning to understand. I thought back to her musings on trust and wondered why I hadn't listened. She had tried to warn me, perhaps—or perhaps she had expected to do this on her own. In the end, it didn't really matter. After I took my step back, I felt a blow on the back of my head that brought me to the brink of consciousness. I dropped to one knee, trying to keep myself upright, and had the staff ripped from my hands. I tried to keep my balance but eventually fell. As I did, I saw Brok walking towards Rayna with the staff in hand, and she was reaching out for it, excitedly.

Rayna took notice of my fading consciousness, but also the rage that was keeping me from fading. Her and Brok had already begun to exit the Church, but she returned to my side, and knelt down by me. "It could have been anyone," she said. "I'm sorry it had to be you." She patted me on the back and returned to her feet, nodding to Brok, who had stepped around behind me.

The last thing I saw before Brok struck me again was Lissa, cowering in the corner. When I woke up, it was just the Wisp and myself. Rayna and Brok had long since absconded with the staff and the Emerald of Brakas, and left us with the body of a priest.

I looked to the podium, feeling the helplessness that often drove people to the Gods in the first place, needing a sermon more than ever. There, in brilliant calligraphy on the front of the bright oak wood, it read "Father Paxton."

BOOK TWO:
THE LORD OF DRAGONS

Betrayed

As I sat on the stoop in front of the church, the wide stone stairs that ran only a short distance up from the ground below to the flat stone platform that the building was resting on, I paused to consider the situation I had found myself in. Rayna had left with the Stone, and left Lissa and I inside the church. When I awoke, some time after they had left, Lissa told me that she had closed the doors to keep any of the monsters out—though resting amongst the skeletons was hardly my idea of safe.

Brakas was still ruined, rubble and debris scattered among the ground like memories of a city that had long since faded from thought. It wouldn't be long before all of the lives these cities once had —brilliant and telling in their own right—would fade into nothing. They would become nothing but stories that people told of the world as it used to be, and likely never would be again, until the stories themselves began to fade, their luster lost and people's undying yearning for *new* stories would take hold.

Even if I had succeeded, and collected the Stones to return the light; it would not have rebuilt the world as even I barely knew it. It would not have returned the lives and souls of all of those who were lost in the initial onslaught of the armies of the undead, or the attacks by the dragons, or through the battles we waged, deep underground when more pressing matters were facing humanity.

Was there anything I *could* have changed? Could I have seen Rayna's betrayal coming? *Was* it a betrayal, or had I simply been too trusting? She had taken the Stone from me, after all. And just after I had worked so hard to retrieve it. I was starting to feel the aches and pains from fighting Father Paxton as I rested, so there was no question of effort on my part; though the pounding in my head was exclusively the work of Brok, the Dawnflayer.

But still, there were questions that plagued my thoughts: Why had she gifted me the Faerie magic that allowed me to see in this darkened world, flawed as it was; if she only meant to use me in the end? I wondered if she would have helped me at all during the fight with the Father, or let me perish?

Or perhaps my arrival in Brakas only served to interrupt her plans to retrieve the Stone herself. After facing Brok earlier in my travels, I was confident that the two of them would have been able to face the Priest on their own. The real question then would have been why they waited until I had arrived? Surely they had been in the city long before I, as I had made the journey to Castleford to the South where I met Azazel, all while they were—again, presumably—heading directly to Brakas.

What had they been doing during that time, if not searching for the Stone? What business did they have underground? Had they seen Lissa, too?

I couldn't tell what was making my head hurt more: trying to figure out what had happened, or the impact from the Dawnflayer's strike. I snapped out of my trance when I felt Lissa's cold hand on my shoulder, the icy touch radiating even through the layers of leather that I was wearing. "Where will we go?"

Frustration boiled over, and I rose. I brought chin down to my chest and took a deep breath. "'We' are not going anywhere," I said coldly and under my breath. I didn't even turn to face her. "*I* am returning to Castleford. *You* can go wherever the hell you please."

I gathered up my things—I had left my weapons and pack sitting on the steps while I ruminated on the events of the day—and began descending the small staircase. She hurried after me.

"You can't leave me," she pleaded. "I don't know what to do."

I stopped, but only for a moment. I turned to her and saw the scared look in her eyes. "You think that *I* do?"

She nodded slowly, more hopeful than confident.

I shook my head, laughing. "I have tried to do the right thing, and have ended up with more wounds than wins." I held my arms out to my side, gesturing to the world at large; what was left of it, at least. "I tried to do right by you, by Rayna, by Azazel, and by all that remains of the world that I can't even *remember*; I've tried for as long as memory serves me to do right by all, and all be damned, for it has earned me nothing but aches and pains and one too many brushes with death."

Lissa took a step towards me, hesitantly reaching out a hand to me, expecting me to move away but I couldn't. I was frozen in place, but not by determination or anger or anything of the sort; trepidation radiated through me like a lightning storm, seizing my muscles and taking my motor functions away from me. It was all crashing down around me as I took stock of my life, and for the first time, I felt true terror at the prospect of the unknown. I had no idea where my path would lead me, or why it had even led me that far. I felt completely out of control of my own destiny, and I couldn't handle it. I did everything I could to maintain my composure, but my refusal to meet her gaze gave me away. As I stared at the ground, I felt her hand on my shoulder once more, and before I could do or say anything, she had pulled me into an embrace.

I was sure it was meant to be comforting, but all I could feel was the cold seeping through my clothing, and I involuntarily shivered. She pulled away, and I could see the look in her eyes, and I wondered if mine looked at all the same. She was just as scared and as lost as I was—she just wasn't as afraid to show it.

I thought for a moment, and brief as it was, Lissa seemed to hang on every aching second as she waited for me to say something. The hope was draining from her face as I tried to regain my composure, to the point where I couldn't look at her anymore. I was beginning to feel as though I was stealing it from her, the hope; I couldn't handle the weight of that guilt on top of everything else that had happened.

What did Rayna mean to do with the Stone? I had explained my intentions to her quite clearly and if she had wanted the same, they wouldn't have attacked me from behind. If we had the same goal, would it not serve us better to work together towards it?

Were they my enemies?

The thoughts weighed heavily on me, though I tried to lift my head high and look forward. As far as I was concerned, my quest was done. It was not something that I had expected—I never saw myself as someone that would give up quite so easily—but at that moment, I thought of nothing more than returning to a simple life. The undead and the dragons, the magic and the swords... All of it could disappear and I could have been happy—though whether or not I *would* have been was another story. I thought about dispensing medical herbs and the little shop that would undoubtedly come with it, tucked into a corner somewhere and filled with oak furniture and the smell of various spices. I thought about the regulars; customers that I saw almost every week, and the pleasantries we'd exchange. Tales of times long past and gossip about the other shopkeeps, just down the way from me. I thought about the bright daylight coming through the window and—

I let out a heavy sigh and looked upwards. The sky peered back at me, still an array of blacks and purples and greens. It was still a sight to be seen—one that I wasn't quite sure I was willing to trade for darkness, or whatever artificial dome Azazel had erected over the town to the South. Hanging high in the sky was the Black Moon, a void where no light could live; a black coin pressed hard into the canvas of the pure sky and a staunch reminder to me of how inescapable destiny may be. I couldn't shake the feeling: someone needed to put things right; someone needed to restore the world as it once was and I wasn't sure I could trust anyone but myself to do it.

I knew then, more than anything that I could no longer trust Rayna and Brok to set things right, and the shadow that was cast over my happy vision of a simple time—that I could never know—lead to a frustration that kept me thinking in circles.

I had put so much trust in them that I was blinded. I was blinded by the way things always have been. And people cannot escape their base natures. Whatever it was that Rayna was planning to do with the Emerald—and I couldn't help but wonder if she sought the other stones as well based on the one comment she had made; just played dumb during my story. I couldn't even be sure that her intents were malicious; believing her own distrust so much that all are enemy to her. No matter what the plan was, I had to interject. I had practically handed her the Stone; any further harm it could cause, whether she would use it for evil or simply use it incorrectly, would be squarely on my shoulders.

And all the while, Lissa just watched as my face went through a thousand different expressions, working through my thoughts until I found the one that pushed me forward. I took a step towards her, my hands no longer shaking, my face sharp as steel. "I don't have any answers," I told her. "Like you, I only have questions."

She cocked her head to the side, waiting for me to finish.

I stumbled over my words, not quite sure what I was trying to accomplish. With the benefit of hindsight, it seems to me I was trying more to convince myself than her. "*We* will go to Castleford, and we will start getting answers to our questions."

She smiled at me, and I did my best to bury the doubt I held within me. I feared from the start that there would be no happy resolution for Lissa. She was, after all, a wisp—a spirit trapped here, destined to fulfill a task.

Even still, she was different from the others, given a physical body instead of ethereal light, as the others had been. None had ever been so *real* as her. And while the others had their duties fulfilled by guiding me to things that have aided me greatly on my quest, small as those efforts may seem in the grand scheme of things; Lissa seemed to be bound to a quest far greater than seeking out items. Her soul was bound to this world, as if by the same force that guided my ambition and desire to see the dawn returned. Neither of us could be quite sure why...

But I knew a Wizard we could ask.

Red Skies

The return to Castleford was largely uneventful and quiet. As I was still reeling from the Rayna's sudden turn, I had little to say. Our party had been reduced to just the two of us so quickly after I felt good about it blossoming to four. Even at such small numbers—two *or* four —I couldn't help but remember what Rayna had said to me in Dewpond about trust.

On the way back, we opted to avoid the Necropolis. We were still unsure of the nature of Lissa, other than her shared similarities with the Wisps, whom I had seen countless times. And not only was Lissa the only one that I had ever seen pursued by the dead, we did not want risk attracting helcats, either. The beasts had a better sense for capturing the dead than they did the living, and I wasn't sure I was up to the task of keeping *that* abreast of our surroundings, though I had little choice.

When we arrived at Castleford, we were greeted with a new sight. The Castle still stood high on the cliffside overlooking the city; only behind it there was a red orb of fire, burning just above the tallest tower: a new Sun, red as blood, that was spreading its crimson light like a fog over the unassuming town. The sky bled with the red aura of the fake sun that hung in the sky, and the color it gave off filled me with an unnatural feeling. There was no heat to be felt standing under it, and the light was muted but heavy. It hung thick in the air like a smog, and the closer we got, the harder it became for me to see. I rubbed my eyes, the strain becoming too much for me to handle when I felt Lissa's cold hand on my arm.

"Are you well?"

I gave her a look. There was concern painted on her face until our eyes met, and she looked away. I was becoming invested in finding out just who she was, and every time we shared one of those looks, I felt like it was only a matter of time before we learned something. It was as though something was actively breaking the connection between us; a realization that was bubbling just beneath the surface, waiting to erupt like a geyser of truth. I wanted to tell her that I would be fine—that *she* would be fine—but I couldn't bring myself to lie to her. I wasn't sure that anyone would be fine: whether it was her; me; all of mankind—the most I could muster was a nod, and neither of us had any choice but to accept it, and allow it to guide us, if even for a moment.

There was something ominous about the magic we were seeing, though. I got as close as I could to the city before I grabbed blindly for Lissa's arms, halting her. "No farther," I said, casting my eyes down to the ground and shielding them with my hand. My head was pounding in time with my heartbeat like a drum. "Something—" I started to speak, wanting to tell her that something was wrong, but my words failed me, and I trailed off into gibberish.

My vision began to shake and my eyelids would not let themselves be opened, protecting themselves from a pain I couldn't quite discern. It was though someone were holding them shut, fingertips pressed tightly on the fleshy lids covering my eyes so hard I could feel them bearing down on them, pressing them deeper into my skull as if to take my sight wherever I was about to go. There was a screeching in my ears that felt like thousands of tiny knives jabbing shallow into the base of my skull in waves. I dropped to my knees, my head in my hands, and heard Lissa calling out to me.

But I was already gone.

There was a flash of light, coming from behind my eyes. It hurt like nothing I had ever felt before, but the light faded quick and was replaced by a silhouette, thumping like a fist clenching tight to the rhythm of a drum.

I heard a heartbeat, so loud that I thought was mine. I clutched at my chest and realized that it was coming from somewhere else—the silhouette. It was beating in time with the what I was hearing, and each thump sent a wave of tiny knives scraping over and under and all over my skull until I wasn't sure if the pain was causing me to scream or not. I could feel a tug on my jaw, and a rasp in my throat, but I could hear nothing save for that incessant beating.

It had to stop. I may have screamed that, but I am still not entirely sure; all I know is that when I opened my eyes, Azazel stood before me with a look of concern on his face.

"Oh! The traveler returns," he said. "In more ways than one, I gather. And little worse for wear, too."

The throbbing began to subside as the light bled away and was replaced with dark. It took a second, but my eyes adjusted, and the bloody Sun hanging over Azazel's shoulder came back into view. All of the other questions I had faded as I focused on the vision I had, and I thought to ask Azazel of it immediately. Somewhere, in the back of my mind, I could still hear the heartbeat.

He stepped towards me, his hands clasped together. "But if he returns, does that mean he has the Emerald?"

I planted a foot, and rested my arm on my knee, slowly making my way back to a stand. "No, he does not." I grunted in effort, wondering how long I was trapped in my vision. I could not see Lissa. "And something has happened."

Azazel was bewildered by this, watching my eyes and face the whole time I returned to both feet, looking for any signs that I may have been joking. Unsatisfied with what he observed, he took one final step towards me. "If you don't have the Emerald, I hope you at least have news."

"We found it," I said. "Someone took it." He did not seem concerned about the state he had found me in.

"Who?"

"The woman who gave me the Sight," I said. "The woman I met in Dewpond." I looked downwards, closing my fist tight in anger, my gloves crunching a satisfying, leathery crunch. "She betrayed me and took it from me."

Azazel nodded, as if plotting. He was working on a contingency. "Do you know where the woman was heading?"

I shook my head.

"Well, do you know what she intends to do with the Stone?"

I furrowed my brow, shaking my head once more. "She acted as though she didn't even *know* of the Stones before she took the Emerald," I said, the deception ringing through my mind like a bell. "She played me for a fool."

Azazel stared into the distance wistfully. "Perhaps she means to finish what they started," Azazel said, nodding towards the Necropolis. The green dome still shone around the center, polluting the night sky around it. "I've kept them at bay as much as I can, the interlopers who wish to learn the truth of the Cathedral—the true home of Darkness—but I fear that my magic is no match for the magic of the Stones, impressive as it may be."

I couldn't be sure what he meant—he still hadn't told me who "they" were, let alone what it was they were trying to accomplish. I couldn't be sure about anything. I felt as helpless as I had been all my life, back to the start of a journey I wanted no part of. I felt the overwhelming urge to ask what it was I returned to ask for: a chance to live out my life as nobody. Something deep down inside of me kept a firm grasp on that urge, holding it just beneath the surface, never quite allowing it to break free, like it was caught in the coral just beneath the water, doomed to flounder until it drowned. "Can she do that without the other three Stones?" I asked.

Azazel smiled. "She doesn't break the dome entirely with just the Emerald." I felt myself start to relax, but Azazel was just as quick to notice. "That doesn't mean she can't get through it, unfortunately; create a temporary hole that she might pass through, and make her way to the center. The process was begun, all those years ago, to bring about the Long Night, and a new age of Darkness—I fear the steps to complete such a move have become shorter."

There was a pause, a silence that hung in the air, for only a second. "The Darkness *is* impressive, isn't it?" The wizard began to muse, taking slow, dramatic strides past me, towards the horizon that featured the Necropolis so prominently. "It's a wonder that you are even still human. The Darkness has a way of seeping into the souls of humans; it *feeds* on them and grows until there is nothing left but black, the absence of everything." He held up his right hand, flicking his fingers outwards, exposing his palm. A small flame emerged from the space just above his pale white flesh, and I felt a sting in my eyes. He noticed my wince, and closed his fist, extinguishing the flame. "The hatred and the anger and the self-righteousness that burns within all men is but a conduit for the Dark to infect, and bring you to the brink of what you know and accept. But the best that mankind had to offer discovered a way to stave off the Darkness!"

I turned to look once more for Lissa. It almost looked like she was trying to be invisible—though it occurred to me that Azazel hadn't so much as acknowledged her presence since our arrival—or at the very least *stay* invisible. I couldn't blame her. Something about the way Azazel was speaking, or the content of his speech was making her uncomfortable. I could see her squirming, and I began to feel something welling up inside of me as I replayed the events to this point, wondering if Azazel's Darkness *had* infected me.

What had started as such a simple act of anger—though still a fitting punishment, I must attest—had led me to something far greater and more meaningful, and I couldn't understand. Why? What would have become of me if I hadn't repaid Rat and his friends for the kindness they showed the people of Brakas? What if I had ignored the library in Dewpond? What if I had perished at the first encounter with the dragon?

By God, there were *dragons*.

I took a step towards the ageless Wizard. "How many of the stories I heard as a boy were true, Wizard?" I almost commanded him to answer. The question came out laced with sarcasm and anger, though I wasn't sure what I had hoped to accomplish with either. "I have known two versions of the world in my life so far—neither have prepared me for the things I've seen. So, tell me; how many fables must I study if I am to set out again?"

He peered over his shoulder at me, and I could only see his eyes as they narrowed, a ruby-tinted flame sparking at the corner and I could tell without seeing his mouth that he was smiling.

"*All* of them."

In the Mountain's Shadow

There was a period of time where no one spoke. I was too frustrated to come up with anything productive, and Azazel likely knew that I was too frustrated to listen to him anymore. Lissa just didn't speak, finding a spot on a large boulder to take a rest. She kept her eyes on the horizon, and it seemed that she had stopped paying us any mind at all.

After some time, Azazel sighed and welcomed us to follow him back to Castleford. I asked him about the dome—the one that I couldn't get close to the last time I was there—and he informed me that he had traded it out for a different type of magic, pointing to the orb in the sky.

It burned red like blood, the ominous glow sending a shiver up my spine. I felt goosebumps beneath the leathers I was wearing, and as I looked at the bloody Sun, I suddenly felt cold and hot all at once, sweat pouring down from my forehead as the shivers ran up from my toes, meeting somewhere in the middle as an unsettling feeling in my gut. There was something unnatural and alluring about it all at once, and I wasn't quite sure how to rectify those two things in my mind. It was sickening and terrifying and it made me look at Azazel with a concern that I had not afforded him before.

More than anything, looking at the bloody Sun *hurt* my eyes. The instinct to protect myself from pain tried to tear my gaze away from it, but no matter how hard I tried I couldn't look away until Lissa grabbed my arm, shaking me lightly. I turned to face her and felt the wave of panic wash away. The feel of the cold of her touch through my layers was enough to bring me back down like a splash of cold water to the face, and I let out a long sigh.

Azazel took us through what was the center of the town. It wasn't as large as the other cities that stood at the four points, but Castleford was large when you took the cliff into account. It jutted out from the

mountain in such a way that it looked like a stage, overhanging that
quaint city below it; if you could call Castleford a proper city at all.
Below it was a deep throng of trees that were staggered in such a way
that the forest seemed designed, rather than natural—though many
wondered if it was a sign that the land itself was blessed with meticu-
lous architecture, especially given the perfect shaping of the cliff and
mountain to the South.

And on that cliff, standing monolithic and silhouetted by the
bloody Sun, was Azazel's Castle. The Castle itself I had heard stories
of in my youth; stories of a quiet man that the village thought would
protect them. But after they grew to fear him—his silence struck them
as odd, and they didn't *like* odd—and marched on his Castle, he abandoned them, disappearing for centuries and leaving them to fend for
themselves. It was then that the wildlife began to descend on the village—hounds from the East and Wargs from the forests south of the
mountains; all things that the spiteful man's magic had secretly been
keeping at bay.

Now that I had spoken to him—*seen* his magic at work—I could
not believe I was standing before a man more than two hundred years
my senior. Even still, there was something about him that was irking
me. Something about the way he spoke of the Emerald, and the Stones
in general, that sounded more than desire to me. I searched every corner of my memory for stories pertaining to magical Stones and ancient
Wizards, but found none that connected.

There were none at all about Stones.

As he took us through the streets, I saw that the rumors of people
returning to the surface proved true. It did not seem like a town returned to life—I saw no vendors or businesses of any kind, and there
were no taverns open or kids playing or people heading home with
their hauls from the markets that weren't there: there was only silence.
The people glided through the streets in a daze, as if they weren't sure
where they were going, where they were coming from, or even where
they were in that very moment.

"They still need time to adjust," Azazel said remorsefully, noticing
that I had noticed the townspeople. "When I brightened the sky once
more, it may have sent them into shock." He nodded quickly. "They
just need some time to adjust."

We reached the base of the mountain and stopped. Though there
was that small, perfect forest separating Castleford from the trail leading up to the cliff, it was nothing to navigate. We were through it with
little effort, before standing at the stone steps that would take us up to
the Castle. They were steep and slick, cut into the stone and dirt that

gradually transitioned to the cold rock face of the mountain, some covered with moss and morning dew drifting from the trees that nestled up against the rock wall. I followed as the Wizard seemed to climb them with ease, watching his footing and trusting I could follow suit. I peered behind me to see Lissa standing at the base, looking up to me with her hands clasped together in front of her.

"I don't think I can make it," she said exasperatedly.

I nodded and looked back towards Azazel, who seemed to not notice that I had stopped. "Then you can wait for me here," I said, rushing back to the wall.

I returned to the climb, double-time, to make up the ground that I had lost. I was growing ever curious about what it was that Azazel wanted me to visit his Castle for, and I tried to steal a glance at the structure as I climbed. I slipped on a particularly slimy rock and lost my footing for just long enough for my heart to skip a beat, but my hand found purchase on a rocky outcropping and I stopped myself from falling. I looked down, and it seemed to me that if I started to slide, there would be no stopping it until I reached the bottom; only many more rocky outcroppings to hit on the way down.

When we reached the top, I turned to face the castle. Azazel had stood beside me. When I looked at him, he was staring in the opposite direction, towards the mountain. I turned to follow his gaze and saw the cave opening in the side of the mountain—almost as tall and as wide as the castle itself. It stared back at us, cold and black as the Long Night had been in the beginning. I felt the same chill I felt when looking at the Azazel's Sun.

"You know what this is?" he asked me.

I shook my head. I had heard stories about a great many things in my life, but something about the awe of the cave mouth was emptying my mind as quickly as I could try and think of something.

"This," he took a deep breath, "is where dragons dwell."

He led me into the cave, which was deceptively shallow, only stretching a few dozen paces from the entrance before coming to an abrupt stop. Even with the sight, I was unable to notice anything about the wall, but just before I asked Azazel what it was he meant to show me, he waved his arm in an arc in front of him, a red fire shooting upwards, illuminating the wall.

"Or where they *used* to dwell," he corrected himself, his voice laced with a distant, unspoken sadness.

Carved into the stone of the cavern wall, there was a door. It looked metal, but even with Azazel's light it was hard for me to tell just by looking at it, but it was something different—it wasn't metal, and it wasn't stone. Whatever the door was made of, what struck me as odd was how *warm* it was. Across it, there was some sort of writing that I could not recognize, a language man was never meant to speak or understand. And within the writing, towards the center of the door, was the black silhouette of a dragon, with four divots shaped like a diamond in the center.

"I'm sure you have seen the dragon, the one with the Rider?" Azazel asked.

I nodded towards the painting. "Is that the one here?"

Azazel shook his head. "This is something *far* more dangerous. When the light left us, much as the morning Sun would spark us awake to face the new dawn, the Dark woke the dragons that remained. There were two, held at bay by the powers of those that came before—those who brought upon the dawn; but their power was made stronger by the light of the Sun." He reached out, his fingers tracing the painting of the dragon wistfully. "Without it, it's only a matter of time before the 'other' through."

"The 'other'?" I asked, stepping up beside him.

"Two dragons remained, sleeping in the light—one more was locked away, as if to pay for what she had done to mankind," he cleared his throat and looked at me, then back to the door. "Here she waits as the power that keeps her fails, even now."

"Did you close it?"

Azazel let his hand fall to his side. "My Castle and I returned as we were called upon. It was my duty to watch over the town, and keep all manner of threats away, including the ones in this cave."

"Why are you showing me this?"

He drew a deep breath and exhaled. "I want you to see what I need the Stones for."

"Why is it so important that I am the one? Why is it that you count on me for your errand, when you, a man of magic, could do so much better?"

He shook his head. "If I leave, this town will no longer be protected. If it is your wish to cease this quest, I cannot force you; but know that there are few that pass through here, and fewer still that could have defeated Father Paxton."

"I've already lost one Stone," I said; but I said it without any sense of remorse or sadness. It had escaped my concern, numbed by the revelations that had been laid out before me.

"You can get it back," he said, placing his hand on my arm. "She is heading for the center of the Necropolis, I am sure of it. That is where this ends." He dropped his hand and turned away, walking back towards the painted door. "I need all four of the stones to seal this door for good, and keep the Black Dragon asleep."

"And what of the two beasts that were already made free?"

He sighed. "They will need to be dealt with in *other* means."

I scoffed out loud. If all of the stories I heard were true, there was no way to slay a dragon. They were immortal beings, and by most accounts *invincible* as well. They were covered in scales that were made of something that no other beast had. No magic or sword would pierce them.

"You must get the other Stones," he said, his voice turning grave. "We haven't much time."

"*Other* Stones?" I asked, thinking he meant the emerald.

He turned to me and his eyes were aflame again. He held out his hand, and nestled into his palm was a small red gemstone.

It was the Ruby of Castleford.

The Orb

I only stayed with Azazel for a brief time after that. He grew tired, and the Twins appeared as if from nowhere to escort him home to the Castle. The sister stayed behind and had asked for my sword. When I presented it, she ran her hand up and down the edge of the blade, muttering something under her breath. Red flames, not unlike those that Azazel had littered throughout Castleford, grew from hilt to tip, engulfing the entirety of the blade, burning so bright that my eyes hurt to look at it. And just like that, the flames were gone again, and the sister was handing back my sword.

The goal was simple, Azazel had said: even the odds.

Rayna had at least one of the stones. If she had learned how to use it, Azazel and I both agreed it likely that I would not stand a chance against her; I barely did with Brok by her side.

It was clear to me before he even said it, but the Ruby seemed to be giving Azazel powers as well, which is why he wouldn't allow me to borrow it, even for the journey to the Necropolis to confront Rayna. He needed it to keep the doors closed, he told me, and I had no reason not to believe him. He had—much as he had told me he would—kept nothing secret from me, at least as far as I could tell. There was so much more I wanted to ask him, but I was beginning to believe that there was, in fact, no more time for questions. I had seen the dragons that now roamed freely amongst us, and I was not keen on the idea of facing them. But what of the Rider? It was the one question I wished I *had* asked before leaving Castleford.

When I had reached the bottom of the mountain steps, Lissa was still waiting for me. She welcomed me from the exact spot she had been when we parted. It struck me as odd for her to stand in place, let alone out in the open, the whole time I was gone. And while I made no comments about it, I couldn't help but notice how exposed she would have been to any attackers. Either Azazel's magic kept the dead at bay, or she was proving luckier than she was in Brakas.

She asked me where it was we were meant to go.

"Dewpond to the West," I said, "or Alduin, far to the North."

"Hadn't you said that you encountered her in the West already?"

I nodded. Rayna and I had first met in the library in Dewpond, which was the building that Azazel immediately directed me to. It occurred to me that much like the church in Brakas, the library possessed the large Spire that seemed to pierce the heavens; a connection that I had not immediately drawn, though had sprung up with enough veracity that I knew a seed had been planted, germinating in the back of my mind. It was more questions, I realized. Once again, I was on the road with no conscious desire than to be beneath a roof and in a bed. I could have slept the rest of my days away, and I wouldn't have had but a single complaint about it, I was sure.

So why, then, was I walking away from that?

When we were safely out of the city, and I was sure that we were alone, I asked Lissa to step back. I drew my sword and looked the blade up and down. The twin had not provided much in the way of instruction, so I just stared at the sword in silence, picturing the flames that I had seen earlier, when—

Whoosh!

The light from the flame once again burned as it erupted, climbing the blade with haste. I felt no heat from it, even though it started so close to my hands. It brightened the area that we were standing in; a shallow valley surrounded on all sides by a thick tree-line. We could still see Azazel's bloody Sun hanging just above the trees to the Southeast. The ground below was just a mat of dead grass, and the remnants of a dirt path that had long since been reclaimed by nature.

In the light, I also saw Lissa's horrified gaze, drifting upwards.

I followed it to the skies, and amidst the purple-green hues dancing among the blacks of the nothingness that stood beyond, I saw that lithe black shape, the massive wings flapping with great heaves that sent gusts tearing through the air towards us, even though we were quite a distance apart. And atop the back of the dragon, I saw the Rider once more. In his right hand, he held a spear—eight feet of solid wood with an ornate steel blade at the end, though I had no doubt its cutting ability. His left hand was empty, but I could see the shape of a shield strapped over his shoulders, nearly as large as his torso was. It was the best look I got at him, but I still couldn't see his face; his helmet was made to look like the maw of a dragon, and the shadows cast by the jaws obscured any of his features from coming through.

The dragon roared, and I found my sword stance. The flames still clung to my steel like they were a part of it, and I knew that we very likely could die then and there.

I stared at the Rider and although I couldn't see his eyes, I couldn't help but feel that he was staring right back at me. It was like we were talking without speaking, and my heart began to slow in my chest. The dragon's wings became a rhythmic flapping that drowned out all other sounds, even that of Lissa screaming somewhere in the back of my mind. The beats of the wings were slowly replaced with the beat of a heart, and—

"Move!"

I felt hands on me, and I snapped out of it. I looked over to Lissa, who was grabbing my upper arm with both of her hands and pulling. She was still looking upwards, and I did the same in time to see the flames building in the dragon's mouth.

We ran for the trees as fire scorched the ground where we had stood mere seconds before. The dragon's roar filled the sky so that nothing else could be heard, save for the crackling of the wood as it sprayed the tree-line where we had entered, flames rising up the trunks of the tall oak trees like hands, reaching up from the ground trying to pull them under. It didn't seem to go far beyond the clearing, and we watched from a hollowed out stump as the dragon circled, shrieking to the heavens.

Why wasn't it razing the forest? It was something I couldn't quite figure out. The dragons didn't seem opposed to destruction, so why not burn it all just to make sure?

I decided not to dwell on *why* we were still alive and began to think about how we could *stay* alive. When the dragon turned its attention to the South, listlessly flying away, I pushed Lissa along and we began to travel north once more until we began to hear a rustling sound in the trees. Without speaking, we knew that the sounds could not be the dragon. The beast and the Rider had already departed, so this was something new that was moving among the darkness.

The sound was something much smaller than a dragon and was coming from the ground, though it still carried the weight of many men. My head whipped left then right, trying to follow the sounds of movement that I couldn't quite be sure I was hearing. I wasn't sure if the Sunsight was beginning to fail me, or if the volume of trees surrounding us was so dense that it felt like the Darkness was encroaching and threatening to envelop us.

My sword was still drawn, though I reached for the mace on my back with my free hand, feeling a slight edge still with me after the dragon had left. As I closed my fingers around the weapon, I was taken off my feet, sent flying forward onto the ground on my belly. I rolled over to try and see what had hit me, and saw Lissa looking past me. Once more, I followed her look and saw an orb-like shape disappearing amongst the trees, rolling along the ground like a ball.

I reached for the mace once more, but it was no longer on my back. I looked around and saw that it had been thrown from me when I was hit. It was only a few paces away but I knew I would need to be quick if I wanted to retrieve it. I could hear the sound from the trees again, encircling me, growing and decreasing in volume as though it were trying to play with me. I spun, thinking for sure I would catch sight of it—but I had fallen for its tricks, and I had turned *away* instead of *towards*.

In the moment of impact, I tried my best to discern what was happening. I was hit from behind again, so I wasn't able to see the attacker; but I was able to feel some things. The things I felt just didn't make any sense to me. I felt hands grazing my back, some were pushing out, knocking me forward, while others seemed to be coming from different angles, with knuckles and fingers and thumbs jabbing into my back. And when I was hit, it was my lower back that was hit first; as I tumbled forward to the ground, I felt the groping hands travel upwards, taking swats as they rolled *over* me and back into the darkness. I had to pull my chin to my chest to avoid the final strike, but I was able to get my eyes back up in time, taking the brunt of the fall that almost knocked the wind out of me.

I was unable to breathe still as I looked at the shape that awkwardly traveled towards the trees. It was a strange amalgamation of bones and iron, rolled into a ball like twisted yarn. Hands and arms and legs and feet jutted out in all directions, most skeletal, while others still had pieces of flesh and sinew hanging from the stained bones. Amidst the mess of bone and flesh and sinew, there were also weapons lodged inside—swords, broken spears, daggers, and even a piece of a tower shield, it looked like. The orb stopped just shy of the trees, and whipped around so that it was facing me—if it *could* face a specific direction.

I still held my flaming sword, now with both hands, as I stared down the monster. The familiar orange glow emanated from the core, and it contorted its arms so that it could reach inside itself. Four hands emerged with weapons that had been absorbed into it. One hand held a dirk, the blade no longer than my hand; another had a sword, though the tip was broken off, and what was left was only slightly longer than the dirk; the third hand was holding a double-sided dagger, the points curving in opposite directions; and the final hand presented a shield, wood with iron lining, only a small fraction of the great tower shield it used to be. I stared it down, and I wished that the dragon *had* burned the whole forest.

I thought about what to do next. I kept telling myself to go on the offensive—I just wanted this dealt with—but something was keeping my legs planted. I thought it was my instincts taking over, and I was at their mercy to just stand there and wait. I had become quite adept at waiting.

The skeletal orb shifted, and I could hear some bones crunching as it attempted to make a new shape. It began to flatten itself, bringing in each side and compressing everything as it did, causing more sounds of snapping that sent shivers up and down my spine. It fashioned itself into a disk-like shape, keeping the four arms wielding weapons free at its sides. It lurched back and then threw itself forward, racing along the ground like the absconding wheel of a cart, something, buried deep within the inner workings, whatever madness that was, shrieking the whole time.

It led with the broken sword, and I parried it with my blade, feeling a brief burst of confidence, cut short by the shield bashing into my back as it passed. I tumbled a few steps before regaining my footing, and I turned to face the skeleton lord—now wheel—as it took a wide turn and came at me once more, on my right this time; the side with the daggers. I held my sword in front of me, trying to cover as much of my midsection as I could with the blade, to block both. I heard the metallic *clang* of the dirk, but the wheel pulled the double-bladed dagger back into itself, reaching out for a glancing blow when it had already passed. I felt the cold steel touch flesh, having found a spot just above the elbow on my right arm. It warmed with pooling blood, but I did not feel any pain—not in that moment.

On the next pass, once again on the wheel's sword side, I had an idea. I wasn't sure how it was going to work, and I could feel Lissa's look as I attempted it: incredulous and concerned for my sanity. As the wheel rolled towards me, seemingly picking up speed, I dropped to my belly once more, trying to flatten myself to the ground perpendicular to my attacker. I waited as long as I could to drop, hoping that it wouldn't be able to correct in time, and veer away from my trap. I was right. I felt the pain shoot down my back as the concentrated bone began to roll over me, but I fought through the pain and pushed myself upwards with force.

The mass of the wheel was impressive. It took almost all of my strength, but I was able to get just enough lift that there was air between the wheel and the ground when it left me. It tried to swing at me with the broken sword as it fell back to the ground below, knocked off balance. It wobbled left and right as it tried to find its center, but to no avail. I willed more strength to my arms as I took two massive strides towards the stumbling wheel and swung. I knew the sword would be mostly ineffective against the core of concentrated bone, but I was able to cleave the arms with the sword and the shield. It shrieked in frustration—I wasn't sure it could feel pain—and I heard the dagger-wielding arms whipping through the air frantically as it struggled to regain balance, off-set by the loss of two arms.

I took a step back and dodged out of the way when it tried to roll at me again. It tried to turn, but it seemed shaky without the other arms. I watched as it tried to quickly rearrange itself, but as soon as I took a step towards it, it stopped and launched another easily dodged attack in desperation.

Each time I moved to avoid being hit, I moved closer to the mace. I ducked and rolled out of the way of another dirk slash, and when I returned to my feet I held the flaming sword in my left hand, and the mace in my right. It was becoming a familiar stance to me, and it filled me with a confidence that I didn't know I needed. I smiled at the skeleton wheel and beckoned it to strike once more.

I swung down with the sword, cutting free both daggers with ease, coming across with the mace weakly to knock the wheel off-course. It seemed to zig and zag as it rolled away from me, once again trying to find its balance; only I didn't give it the time. It was unarmed for the moment and I didn't want to waste the opportunity, so I ran to it and spun, swinging the mace with all of the strength I had left. The core exploded in a mess of white and grey and yellow, and the shrieking sounds cut short. Amongst the myriad of bones that were strewn amongst the forest grounds, I found a skull with a withering black stone set into the forehead. It seemed to be opening and closing its jaw in an attempt to move, but it was just bouncing in place. I watched it and took notice that it was the only piece still moving—must have been the only thing that kept it alive—and took care of that with my boot.

I had not seen that kind of Undead before, and I was starting to wonder if what Azazel alluded to had been true: was someone bolstering the powers of the Darkness? What new madness would there be as the evil that Azazel warned of grew stronger?

Did Brok come from whatever world these creatures—these abominations—were crawling from? I took a deep breath and pushed the questions aside. There would be time enough for answers once I was face-to-face with them once more. And the faster I found the stone at

Dewpond or Alduin, the sooner I would be ready to face Rayna. Though I wasn't sure what that encounter would be. She had attacked me once, yes; but if she meant to kill me she could have done it in the Church.

I was going in circles. I stood amongst the bones of what had to have been almost a half dozen people and looked around. The trees were still thick, and although I could feel the Sunsight being strengthened by my recent victory, it was still hard for me to see much of anything in that forest. I turned to Lissa and asked her if she was ready to move.

She was already gone.

INFESTATION

"Who goes there?" A voice rang out in the darkness, echoing off the damp stone walls that encased the dark alleyway. It took me by surprise, though I sensed something familiar in its cadence. "If you mean to kill me, do it quick."

By the sound of his voice, there wasn't much life left to take.

I moved closer to the sound of the voice, trying my best to pinpoint where in the maze of alleys it was coming from. Dewpond had become far more dangerous than it was on my previous visit, with helcats moving in—which had seemed to diminish the wisps in the area to few—as well as Sentinels, like those I had faced in the Catacombs beneath Brakas; larger sentries with oversized weapons to match. This was all on top of the Undead that had already roamed the city. As I looked on, during my approach, I saw movement collecting around the Library, as though there was something to be found there.

I could only imagine what they were looking for.

As I rounded a corner, I heard the sound of plate-mail shifting, and I whipped my head around to see where the noise had come from. There, sat against the wall with his hand covering a still-bleeding wound in his side, was the Knight I had seen outside of Castleford.

I quickened my pace, taking a knee beside the Knight. As I got close to him, he seemed to finally recognize me. I wondered how the Knight had survived all this time if he couldn't see that far in the dark before it occurred to me that the dark may not have been obscuring his vision. "What happened?" I asked him.

He was not long for this world.

"Ah," he exclaimed, relieved. "It *is* you. And here I thought I might be able to accomplish something before the darkness took me." He looked down at his hand, which I could see was covered in blood. He scoffed, and looked up at me, showing me his palm. I saw his sword, still on the ground in a pool of blood was running off the entirety of the weapon, hilt to tip. "You can see better than I, but I wonder what that gift will cost you." His hand fell to his side, and he looked away. "The scars of our past are opening; we have ignored them for far too long."

I tried to follow what he was saying, but grew tired of ramblings. Lissa was still lost to me, and Dewpond was overrun with all manner of dangerous things; I had little time for cryptic warnings and messages, though that seemed to be the only language anyone spoke in this new world where trust did not—and was seemingly not allowed to—exist.

"I've been all over Alghast," the Knight continued, his voice softening and growing weaker. "I've even seen the mountain to the North; the tip of our corner of the world. I have seen the Spires in all of the cities—though I could not find Castleford's, which I found quite peculiar. I saw so many things, all reaching for the sky; all reaching for the heavens, as if to say this world is not good enough for us—we must ascend!" He looked upwards briefly before turning his eyes downward. "We took the world by force and still we spend so much time thinking about where we will go, instead of where we are; instead of where we were. We are so quick to forget! That is why I cannot stomach being only a memory: memories fade; legends live forever!"

I didn't have a response, though I thought on one for a moment. There are those who were talked about frequently long after they were gone; names that I knew from songs like Sirk, assassin of Brakas that quietly helped liberate the city from pirates ages before even I drew breath. They were names that I attached no faces to, only deeds; as though the names were more important than the person. I thought about the stories, and all the moments in-between, the quiet moments that Sirk might have shared with someone—did he even *have* someone? Instead, we only hear of the blood he collected on his knife. We know his exploits and we have defined an entire man's life by them. I didn't want to be just a name—a fading memory would be fine, so long as I wasn't here to see it fade.

I heard the sound of a skeletal orb somewhere nearby, the bones and metal skittering on the stone streets as if all around us. I looked back to the Knight, placing a hand on his shoulder. I opened my mouth to ask him if he was okay to travel, and stopped myself. I took note of the wound in his side, and the weakness in his voice, and knew that he would only slow me down. It was a heavy thought, but it was one that I couldn't ignore. I couldn't be sure what would happen to him after I left; I just knew that I couldn't let it concern me. I withdrew my hand, and he bowed his head.

He knew what it meant.

"The fire in the library went out," he said to the ground. "The fires everywhere are going out. The scar—the *wound*—is festering; the shadow will spread until it covers all of these lands."

I heard another orb roll by, and stood.

"Wait," he said quickly. "I won't be needing this... Not anymore." He held out a small crossbow and a quiver of bolts. "Wasn't much good with the it anyway; not in the dark. You seem to me far more capable of aiming in the Night. Just be careful, it takes a moment to reload. Hard to do in the thick of battle."

I took the weapon from him and strapped it to my belt. I turned back around to face the alleyway and moved slowly. I had spent too long listening to the Knight, and things were starting to dim. It was a twisted thought, and one I couldn't believe that I was having: that a dying man had stolen much needed time from me. I couldn't tell for sure, but it seemed like the Sunsight was beginning to fade faster. That, to me, only meant I had to fight more than I cared to.

Finding my way to a crossroad, I noticed that one of the streets had an elevated walkway, running along the second story of a strip of similar buildings, all boasting storefronts on their first floor. The second floor was largely untouched by fire—at least the front of it—and the balcony still looked to be holding strong. There were stairs wrapping around the front of the building, though they looked like they had seen better days. I followed the walkway down the sides of several buildings strung together to look like one, though they were painted with different dull colors. Even with my vision beginning to fade I could see the green, red, and deep browns that marked the separations between buildings. What remained of slanted roofs—each at slightly different angles—hung over the sides of the buildings, covering the walkway. And at the end of the street, I saw a lone undead standing with his back to me.

I climbed the stairs quietly and carefully, lightly stepping to make sure that the wood would hold. I saw an opportunity to try the crossbow that I had just received, and slowly made my way down the walkway, taking care to avoid any creaks or groans that the wood may have made beneath my boot to give me away.

In the distance, I finally saw more of the library than just the spire. I was still moving towards it, but I knew that I needed to find more light. The Knight was right, it felt like the Darkness was growing stronger.

I drew the crossbow and dropped to one knee, using the railing to obscure me from view in case I missed my shot. He had been right, it

would take me some time to reload; I had never used a crossbow before. When I was young, my uncle had been tasked with learning how
to repair them, and I watched as he played with the mechanisms and
tried to explain to my young, uninterested ears how the whole thing
worked. I hoped all of that would translate to a hidden proficiency,
allowing me to wield the crossbow with ease.

It did not.

The first bolt I fired sailed wide to the right, bouncing harmlessly
off the stone ground. The sound drew the attention of the soldier, and
he shambled over to where the bolt had connected, not once looking
behind. I tried to quietly draw the string back and load another bolt,
but my hands slipped more than once, it was so fine and taut. When I
finally had another bolt loaded, I looked down to see the orange glow
begin to swell.

He hadn't seen me yet. I knew that much because I hadn't heard
the shrieking sound they make when they usually discover a foe, I
assumed, to draw in reinforcements. He hadn't seen me *yet*, but he
was definitely suspicious. It was only a matter of time, or a small
movement at the wrong moment, before he discovered me. I had to
hope that luck would find me on the second shot.

I squeezed the trigger on the single-handed crossbow and felt it
jump in my hand as the second bolt was let loose, cutting through the
air and finding its home just behind the left eye of the soldier, the glow
leaving it immediately as it fell lifeless to the ground, my eyes burning
brighter.

I decided I would need more practice with the crossbow, though I
could not afford to stop and train. As I moved through the city towards the library, I did my best to avoid the skeletal orbs—they were
only a pain in how erratic they were—as well as make use of the
weapon to thin out any roving groups of Undead. By the time I stood
on the familiar stoop, looking up at the now-darkened building before
me, I was far more confident, but far lighter on bolts.

The final approach to the library had proven to be much easier
than anticipated, with the number of creatures roaming the streets di-
minishing as I grew closer to the building, as though they were ultimately disinterested in the Library—it wasn't *theirs* to search, I would
quickly learn; but they were still far closer than they had been on my
previous visit to Dewpond, and moving closer still.

That's when I saw the fading light coming from the foyer of the
Library. As the Knight had said, the fire that Rayna, Brok and I sat
around on my previous trip to Dewpond had waned and almost gone
out entirely, only a soft orange light warming the stained glass win-

dows from within. I stepped through the doors, pushing the left one open with my shoulder as I gripped my sword tightly with both hands. The Ruby fire was another skill I had been working to master, and I had learned that its strength was immeasurable, rendering the sword far more useful on most things I had encountered. I kept it extinguished as I entered the Library—opting for surprise rather than showing too much.

The Library was almost as I remembered it, although the shadows cast by the dying fire in the center of the room seemed to dwarf whatever light had remained. I expected my eyes to hurt, realizing that I had not been in the room with the fire since getting the Sunsight; but to my surprise, I felt no pain whatsoever. I looked straight into the heart of the flame and it seemed to pulse along with that heartbeat, still thumping somewhere in the back of my mind. I was mesmerized by it, and took a step towards it, reaching out to see if I could feel its heat.

There was a roar from somewhere deep within the stacks that rippled through the building, shaking it as though the earth beneath us had begun to move.

The Library was a long building; longer on the inside that it would seem on the outside. Many would claim that this illusion was not their minds playing tricks on them, but a twisted truth of the architecture, contorting and evil to its very core. In the Darkness, the effect was even more terrifying, and I felt as though the building itself could swallow me up, never to let me go.

I tried to pinpoint the source of the roar, staring down the long center aisle and trying not to feel the building closing in around me. The stacks stretched up to the second story, each with a ladder attached to a slide that ran the length of the shelf. On the ends of the stacks, just above the placards indicating the subjects contained on the shelves, were lanterns made of bronze. I felt a gust of air from behind me as the last of the flame went out. I was almost able to follow it as it was drawn into the torches; first the ones closest to me, then in sequence until the entire way was lit.

I then saw what had made the roar.

It stood between the stacks, which were about ten or so paces apart, lumbering in the shadows with the lanterns above it rocking about. I could see the shape of it just fine: it was tall—its head was just below the balcony on the second floor. It had a muscular upper body, its arms like tree trunks, hanging from shoulders like boulders attached to a chest like a rock wall. Each hand was held out to the side: one was open, displaying the sharp claws that grew from the tips of

fingers the size of my arm; the other was holding an axe that was larger than the whole of me. I had to crane my head around to confirm
that I saw its bottom half correctly. It had four legs, reaching out of an
abdomen that was wider than it was tall, nearly scraping the ground
as it swayed uneasily on the four thick legs. It wasn't until the lanterns
calmed that I saw its face. It had more of a snout than anything, painted with a permanent snarl thanks to long, sharp teeth sticking out between its lips from the top and bottom. Its eyes were small, reflecting
the dying light of the Library, sunken behind pointed cheeks, with no
proper nose to be found; just nostrils on top of the mound that made
up the snout. The ears were pinned back against its scalp, a chain running from the middle of one flat, pointed ear around the back of its
bald head to the other ear.

I opened my mouth as if to say something—what *could* you say to
such a beast—and the monster ahead of me simply grunted.

"Sapphire," I thought I heard it say, sounding almost like a com-
mand.

I closed my eyes and envisioned my sword aflame. When I
opened them again, the vision had become truth. Another trick I had
learned while carving my way through Dewpond to reach the Library.
Though it *was* the first time it had worked on the initial attempt.

I readied myself for the attack, but once the creature started moving, I froze. Each lumbering step shook the stacks closest to it, books
tumbling out to the tile floor below, centuries of knowledge spilling
out like water from a glass, doomed to be ignored and forgotten. For
being as large as it was, the beast moved quickly. It was almost on me
before I could even come up with a proper plan of attack, forcing me
to come up with a plan of defense instead.

Scanning my surroundings, I dashed off to the right, heading for
the nearest stack. The ladder was situated close to the aisle and I
mounted it as soon as I was able to reach out for it, grabbing it with
my free hand and swinging myself onto it. I clambered upwards, even
with sword in hand, driven by a desire for the high ground.

The second floor was constructed around the bookshelves, with
walkways coming out from the main floor that ran along each side
wall. The walkways extended the length of the stacks, with every
fourth one connecting as a bridge over the entire room, starting with
the first, so that the higher shelves could be reached. I had not known
the Library well enough to know its history, but I often wonder what
came first: the second floor or the high stacks?

When I reached the top of the ladder, I scrambled for the railing,
hearing the rumbling sounds of the monster's steps growing ever

closer. I pulled myself up and over just in time to look down and see the giant axe cut the ladder free from the shelf, sending the wood splinters out to the either, hitting it with enough force to shatter it. While I was distracted, the large empty hand of the beast slammed down on the railing just a few steps from me, crushing it into the floor. It retracted its hand, and an idea struck me.

I lifted my sword in my right hand and spun it in my palm as I rose, taking the quick steps to the new gap in the railing that the monster had so graciously created. It was still standing below the bridge, unmoving as though it had lost sight of me. I sprang forward and plunged the blade of the sword downwards, aiming for its head or at least somewhere that could help slow it down.

It must have heard me running as it shifted quickly, moving its torso out of the way and ducking its head under the walkway I had jumped from. My sword ended up piercing—though barely—the hide, and the monster reared back and screamed out in pain. Dark blood pooled where my sword had gone in, and I felt the muscles tugging at the sword as the convulsed beneath the skin. It twisted its upper body enough that it was able to swing a free arm around, connecting weakly with its forearm. The strike was still strong enough to send me flying, my back hitting a bookshelf hard. I felt the wind leave me for a brief second, but when I had my faculties back I had to quickly roll out of the way of a falling axe strike, hearing the wood crunch behind me as it planted itself in the heavy oak of the shelf.

I slashed at the arm holding the axe and was able to break the skin. It looked barely like a scrape, but it was enough to get the thing to let go of the axe; long enough, at least, for it to backhand me once more. I struggled back to my feet as it pulled the axe free and once again turn to face me. It raised the weapon above its head and rushed me. It brought the blade down hard but I was able to move out of the way. The tile on the floor exploded outwards when the axe made contact, and I felt the floor beneath me shift as though shuddering.

I tried to get around behind it, taking paltry slashes at the legs. It was enough to draw blood, but I couldn't help but wonder if I was being anything more than a pest to the thing. It didn't seem to be reacting to my strikes anymore; not nearly as much as it had from the plunging attack. I looked around for more ladders, but I wasn't the only one that remembered the effectiveness of that attack—any time I tried to make a break for one of the ladders, I was blocked. It began picking up and throwing nearby benches and tables at me just to keep me from them, eventually aiming to destroy the ladders themselves. It was clever for its size, I'll give it that.

The axe strikes continued. Some were sweeping horizontal strikes that chipped away at the lower levels of the stacks; most were straight downward strikes. The floor was beginning to look like Brakas: debris strewn everywhere from the attacks, whether it splinters of wood or torn pages or cleft books; all of it accumulating beneath our feet. And as I moved to try and get better positioning to continue my seemingly fruitless assaults on the beast, I felt the floor shudder under our weight once more, pleading with us to stop.

We did not listen; we couldn't! We continued our dance, the beast and I, until I could see the shuddering, instead of just feeling it. There was a creaking of wood, a symphony of destruction as the creaking turned to cracking and a wave rolled through the floor before it all began to fall downwards. Whether it wanted to throw tables, chairs, its axe or even itself at me, I didn't care; I dove for the closest ladder as the floor finally collapsed beneath us.

I managed to grab the bottom rung of the ladder just as the floor gave way and felt my body fall out from under me. The muscles in my arm screamed with agony as my full weight jerked downwards and then dangled over the precipitous drop that had opened beneath us.

There was a spiral staircase heading down, attached to the stone walls that wrapped around the oversized well that was situated beneath the Library. There was, at one point, a pulley system here that took things down to the stores and Catacombs below; but it had been retired when the library was fully constructed. The basement of the Library was several small rooms that were connected to the central hole that ran all the way down into the Catacombs, though where it exited I couldn't be sure. The monster fell straight down the center of the hole. I had turned just long enough to see it through before breathing a sigh of relief and reaching up with my other arm—

Suddenly, I felt a forceful tug at my leg and I screamed out in pain, my arm nearly torn from its socket. My grip on the ladder weakened and with a second tug I was pulled free, dragged down by the beast I had been fighting, to the abyss below.

Homecoming

When I came to I was lying on something large and slimy. I pushed myself onto my elbows and caught a glimpse of my sword lying on the ground a few feet away. I had landed on the mace—still on my back—when I fell, and there was a pain in my thigh from where the tip of it had dug in, but it was far from the worst I had endured since emerging. I tried to get a sense of what I had landed on and where I was, but my head was still pounding from the impact. My body had begun to relax from the fight, which allowed me to feel all of the aches and pains that were just waiting to be addressed.

The monster!

The thought returned to me like a flash of lightning and I spun my head around to look for the creature that had pulled me down. I couldn't see it anywhere, until I looked below me.

I was laying on top of it.

I scrambled to my feet and over to my sword, fearing that the creature would also awake any moment. I nearly missed as my fingers scraped the ground, raking the cold, hard stone of the floor, trying to reach for it as I took long strides away from the beast. When I turned to face the monster, ready for another fight, I saw that the creature was no longer moving. In fact, a pool of black blood was starting to pool beneath it, spreading out like a viscous puddle during a heavy rain, and I leaned over to see the wound.

It looked to me that when the creature had fallen, it dropped the axe in an effort to free hands to save itself. One of the hands had grabbed me, but we both ended up falling. Unfortunately for the monster, the axe had landed in such a way that the blade was sticking upwards. Unfortunate for the creature; *very* fortunate for me, as I was still unsure how I was going to be able to beat the thing on my own. It had landed on the axe when the ground finally met us, looking as though it had found the spine, just below the neck. One of the fingers on its right hand was twitching; it was the only movement I would see from the creature again.

My fall had been broken by the considerable mass and the thick hide of the creature. And although I was safe from the drop, I could not bare the pain of the fighting anymore, and allowed myself to stumble to a nearby wall; but only when I was sure that the monster was dead. I propped myself up with one hand on the wall and tried to shake the ache loose, to no avail.

That place seemed so familiar.

The smell of death hung in the air and I was sure that blood had been spilled fairly recently, other than the grisly seen before me. I tried to map everything out, noticing that the stairs that led back up to the library had been knocked out for the last two stories, though I wasn't sure that was from our fall or something previous. I looked around the rest of the chamber, and saw the three doors that connected it to other rooms and tunnels and it suddenly dawned on me:

I was back home.

While I had come from—and reemerged in—Littlehollow; I had spent most of my formative years in the Catacombs beneath Dew-pond. When it came time for my expulsion from the survivors, I had requested to return home, thinking that I would surely die before long, once I reached the surface. How I have persisted, even I am unsure at times.

Where I stood was only a short walk from where the medical stores had been, where I found Kat and her friend from the North stealing, where my actions would become the catalyst to let those simmering tensions finally boil, and open conflict amongst the sur-vivors began. In the other direction were the barracks, where I had slain Rat and his posse in their sleep for the massacre in the Brakas catacombs, all in the service of what I thought was right. My body count that night was far less than theirs, but the people of Dewpond saw only what I had done—they paid no mind to the massacre I had seen. It was all coming back to me in waves and I began to worry about the reaction from the people if I was discovered down there. Surely the ruckus from our fall would be drawing people out? I watched the doors with bated breath, waiting for them to crash open and for the shouting to start.

First, there would be the shock; whether it was upon seeing me as I was now, clad in armor they had not sent me out with, armed and battle-hardened in a way that I maybe hadn't been when I left; or the shock would be at the sight of the four-legged brutish beast that lay in a heap in the center of the room, propped up on its own axe.

Second, there would be panic; people yelling and screaming at me for once again dooming them, bringing down creatures from the surface and opening quite a large hole through the floor of the Library above. Once again, I had left them vulnerable to attack, they would remind me.

Then it hit me harder than the beast ever had: there was no people because they were likely dead. And I recalled the large, iron door in Brakas that I had left open. There was a maze of tunnels beneath the Necropolis, but I had no doubts that the Undead would find their way through to Dewpond. I had doomed them all by sheer complacency.

When man escaped below ground, we had a system for dealing with our dead that prevented us from ever having to worry about them rising. This comfort is one of the reasons why I had neglected to be concerned about the amount of corpses still lying in Brakas. When someone perished in Dewpond, their body was taken to one of the furnace rooms, where fires were kept stoked to warm the Catacombs. In there was a large iron furnace and in *that* we kept our dead.

The sheer volume of them in Brakas must have kept them lifeless for the time it took me to get there. It did not seem like a quick process en masse—especially considering the times above ground when the dragons began their assault. We saw so few of the dead rise before we fled the surface, though we hadn't the time to consider it odd. Perhaps it took time for whatever twisted magic was at work to strip so many bodies of their souls and turn them into the thoughtless husks that they would undoubtedly become, through no fault of their own.

I cursed myself for leaving the door open and again for having to likely fight my way out of the Catacombs, regardless of whether or not there were any survivors. I did not seem to be well-liked as I was sent above ground, and many seemed keen to the idea of throwing me into the furnace—the type of public execution that I knew was only a few short years away, with how things were going.

I *mostly* remembered the layout, thinking to look for some of the storerooms. I could have used some more crossbow bolts and I was running low on food and healing salves. I still held my sword, but I kept the blade pointed down. I didn't want to seem like I was *there* to fight.

As I moved towards one of the closets that we kept weapons in, just a few doors down from the medical stores that I used to be tasked with protecting, something caught my eye. There was an eerie glow coming from somewhere just beyond the crack in the mostly closed door. Through the crack, I could see into the room, and the memory of what had happened there—the start of all of this, as far as I was concerned—began to rush back to me. I pushed it aside when it dawned on me that the light I saw was a familiar blue.

There was a wisp's light coming from inside the medical store room.

I cautiously moved towards the door, which was only slightly ajar, the blue light escaping through the crack. We had not seen Wisps below ground—in fact, I did not even believe they were real until I emerged—so the sudden appearance of one struck me as alarming. I slowly gripped the door and pulled it open, squeezing my other hand tight around the hilt of the sword. I hadn't been having much luck with doors as of late.

The storeroom looked as though there was an attempt to ransack. Many tried to steal from here in desperation but were stopped; the contents of the shelves simply strewn along the floor, on or under pools of dried blood. There were no bodies, only puddles that indicated where bodies once were. Over by a pile of bundled herbs, I saw the light grow stronger. I walked towards them, and amidst the brightest part of the light I saw a shape taking form: it was a woman, and from behind it looked as though it was Lissa!

I reached out to her, and she opened her eyes wide, jumping backwards with fright. "What's wrong?" I asked.

She shook her head at me, her eyes darting all around the room. I looked around, to see if I could follow whatever it was she was looking at, but there was nothing remaining in the room but her and I and the signs of death, brought on by my own disregard for history. My heart sat heavy in my chest, indeed.

"You!" she said with an accusatory tone, pointing at me and backing away.

I looked down to see that she was, in fact, pointing at me. Looking back at her as confused as ever, "Me?" was all I could ask.

"Ian—" she trailed off, her voice shaking with sadness offset by an anger that I could tell she had been yearning to name. Watching her face I could see the twisting and contorting as she was finally able to find a home and a reason for all of the frustration she must have felt, not knowing who she was.

Ian, I thought to myself. *Why do I know that name?*

I tried to think of something to say. I had never seen Lissa so frantic, even with the things we had seen in our short time together. She had become a fantastic hand; quite adept at healing and alerting me to the presence of enemies. She had not shown me fear in quite some time. I stood in uncomfortable silence, frozen by confusion.

And then I remembered.

Ian was the name of the man I had killed, in that very room, all that time ago. But why did Lissa know about him? Was there a lingering presence in the room—another spirit that she may see that I did not? I looked around again, wondering if that's what her eyes were following, but I still saw nothing.

"*You* did this." She said with authority. My eyes shot back down to her, resentful of her statement even if it was entirely true. I wasn't ready to accept that yet. "*You* did this to *me*."

I took a step back, and cocked my head to the side. I stared into her eyes, seeing the anger and the fear and the sadness inside them before pulling back and looking at her *face*.

I knew at once where I had recognized her from, as though being in the room triggered a memory that I had repressed. It was one thing for me to remember what I had done; another entirely to remember everything about the people I had done it too, and that was a new a cross for me to bare. The face on the Wisp that sat before me, as it always had been, was one that I should have known, for it belonged to a woman who's life I directly affected, and possibly indirectly ended.

It was Kat's face.

Kat, the woman I had banished to the surface in front of the entire community for what she had done. Kat, the one who *got* herself stationed at the medical stores simply to sneak her friend in one night in an attempt to *help* someone. It was *that* girl that stood before me, ethereal and corporeal and—

Dead.

Wisps were spirits of the dead, tangentially attached to some part of the living world. They remain to fulfill a purpose that they didn't feel they had accomplished in life. Most of them are simple in nature; just needing a good scrubbing of the soul before they head off to be judged. That is why most of them guided me to items they knew about, perhaps things they had stashed while living that they knew would be of no use to them. They just wanted to feel like they helped one last person.

But Lissa—Kat—had been unlike any Wisp I had encountered before. Even after Rayna gave me the Sunsight, and I was able to see more than I had since the light went out, the Wisps never appeared as more than a ghostly light, and perhaps a shadow of the form they once inhabited—even then, it was only a few times that I saw more than just blue. Kat was fully formed and physically *here*. I felt her touch me. How had I not recognized her before? Why had her face been so unimportant to me that I forgot so soon?

I looked back up at her, and sheathed my sword. I held my palms out to her to show her I meant no harm. I took a cautious step towards her. "Kat, listen," I started, stammering. "You know that's not who I am. Not any—"

"But it *is*," she said through tears. "I was just fortunate to be on *your* side this time." Her words were biting. "Why can't you go?" she cried out. "Why can't you leave this place?"

I lowered to one knee in front of her, and bowed my head. I heard shuffling in the tunnels, her cries likely alerting the dead to our presence. "Kat, I did what I did for, what I thought, was the greater good; but all I did was destroy everything I once cared for. My desire to do what I thought was right has given way to far more deaths than just your own, I can see that; I *know* that now." I looked up at her, my eyes like fire. "If you remain here, in the living world, *our* world; then it is for a reason. The fact that you seem attached to *me* means that *both* of us can have our chance at redemption."

She looked at me with that same mix of confusion and anger that she had in her eyes before, being replaced by a pensive look as the words began to sink in, and she finally asked the question that even I still did not hold the answer to:

"How?"

Moving On

We reached the surface after fighting through throngs of undead, some of which I thought I may have recognized, and returned to the Library. I recounted my encounter with the monster in the building as Kat gazed upon the gaping hole left in the floor.

We moved up to the second floor, and began checking the few rooms that were up there, sleeping quarters and storage mostly. There was nothing left but boxes of books and a few poor souls that had been locked in the rooms, now returned and Undead.

We looked everywhere in the Library that we could, until we reached the far end of the building, on the very last bridge between the two balconies that ran snug along the very back wall of the building, the mighty stone frame around the window cutting into the bridge by about half a foot. There was a large stained-glass window that depicted the Compass of Alghast, the four gemstones featured: Onyx for Alduin; Ruby for Castleford; Emerald for Brakas; and Sapphire for Dewpond—the one that I could not seem to find.

We scoured everywhere. We overturned every nook and cranny, and did our best to comb every aisle of the building—both floors, though searching the first proved difficult with the now gaping hole in the floor—and found nothing. I thought that maybe the Spire would have had a spot for it, but I could not find one on any level that we were able to reach. It was almost as though it didn't *want* to be found.

Or it was already gone.

I closed my eyes, feeling a familiar frustration welling up inside me. It *had* to be Rayna. It *was* the building where I first met and spoke to her. If she knew enough to betray me to take the Emerald, her ignorance was likely all staged. Surely she must have taken the Sapphire while she was here. That must be why she decided it was time to move on to Brakas, and another Stone. But why skip Alduin and Castleford? Were those ones also missing? I began to grow tense at the thought.

I clenched a fist and slammed it against the railing.

"She has two of them?" Kat said.

"She must," I said, thinking there would be no other way.

Kat turned away, stroking her chin. "If she already had one, why couldn't she face the priest?"

She was right. Rayna had more than enough of a head start on the road to Brakas. She had every opportunity to face Father Paxton before I even entered the ruins of the city. Until then, the only reason I could see that I fought the Father instead of anyone else was because I had been locked in with him—one of us was going to perish that day. Though if Rayna *did* possess a Stone before we even found them, why had she not faced the priest on her own? He was not hidden.

Unless she hadn't learned to control the stones yet.

"I don't want to risk that," I said aloud. Kat turned to look at me, concerned. I stepped away from the railing, and looked to the northern point. "She told me she came from the North," I said, half to remind myself. "There is a good chance she already has the Onyx, as well."

Kat sighed. "Perhaps that, too, was a lie."

"*That* I am willing to risk," I said, staring at the northern point as though I could see a glow coming from the black gemstone there, meant to represent the Onyx. "If she already has three of the Stones, we know where the fourth is. The Wizard should be able to take care of himself, at least for the time being. We should head for the one that we *don't* know about. We can waste no more time searching here; it is clear to me, though I do not wish to accept it, that the Sapphire has been pilfered." I stopped and thought of the beast I had fought, falling silent. "Though it seems to me as though it was not the enemy that found the Sapphire—why would they post such a sentry here if that were the case?"

We made way for Alduin with haste. We cut through the upper part of the Necropolis, despite my wishes to avoid helcats at all costs. The Undead were easy to deal with—even in groups of four or five, I could easily hold my own—but helcats were far more nimble. If we found ourselves against more than one, I feared the worst. I was able to dispatch of the first few that surprised us with some effort, but once we caught on to them it was short work with the sword, with Kat offering herself up as a distraction. They seemed to be focused on her until they spotted me, seeing me as a threat to their bounty. Lucky for us, Kat seemed to be able to detect *them* just as they were able to detect *us*.

She seems stronger somehow, I remember thinking to myself. Since she discovered who she was, she seemed to have found some drive and determination; the confusion no longer stunting her progress towards waking up to the new world. She was finally able to focus on a task, instead of ceaselessly wondering what happened. I was amazed that she wasn't in mourning for herself; though she knew just as I did that there was no time for that. She had bounced back from her own revelation in quicker fashion than I imagined I would have, and I began to grow and admiration for the woman that stood against the order, rather than for it as I had, in the name of helping someone else. Her fear in the moment—which I was also beginning to remember—should not have been viewed as weakness, but a sign that the consequence of failure was so small in her mind that she had not even prepared for it. It wasn't ignorance, it was a belief that failure *wasn't* an option.

Unfortunately for her, she was wrong.

When we reached the southwestern border of Alduin, we took a break in a small clearing, surrounded by thick, dark trees. It was beginning to grow cold, a southern wind from the Necropolis moving in, carrying with it the chill of the dead, no longer in their graves. It was a brief moment that I was beginning to grab hold of, for they served as constant reminders for why I was pushing forward, even if I was not conscious of how motivating those moments were. I thought about the world that we found ourselves in, my eyes drifting upwards to the perpetually night sky.

As if Kat was in my thoughts, she shook me from my daze with her soft words. "It's almost more beautiful than the old sky," she said, the bite in her voice all but gone.

I nodded, before shooting her a curious look. "I should have assumed it, but you are able to see clearly?"

"Of course," she kept looking skyward. "I'm dead. I *died* to *live* in darkness." She lazily looked my way. "*You* merely have to adjust."

It amazed me how she had changed; as if the soft, unassuming girl that Lissa had been was buried beneath the personality of Kat, now fully in control. Though it made sense when I was a stranger to her—people are often timid around those they do not know in times of panic and fear—her change was so complete that it was still jarring to me.

And I was not a stranger to her anymore.

I drew in a deep breath, and looked back to mural of the sky, and the worlds that hovered above us, far away, wishing that I could be on a happier one; a brighter one. "I would not be here if not for my sense of 'duty' to them," I said. "Though I gather that neither of us would be."

"You are correct," she said. It looked as though she wanted to say more, but we spoke just as much in silence as we did with our words; an endless argument about who was wrong and who was right, summarized finally when we spoke again:

I looked at her, cold and stoic. "But the blame is just as easily placed on you."

A sharp silence hung in the air as she let my words sink in, but only for a second.

"You," she was nodding, looking back up towards the sky, "are correct."

"If you needed help you should have said something."

"You didn't see how things were going," she said, her voice shaky. "How things were *going* to go. They told us that things were going to be all right—that the people were to be all right—and you believed them. All of this would have happened eventually! You think I was going to be the only one to do what I did? People have friends, all over —it's what we do, as people; seek others. I am not the only one that would have taken what we did not need, and give it to those that did. And if not on our watch, then the watch after ours," she stood, seemingly hovering over me. "And the one after that, maybe, someone would have tried to help a friend, only to be sent to die up here by someone who had no sense of duty for themselves, so they had to borrow it from the community."

Her words cut, but it was nothing I hadn't told myself in the time since, or before. I opened my mouth to rebut, but nothing came out, just stammering.

"Fate chose me," she said quietly, turning back to look at the sky. "Fate chose *us*."

"To do what?"

"Live? Die?" She looked at me, shrugging her shoulders. "*Try?*"

Fate was a difficult thing for me to accept. To me, coincidence was far more likely. But I was beginning to see it: a picture in my mind of the comfort that acceptance—the acceptance that you cannot be in control of everything—must bring. To believe that everything is random occurrence must be maddening over time. The constant question of "why?" weighs heavy on the minds of those that can't believe there is a purpose for them, but refuse to accept that life is always moving forward, even while you stop to figure out why you do the things you do. It was just so hard for me to entertain the thought of something else controlling my destiny, even though, in times of reflection, I knew full well that I still relied on others to guide my hands. Whether it was merely for their acceptance, or to prove my worth, I couldn't know.

The idea that this is what I was *meant* to do still seemed ludicrous to me, even after I have displayed a certain aptitude for it. I *was* still alive after all—though having *that* thought while looking at Kat was a bittersweet one, at best. The part that was so hard for me to accept was the "Why me?" more than the "Why?". What was it I had done that put me on the path that would lead me here? And what madman, at the helm of all this, would decide on *me* to *save the world?*

The thought was hurting my head. It seemed circular in some way, tracing events as far back as I could remember to see when and where fate began to interject in my life, coming up with nothing. I wanted so badly to know the reason, but I could see that Kat was someone who believed *that* was the question that didn't need an answer. To her, it wasn't a question of "Why me?", but "What next?", and I couldn't get past that. I wanted to, but something kept bring me back to the former question, etching it into the walls of my mind so that I may never forget to ask it.

But the other question was so enticing now. I was beginning to fill a sense of nervous excitement. I could not know how much farther this madness could go—I don't think anyone could have known—and that unknown, that fog that hung over the future, was begging to be cleared. I finally felt *ready* for what we were doing; ready for the path that fate chose for us.

What next?

ALDUIN

The city of Alduin was renowned for its wisdom. As the northern tip of Alghast, those that settled the great city considered it the 'brain' of the entire realm, offering strategy over strength in times of need. Which is exactly why—many say—they were the first to fall; a winning strategy by the forces of Darkness.

Deep in the center of the city was the Alduin Academy, impressive in its own right without the Spire that stood out from the center of the roof, a common feature amongst the cities, and usually attached to one of the few structures still standing. The Academy stood six stories tall, and wide enough that taking a trip from one end to the other would take considerable time. In the center, bisecting the 'wings' of the school, was the administrative building. It was where the instructors and self-proclaimed 'prophets' would mingle, sharing their conspiracy theories on the fate of the world, and attempt to recreate the faerie magic they had heard so much about. Most of the priests were sent here for some manner of teaching, but the student body largely consisted of the future leaders and politicians—the people that have the smarts to know where to send us, people that know how to use a weapon. The central building added two more stories, with a roof that slanted into a pyramid, the Spire standing straight out of it.

Beyond the school, Alduin was a largely unimpressive city, architecturally. There were districts—markets and slums and middle-class —but none seemed too dissimilar from the other. The poor lived in houses only marginally worse for wear than those who weren't. It was rustic boxes, all in a row, amidst colors that seemed to only exist there. There were browns and blues and greens and none of it seemed to be colors that I would think adorn housing—but in Alduin, things were not quite the same as they were everywhere else. There was a madness that hung over the city, as though the collective knowledge of our history and our future was poisoning the minds of the people of Alduin.

And the closer you got to the school, the more the madness was offset by flora and fauna that had glowed in the sunlight; bushes of pink flowers and gorgeous trees dotting the horizon with fields and fields of the greenest grass you've ever seen, wilting listlessly in a perpetual breeze.

It didn't look like that anymore.

The homes were largely made of light woods. From the construction to the coloring, the homes were soft. It wasn't something that anyone had ever been concerned about—they *were* the closest city to the mountain to the North, long thought of as a volcano, stories of ancient eruptions laying waste to the area surrounding it. It made sense for them to build only what was necessary, save for the school, of course. But when the fires hit, they hit Alduin *hard*. Enough that one could easily assume the mountain north had finally let loose the lava and fire burning up inside.

But we knew better as we broke through the tree-line of the forest that surrounded the entire city. When we saw what was left—all but the Academy had been decimated—we knew that *both* dragons must have been here. It was the only way to explain the utter destruction, as there were no other signs that the volcano had erupted. Either that, or repeat trips had been made over the course of the years since—but we couldn't surmise why. Something in Alduin had prompted the wrath of the dragons far more than any of the other cities. It was a wonder the Academy still stood, though the East Wing was worse for wear.

I had always heard the stories of the last time the 'volcano' erupted. They called it Mount Darkheart, which I'm sure meant something to someone a long time ago. Much like many of the stories passed down, it meant nothing to us as we hung on our older peer's words and listened more for entertainment than knowledge.

It happened hundreds of years before, when the mountain had yet to fully breach the surface, poking and prodding just beneath the ground, looking for a place to break through. Feeling trapped, it unleashed its anger and burrowed through the dirt and rock without concern for what lay above, so that it could reach the sky. The fires it unleashed burned away the land, and when they pooled just south of the new mountain, they ate away at everything, creating the valley that would become Alghast.

It had been one of my favorite stories of how this all came to be when I was growing up. The Mountain was a God in this story, and something about that resonated with me. As I got older, I began to think about it less and less, as if the question of why the world existed as it did no longer mattered to me. Many believed in higher powers—

others believed that we were left here, forgotten, while the rest of our kind would prosper; wherever they might have been.

Staring at the ruins of Alduin, I could see that there was no sign of the fire from the mountain north; no pooling embers or lava, and the skeletons of the trees and bushes—while scorched—still stood. No, these fires came from the sky. I was sure of that. I only wondered *why* this place was left so utterly destroyed, compared to other places we had been. Why had Dewpond (mostly) and Castleford (almost entirely) been spared the same fate as Brakas and Alduin? What vengeance did the dragons owe them?

Surely, the care taken to preserve the buildings attached to these Spires had something to do with the Stones. I only wondered what the Stones and Spires had to do with the Light. I wasn't prepared for more questions, and I had grown accustomed to not receiving anything but frustration—and yet *more* questions—from the answers. The world was a twisted and confusing place.

The world was a different place.

The more I looked at the Spire, striking out from the Academy, the more I began to think that it was there *before*, the Academy built around *it*. There was a look to it, the color or the way it shot up with such a steep incline that it doesn't look like it will ever end, until it comes to a point, so fine that it just becomes part of the sky around it. It was narrow enough that with bright enough light behind it, your eyes might not even be able to see it. It didn't feel like any part of the building it was attached to, much like the Library in Dewpond. And, much as in Dewpond, it cast an impressive shadow over the entire city. In fact, many used the shadow to tell the time.

So far each of the Spires had been in the building that stood as the center of the town—not even just the physical center, but the center of the whole town's methodologies: the library for Dewpond, curators of history; the church in Brakas, the spiritual capital of Alghast; the Alduin Academy, renowned for their wisdom; and perhaps Azazel's castle? The absence of a Spire in Castleford was curious.

It confused me that Azazel's Castle had vanished for so long, leaving Castleford without its Spire; but I had seen the wizard's illusions at work. It was not a far leap for me to believe that he simply *hid* his castle from the people below, all the while watching over them as they fell to their own complacency, too dependent on his protection. At least, that was how the stories went. And now I depended on him, eagerly awaiting my chance to sit and ask him many questions, as he seemed like a man that had many answers. I had to know, if he knew:

I had to know *why*.

I wanted to know how things got the way that they had, so that once we fixed this, and put things right, we could *learn* from our mistakes instead of being enamored by them. The stories and legends could be used as cautionary tales instead of morality plays. We could focus on the world at large, instead of just an image in time. I wanted to believe that we could be better, until I reminded myself that there wasn't much of a *we* anymore. I felt a deep sense of mourning as I pictured the houses of Alduin, lined with small gardens, each unique in its own way, unseen by anyone that didn't spend each and every day of their lives here; now merely ash. The memories of families and neighbors who did nothing more than *live*, burned away with their homes, doomed to be forgotten forever; their stories never told.

It was like they were never even here.

It made me angry. The destruction of these lives, of these memories and these histories, big and small—it was more senseless than I could even fathom. *What was worth all of* this, I wondered, *what was so important that all of this death needed to happen?* There weren't even any bodies left—if there were, they had already returned to their feet, likely hiding around a corner with a rusty dagger, swaying back and forth even though there was no wind, waiting for me to walk by and give it purpose. It was not a person but a shell; a vessel formally inhabited by a soul that could very well be lost, itself. All others, returned to the dark.

The anger gave way to nothing, as the bleak future began to present itself.

It appeared to me as a mural, but it was all painted black.

Who Goes There?

Alduin was the first of the cities to slip into the catacombs when the Long Night began. They spoke of the "heart of the North" awakening something to the South, warning that fire was coming to strip away the light, and leave us in Darkness. It sounded like lunacy at the time, but I had come to posthumously appreciate the wisdom of Alduin. I was beginning to learn the importance of the moments surrounding the stories we were told as young ones, and it seemed to me that the warnings were there; we just deemed them stories to entertain, anything else to be called madness.

When the first sunrise failed to appear, they began to stir, moving what they could down below and fortifying their defenses. They had carefully stocked themselves with everything they thought they would need for however long it took. And while it was clear that they knew what was happening, they knew they couldn't stop it on their own. The other cities had only baulked at them when they heard the "frantic ramblings" of Lady Artemis, headmistress of the Alduin Academy.

Their posh lifestyles above the ground had left them unaccustomed to the lifestyle of hiding, however; they were not prepared to deal with the hunger and the pain and everything else that came with it. They began burning through supplies, and eventually they *had* to learn to fight. Logic then prevailed, and they decided to fight *us* after we killed one of *them*. They had a common enemy, allowing them to finally unify and relearn to work as one.

I had come to realize how the simple actions of one man had such a ripple effect through the what remained of humanity. And while it may be easy to assume which man I thought that was, considering everything I knew to that point; I realized that there were many who could be handed the blame, depending on how you viewed things.

When *I* thought about it, I put the blame on myself. I am the one that drew blood from the silence, and sent a woman above ground where she—clearly—died. I am the one that drew the blood that marked the start of the fighting between the West and the North, a ringing bell that led to the sons of the West getting a taste for blood, and combat, and *victory*. And when that thirst became too much for some men to resist, it was *I* that traveled east, through the maze of tunnels beneath a city of the dead, leaving the door open, allowing the undead to spread below as they had above. I was doomed to err in my attempts to do what I thought was right. I followed my instincts, and each time they led to more horror.

But I didn't take the light from the sky, did I? I didn't take the minds from the men we trusted, and I didn't drive us underground where we had to learn to survive in the dark. I didn't tell us to kill, or keep killing. I didn't tell us to fight. So many decisions I didn't make along the way; but who was it that made the *first* decision?

We were walking towards the Academy when we heard some shuffling from a stone enclosure. It looked like it had been used for food stores before the Sun went down, but it was obvious to me now what it had always been. It was heavy stone bricks secured with a heavy steel door. It stuck out amidst the rest of the neighborhood it was in, imposing brick amidst the more simple nature of the surroundings. I motioned for Kat to stop, and went to investigate.

Most of the surrounding area had been gardens—now the dried remnants were but ash beneath my feet—though there was a row of houses to the left that were blown away, the foundation all that remained. I could see flashes of the lives that had lived there before; the table where the family would eat; the bench where the young man wrote in a leather-bound book that was almost as big as him...

...None of that happened now. There was an eerie silence that enveloped me like a fog, thick and oppressive.

Underground, there were no "family dinners". There was no bench for private writing. You slept in a room with eleven other people, maybe more, unless you were on duty. If you were on duty, you slept at your post, so that you would be ready to relieve the previous person immediately.

It was all for the "greater good" in someone's eyes. And they probably believed it—most of us just got used to it. *All* of us were just happy to be alive, most days. We were happy that the dead had stayed mostly above ground, and that the things we were truly afraid of, but never talked about, seemed to be kept at bay. We were safe, we thought.

But we stopped being "we" and we *all* became, pure and simply:

Me, myself, and I.

As I stepped to the steel door, the slat that was just about eye level slid open. From behind came a voice, a man's voice, deep, but almost put-on. It sounded forced. "Who goes there?" he barked. I could not see far beyond the slat, and the man seemed to be standing a distance away, afraid of coming too close.

"We seek to end this Night, once and for all!" I said with confidence and bravado, enough that I surprised even myself.

Alduin's catacombs were fortified. When the battles started down below, they mostly took place in the tunnels connecting our cities—the four points were connected in the shape of a diamond, with an intersecting cross beneath the Catacombs, if you could see it from high above. It is not dissimilar to the symbol that represents the land. Though it was clear that the tunnels were constructed after the Catacombs beneath the Cities and the surrounding hubs had been, and in haste. Many had collapsed over the years, and created enough dead ends that if you did not know the tunnels well, they were a terrifying place to fight.

"And how do you plan to do that?" He asked with a laugh, the natural pitch of his voice coming through, much higher than it was before. "Do you plan to bring back all the dead and return all me crops? Can you make me a rich man, too?"

I stood silent, unamused.

"You're gonna kill us all, I hope you know," he said, quietly.

"Listen," I said, taking a step forward. "You don't—"

"I know that promising to put the Sun back in the sky is beyond one man."

"I have gone *beyond* one man," I said. I felt a fire in my chest, allowing myself to be challenged for the last time. I hadn't wanted this —but I wasn't about to be told I couldn't do it. "How many of *you* remain?"

His eyes appeared in the slot, bright and blue. I could see the smile in them, but there was something else. There was a cloud or a glaze that covered them as they darted nervously before returning to focus on me. The man had either been awake for days or dead drunk. "That's none of your concern. But, if you think you know better than the masters did; you can probably find what you're looking for at the Academy. I doubt it will make much difference anyway; the world's already gone to shit."

"We will start again," I said softly, after a pause.

The man scoffed at me. "*Us?* You know as well as I do, friend: we are a legion of pure impulse that must be *guided* to a neutral ground. I don't dare think of the world that *we* would start. We'd likely only be here again—"

"He's wrong," Kat said to me quietly.

The man at the door didn't stop. "—and I'd just as much live out one apocalypse in my lifetime. In fact, while you may look young, I can tell from your eyes that you're older than me. You probably remember seeing the fires, don't you? I only remember the feeling of them: the burning hot air brushing at my skin as my mother whisked me away and down below." His voice was taking on a sing-song tone. "I remember the smell though. To this day I can still *smell* the smell, sometimes. The smell of the people that were unfortunate enough to be outside for the first fires.

No, I don't want to see us birth a new world. We are *far* too broken for even the one we were left. Even in the face of annihilation, man still fought man over what they had, that the other one didn't. There is no 'greater good' to achieve because the 'greater good' is still just the creation of a person. And while we think we can share that with someone else, and persuade everyone to see what we see, we can never be sure that the image remains the same; that it isn't altered somehow, someway, once it leaves our hands." He chuckled to himself. "No, I have learned to adapt, as all great men do. I will take the world we have now over the one we start tomorrow. I hope tomorrow never comes." He stepped away from the slat.

"Though I wish you the best on your travels."

The slat slammed shut.

I looked at Kat, my tongue paralyzed by the man's words. I had hoped that she had something to say, but her eyes were cast downwards at the ground.

I shook it from my head. I didn't disagree with him—I had seen what humans are capable of and I had seen what *I* was capable of; but that didn't mean that there weren't good people left; did it? That there weren't trustworthy people that we could look to for guidance in times of need, like a light to a traveler in the dead of night, all to guide him home.

It was okay to *need* people, wasn't it? We were supposed to be in this together, weren't we? Instead of ripping each other apart in the name of power and wealth and food and supplies and pure sport? Did we get it wrong? If the stories were to be believed, our only purpose was to be food; sport for a creature that underestimated us. It was up to *us* to decide what we were, and *this* is what we chose?

No, there was still another chance. The fires of the dragons, and the blackening of the skies, and the waking of the dead; it all should have brought us closer together. Instead, we continued to separate and barricade and close ourselves off. We didn't think of ourselves as the realm of Alghast, but the survivors of Dewpond, or Alduin, or Brakas, or Castleford; never just *survivors*. And never just *people*.

I felt my fist clenching at my side, frustrated by the words of the man behind the door. It wasn't the content of his diatribe that bothered me, either; it was his belief in it. The immediacy of his response was one of someone who truly believed in what they were saying and I refused to believe that there was so little hope. I was *mad* that he felt hopeless, cursing the ones that made him and so many others that way. Hope was all we had; they weren't supposed to be able to take it.

Kat put her hand on my arm and I looked down at her hand. My anger did not break, I merely followed her gaze to redirect it, looking to where we would head next.

The Academy

We made it to the building with relative ease—save for a few shambling Undead, not even clad in armor. It was a roaming helcat that gave us the most trouble, just before approaching the front of the Academy. It had been especially fleet-footed, and was using some rocky encampments along a narrow path that ran down slightly into the trench before emerging again, just outside of the main gate of the Academy.

The building was even more impressive up close: each wing stretched for as far as the eye could see, the ends being consumed by the fog that had settled over this eerie center of town; and to see the Spire's end from where we stood was, like the others, impossible. Twenty or so paces from the front doors was what remained of a fountain, and I surmised by looking at it that it was collapsed by time, if nothing else. For the most part, the yard was untouched by fire. Though, without the light from the Sun to feed it, the grass and everything else had withered and died, leaving behind only greys and browns and not even the faintest hint of green.

The East wing, to my right, had collapsed at the far end, at least that's what it had looked like from a distance; but now that we stood closer to it, I could see that pieces of the building were scattered out on what remained of the lawn. There were scorch marks on the inside of the building, but we saw none on the outside, and it wasn't a far leap to determine the blast had come from within the building.

I felt a small tinge of trepidation as we approached the door, and reached out to grab the handle with my left hand, my sword in the right. The weight of the mace on my back was growing tiresome, and had I known how little I would need it after receiving the Ruby's fire, I would have left it in Castleford. I had full control over the fire by the time we reached Alduin, and was ready to ignite my blade at a second's notice, hoping not to see anyone—living or dead—when I opened the door.

My wish was granted as I looked in on the foyer, which was vacant of anything living. The walls were stained a deep brown, and in the center of the room was the main staircase. It stretched almost as wide as the room itself, with a bright red carpet running most of the width, only slight ribbons of the dark wood beneath showing on either end. The bannisters were works of art in and of themselves, immaculate carvings all the way up and down, each a mirror image of the other. A chandelier hung high above us, mounted to the underside of what seemed to be a third-floor landing, and I stared at it for a moment before realizing what was odd about it—

Small orange flames were flickering in the bulbs.

It was magic, it *had* to be; but did that mean that someone was still there? I spun around, scanning and rescanning the foyer for any signs of life; but there were none. There were doors on every wall of the first floor, and all but the front on each other floor. This seemed like nothing more than a stairwell, disguised as a main hall, which meant there were many more rooms for people—or *things*—to be hiding in.

Kat followed me in, and while she couldn't sense anything, there was a feeling in the air that I couldn't quite describe. It was heavy and thick and stifling and it sat on your chest like a hound, unmoving and staring at you with that vacant look, challenging you to move. It filled my head with thoughts of despair and death and I could see me lying in a pool of my own blood, reaching up for something or someone, unable to speak.

And behind it all was that heartbeat, pounding between my ears. It came from inside, pushing out, and it was as though something was pushing against the back of my ears, trying to break free. I felt myself grabbing at them, dropping to my knees. Kat would tell me I was screaming, but I could hear nothing other than that *damned* heartbeat. I felt her hands on my shoulders, shaking me every so often to try and snap me out of it. Somewhere in the distance I heard her voice, calling out to me. Then her shaking became quicker and more frequent, frantically trying to bring me back from wherever I had gone. I closed my eyes, only for a moment, and her voice faded. And as her voice faded, her touch faded.

Then all faded.

When I opened my eyes I was in a classroom; dark, even with the Sunsight. All the desks had been pushed out to leave a circle in the center of the room, where I was on my knees. I let my hands fall from my head as I stared at the front of the class with confusion. On the chalkboard, it read: "Awaken".

There was a flash, and I swore I saw something red. I felt heat for that instant, almost overwhelming and I immediately started to sweat. There was a loud *thump* of the heartbeat, back for only that second, before I was returned to silence. When the flash had cleared, and my vision returned, the word on the chalkboard had been erased.

Then my eyes were drawn to the dark shape behind the podium, moving.

I rose to my feet, cocking my head to the side. I furrowed my brow and tried to imagine what the shape could be, and if I was even still awake. It felt like a dream, something ethereal and floaty that I couldn't quite wrap my head around. I felt a tightness in my chest like anxiety, as though I didn't belong there.

The shape was smaller than me and as I got closer I could see it looked human—for the most part. It was hunched over, the arms wrapped around the legs as it rocked back and forth. The arms were thin, almost skeletal; but I could see flesh hanging loosely from the bones, as if there were little left between the bones and the skin. As I got closer, I could hear its whimpering cries, and it turned to face me.

Its face was hollow. There was no tongue, no eyes, no ears, no nose —nothing remained but black, empty holes. It dropped its jaw and screamed at me. It began to rise to its feet, which were bare and just as sickly as the rest of the monster. The thing was wearing the tattered uniform of the Academy, and I couldn't tell if it had been a male or female student. Either way, it hadn't mattered, as it was nothing of what it once was; much like the Undead outside. It looked like it had long since grown out of the uniform, the way its arms hung loose in the sleeves.

I stepped back from it as it reached out to me, and I heard the sounds of bones cracking and skin stretching as the arms of this *extended* towards me. I could only watch in terror as the thing reached for me, its hands closing in faster than it could walk. I felt my hands hanging empty at my sides, and saw no sword to speak of—had I dropped it in the foyer? I bowed my head and closed my eyes, waiting for the hands around my throat.

But nothing happened.

When I looked back towards the student, it was gone. I scanned the room ahead of me and saw nothing. I wondered if it was all just a dream; if I was still in the foyer. The heartbeat and the headaches were becoming more common, and something about them always left me feeling off. I took a deep breath and closed my eyes, hoping that when I opened them, I would be back in the foyer with Kat, and we could continue to look for the Onyx so that we could leave at our earliest opportunity.

"Wake up," I heard a voice whisper, not a man or a woman but *both*.

I opened my eyes, and the student was barely a hair away from my face, and I could feel it staring from the black holes where its eyes should have been, just as real as I could feel the skeletal hands on my face. They were still warm, but there was no moisture left in the skin. It scratched against mine like sand, and I winced at the terrible feeling as the face moved closer. If it had a nose, it would have been touching mine, and I felt no breath escaping its lips. From within the darkness of one of its eye sockets, I thought I saw the glassy, tear-filled eyes of a person—the person this thing *used* to be, likely—staring back into mine.

"Wake up," the voice said again, clearer. It sounded *sad*.

I felt the urge to cry but couldn't quite understand why. The weight of the building shifted on my chest and I felt like I couldn't breathe anymore. I looked into the eyes as they drifted away, back into the darkness. Movement from the jaw took hold of my attention, and the thing *screamed* again, and pushed me away.

I reached for the mace on my back and felt that it was gone as well, watching as the creature in front of me dropped onto all fours, and skittered up the wall to my left. I watched in horror as it reared its head back towards me, the bones in its neck cracking as it twisted, and it howled once again before leaping off the wall, correcting itself to a pounce.

I stumbled backwards, reaching for something to break my fall. When I found nothing, I let the ground take me, and kicked out with both feet, catching the monster in the chest before shifting slightly, to kick it off towards the front of the class.

It crashed into a pile of desks with a bang. When I saw it clawing for the ground to pull itself from the tangled mess it was in, I quickly rose, knowing all the while that it would likely not have been killed by the vault. I turned to look for a door at the back of the room, and when I spun, there were hands on me.

There were hands everywhere.

I felt numb as I looked into the crowd of students, each with hollow skulls and skeleton touches and how had so *many* of them gotten behind me? There had to be twenty of them, and they were all reaching towards me. I tried to scream but couldn't find the sound in me. I couldn't find anything in me anymore. They stood between me and the door, but I couldn't see the door anymore.

And then, all at once, the hands fell from my face. I felt a thumb and forefinger grip my chin, turning me around. The hollow face of the first student I saw somehow managed a smile as it leaned in towards me. "Wake up, before *she* does," it said, crystal clear in a woman's voice.

GOOD MORNING

I blinked and I was back in the foyer, sitting up on the carpeted floor with Kat at my side. I had laid down, or fallen over at some point; I began to wonder how much time had passed while I was in my nightmare.

"Where did you go?" There was something about the way she asked, so alarmed and confused, that caused a lump in my throat to return.

I managed to only choke out a question of my own: "When?"

"I lost you for a moment," she said, with some concern, scanning the room as if to see where I had left—and where I had returned—from. "You were here, then you weren't; then you were once more." She shook her head. "Where did you go?"

If the dream wasn't a dream, and what I had seen had been even tertiary to reality, then surely it meant we weren't alone—

I heard the familiar shriek ring out from behind the doors in the main hall, seemingly all of them at once. The cacophony was deafening, and Kat ducked beside me with alarm when the screams rang out, even though I felt the same degree of terror, welling up inside me. The only difference was I had an image of what was making the screams in my head; she hadn't been so lucky as to meet them, yet.

And just like that, the screams fell silent.

I fumbled around the ground and found the hilt of my sword, feeling comfort that I would be able to fight back, should the things in the dream come for us.

I nodded towards the stairs, Kat nodding back swiftly in agreement. We wasted little time, taking the stairs two at a time as we climbed, the central column of the spire running up the back wall of the hall. After the first, grand staircase, the stairs broke off into two sets of alternating staircases that then crossed past each other through the center for the rest of the floors. Each floor had a landing that wrapped around the wall, with a large stained-glass window at the front of the building, two doors separated by the central pillar on the other. My thought was that the gem might be attached or near to the pillar, and I wanted to make sure that the main hall itself was clear.

When we got to the third floor—of many—we found barricades of desks and tables and chairs had been erected on the stairs. I thought to climb around them, but each floor was nearly two of me tall; even from the third floor if I slipped and fell it was unlikely that I would survive, and there was little to grab on to on the way down.

It was more likely that these were not the only stairs up, and although the thought wasn't something I *wanted* to entertain, I knew that I *had* to move on from the hall, and begin checking the other rooms.

It was just my hope that we wouldn't have to comb the whole school.

Wouldn't want to wake *her* up, whoever she was.

We returned to the landing on the third floor, and checked the doors on either side of the central pillar. Neither of them would open, locked as if by some force. There were tall, narrow windows on the sides of the doors, but something had blackened them out; we couldn't see through them. Each of the doors on the second and first floors shared the same traits, so we had to begin branching out to the wings.

We started with the West wing as it appeared from the outside to be still intact. I was hoping that we would be able to find our way up at least past the barricades—the wings were two stories shy of the central building, after all, so we hadn't expected to go much further beyond that. We could only hope that no more obstacles were laid out before us.

The layout of the building was fairly straightforward. Off the main hall, there were long hallways that stretched down the entire length of the front of the building, much like the bone of a bat's wing, complete with perpendicular halls shooting outwards much the way the membrane of the wing is separated. In between the hallways were the 'sections' of the wing, whether it was for different sorts of classes, or libraries, or activity rooms. The top floors were the only ones that were the same all the way through; that was where the dormitories were—men's to the West, women's to the East. Many joked it was because the women were always first to rise with the morning Sun, ready to face the day long before the men even dreamt of stirring.

We had never been in the building before, but I had hoped aloud that there would be stairs leading upwards at some point in each of the hallway sections. And while I had been mostly correct, we found that the West wing of the Academy had been gutted.

There were holes in walls, large enough for Kat and I to pass through side-by-side. Ceilings had collapsed and rubble was strewn about the floors, some of which looked to be on the verge of collapsing themselves. Desks and chairs and shelves and cabinets were laid to ruin, shards of lumber littered everywhere. The skeletons of books were left with pages ripped from their spines and left about like trash.

And each and every stairwell we found had fallen to pieces.

Whether it was done purposefully or not, I couldn't tell. There were claw marks on the walls where the stairs had been knocked out going from the first floor to the second. The second to third floor stairs had also been mostly destroyed, but it was a lazier effort somehow. There were also dried pools of blood on the ground around the foot of the stairs, and I began to paint a picture in my head of what might have happened.

When the dead rose, it took everyone by surprise; even the Academy-trained were bound to be shocked by the sudden assault of un-dead soldiers. But in their cunning, they though to seek higher ground, eliminating passage for the all-but-mindless corpses that had laid siege to their school and city.

The second set of stairs, the ones going from the second floor to the third; they told the tale of how well the plan had worked. By the time they had to move to a higher floor, their numbers and resources had clearly thinned, and they were nothing what they once were. Their minds had grown soft and their muscles softer still, and they were left with nothing to protect themselves.

When we reached the western end of the school, I entered a class-room that had remained suspiciously unharmed. There was a light coming from some corner of the room, blue in color yet warming to the skin; I was helpless to resist. I walked towards it, and it grew brighter and brighter until it wasn't blue anymore, but white.

And then it went away.

There was a *bang* and I spun my head around to see that the door to the classroom and slid shut. The blue light surrounded the frame of the door, and I took a handful of lumbering steps towards it, and tried to pull it open to no avail. Something magical was holding it shut.

There was a rustling behind us, and I heard Kat gasp.

"What is *that?*"

I knew without looking; it was the thing from my nightmare, the one that took me from the main hall to warn me of *her.* The uniform it wore was tattered and hung loose from the pure skin and bones that remained. The skin hung looser from the face on this one that it did on the one from my dream, and I couldn't take my eyes from the drooping cheeks until they dropped suddenly from my view.

It was on all fours and heading for the wall, skittering fast like an insect trying to hide from light. As soon as I saw it move, I drew my sword. I took a deep breath, and when I exhaled it, the blade became engulfed with fire. My eyes followed the thing as it climbed the wall on my right, and then began across the ceiling until it was almost directly overhead.

I watched closely as it released its grip on the ceiling and let its upper body hang, swiping at me with its elongated arms. I ducked out of the way of the strikes, but this one was adept at stretching its limbs out, much like the one I had seen in my vision—my dream? I wasn't sure anymore. I was unsure of how far they could reach, but the confines of the room made me uneasy about the prospect of testing that.

I tried for a few slashes of my sword but found no purchase. The thing was nimble, and dodged quicker than I could reset and swing again. It returned to all fours on the ceiling and skittered down the wall behind us, where the door still glowed. It tilted its head back, farther than anyone should be able to, and let loose a haunting shriek. I watched it prepare to strike, and knew the pounce was coming.

As soon as it left the wall, I fell backwards and stuck the point of my sword outwards. When I landed on the floor, the pommel of my sword was driven into my stomach, and I had the wind knocked out of me; the weight of the squirming student creature sliding slowly down the blade, the fire burning away at it as it tried to pull itself free. The pommel was grinding into my gut as I heard the dry, loose skin sizzling as the Ruby's fire took hold, passing over the entire creature like a wave.

When the thing stopped moving, I rolled onto my side. As I stood, I used my boot to free my blade from the body. It burned away to ash right before my eyes.

"The door," I heard Kat say. I turned to see that it once again stood open, like it had when we entered, opening silently while we were distracted.

What magic ruled this school?

I nodded to her, and we took our leave of the room—though something from the feeling in the *air* has stuck with me ever since. Something in that building was different from the ones that we had been in before. It felt like the walls were *alive*. It felt like we were being watched the whole time we were there, and while I would soon learn the truth of the school, it was in that moment that I began to feel that something was amiss.

When we returned to the hall, the walls were alight with the blue hues we had seen in the classroom and around the locked door. The light spread across the walls like vines, weaving and intricate but random pattern that stretched across some doors, barring them closed, it seemed, while avoiding others altogether. It was as though the building itself was now awake.

Though I was quick to wish that all of the doors *had* been blocked, a student creature moving on all fours and crawling slowly out of a distant room. Another came around through the top of the door, before stopping and looking in our direction with the black and hollow pits where eyes once were.

Whatever was in the school had begun to wake, which meant we would likely be fighting our way through the rooms until we found where the Onyx was hidden; its power no doubt part of the reason for all we were seeing. I wasn't happy to do it, but I knew that it couldn't be avoided. We both knew that we weren't going to make it to the second floor on the West wing, with all of the stairwells knocked out, so we cautiously made our way back to the main hall. We tried the doors to the West on the second and third landings, but they wouldn't budge. So we decided to begin checking the East wing.

What was left of it, anyway.

Nothing Remains

When we reached the East Wing of the Academy, we stood at the doorway for a moment to try and make sure that we weren't walking into a trap. It wasn't the monsters or the magic we were worried about, but the building itself—it was hard to tell the damages to the East Wing from the outside, and we wanted to make sure we weren't about to get buried in rubble.

It would be a terrible way for it all to end.

It looked to me like most of the damage had been on the upper floors. The main floor was, for the most part, unharmed. There were some piles of rubble—one of which that would block our way to the very end of the hall about halfway down—but the building was still intact all the way down to the end. There was the whistling of wind coming from somewhere above, and we used that as a guide to find our way upstairs.

There were only a few students along the way, and while I was not used to the erratic ways that they moved, I found that as long as I could get them to pounce, I could counter fairly consistently. These things didn't seem to share the same mind, like the rest of the undead, so they didn't learn from me—not that the corpses outside of there showed much in the way of intelligence—but there was something *smart* about the way these things moved.

More than once I thought I heard one of the students talking to me, grunting something while pouncing or hiding words in its powerful shriek that still sent shivers up and down my spine; whispers of warning or pleading to leave this place. They also didn't glow the way that the Undead did, so the shriek began to serve largely as the only warning that we had been discovered. Even then, as we moved through the halls, the creatures began to stifle their cries, opting instead to try stealth.

Kat remained at my side, though she would generally move to a

corner of the room or some kind of cover when fighting broke out. After we reached the main hall, I offered her the mace on my back.

"No," she shook her head. "It's not mine."

I had looked down at the mace, and then back to her. "Honestly, it
never felt much like mine, either," I said. "And you should be able to
defend yourself, especially if something happens to me."

"If something happens to you, then I failed." She put a hand on
mine, and pushed it down, rejecting the weapon once and for all. "But
I cannot fight." She fell quiet and looked down to the floor. "It takes
much effort, even for me to touch you," she said, looking then into my
eyes. There was no sadness there, even though it permeated her voice;
her eyes were cold and dead. "I cannot wield a weapon; I can only do
what I can to keep you alive—to get the Stones and make it right. We
have to make it right."

We had found the first aid room in the block closest to the main
hall upon entering the East Wing, and were surprised to see that it was
left mostly untouched. Whatever had happened in Alduin, especially
at the Academy, must have happened quick. Quick enough that people forgot to raid that room in particular, I was beginning to think—
though if they had, the thought occurred to me, it may have stayed my
sword from drawing blood that much longer. Either that, or whatever
had happened to make the school *come alive*, as it were, might have
driven people away from the supplies.

But why were we able to walk in? Perhaps whatever was defending it saw no need, now that it has had a few decades to work au-
tonomously. The state of the school made me think that there were no
actual people left wandering the halls; just the nightmarish shells of
the former student body, left asleep until someone—us—disturbed
them from their slumber.

It was as though something had been taken away from them.
Something that left them the way that they were, shells of their former
selves. But unlike the dead, their souls appeared to be trapped within
the husks—or at least what remained of them after they had been
feasted on. And the desperate way they were warning me about waking *someone* up, I shuddered to think what terrors still slept.

Not that I could surmise much, anyway. They were all quite
skilled at the pronoun game, and it wasn't until we finally found our
way to the fourth floor, having to slip around behind the central hallway, through a short classroom into a back hall that was used for
maintenance. We found a ladder that lead up to the second floor, and
from there we were able to find a clear path up the stairs to the fourth.
We made our way back to the main hall, and I was beginning to grow

weary from combat and looked forward to a moment of rest. At the end of the hallway we saw the familiar piles of desks and chairs and other furniture that had been piled against the doors leading to the central stairwell and foyer.

The fourth floor of the central building was largely the same as the others: one set of large doors each for the wings on either side, and two single doors on either side of the Spire that was rising up the back wall of the room. From the outside, we could figure that the Spire was closer to the front of the building, so although I had never been there, I knew that the central structure stretched out much farther back from the doors we still couldn't get through, the same blackness covering each of the windows to the left and right of the doors. We rested for a moment before moving on.

We reached the fifth floor, and the double doors to the wings had been replaced with big windows that opened up onto balconies over-looking each. On the one to the West, I found a heavy cloak and a shield that had been adorned with the sigil of the realm—a four-point diamond with the colors representing each gemstone at the points, a cross intersecting where the Necropolis was, in the middle of the dia-mond. I picked up both items, and threw them on. The cloak was heavy enough to soak up some blunt attacks, where the shield, at the very least, would save my shoulders from the constant impact with the ground from rolling.

The balcony to the East had collapsed, but from the window we could see the damage done to the wing. It looked like it had started from the third floor. One of the larger classrooms was at the center of the blast, which exploded outwards, taking most of the floor above it, as well as the ceiling and most of the walls of the one below. The col-lapse of all of the floors had happened in such a way that the wreck-age from the third and fourth floors plugged the hole left by the col-lapsing second, which is why we didn't start to feel the breeze coming through the rubble until we reached the second floor on the Eastern side of the building.

The other doors on the landing were the same, though the long windows on either side of the doors were clear. I opened the door on the left, with relative ease, and stepped through to see that both doors opened into the same room, wide, that stretched back about thirty feet. Each wall was lined with desks, and each desk was littered with pa-pers, and each paper was scribbled and drawn upon; shapes that I had not seen before that left me with an unsettling feeling—just what had they been teaching here? And in the center of the room, four long ta-bles were pushed together into a rectangle that stretched a good length

of the room. There were four chairs *inside* of the tables, and many surrounding it. In the very center was a chair that sat a couple heads
higher than all the rest, on some kind of swivel.

The ghastly light from the rest of the school was there as well,
torch flames hanging in the air attached to nothing, just floating as
though part of the air. It lit up the room enough that I was able to see
—the Sunsight had long since waned, as it didn't seem that the students were kept alive by the same power as the undead. Defeating
them did nothing to replenish whatever twisted energy it was that I
needed to maintain my vision in the dark.

Aside from the furniture and the fire, the room was empty. It
wasn't the first time we had encountered an empty or seemingly empty room; there had been a few classrooms in either wing that appeared
to have nothing of use, and were bereft of the student creatures. There
was something about that room that felt *oppressive*, as if something
was trying to keep us there. My mind began to race, as if beyond my
control, and I felt as though it was something *else* that was searching
for something.

I heard the low sound of cracking wood coming from somewhere
beneath us and tried to trace the source. I followed it to where Kat
stood, across the room from me, by one of the student desks examin-
ing a paper she found there. But it was too late; the sound grew louder, and floor exploded upwards, black tendrils, glowing with a deep
blue aura, were shooting upwards from beneath. Kat seemed to begin
to glow as well, and the blues appeared to meld. As the tendrils
wrapped around her lower-half, she locked eyes with me and was
pulled beneath the floor.

I screamed out for her and crossed the room as quick as I could.
When I got there, and peered into the hole, I saw nothing but darkness. I tried to keep my distance, for fear that I would get grabbed as
well; but the black didn't seem to move at all. Veins of blue began to
pulsate in the darkness, and I saw that it wasn't the absent of light, but
a thick layer of whatever was blocking the windows in the hall that
had sealed the hole. I thought about poking at it with my sword, but
worried about how many more holes the thing would make before it
was done playing with me. I needed even footing.

I had a pretty good idea where the Stone would be, though, when
I saw that the spire was even more present on this side of the doors. I
doubted I would find it climbing. Each of them seemed to give some
kind of power—I just couldn't be sure which because I had yet to hold
one for any length of time.

The Ruby from Castleford gave my sword fire, as well as it gave

Azazel the powers to sprout a new Sun, hideous as it may be. Whether or not the Sun was also a product of his Wizardry, I was not sure—I did not know the extent of his *own* magic, let alone his magic *with* a Stone.

The Emerald from Brakas was something different. The bodies in the church, reanimated skeletons and the force-fields that the Father was using against me, not to mention his ability to warp from place to place. And while he was able to unleash blasts on me using the stone, they seemed to be mostly concussive in nature, offering little in the way of pure harm and more annoyance and discombobulation unless given proper time to charge.

Perhaps the user's time with the Stone was important to the powers they were able to wield? If it was like most talents, it would likely take years of practice with them to be able to master them. Is that why Azazel was unfazed by learning Rayna possessed one of the Stones? Because it would be a long while before she was able to master its magic? At least enough to be a threat?

And what of the Sapphire of Dewpond? It was, to that point, missing in action. To this day, the mystery surrounding that Stone eludes me. And as I stood in the Alduin Academy, I feared the magic of the Onyx—surely, it was what had infected the very building I was standing in, which, to me, only meant that it was still there. It didn't appear as though it was attached to the Spire. In fact, it didn't appear that anything was attached to the Spire; every floor I entered, it was untouched and smooth, standing as black and monolithic as they had from the start, just as curious as always.

Up didn't appear to be the answer.

ENVELOPED

It was clear to me that I needed to head down to the lower floors of the central structure. I had thought it was four separate stories, but the blackness on the windows, and the tendrils shooting through the floor to take Kat, all made me think that something not unlike what happened to the East Wing had happened there. In my mind I saw the central structure gutted, but only to a point. I wondered what kind of monstrosity could be lying in wait inside.

Whatever it was, it had Kat.

Much in the same way she had pointed out earlier that she will fail in her quest should anything happen to me, I was beginning to feel the same for her. The thought of going on alone was already weighing on me, and I couldn't even be sure that she had been killed. If that's all the blackness wanted, then it could have done that in front of me instead of taking her down below.

I had to go through the large room on the fifth floor, walking through a set of double doors on the opposite end to find another stairwell, much more narrow and less ornate than the one at the front of the building, that went down. Though much like the main hall, the doors at each floor were blocked shut by something on the other side, barring my entrance.

All except the one on the first floor.

I pushed on the double doors, expecting the same resistance I had felt before, but to my surprise they swung open with ease. I was met with a wall of stench, constructed of heat, and death; I had to turn away. It was unlike anything I had experienced to that point. I tried to keep from retching, but something I had seen had burned itself into my mind.

My eyes closed, I still kept seeing the flashes of what was in the room. Much like I had surmised, the ceilings above, up to the fourth floor, had been ripped out. Small patches of the floors above still stood, though I couldn't speak to how sturdy they were. Everything was covered in blackness, like a physical shadow, that had reached out and took Kat, as well as blocking the sight from all of the windows into the chamber. The veins of blue emanating their glow appeared to carry with them a deep hum that made some part of my ears hurt, even though I wasn't sure I could hear *anything*.

But it was the thing in the center of the room that I couldn't get out of my mind.

Wrapped in something not unlike a cocoon, made of the same blackness, though the strange substance had become transparent at the core. Inside of the crystalized cage of shadow was a woman, her arms draped over her nakedness and her eyes closed. She was smiling as she slept, and appeared to be at peace. She was held in place, high above the first floor—somewhere around the second, if I had to guess without looking a second time—by a trunk of the shadowy substance that ran up and down the center of the room before spreading out, covering the walls like living paint.

I forced myself to turn around; to look again. The room was bright and dark at the same time. I didn't know what was shadow or wall or floor or furniture; it was all covered just the same. And in the black, I could see that the blue lights weren't staying still; they were moving towards the center column, where the woman was resting comfortably, as though it was delivering something to her; *feeding* her as she slept.

I took a deep breath and scanned the room for Kat. There were lumps in the walls where the blue seemed to be the strongest, most of the lights moving outwards from these, and something in my mind told me that there were bodies under there; bodies in shadowy cocoons, being sapped of *something*, that was being taken back to *her*. It wasn't a gut feeling, or deduction—it was as though something had entered my head and *showed* me what was beneath the black.

But which one held Kat? And how long until she looked like one of *them*—like the creatures we had faced on the way there? The hollow husks of the former student body, remnants of the things she *didn't* want.

When I stepped through the precipice and into the room, the shadows retracted at my feet. I didn't notice until I could hear the bottom of my boots on wood, and looked down to watch as it slid away from me. It was alive, whatever it was. I wondered if the woman in the cocoon was the one controlling it all? I held my sword in my right hand, the Academy shield in the left, and continued to scan the walls for any signs of Kat. I moved farther into the room so that I could look up the back wall, where I had entered from, but the mounds were cov-ered entirely—there was no way for me to see who or what was be-neath them while the black still covered the walls.

But there was *so much* of it; I didn't know how to even start clear-ing it out. I couldn't walk the room to get it all to go away, for I was quick to notice that it had begun filling in again behind me, leaving only enough room for me to begin walking in any direction without making contact with it.

I couldn't be sure why it seemed to fear me, but I wasn't about to question it too much. It had afforded me some comfort to know that it wasn't actively trying to grab me the way it had Kat, even though it only brought up more questions about its intentions.

I saw one of the mounds begin to move, and lowered my stance. I kept an eye on the ground around me, to make sure that the shadow wasn't about to close in, while also watching the movement above closely. The mound was somewhere close to the third floor, but I could hear muffled sounds coming from within. There was no more blue coming from it, which led me to believe that it had finished feeding. The shadow began to dissipate, and a body dropped out, plummeting to the ground in front of me with great speed.

The black seemed ready, a large hand-like appendage forming out of the ground to catch the body, setting it down on its feet in front of me. It was another student creature, freshly hollowed. It screamed at me, and I took my breath, and lit my blade aflame—

A shriek filled the room, terrified and loud enough to make me recoil in pain. I looked to see the black *jump* away from me and my sword the moment the flames lit, like an insect fleeing from fresh light in the dark night. There was a *fear* of the fire, and the power that my sword held; I could feel it in the desperate movement of the shadows.

It is spread too thin, I thought to myself, *to challenge the fire.*

I struck down the student with relative ease and watched with a smile as my path cleared quicker than it had before. The path behind me seemed to stay clear longer, as well; as though it didn't want to risk me returning to where I had been. It had revealed itself to me, and I was no longer the one being intimidated. I believe it was desperation that finally sounded the morning bell, the black beginning to under-stand what it needed to do in order to defend itself from this new threat: Me.

The woman began to stir.

Like blood pumping from the heart, the black seemed to pulse on its way to the cocoon in the center by way of the tendrils attached to the floor and ceiling holding her in place. I watched in horror as the walls and the floor began to clear of the shadowy black, leaving only the rubble of the destruction in its wake. The woman's eyes shot open, and she gasped for air—only her eyes weren't normal anymore. When they open, they were white and pure; nothing else to be seen in them. But over the course of seconds, I saw as they filled with black, starting cloudy before consuming all white that I could see.

"Stop her!" a voice called out from the wall.

"Kill her before she wakes!" said another.

"Run!" a familiar woman screamed.

I readied my sword and dove for the lower tendril, readying a horizontal strike that I had hoped would cut clean through. Instead, the ooze formed a thick tentacle-like appendage that struck out at me, knocking me back. I lifted myself to my elbows before I saw the co-coon lowering, all the black on the walls and ceilings returning to the center, feeding into the cocoon and disappearing before nothing was left except for the woman kneeling on the ground half the length of the room from me.

She swayed her head back and forth, her eyes staring up at noth-ing in particular, her jaw hanging open. She was still naked, and seemed little concerned with covering herself up. In the center of her chest, between her breasts, a black stone was set upon her skin. I watched her face, waiting to see what she might do, when I saw Kat lying on what remained of the second floor, unconscious, just over the woman's shoulders.

"Welcome to the Alduin Academy." The words came from the woman's mouth, but it was not her voice. It was not *only* her voice, that is; but the voice of hundreds, speaking all at once. "Join us, and we can answer all of the questions that plague your little mind." She was still staring off into the distance. "Share with us, and we shall share with you—together we can live forever in these great halls, where all the world's knowledge lives!"

"Who are you?"

"The Alduin Academy," it said. "Centuries of knowledge, passed down like a curse; warnings unheeded by humankind. All the things that you wish to remember, I hold; all the things that man would think better forgotten, I hold as well." It rose to its feet, turning the woman's gaze to meet my own. I felt our eyes lock, as though struck. "Though logic can be second to feeling no longer," it barked, and my heart sunk. "Perhaps it is time to return the world to the great mother."

I opened my mouth to speak, but was interrupted by a blast, shooting outward from the woman, sending me flying into the wall just beside the double doors leading to the back stairwell.

When I got up, I saw the woman convulsing in the center of the room. Her skin seemed to be bubbling, much the same way the surface of boiling water will bubble, before the shadowy black erupted from beneath and began enveloping her like a shell, bigger and bigger until she had grown three times her normal size, and was big enough that the top of her head was brushing what remained of the second floor.

She had been covered head-to-toe in black. And although the form was still mostly human, a cluster of black tendrils—maybe a dozen—were sticking out from her back at varying lengths. They writhed like snakes of different sizes, with the two closest to her shoulders folding forward, towards me, like horns. Her legs were like trunks, the shadow puddling at her feet as though it wasn't completely bound to her, a peculiar observation that I would have to remember, I thought. Her arms had grown longer since being covered, the clawed hands nearly scraping the ground even as she stood upright.

The sight was horrifying. The shadow came from the Onyx, of that I was sure. It seemed as though it was feeding on the knowledge of those that it had captured, and turned that into whatever energy was helping it spread. I wondered, if this thing had been feeding the entire time we were underground—especially if all of the students had remained here, like I suspected—than it would surely have had enough time to feed on most, if not all of the student body. It explained to me why they were driven not by the stolen power of the light, like the other undead, but something else entirely. They were merely husks of their former selves, defending the school as though it was the only instinct they had left.

It *was* their home, after all.

It had to be the headmistress, I thought as I looked upon the creature before me. Much the same that Father Paxton had seemingly taken to using the Emerald, it seemed obvious to me that the headmistress, Lady Artemis, had found a use for the Onyx.

But why?

She was in no condition to answer any of my questions, having been completely overtaken by the black; but it was one that I felt needed answering: like so many others that had come before it. And even as the questions kept mounting, I still found myself too late to arrive to find any answers, only more perplexing scenes such as this one—the former headmistress of the realm's greatest school, encased in black shadow that has turned her into a hulking beast, borne of the knowledge and life-force of the student body.

She took a lumbering step towards me, shaking the whole building as she did, and it snapped me free from my thoughts. I gripped the hilt of my sword tight and raised the shield, without thinking, just in time to block the whipping strike of one of the two longer tendrils, the force nearly breaking my guard.

I dropped my shield and looked to see if there was an opening for a counter attack, but I found myself distracted by strange movement. The surface of her skin, the skin given to her by the Onyx, was beginning to ripple. It all moved, almost in a singular wave, up and across her body to her right shoulder, and then down the arm, where the substance was beginning to pool, creating massive ram. She drew her elbow back, and shot it forward, the clubbed fist suddenly coming towards me at an alarming speed.

I dodged to the right, lifting the shield as I did, the steel catching a small part of the impact. I was sent crashing to the ground faster—my poor shoulders—but I was able to roll through and back to my feet. I slid along the ground for but a second, and watched: she was unguarded on the left, still frozen in place from her attack. I spun my sword around to get a feel for the weight, and dashed forward. I swiped downwards, across the torso, without any resistance.

My sword went right through her, like cutting through air.

The body appeared to separate just hairs before the flames of the sword touched it, as if pulling itself in to avoid the attack. I had expected the blade to make contact, at least, with the woman contained within; only there was no longer a woman there, just the black shadow that the Onyx had created, the skin that now encased her. What was left of the legs pooled on the ground and flowed around me to rejoin the ram, which had begun regrowing its arms and legs, turning to face me once more.

Of course, I thought to myself, *she was transferred through the arm. She can move within the body.* That would make things more difficult. If it could move her to safety and avoid my strikes, it would be nigh impossible to kill.

Though, she did look... *smaller* somehow, as if some of the skin had been burned away, maybe by the fire on my blade. Perhaps the powers of the Stones can counteract the others?

While I was once again lost in thought, a tendril shot out at me, aiming to pierce my chest. I brought the shield up as quick as I could, but I had to hold it too close to ensure I blocked the attack; the force of it sent me stumbling back and to the left. I used the stumble to my advantage, though, letting the force spin me so that I could bring my sword around. I sliced downward, cutting through the tendril with ease. The appendage itself *shrieked* as it burned, the fire traveling quick, but not far. Still; it had done what I had hoped.

She was smaller still.

But that also meant that what she lacked in size she now had gained in speed. She moved around much easier, sometimes her legs allowing her to move along the ground like water. It was eerily beautiful to watch her move, so lithe and dance-like, almost majestic. She had lost some of the range to her attacks, but after a quick, ineffective shot with the crossbow, I knew that I would need to get in close if I had any chance of defeating her. It was becoming *much* more lethal to do so, but I had no other choice.

I kept my shield up but it wasn't enough. Tendrils were able to cut through my sword arm, just above the elbow. It wasn't deep, but something about it *stung*. I briefly looked at the wound, and I could see that some of the shadowy substance remained on my arm, disappearing quickly into the wound. Is this how it started? When I saw an opening, I went to strike with my sword, aiming to cut off a leg.

At least, that's what I had *wanted* to do. I had misjudged my opening and she was able to dodge to the right, just over the attack. She swung her arm around, the tendrils melding with the arm as if to bolster its strength, hitting straight across my shoulders.

I flew forward, the wind knocked from me. I struggled to regain my breath, and having dropped my shield from the attack, I was able to clutch at my chest with my free hand. Just as suddenly as the previous attack had come, she was on me. I could feel the shadows oozing over my shoulders from where she had planted her foot on my spine.

"I will know what you know," she said. I heard her voice grow closer, her hot breath brushing my ears as she leaned down, the shadow pulling back from her face. "And what we know is who we are— you will live on forever in me, as they do." She looked around the room at the marks where the cocoons of her students had been. I couldn't see her face fully, but she almost seemed sad that they were now gone, empty; their forms abandoned her and the collective sadness of the student body coming forward in her crowded mind.

My head hurt immediately. There was a fire burning somewhere behind my eyes, and I couldn't feel anything anymore. I know I was screaming, but not in pain. There was something fighting its way out of me, and I can't, to this day, put to words how it truly felt. It was painful and exhilarating and scary and *good*. Without much warning, my arm was across me, and I was able to breath. When my senses returned to me, I felt wetness on my face, and heard the sound of a woman screaming.

I was laying on my back, and from what I could tell I had, with some level of instinct, swung my sword across; the magic within somehow reacting to my pain, defending me from its sibling Stone. I had cut clean through the leg of the shadow—

Only there was no more shell for Artemis to hide in.

The skin had abandoned her, fearing for its own safety. I stood, still drawing deep breaths and clutching my chest. I wearily stepped towards the headmistress as she grabbed at what was left of her leg, cut just above the knee. As the blood dripped from the fresh wound I knew what the wetness on my face was, and wiped it away.

When Artemis looked up at me and saw that I was covered in *her* blood, she began to back away, screaming out when I reached for her. I didn't mean to do anything more to her, as it was clear to me that she didn't mean to do anything more to me. The fight was over. I only wanted what I had come for.

I grabbed for the Onyx on her chest, and pulled it from her. She pawed at my hands weakly as I ripped it from its place in her chest with ease, and knew that its power had abandoned her. She was no longer a viable host. Her screams ceased immediately, and she froze in place. I watched with a twisted fascination, rather than horror, as she began to turn to ash, her face frozen in shock and betrayal; not pain.

The sight was fascinating enough that I didn't see the remnants of the shadowy substance—which wasn't much at all—leaping through the air and landing on my hand, before slithering back into the Onyx that I now held. I held the stone up to watch the tar-like substance be *absorbed* into it, like it had belonged there all along. It was home. It took me by surprise when the stone then shot a small tendril into my palm, pulling itself *through* my glove and into my flesh.

I ripped off the glove in desperation, seeing myself suspended in a cocoon for all of time, until some wary traveler found *me*, and saw that the stone had embedded itself in my hand, and dropped my sword to grab for it, hoping to pull it free.

A flash of light stopped me. My mind was screaming. There were lights flashing in all directions and I couldn't find anything to focus on. I felt the back of my eyes pounding to the beat of an unseen—and unheard—drum.

The light burned bright, to an almost blinding degree, and then stopped, giving way to the sight of a classroom, where Artemis stood in the center, surrounded by faithful students who watched in awe as she showed them the Onyx planted in her chest. As the students walked towards her, she nodded to someone or something. Just then, a whip-like tentacle emerged from the Onyx for each student in the room, shooting out with a flash and piercing their foreheads. The tendrils held them on their feet while they sucked the life from the young pupils, lines of blue and black appearing in their skin, running up towards the shadowy tendril.

Artemis seemed overwhelmed by the sudden influx of power, and began to shrink in pain, down to her knees, and then all fours, before nearly curling into a ball on the ground.

The tendrils returned to their home in her chest, and all I could feel was the beating behind my eyes, but there was no sound; no sound but the slow, drawn out breaths of Artemis as she lay on the ground in front of me.

And just as quickly as the tendrils shot out of her, she threw her head back and screamed, a burst of energy erupting from within her. I thought I saw a section of the wall tear free, and the rising Sun off in the distance; the sight of it made me emotional, for it had been a while since I saw a Sunrise, even in dreams.

Then there was the heartbeat.

The heat was unbearable as the lights began to dim, and I saw the deep reds of the heated rocks that surrounded me. Fires burned to the left and right of the stone walkway before me, a lava wall at the very back of the chamber. At the end of the walkway, suspended in the air, was the heart.

It was as large as the whole of me, if not a little bigger, thumping in time to the drum that had been beating just behind my eyes. The fire around me seemed to pulse to the rhythm of the heart.

I looked down from the beating heart, and saw before it, floating delicately above carved stone cradles, were four large crystals. Each one was a different color, and stood about as tall as I was and a little more narrow. I could tell at once that they were the crystals that the Stones we now sought had come from; one was black like Onyx; one was green like Emerald; one was red like Ruby; and the other was blue like Sapphire.

There was a low rumble, and the heat began to intensify. I started to sweat and looked down at the stone in my hand. It seemed satisfied somehow, as though it were mocking me from where it had made its home. I could hear it laughing in the back of my mind, but that just gave me something to focus on. I had a thought to shake clear, and as I did I closed my eyes tight until the pounding stopped.

When I opened them, I was clear of the vision. I was on all fours in the rubble of the central chamber of Alduin Academy. The stone was still in my hand, and I had thought again to remove it but knew that just by keeping it with me it would find a way to attach itself.

I rose to my feet, and blinked until my vision cleared up. I looked up to see if I could find Kat, hoping that I remembered right that she was by the doors, but saw nothing on the second floor.

"The beasts grow stronger," said a voice from behind me. "But the night just became shorter."

I turned to see Kat standing there, looking at my left hand, where the Onyx now resided. I looked down at the stone, and then back to her, nodding. "I fear there is much to do," I said.

"I fear there is, too."

Prelude to Revenge

After we escaped the Alduin Academy with our lives—and the Onyx—we knew there was only thing left for us to do: it was time to head to the Necropolis.

We couldn't be sure whether or not Rayna was in possession of *both* the Emerald from Brakas that she had taken from me; as well as the Sapphire from Dewpond, where I had first encountered her and her Dawnflayer companion, Brok. To us, it didn't matter whether or not she had both or just one of the Stones—she appeared to be standing in the way of our returning things to the way that they had been; if not for us, than for those that still lived beneath the ground, so that they might return to the surface where man belonged.

We had found purpose in our travels that neither of us seemed to find on our own, in our lives before these ones. We had a chance to set things right, and make amends for the things *we* felt we had to; not the ones others thrust upon us.

In truth, I didn't know what Rayna's intentions were. If she had aimed to kill me, she had the perfect chance, and faltered. Maybe she didn't believe I would pursue her, of that I cannot be certain. She had given me the Sunsight on our first meeting, after an unannounced "sparring" match with her companion; a helpful act that didn't seem to fit someone who was trying to bring about a world of darkness. Was it only because she thought I would head to Castleford, and end my journey there?

I didn't head south from the Academy with the intent of killing her, or even fighting her; I merely wanted to speak to her, plead with her to help us bring back the Light. I wanted to know *why* she needed to take the Emerald from me, instead of letting me in on her plan. Was it just that she didn't trust me? I remembered her speaking at lengths about trust, when we first met; but I began to wonder if there was something else that she was hiding.

The Onyx that I had in my hand—quite literally, to my dismay—could prove useful. I thought of what it had shown me when it first bonded to me; Artemis blowing out the East Wing of the Alduin Academy when she acquired her first batch of power. It seemed to know things, or be able to know things, so there was a chance that I might be able to use it to find out what Rayna was truly thinking. If she didn't want to offer that information up on her own, that is. I just wasn't sure how to use such abilities, or how to prevent the same thing from happening to me that happened to Artemis.

As we left the Academy I found myself nearly blind—the students were kept alive by the power of the Onyx, not fueled by stolen Light, like the Undead and other beasts appeared to be. Defeating them did nothing to replenish the Sight. After striking down a pair of wandering Undead, both with rusty daggers and ragged robes, I could see clearly.

We had been caught off-guard by a roaming helcat just as we reached the edge of the Necropolis, and it was able to pounce from a higher ridge, slamming into my right shoulder from behind. I dropped my sword, which I was beginning to keep drawn at all times while we were traveling, and almost fell to the ground myself. I followed the cat's movements with my shield raised, and when I took my eyes off it for only enough time to confirm the location of my sword on the ground, it was already on me.

I was able to push away with my shield, but it had gotten close enough that its grip on the steel was too strong. When I tried to throw it off me, the shield went with it. I watched as my only defense was taken from me. I looked again for the sword, behind me now, but had my attention drawn back to the cat when it hissed at me, and came running, rolling the shield over and springing off it, into a run.

There was a flash behind my eyes, as though everything went black for just a second. When I realized what had happened, and snapped back to reality, there was a wall of black in front of me. I felt the force of the helcat's strike ripple up through my left arm, and saw that I had raised it as though the shield was still there. And it was! Only now, it was black, and seemed to be coming from within my arm. And in my moment of realization, I realized I had the helcat suspended by my new shield, and threw it to the ground with a crash. I grabbed for my sword as the shield retracted into my arm, and just as the helcat attempted to rise, I drove the blade through its chest and into the ground.

I stared in amazement at my new power, but felt my eyes grow heavy, the light in them beginning to fade once more. It was happening far more rapidly than it had before; a bad omen that I had to push from my mind. I grabbed again for my sword, the shield retracting itself as I stood over the mortally wounded helcat. It was still breathing, but was not long for this world. I did the only thing I could for it:

I put it out of its misery.

The sight returned to me, as it had so many times before. I breathed a sigh of relief as I began to parse what had happened, collecting the shield from the ground. While I appeared to have a new level of powers, thanks to the Onyx; they were taxing on the Sunsight. Using the Onyx shield would only blind me quicker—and even then, I wasn't sure how to control it. It had come out on its own and returned on its own, without any thought on my part. Was it driven by instinct? *Could* I learn to control it?

The drain it had caused on the Sunsight was not permanent, as I had initially, but only briefly, feared. I was beginning to understand some things about the world that had rightfully eluded me in my youth. There was no need to complicate the mind of a child with the possibilities of the world, at least not in any serious terms; it would only serve to scare them off growing up. To learn of the world through the context of myths and legends; it was a way to learn the base lessons, without the grisly details of the troubles it took to get there.

I tried to recall if engulfing the sword in fire would have had the same effect, but being that it was magic borrowed from the stone, rather than the stone itself, I thought maybe it had its own limits. It, too, might run out one day soon. I regretted using it as much as I had in the Academy.

We reached the crest of a hill, still a fair walk away from where the dome covering the center of the Necropolis stood, standing in shades of green. It looked weaker somehow, now that we were closer, than it had when we stood with Azazel in Castleford. The colors had faded, and even as we stood I could see them fluctuating in an out of view.

"Look," Kat said. I turned to see her looking not at the dome, but somewhere off to the East. I followed her gaze, and saw what she saw: groups of Undead were heading *towards* the center of the Necropolis, as though something were calling them there. The orange glow they gave off when alerted to the presence of an enemy was pulsing, fading and intensifying with each step. They seemed to be oblivious to our presence, but I kept my sword ready all the same.

There was a crack of thunder above, and I looked to see that the purples and the greens and the stars of the sky above had gone black, covered by impenetrable clouds that carried with them the darkest omens. And as I turned my face upwards to the clouds, I felt a drop of rain land on my cheek. It was warm as it ran down my face, beneath my ear, and down my neck. I could feel it every bit of the way, and just as it calmed me, it filled me with a sense of foreboding. Was this the first time it had rained since I reemerged?

And almost as if on cue, there was another loud crack. Not thunder this time; no, this was something else. This was coming from the center of the Necropolis. I turned to it just in time to see the spark of light, followed by another loud crack as the sound hit us, still on the outskirts of the Necropolis proper. The green of the dome gave way to pure white, and for the first time in nearly three decades, there was light bright enough to reach all in the realm, if only for a second.

The dome exploded.

The Cathedral of Woe

Kat and I made our way through the Necropolis as quickly as we could. The labyrinth of graves was thicker than I had imagined, made worse by several sinkholes that had resulted from the bodies, when they removed themselves from the soil.

There were many things I wanted to stop and investigate, but we didn't have the time. Something or someone had destroyed the bubble that was protecting the Necropolis from outsiders. I thought I knew at least part of what had happened, and I think that Kat knew it too; we just couldn't afford the time to talk about it.

It had to be Rayna. Though I wasn't sure why it took her so long to get through. Whatever she was planning must have required more time to prepare. And hadn't Azazel claimed the Emerald alone was not enough to destroy the dome? What had happened?

Another question that I—and perhaps the Onyx stone, if I could figure out how to use it—would have to ask her when we found her.

The Cathedral of Woe stood in the center of the Necropolis, untouched by the fires and destruction that had rained down everywhere else in Alghast. And even though it was one of the few remaining structures of the world I *used* to know, as I stood and stared up the small hill that it sat on I felt an overwhelming sense of dread. It was as though hundreds of ghastly hands were reaching out from there, and trying to pull me along weakly, their arms just going through me and leaving me with the ethereal chill that I was feeling, deep in my bones.

It was rectangular, with thick stone support pillars running the length of both sides, connecting to the large overhang of the flat roof. The building was large, easily two stories if split in such a way, but I could see from the outside that unless there were landings built inside, it was all one floor. In between the pillars I could see the dark of the stained-glass, shadowy images painted on them surrounded by darker purples and blues and cooler shades likely meant to calm the mourning, despite how morose they were to look at. The entire building sat on a stone lift that was about waist-high, with wide steps cut into it ahead of the main double doors leading inside. And at each corner of the stone slab that the Cathedral lived on were statues, each one facing outwards, holding empty hands to the sky.

There was a loud crack and a crash from inside the Cathedral, and I shot Kat a concerned look. Something was happening in there already, and it took me longer than I thought—still only a moment, mind you—to find the courage to take that step towards the door.

After everything I had seen to that point, everything I had face and experienced and *learned* about the world, I still found myself dreading what waited on the other side of those doors. I turned to Kat, and took a deep breath. "You had better wait here," I said.

She only nodded.

"Hide from the dead. I won't be long."

The doors were almost twice as tall as I was, black and iron. The rivets that ran along the edges were almost as large as my fist, and I wondered why a Cathedral would need such heavy doors. I knew there were more pressing matters, so began to push on them where they bisected in the center, opening them just enough that I could pass through.

The inside of the Cathedral was anything but a church. There were no pews or altars, or banners hanging. The rune of the realm was chiseled into the back wall, but save for that and the windows there were few other markings. Bodies were strewn about, some fresh, others not. In the center of the chamber there was a heavy iron grate in the floor covering a large, round hole in the ground. The beams were circular and irregular in design—at least, I couldn't parse any sort of pattern from the ground where I was; it was far too complicated and large. And whatever magic was lighting the Cathedral—it was bright as day inside—was invisible from the outside.

I wanted so badly to look down into the pit. There was a heavy feeling in the air that I hadn't felt in quite some time; a feeling that I couldn't quite make sense of. All at once I was frozen with fear and anxiety, my mind reeling and my heart aching, as though it were all about to explode. I snapped out of it when I finally looked across the room.

On the other side of the iron grate, Rayna and Brok stood over a fallen and cowering Azazel, the Wizard holding his hands up in defeat. Rayna's own hand was glowing green, and it seemed to me as though she had figured out, at least in part, how to control the Emerald.

She looked weathered, angry; wherever she had been all this time had not been kind to her. It looked to me as though Brok had obtained a large scar across his face and chest, and lost the use of his left eye in the process, leaving it milky and white.

Whether or not they heard me enter, I wasn't sure. They both seemed so preoccupied with the wizard, that I decided to try and sneak up on them if I could. The storm outside may have masked the sound of the doors opening, but it would only take someone stealing a glance in that direction to know that they were no longer alone.

There was a blind spot along the right wall, obscured by the thick support pillars that ran just a few paces out from the wall where the gaudy windows lived. I slipped into the shadows—what shadows there were, in the bright light that seemed to reach for every corner—and tried to move quickly and quietly between them, closing the distance fast.

"Where is it?" Rayna asked in a commanding tone, her voice growing louder as I grew closer. "I won't chase you any farther."

I was getting close enough that I could *hear* Brok taking a step forward, and the quick cry of Azazel shortly thereafter. I couldn't wait any longer; it looked as though the Dawnflayer was getting ready to begin an assault on the Wizard. Perhaps their intents truly were villainous. I stepped out from the shadows and called out to Rayna.

She spun, alarmed, and Brok followed suit. She looked annoyed, then worried when she saw my sword, ignited with the flames of the Ruby—I would simply ask Azazel to replenish the sword with magical energy when I was finished saving him. She opened her mouth as if to speak, but I afforded her no time for distractions.

I dashed forward, swung my blade across from the right, expecting her to dodge. She jumped backwards, and my strike missed, but it got Brok to move. He lifted his fists above his head, clasping them together and bringing them down fast where I had stood, only I was able to quickly push off and his fists the collided with the hard stone ground beneath us.

"I see I was right to distrust you," Rayna said, breathing heavily. "You're in league with the him; with Azazel?" Brok was returning to an upright position, and the three of us stood in silence for only a brief second before Rayna began seething. Her voice dropped. "That is the magic of the Ruby in your blade, is it not?"

I looked at the sword, and then back to her. I saw a quick glimpse of her standing over the Wizard, as she was when I entered the Cathedral. I saw a vision of the horrors she would have inflicted on him, if I had not interfered when I did. I began to grow angry as well.

There was also the matter of the pit in the floor—the one covered by the intricate ironwork. It was covering a deep well, and I could see that the stone walls running down gave way to nothingness; shadows and darkness. There was a terrible cloud of foreboding that I felt as I thought about looking deeper into the pit. Voices in the back of my head began speaking, in a tongue I couldn't understand.

"The light," I said, quieting the voices. I thought it would be here, I was sure of it. What had she done with it? "What is it you mean to do?" I took a step forward, pointing to her with my sword. "Do you plan to take its power for your own?"

"I gifted you with sight, and still you are so blind," she said almost disappointed. She looked to where she had left Azazel, only he had vanished. "And you've cost me my revenge with your ignorance. I have nothing more to say to you. But my blades," she drew her sword in her right hand, a small dagger in her left, and readied herself for combat. "My blades would like to have a word with you." Brok roared, and I held my sword out at my side, my shield ahead of me.

After a pause, while we waited for someone to make the first move, I saw Rayna clench her right fist tighter around the hilt of her sword, and I could see that she had installed the Emerald into the gauntlet that she was wearing. It glowed a brilliant green, and surrounded her before she vanished from sight, smiling.

Brok roared again, and came running at me. I was caught off guard by Rayna's sudden disappearance, and barely dodged to his right, slashing at his legs. He had once again grown in size, much as he did during our first encounter, and I could not afford the energy to reach any higher for strikes. They would not have enough power behind them to do damage, and would only tire me out faster. So I struck for the legs, hoping I could take the brute down. The addition of the flames seemed to help; he yelped loudly as the skin around the shallow cut seared like meat cooking on a campfire.

Even then, he only stumbled before turning his attention on me once more. He swept his massive left mitt along the ground, hoping to send me flying upwards, but I rolled out of the way and watched as he turned in absolute panic to get me in his sights. That's when it dawned on me:

He was blind on one side.

Just as I was beginning to process how to use this to my advantage, my vision blacked out for a second, and I saw a flash of green somehow behind me, as if a sense was showing me something my eyes could not see. Not questioning it, I ducked just in time avoid Rayna's sword thrust. I shot an elbow back, and thought I would connect with her gut, but she still seemed to have some sort of energy field around her that blocked my attack. By the time I was able to turn, she was gone again.

And I was flying across the room.

Just before I crashed into the wall, I felt something slow me in midair, like a cushion of wind that stopped me just enough that when I landed, it was only a modicum of pain. I looked around to see if Azazel was somewhere around, helping me in whatever ways he could, despite how weak he looked at Rayna's feet when I entered.

Brok was already on the move, so I didn't have time to fully recover from his attack. I was unsure what magic had saved me from the impact, but knew that unhindered it would have left me helpless. I was back on my feet as quick as my body would allow me. He pulled back his left fist, and shot it outwards with enough force that it would have crushed me, even if I was able to block it with my shield; but Brok was slower than he had been when I fought him before. The road had tired him, as it tired me, I had thought, and I was able to sidestep the punch to the left.

There was a tinge of regret in my stomach before I even did it. I grunted, but more through my own hesitation rather than effort, as I used the brief seconds in his blind spot to my advantage. Moving just quick enough that when he turned his head to follow me I was able to stay out of sight. And when he began to turn to his right, I saw my chance.

There was little left in the Cathedral, but there were some elevated platforms on the left and right, leading up to the raised landings that ran under the windows. It was only a few steps, but through our little dance we had found ourselves fairly close to one of the support pillars. When I knew I had a second, I quickly mounted the stairs, and jumped. I pushed off the pillar for just that little more height that I needed, and as I was in the air I felt that tinge of regret, as though I was making the wrong choice.

Then I stabbed my sword into the Dawnflayer's back, just under the left shoulder blade, pushing hard to make sure that it got as deep as it could.

Brok threw his head back and roared in pain. The tip of the blade was exiting through his chest, and the flames on the sword were blackening the skin around the wound. He reached over his shoulder and grabbed me by my cloak. With his last gasp he tossed me limply from his shoulders, and slumped to the ground. Before I had time to retrieve my sword, or even rise to my feet, Rayna reappeared, screaming in anguish.

She walked over to him, and I noticed that she was limping. I had wondered why she had stayed out of the fight, but much like Brok she did not seem to be ready for a battle. I shook the thought from my head, hoping that the sympathy that it brought with it would dissipate as well.

I heard the clatter of steel as my sword hit the ground between me and them. Rayna had pulled it free, and was resting a hand on Brok's slumped shoulders. He didn't move, and as far as I could see he wasn't breathing, either.

She looked at me with disdain as I quietly reached out, and grabbed the sword off the ground. Her eyes began glowing green, just as her hand did; soon her whole body was engulfed in a green aura like fire. It expanded outwards in bursts, and she reached out to me. There was a blinding flash, and suddenly everything was dark.

Except I could feel rain on my face.

There was a flicker of green, and I tried to focus, and faintly I could see Rayna's face in the dim light. The aura had faded, but she stood before me. I could feel the cool air on my face, and knew that we were outside.

And I could no longer see.

In the Dark

I heard rain and thunder, and somewhere in there I thought I heard the deep, gasping breaths of Rayna as she stood across from me. I waited, hoping for my eyes to adjust to the darkness as they had before.

"You didn't have to do this," she shouted through the rain. "You didn't have to do any of it. This didn't have to concern you."

Water ran down my face from wet and matted hair. I rose to a knee, having been seemingly teleported while I was still down to retrieve my sword. "And why did it have to concern you?"

"Fate *chose* me for this!"

I stood, and gripped the sword tightly. I lit the flame on the blade, which seemed unaffected by the rain, save for muting the light that it provided me. Much the same as Rayna seemed to glow with the power of the Emerald ahead of me, a soft green, though darker than before; I offered a muted red. They were our only sources of light. "You and I are guided by the same hand, then."

"To think, in another version of this we might have been allies," she said with a laugh. "Fate is cruel, indeed."

"Just give me the Emerald, Rayna." I lowered my sword, and took a step towards her. "Just give me the Emerald, and the Sapphire, too. Fate cannot mean for both of us to succeed."

"First," she said, drawing a single deep breath and steadying herself. "First: I don't *have* the Sapphire; it was taken from me by *him*; and second: you are absolutely right. Fate must favor one of us, so let's see how you fight in the dark!" I heard the sound of her foot coming down hard into a puddle as she no doubt sprang towards me. The aura that surrounded her flickered just enough when she moved that I couldn't follow it, just as my sword's, I would soon find out.

I wanted to know who she meant had taken the Sapphire, but she had moved too quickly to attack. I listened for the sounds of the rushing footsteps in the rain, and when they slowed, I squinted so I might focus on the still flickering-aura to see which direction the attack was coming from.

I ducked to my left, and felt her sword cut through the air next to the skin on my face. It was close enough that I wasn't sure at the time if the wetness on my face was just rain, or also blood; though I felt no pain, just relief that I had avoided taking the whole of the strike.

Rayna stumbled from the follow-through, and I tried to return to a vertical base, sliding instead on the wet stone. I heard her spin around, gasping for breath as she did, and there were footsteps running away.

As soon as I lost the sound of her feet, I stopped in place. I held the sword out from my body as far as I could, and listened. There was nothing but the rain and the darkness—I couldn't even see the green surrounding her. I tried to urge my eyes to adjust, to see the world as I had before. The light in the Cathedral was strong enough that I hadn't even noticed that the Sunsight was running out; it had after all been some time since we had encountered any of the dead, opting to avoid the throngs of them as we made our way to the Cathedral; too many to fight.

In the distance, a flash; a green burst of energy that went dark again before blooming out into a line, growing thicker and thicker—

It was coming straight towards me.

I threw myself back, narrowly avoiding the beam as it drifted off into the sky. Knowing I had no time to admire the spectacle—Rayna would be on me in no time—I quickly rose and tried to trace the energy blast. As if answering my unspoken plea for help, there was a crack of lightning close by, briefly illuminating the silhouette of the rapidly approaching Rayna, her sword lifted above her head.

She struck downwards, and I was able to get my blade up in time to block. There was a flash of light exploding outwards from the contact that lit everything for just a second. I pushed her off with my shoulder, and swung across her waist. She parried down, and the sky was alight again. Each time our swords connected, light exploded from them.

I had backed her towards one edge of the rooftop, as she was growing tired. Her strikes were coming less frequent, and they were becoming easy to block. She had jumped back to avoid one of my slashes, and I lost her. Everything had gotten pitch dark, even the area around me.

The sword had been extinguished.

I stood, panicked for a second. I once again listened for footsteps around me. Instead, I only heard labored breathing.

"True dark," Rayna said. "That's where we go. I won't return if you kill me; can the same be said for you?"

The footsteps sounded, and I parried right, my timing just right as I heard her sword fall to the ground. I tried to grab for her, but the light she gave off was muddled—it was barely green anymore.

Suddenly, there was a searing pain across the back of my sword hand, and I dropped my weapon. I felt a hand come across to slap my arm out of the way, and then a pressure in my side that took the air out of my chest. I gasped and gasped, but it felt like I could get nothing. I reached down with my bleeding hand just as she twisted the dagger in my side, and the pressure turned to pain, and I screamed out.

There was something pooling in the palm of my left hand, which had remained at my side without my thinking. I could barely notice the feeling coming from the Onyx over the pain in my side before it had already been entirely covered by the black substance. I shot my arm out, into Rayna's abdomen, and saw the sharp end of a tendril pierce clean through to the other side. And only after seeing the tendril did it occur to me that I could see again.

I followed the retreating whip and noticed it disappear into a fading orange glow that was coming from Rayna, who was slumped against me; the aura being pulled from her, draining into my arm and filling my eyes with light. Her hand fell from the dagger still planted in my side, and just as I meant to push her off, my vision went black again.

But only for a second.

After the flash, I was in the Necropolis. Only, I was no longer at the Cathedral but in the stacks. There, I saw a confused woman crawling out of a casket. It didn't take me long to realize it was Rayna. She stood, looking over the world as the other corpses began to rise. And while they shambled mindlessly into the distance to drive the people underground, she stood in silence, looking down at her hands in disbelief.

And just like that, the vision was over. Rayna's lifeless body was slumped over me, no blood at all coming from the wound. The shadow had retracted into the stone. I weakly pushed Rayna off me, and let her body fall to the ground. I looked at her with confusion and...

...Clarity.

If killing her restored my vision, then that meant...

I felt another wave of pain coming from the dagger, and looked down to see how bad it was. Blood was pouring down my side, soaking through everything. She had buried the blade to the hilt, and it wasn't moving. I tried to keep breathing, but as I went to take a step, I stumbled and fell, next to Rayna.

I was growing tired. I started to close my eyes, but my thirst for sleep was interrupted by the whooshing sound of wings above.

Not now, I thought.

There was a crunch of stone as a dragon landed, on the front edge of the roof to my right. Rayna and I had fallen halfway across, by one of the sides of the building. I locked eyes with the beast that, because of its size, was not as far away as I would have liked—I could almost feel the hot breath coming from its maw—and I waited for it to set me ablaze with its fires.

Instead, I heard the sound of whooshing once more, and tore my eyes away from one dragon to see another flying over head, Rider on its back.

The dragon did one pass before landing on the back edge of the rooftop, lowering its long neck and shoulders so that the Rider could dismount. He did, and I finally got to see him up close. His armor was black and sheen, scaled all over like dragon. He wore a mask shaped to honor the form of the dragons as well, with sharp teeth and protruding jaws, open and encircling a face that made me think I was hallucinating.

It was Azazel in the Dragon Rider's armor.

He was looking at me with concern as he stepped towards me, tilting his head to the side and studying me. Behind him, the ridden dragon seemed to vanish. It was only when Azazel was standing over me that I stole a glance back to the edge of the rooftop to see that one of the Twins was standing in the ridden dragon's place.

"Stay with me, fair Traveler," he said, turning his attention to Rayna. He walked towards her and lifted her arm. With ease, he plucked the Emerald from where it had been slotted, and walked back to me, studying it. "It doesn't look like we have much time to discuss things, and I'm sure you have many questions."

I began to try and crawl backwards, but it was very quickly that I reached the edge. I held my hand up to him, and tried to find the words to speak. "You?" It was the only one I had.

"Me?" he said, tilting his head to the other side, almost mockingly. "Me what?" He looked back at the Twin, and then to the other dragon, which had also been replaced, before looking down at me. "Ah, yes. Allow me to introduce myself: I am Azazel, Lord of Dragons." He knelt down next to me, and I reached for him with my left hand, grabbing at his armor. "And you will be a footnote," he said, grabbing my wrist and twisting my arm so that my palm faced up, "in the annals of history." He grabbed the Onyx, and ripped it from my skin before throwing my arm away, sending me tumbling along the edge of the roof with it.

My arm hung over the edge as I laid on my stomach. I heard Azazel walking away, and then I heard him say something, but it didn't register. It was some time before I recalled that he had even spoke—I was on the edge in every sense, and knew that a death was coming for me: either Azazel would end me with his weapons and magic; or the dragons would be free to feed on me; or they would leave me there to die. I didn't know which I wanted more, I just wanted it to end.

"Time to wake your Mother," he had said. "But first, how about a jailbreak?"

The whooshing sound of wings returned, and I saw the dragons take to the sky overhead. I didn't have the strength to turn, I had lost far too much blood; but I watched as Azazel flew by the two statues I *could* see, stopping to insert one of the stones into their previous vacant hands. When all of them were in, I felt the rumbling before I heard anything.

The iron grate was opening.

After a few seconds, I heard screeching and roaring coming from below, and even though I had fallen numb to even the falling rain, I still felt fear at the cacophony that was erupting below. Inhuman sounds, the likes of which I had never heard before from any man or beast—even the monstrosities I had faced in my travels could not match the sounds I heard. They shook me to my very core, touching parts of my ears that I had no prior knowledge of. I closed my eyes tight, and began to quietly plead for it all to stop; so much so that I didn't notice the rather large arm reaching for me, and pulling me down from the roof.

BOOK THREE:
WHERE DRAGONS DWELL

The Darkest Night

When I awoke, I rose with a start. I was unsure how it was that I was even still alive. I reached for my side and felt only skin. It was tough, scarred; but it was all me.

I looked around the room I was in, and didn't recognize anything about the way it was built. It was bright, made of wood. It was domed, and it looked like a single dwelling. There were small porthole windows on either side of the dome, and a small door cut opposite the bed I was in, which itself seemed to be made mostly of sticks. There was a small table next to the bed, and some shelves, with various jars of liquids and solids and everything in between in them.

And there was light *everywhere.*

I had been stripped of my armor and my weapons, though I had no want for them when I rose. I had not even wanted to begin dissecting what had occurred at the Cathedral, hoping that it had all been a bad dream, the scarring on my side just my imagination.

Walking towards the door, and even brighter light, I felt a rush of anxiety; not knowing where I was or how I had got there. The last thing that I remembered was Rayna stabbing me, and visions of her leaving her coffin. That's right, she had been an undead—but she still had her soul? Is that how she was able to talk and think on her own? Was she not a husk like the rest? How much of what she told me had been a lie?

I tried to clear my head. No time for those thoughts. I stepped through the door and into the light, my eyes burning as they adjusted in a way that they hadn't had to since my youth.

Azazel.

I had to cover my brow with my forearm, growing impatient with my eyes in the best way I could have ever imagined possible. The shade it cast allowed me to see the trees that dominated the sky ahead of me, with thicker trunks than I had ever seen in any of the forests I

had been to. They reached high above, disappearing into the light
coming from there, up there, hanging off the branches; luminescent
leaves like little stars. It was everything I could do to stop my jaw from
dropping at the sight, and I let my forearm fall, indifferent to the
blinding light and the pain it caused.

The Rider.

I shook my head and closed my eyes, trying to keep free of the
thought that kept trying to push its way into my mind. I took a deep
breath, and when the afterimage had faded I opened them again,
keeping them down.

In front of me was the strangest creature I had seen to that point,
and I know now why people in the stories always said: "You never
forget the first time you see a Faerie."

Even if it wasn't the first time I would truly see one.

It was floating in front of me, hovering with wings that flapped so
fast that they were invisible if not for the humming sound, and the
gentle bob was mesmerizing. Its hair was wood, and stuck straight out
the back of its stout skull, disappearing into the dark brown skin that
tightly covered the high and prominent cheekbones that left the eyes
so sunken that they could only be seen by the small speck of light reflecting from them. Its nose started round and wide and tapered low
enough to almost cover the tiny but smiling mouth. The chin stretched
out as if to meet the tip of the nose, and I thought from the side it
looked like the crescent Moon on some nights. Its body was small,
though its limbs were even smaller in proportion to its body. It wore a
suit, it seemed, made of bark; the shoulders flared out and broke off,
the ends looking like flames. It must have been their armor.

"You wake," it said in a slow, monotonous voice. "You come." It
nodded for me to follow, and as if hypnotized, I did.

"How did I get here?" I asked. I looked around and saw that there
were more small domes, like the one I had awoken in, scattered
amongst the bright green field of grass, spreading as far as I could see.
"And *where* is here?"

"Dawnflayer," the Faerie said, drawing out every syllable. It
pointed to a dome in the distance, but I couldn't see inside.

Did it mean Brok?

I looked behind me and noticed that Kat wasn't following me. In
fact, I hadn't seen her since before I entered the Cathedral. Could she
have been there still? "Where is my companion? She is a Wisp, but she
is unlike any I have seen before or since. She was with me at the
Cathedral. Perhaps she's still—"

"No Wisp," it said. "Just you."

I felt the urge to leave; to go back to the Necropolis in the hopes that she was still there. I hadn't finished my task yet, which meant she hadn't finished hers. I had, in fact, failed my task masterfully, oblivious to the fact...

It was all coming back to me in a wave that I couldn't stop. Rayna was Undead, though with a soul still trapped inside; Azazel called himself the Lord of Dragons and was at the very least the Rider I had seen on my travels, who now possessed all of the stones; and Kat was the lost spirit of the woman I had banished from the catacombs, looking, as I was, for purpose in this world we were left.

It was almost too much, and I didn't realize I had stopped walking. My legs trembled beneath me, and I tried to shake myself free of the memories. "I have to go back for her," I choked out. I felt like I was going to fall asleep.

"There's no going back for you," a new voice said, behind the Faerie that had been guiding me, light and airy and more importantly fast. "The gate has been opened; the world isn't yours anymore."

What gate?

The other Faerie appeared from a nearby hut, and while the head shape was the same, the wooden hair fell differently, parted down the center and partially covering the face. I could detect feminine features, confirming the thought that I had never thought before: Faeries could be male or female. Her arms and legs were longer, and she was walking instead of flying, standing about as high as my waist.

"Zig is under the weather today," she said, nodding to the floating Faerie next to me. "Aren't you Zig?"

Zig nodded.

She gestured for him to go, and he bobbed away into the hut. "You are lucky to be alive," she said. "You *are* alive, don't you worry. You were still warm when you got here; unlike the girl."

"Rayna?"

"Yes, Brok brought her to us as well." She stopped suddenly and extended her tiny hand. I took it and shook it once. "Where are my manners? I am Py, keeper of the Forest." Her eyes were softer than I was expecting, as though she were apologetic.

"The woman—Rayna, as you said—was an interesting predicament. She had been buried en masse, you see. It's as though she was missed in the endless reapings, and lucky or not, her soul remained with her." Py stroked her chin. "I can only imagine what a horror that must have been for her, trapped in her body for so long.

"When the Long Night began, and she awoke, fueled by the same magic as the Undead you have faced; she was finally free. She crawled from her grave, and instead of marching with the others, she joined a Dawnflayer that had escaped from a pit of his own—" Py shot a look to the hut that Zig had pointed out earlier—"and together they came to see us in the hopes that we could revive her completely." She turned back to me, though her eyes were cast down. "We were able to restore most of *her* in the sense that she no longer looked like a corpse, but there was something else in there. The power that had woke her was preventing us from finishing our work." Py took a deep, remorseful breath.

"We were played." Py cast a look down to the ground. We shared a somber second before she popped back up. "As were you, so it's a joy to not be the only ones. At least now we know for sure the name of our troubles."

"What did he do?"

Py sighed, gesturing for me to follow her into the hut behind her.

History Lesson

I had fled the surface of the world when I was very young. The 'world' I knew was the catacombs, not the surface. There were many things I still didn't know about what was true and what wasn't in regard to how Alghast at large came to be.

When I entered the hut of Py, the forest Faerie that—presumably—returned me from the brink of death, or worse, I recognized the rune on her back wall almost immediately.

There were seven points, five running on a line going straight up and down and one each to the left and right of the point in the center. The four points that surrounded the center, with lines drawn between them to form a diamond at the center of the cross, were differently colored, though the colors had long since faded.

I had seen the diamond formation before, as a way of mapping the four great cities: Alduin, Brakas, Castleford, and Dewpond; but I had never seen it with the other two points, one above and one below.

Py lead me to a chair and had me take a seat, which I was happy to do. I was still very tired, and it occurred to me that I wasn't even sure how long it had been since my clash with Rayna in the Necropolis. What had gone on there? I was remembering strange noises and monster howls amongst fading lights and

Time to wake your mother.

What did *that* mean? Had I heard that right? I still wasn't convinced that what I had seen was correct. I had just been stabbed in the side; it was entirely conceivable that it was all a fever dream, and Azazel did *not* appear before me in the Dragon Rider's armor, wasn't it?

Something in my gut rolled over, and I felt like the worst had yet to come. There was so much that had happened, and it felt like I couldn't trust anyone. I didn't know what to believe anymore, as all of my senses had failed me to that point, in some way or another. Even my gut, angry as it may have been in that moment, had been wrong.

"She gifted you some of our magic, I sense," Py said, snapping me from my daydream. "See things a little more clearly?"

I nodded. The Sunsight hadn't been perfect—I still needed to fight more than I had wanted to in order to keep the magic working—but without it, I would have likely perished not long after leaving Rayna and Brok the first time. The road to Castleford had been much more daunting than the one I had taken from where I emerged to Dewpond.

"But not perfectly," she said under her breath, looking off to the side. She brought a hand to her chin, and for a moment her fingers moved wildly, almost like tentacles. She had a point. "Do you know what Light is? What it can do?"

My furrowed brow did the talking for me, as I had not been able to take my eyes from her hands, hoping to see what I had thought I had seen again, if only for my own sanity.

"The Sun gives," she said, looking to the rune on the wall, "and the Moon takes." I followed her look, and thought I finally understood the highest and lowest points and what they represented: the Sun and the Moon. "One is light, the other is dark," she continued. "The Sun fills our world with light during the day and the Moon then comes to draw the light from us during the night. And when the darkest point of the night comes," she slowly brought her hands up and up, pointing to the sky, "the Sun comes to fill us with light once more. At least, that was the way that it was supposed to be." Py brought her hands down to her side. "Dragons *need* Dark, you see? They cannot survive in the Light; that is why the four *gave* the power to the Sun. The time of your people and mine being their food was over. The time of the Dark was over."

She walked over to me and reached out her hands. As they got closer I saw that they were unraveling like rope, each finger separating at the palm, then the wrist, and up the forearm. I jumped back, gasping in horror and hit my head off the wall. I immediately recoiled in pain, in the direction of Py, and upon realizing this climbed out of the chair as quickly as I could. When I looked back to her—

Py was standing, confused; her arms were normal.

Had I imagined it? I was beginning to worry at that moment, more than any other point on my journey, that I was losing my mind. It was a sickness I saw far too often in my life below ground; men just lost control of what was real sometimes. It could be tolerated only so much back then before someone was deemed too far gone, locked in a room for the rest of their days, allowed plenty of time by themselves to go as far beyond the veil as their broken mind could take them.

"I need you to know what the world looks like," Py said, stepping towards me again slowly. "I need you to see what it looked like then, so you will know what it looks like now, and I *need* you to see what you're fighting for; I think you may have forgotten."

I looked down at Py, confused as ever, and suddenly her arms shot upwards and separated into slimy tentacles once more. Before I could react, they were touching my face. My body froze, and my vision was obscured as if I were under water. I gasped for air and my eyes felt heavy. I felt as though I were falling backward, but slowly as though someone was guiding my body down. I tried to see through the cloud in my vision, growing ever thicker, thinking that I saw a face hovering over me. My first thought was that it was Py's, but the features were all wrong. Her head was longer than it was wide. The hair was not wood, but extensions of dark blue skin, tendrils writhing from her skull, hanging like living hair. Her eyes were deep and green, piercing even through the clouds. Her nose was gone completely; a single wide but thin nostril in its place. She had no mouth, per se—there was an opening that ran vertically from just above her chin and down her neck, opening sideways in a wave, revealing rows of uneven and crowded fangs.

And then the clouds took the sight away, and I quietly thanked them for their mercy. I was unsettled enough, feeling as though I were floating in nothing and seeing nothing. Until I saw *something*; I saw something in the distance that was growing closer: a Light. It got closer, and brighter, and more intense until it overtook everything I saw.

All I saw was white.

VISIONS OF THE PAST

I opened my eyes to the sound of a dragon roaring overhead, feeling the wind displaced by the flapping of its wings. I was standing somehow, and I suddenly felt very lost. I looked around quickly to get an idea of my surroundings, but I did not recognize them.

I was on a stone bridge; though many of the stones running along the sides had fallen loose or off the bridge entirely, into the murky waters below. All around me were trees, as far as I could see. And it wasn't very far that I *could* see—it was dark, very dark. I wasn't sure if I still had the power of the Sunsight, as I was able to see more than I had before receiving it; but I strained to see much more than trees, scanning to my right all the way around until I saw the beam of light.

In the sky, I saw the Moon, glowing as it always had during the night, a soft silver coin amidst the otherwise dark and speckled sky. Only now the glow seemed to be coming from the beam that I spotted. I followed it up to the silver orb in the sky and stared in wonderment until shapes, hundreds of them, all across the sky, moved rapidly as if to draw my attention. I tried to follow one of the dark shadows as it darted around, just above the ground where the beam was meeting the surface. I had my suspicions about what it was, and then it shot flames to the ground below.

They were dragons. Enough of them to cast a great shadow, even in the dark of night; enough of them that I didn't notice something strange about the moon and its glow: the silver orb wasn't silver at all.

The light coming from the ground was brightening it, but the Moon itself was as black as the night sky around it. No, it was darker, somehow. There was something about it that was so monolithic that I could almost hear a low droning hum as I looked on, entranced by the darkness that wanted to permeate from it, if not for the light from below to stifle it, as if holding it in place.

There was another roar, louder than any of the ones before, that

came from everywhere at first before I was able to track it to just behind me, growing louder as it approached. When I heard the flapping
of massive wings and looked above, I saw a shape that dwarfed the
other dragons I had seen so far. The beast that flew overhead was almost as large as a building—it could easily fill the inside of the otherwise hollow Cathedral of Woe, I was sure—but it moved quickly.
When it went overhead, the flapping wings almost knocked me to the
ground, if not for me widening my stance to brace myself.

It was heading for the light as well. I heard it roar once more, and
saw the fires churning in its mouth as it reared its head back. And just
as it fired, the beam of light became stronger and brighter and continued to intensify until all I could see was white once more.

When the white faded, I was standing at the edge of a familiar
looking pit. The Cathedral had not yet been built around it, and the
hole was wide and deep and uncovered, looking like a wound upon
the world. I looked down but felt my head begin to spin trying to see
the bottom without falling in. I took a step back and looked around.

I was in the Necropolis, only there was not a grave or casket to be
seen. The sky was still dark, and the Moon still hung in the sky, a dark
disk that I once thought kept the night from going all the way black,
only to find that its intentions were to leave us in darkness should the
nights have been any longer.

In the distance, on the hills to the North, I saw a light breaking
through the horizon. The Necropolis never seemed to be set lower into
the ground than that rest of Alghast, though without the scores of
dead being buried here, it made sense for it to sit lower; it was *much*
lower than I had thought, though. I watched the light breach the horizon, illuminating a line of...*shapes*.

I don't know how else to describe what I saw. As the line got closer, I was able to distinguish different beings within the shapes, specific
forms and traits, but it was difficult. I could never get a clear picture of
what one entire being looked like. Things were writhing, arms and
legs and tentacles. There was screeching that wasn't anything I'd ever
heard before—except for maybe as I lay dying at the Cathedral. But
there were also repeating patterns—they were distinct in their chaos,
and while it would be difficult for me to recall every detail of their
appearance, I could tell enough that these were species; not just indi-
vidual abominations.

Though it took all I had, there was something in me that was persistent enough that I listened, looking to the West. There, in the distance, I saw the same thing: a light and a line, moving towards me
down the hill.

I continued turning, following the line to the South and then to the East. The four lights were closing in on the creatures like shepherds herding an unruly flock of sheep. And they were closing in on me in the center of the Necropolis, next to a pit that had begun to glow with an ominous but warm light that drew my attention back to it.

"What is it you mean to show me?" I asked out loud, whether it was to Py or not, I wasn't sure.

As if in response, light exploded from the pit into thousands upon thousands of beams that went up and then out. You could almost see them as they shot along the ground as if hunting for something. It was something else to see them find what they were looking for, piercing the thick bits of the creatures like harpoons on a rope, yanking them back *hard* and dragging them into the pit below. I froze as the shapes whipped past me to the left and right, though somehow avoiding me. It would have been impossible to see it all, they were moving so fast, but there were so many monsters that it took a couple minutes for the hills to be cleared, all that remained was four figures, holding light above their heads.

I looked down to see that I had been unaffected by the beams of light, even though I was standing so close to them. I tried to remind myself that this was only a vision, that is why I was unharmed. But it all felt so real that I sometimes forget, even now, that it was nothing but an illusion.

When I looked back up, the figures were gone and the Moon in the sky was replaced with a weak-looking Sun. It gave off very little light, but the warmth was noticeable. It was trying to break through the veil of darkness that surrounded us, but it couldn't. Just then, four narrow beams of pure white light shot up into the sky: one from the North; one from the East; one from the South; and one from the West. When they reached the edge of the sky, they seemed to pierce through something, and suddenly the light was spreading outward and began to fill everything; the whole sky was alive in a matter of seconds, and I had to turn my eyes away.

Was *that* what sunlight felt like?

It was a feeling I hadn't experienced in nearly a lifetime, and still it felt as though it were the first time, even though I knew that it wasn't. I remembered the joy that the feeling filled me with and yearned for the pain of staring into the Sun, at least for a few seconds too long. How could I have forgotten what it felt like to be outside on a warm summer day? All I knew was cold and dark; yet there I stood, feeling something that I had long forgotten possible.

Tears formed in my eyes and I didn't know if it was from the intensity of the light or what I was feeling at the time, but I didn't wipe them away. Instead, I took a deep breath, and closed my eyes, looking downwards and nodding. "I know I'm not done yet," I said quietly. "But what do I do next? How do I go on?"

With that, I was suddenly in a town. I looked around but did not recognize where I was. People walked the streets as if in a daze. I looked up and saw a cliff in the horizon, a castle perched on top, and knew at once that I was in Castleford. The beam of light from here was still shooting out to the sky, from a Spire deep in the center of the town; but there was another light, coming from the mountain. Light poured out of the cave on the cliff and consumed the castle. There was a shriek from above as a massive shadow was pulled over the town and into the mouth of the cave. When I looked again, the castle was fading from sight.

The door! The door that Azazel had shown me must lead to where that huge dragon was. He didn't mean to seal it; he meant to open it, and unleash it. *Mother,* he had said. As I remembered that, visions of the shadows so aplenty that they blacked out the sky came to my mind once more. More than the feeling of sunlight on my skin, I wanted very much not to see that again while I still drew breath. Where had they all come from? And if this was a vision of the past, as it felt; where did they all *go*?

I began to wonder about the Stones and their power. To that point, I had seen them held as weapons: Father Paxton, Headmistress Artemis; I had seen them sought for contraptions: Azazel's door, the statues outside the Cathedral of Woe; and I still felt them useful for something amongst the Spires that auspiciously still stood in each of the cities I had been to. Though Castleford's Spire had been absent on my trips, and did not stand where it had in the vision. Was it hidden?

As if reacting to my thoughts, the vision shifted and I saw before me four large Crystals. I had seen them before, in visions shown to me by the Onyx. These were the Crystals from which the smaller Stones had been retrieved.

The walls around glowed red with heat, and the fires and the lava that surrounded was so intense that I began to sweat, even though I knew it was only a vision. I could still *feel* it, as though I were really there—wherever *there* was. It was overwhelming and it only seemed to get worse as I started walking towards the Crystals. In the back of my mind, I felt it before I heard it: that heartbeat, louder than ever, began to swell until I could feel it in my eyes. It grew louder still until I heard nothing else, then it turned into a roar...

And I was floating. I was floating in a cavern surrounded by heat but I couldn't feel it anymore. The walls still glowed red but I couldn't see them anymore. The heart was still beating but I couldn't hear it anymore. And yet, there it was, just before me, thumping quietly as though unaware or indifferent to my presence. I watched it for a moment and with each pump, I felt myself growing angrier and angrier. And as the rage built inside of me, I could feel the rage growing inside of *it* as if in response.

We *hated* each other in that very moment, me and the Heart of the Mountain.

And just like that, I was whisked away; the heat and the glowing and the beating all gone, as if they were never there to begin with. I stood in silence on a cliff—not unlike the one south of Castleford—looking out over a valley of nothing. The land, as far as I could see, was barren; untouched by the hands of man and beast alike, virginal. Surrounded on three sides by mountains, with water to the East, it was a perfect valley. To the North, the Mountain sat asleep. The Sun shone brightly in the sky, and everything seemed to be as it should. Calm, serene, and quiet.

Everything was *so* quiet.

Again, the sky lit up suddenly and I blocked my eyes from the flash, white enough to sting. I heard a cacophony that brought me nothing but pain and confusion, peering through my fingers to try and see what was happening. The wind picked up and nearly knocked me off my feet. Through my fingers, I could see a beam of energy shooting down from the sky into the center of the valley, burrowing deep into the ground.

The pit in the Cathedral, I thought to myself as the light dimmed and I lowered my hands to watch the beam disappear into the hole it had created, perfectly round, in the center of the valley like a festering wound. I knew in my gut that I was looking upon a fresh, untouched Alghast; the Alghast I knew still a long ways away.

There was another low rumble as light emerged from the Mountain to the North: red and ominous, it spread across the sky like fire across a pool of oil. It was as though the mouth of the volcano was a beacon; a harbinger of what was to come, rather than what many had feared it to be. It was worse. It blocked the sun and covered the ground in shadow.

Just as the shiver reached the back of my neck, the rumble turned to a roar. It was many roars, merging into one sound that was so horrible that I was driven to my knees. They were coming from the pit. I struggled to look up and see what was happening: swarms of creatures were emerging from the pit and covering the land, scurrying like insects to invade all corners of the world. They were all shapes and sizes, but most were dark in color. Some had many legs, some had multiple arms, and some had tentacles, not unlike the creatures I saw at the start of the visions. Then there was the first dragon, flying upwards. It was black, though its scales seemed to glow with the red light that filled the sky. It was the most terrifying thing I had ever seen, and it had stopped just above me, floating in the sky.

There it sat, the Black Dragon; its eyes were fixed on me. I could no longer hear the flapping of its wings or the horrible sounds from the creatures still pouring from the pit. I couldn't hear anything as I looked into the dragon's eyes. It guided me, *urged* me to look down, so I did: in its hands, it was holding two limp humans, a man in one set of talons; a woman in the other. It seemed to me that they were still alive; they wore no clothes, and they were filthy, bruised, and battered—

But they were still alive.

It called me back to its eyes and I obliged. It appeared to shift closer to me as I heard a whisper, though I couldn't make out what it said. Words I couldn't understand that might have been another language. Whatever it was saying, it sent chills through every part of me. I felt that if I weren't frozen in place, I would have shivered in fear. Was the dragon *speaking* to me? Was it at least *trying* to?

And was it speaking through my mind?

I opened my mouth as if to respond, not knowing what I would say, if anything, that the dragon wanted to hear. I knew I was in a vision, but even as I thought that the clouded whisper got suddenly clearer.

"Are you sure?" it said.

It had to be. I just didn't know what it was Py had meant to show me. It was clear to me that I was witnessing the dawn of our realm; the fabled time when mankind was simply food and fodder for the monsters that ruled the lands, chief among them dragons. They came from the pit—and were banished there, it seemed—but they first came from above? Did we come with them?

"Does that matter?" the voice said, snake-like and raspy.

I guess it didn't. Where the creatures came from was not what concerned me. It was evident that the sounds I heard on the roof of the Cathedral were very much the sounds I heard in those visions. The pit had been opened; Azazel had used the stones to release the seal and who *knows* what else.

I had so many questions, yet when I opened my mouth to ask them, nothing came out. I felt sick and my vision blurred. I lurched

forward and fell onto my hands and knees. I closed my eyes to stop
the world from spinning, but to no avail. It was only seconds before I
fell to my side; only seconds before I fell asleep.

TRUTH

When I awoke, I felt the wooden floor beneath my hands. I opened my eyes to look down, and although things were darker—greyer, somehow—they were as I remembered them before Py sent me on my vision.

"What did you mean for me to see?" I asked with labored breath, not looking up from the ground. "Was it the pit of monsters?"

"You saw that they were not the only ones to climb from that pit? That man *also* climbed out of it?" Py asked as if to deflect an insult.

I shook my head. "I still have so many questions; what about Azazel? Who is he?" I clenched my fists, the frustration building. "And what about the Stones and the Heart in the Mountain? Where did *those* come from?" I looked up.

Some version of Py stood before me, only it was not the wood nymph I had seen before. In its place was a horrific grey-blue creature that was more sea creature than human. Her legs were gone, dozens of tentacles, thick and thin, writhing in place for her to stand on. Her arms looked normal, although now I could see the seams between the appendages as they blended together to seem more human-like. There were small spines poking out of her shoulders that gesticulated not unlike tiny wings. There was an opening, like a sideways mouth, that started just about her collarbone and ran up what I could only think to be a neck, though it was flush with the chin of the long, wide, head.

"You saw something bigger than all that," the thing said. The lips of the sideways mouth seemed capable of movement, but she didn't speak from there. It was as though she were projecting her words directly into my mind.

I didn't recoil in horror. I wasn't sure why—which might have scared me more than the *thing* that stood before me—but I know now it's *because* of what Py showed me that I didn't fear her. It's as though she had lifted a veil and I could see the world clearer than ever.

Her hand was suddenly on my face. I didn't move. "You have the old eyes now," she said softly, leaning in. Her own eyes, green as the Emerald of Brakas, were captivating, drawing me in. I did nothing to resist. "You have no small task ahead of you. Your quest is not unlike that undertaken by four before, yet you are only one. But do not let this discourage you, for you are powerful in ways that you and I both cannot yet see." She looked up, past me. "Now go!"

I looked back to see the door of the hut, and the rest of the hut itself; it had become dark, the wood itself looking as though it had been left to rot. The shelves and the decor was in tatters. When I looked back, Py was gone. I rose to my feet and walked through the door, and saw that the forest was dark. The trees above, once bearing the luminescent leaves, sat barren in the night; only it wasn't a black or purple or green sky that hung above them.

It was red.

It was the same as it was in the last vision: the one where the Mountain came to life and spread its fires throughout the sky, instead of the ground as the stories once claimed. Was this what Py meant by the old eyes, that I could see the layer of Darkness that kept us in perpetual night? My mind was filling with possibilities and trying to determine what it was I had to do next.

The Mountain had seemed important, but I also thought of Azazel's door. If the Mother of Dragons truly slept there, awaiting him and the Stones to free her, time was running out to stop him from opening it.

If he hadn't already, I thought. I had no idea how long I was unconscious for, or even where I was. It was likely that I was in the forests north of Alduin, the ones where Faeries were said to reside. That meant that Azazel had all the time in the world, not to mention the benefit of dragons, to return home and use the Stones once more.

"You wake," I heard a familiar voice call from one of the nearby huts, weak but still booming. I entered and saw Brok sitting up against a wall, one of the creatures that I now understood to *be* Faeries—the *true* form of them—standing over him. Noticing my briefly puzzled look, Brok also looked to the Faerie, then to me.

The Faerie spoke, his voice masculine but still high: "You see us now?"

I nodded. The Faerie looked embarrassed.

"We thought the light was in the pit," he said. Brok let his head roll back against the wall. His stab wound—the one I gave to him— did not appear to be healing well, black at the edges and still glistening with moisture. "We were wrong; only Darkness down there." He took a deep breath and looked mournfully at the dying Dawnflayer. "Azazel awaits in his Castle for the pit to be emptied. Only then can he recollect the Stones and open the door to release the Mother of all Dragons: the Black Dragon."

I saw a brief flash of the dragon that spoke to me. Was that her? It had been *huge*. The other two I had seen were like dwarves in comparison. I very badly wanted to stop Azazel from opening that door.

"And what of him?" I nodded to Brok.

The Faerie shook his head.

"Azazel," the Dawnflayer choked out. "you did not know?"

I cast my eyes down, ashamed in my own right that I had been deceived. Brok laughed, but the laugh turned into a cough before he fell silent once more, asleep.

"Why didn't they tell me any of this before?" I asked, hiding my frustration. *We could have worked together,* I thought.

"The Dawnflayer and the Undead girl had their issues with trust; and with good reason. You were not the only one that had been deceived by his lies." Brok adjusted, groaning and weakly reaching for his wound. The Faerie tried to tend to the Dawnflayer, but was waved off. "In their minds, it had to be just them. And now she is laid to rest, once and for all, and her companion is not far behind. What a world we've left for ourselves."

I looked over to the Faerie, who looked back at me. "He refuses treatment," he said.

I looked back to Brok. "We have all made mistakes, Brok. I'm sorry that it went this way."

"Don't let it go to waste," the Faerie said. "Get to the castle. Maybe someone there will answer your questions." He looked off into the distance, into space, and it seemed as though he were done talking.

"Go," Brok said under his breath, almost quiet enough that I didn't hear him.

I stood, looking down at the once intimidating Dawnflayer. He never looked *smaller* than in that moment. He had stood with Rayna for so long only to fail. I couldn't afford to do the same. If there was a chance that I could make it to Azazel's Castle and stop him while he didn't have the Stones, I had to take it.

I had thought about returning to the Necropolis to collect the Stones myself, but if the visions and warnings were true, it would be rife with monsters. It would be suicide to attempt. I would have to figure out how to return the creatures and reseal the pit later.

Though even if he didn't have the Stones, he still had dragons. It was apparent to me that he was, in some way, responsible for the Long

Night in the first place. We were just pawns in his game; the last survivors to do his dirty work to collect the Stones while he rested. His
magic seemed to be growing more powerful, and I wondered it was
only now just regaining his powers, from the years in isolation. That
meant that it was entirely possible that the Undead, the helcats, the
skeletal orbs and everything else I had faced to that point was under
his control, and likely filled his castle.

It almost didn't seem better than going for the pit.

But those things I knew how to deal with. The monsters that were
hopefully still pouring out of the pit were another story altogether; I
didn't want to charge headlong into an army of either of them, but at
least one was familiar.

I returned to the hut where I awoke and collected my sword and
shield. My mace must have fallen off at some point during my battles,
likely still at the Cathedral with—

Kat!

She had slipped my mind. Was she still there? I had hoped that
she found a way out, as she had not traveled with me to the forest. I
worried that I wouldn't be able to reach her, even if I wanted to, had
she stayed near the Cathedral.

What if she had vanished? Her quest had come to an end, guiding
me to a clear and distinct failure on all counts. A failure that I had
aimed to correct, as soon as I regained my bearings; but I knew not the
semantics of Wisps and their unfinished business. With a path ahead
of me, and the Black Moon hanging amidst the red sky ahead of me, I
began walking.

Lost

Getting out of the forest proved to be difficult for me, even as I followed the path for what felt like an eternity. It seemed that no matter how far I walked, I never seemed to break through the tree-line and out into the world. I was growing anxious, feeling as though the trees were closing in on me. After a while, I was no longer sure that they weren't; the area afforded for me to walk becoming ever more narrow.

There was something welling inside of me, a twisted agony in the pit of my stomach that made me want to turn around and head back to the forest village of the Faeries; but I had been walking for so long that it felt to me like it would waste even more time to double back. I had been face-to-face with *dragons*, I wasn't sure why trees were giving me such pause.

And still, they were. There was a horrible omen, a palpable dread seeping out of the trees like sap, turning to a mist when they hit the atmosphere, falling gently down to the forest floor and spreading. I looked down to see the mist climbing my legs, reaching out to me with thousands of tiny hands—

A sound in the trees broke my concentration. It was a rustling, but loud, as if something large was moving amongst the branches above. I tried to follow the source, but it seemed to be coming from all around me. And just as soon as it started, the sound stopped. I stood for a moment, my chest rising and falling with each heavy breath as I tried to slow my heart to no avail. A chill ran over me, and even as I scanned the woods ahead, I felt the hairs on the back of my neck standing, gooseflesh running up and down my covered arms.

There was a muted thud behind me, of something heavy landing on the soft forest floor. I turned around to see the creature standing there, squatting on meaty legs with its massive fists planted in the ground in front of it for balance. Two smaller arms were rising out of its back, leaner than the ones that kept it upright. I noticed similar

seams to the ones on Py's arms and imagined that it was also a network of tentacles, formed into some kind of facade. The head was
round, and aside from a small space for a face—which consisted of
two sets of three very bright eyes, each moving in unison and darting
all around, taking in everything—the entire head was covered with
squirming tendrils, about as long as my forearm.

It lurched towards me, walking on its fists as though they were
feet. I reached for my sword, while raising the shield. The thing
stopped moving as soon as I armed myself, and I froze as well. It
cocked its head to the side; at least, I think it did—it was hard to see
distinct movements, as the tendrils were always shifting, writhing like
a swarm of snakes held by the ends of their tails, trying to get away.

We stood watching each other for a long moment, a spark of
recognition flying between us. The sight of the thing scared me, but I
was feeling an innate anger and resentment towards it; as though it
had wronged me in some way; and not just this thing standing before
me, but all of them. There was something deep inside me that made
me hate this creature that stood before me, as though it stood for
everything that had driven us underground in the first. It embodied
the world that would have us hide, and I couldn't take that—not in the
anxious state I was already in.

"I wouldn't stop," I heard a woman's voice say. "Humans were
responsible for his imprisonment, after all." It was Py's, somewhere in
the back of my mind, as though she were a part of the forest itself.

"And why did we do that?" I said quietly, not wanting to alert the
beast with my talking. "Was it because this monstrosity is just one of
the many things that used to rend our flesh, and suck the marrow
from our bones; all in the name of a good meal?"

But it was just as she said: it saw me as the thing that it hated
most. After all, I looked just like the ones that locked them away for all
this time, much the same as I felt towards it. It slammed its fists into
the ground, and the arms on its back split into an array of tentacles,
about a dozen, that flailed about wildly, as if to distract me with the
spectacle.

And just like that, the hulk was bounding towards me, kicking up
dirt and dry leaves as it crossed the short distance. I tried to swing my
sword, but it caught me with a backhand before I could connect. The
back of its fist connected with my shield, though I wasn't ready for the
blow, and the shield was driven into my side, knocking me down to
the ground. I rolled through, returning to my feet and readying both
sword and shield. My shield arm was on fire, twisting awkwardly
when it was hit; but I pushed the pain to the back of my mind.

It came at me again and I thrust forward with the sword, stabbing for it. It swatted the sword away from me with ease, and I was able to follow it as it clattered to the ground at the base of a nearby tree. I raised my shield in the hopes of absorbing most of another blow, but the hulking brute broke my guard with another backhand, sending the shield flying in the other direction. I stepped back, defenseless. My left arm was screaming in pain, and my right wrist hot as well from being twisted when the brute disarmed me. I looked into its eyes, no longer darting from here to there but focused on me, and the pain in my arm began to subside. The brute pulled back its right fist, ready to strike, and time seemed to slow. I looked down to see something dark coming out of my arm. I looked up to see the fist flying towards me, and without thinking, I raised my bare arm…

And the black shadow from the Onyx created a shield, absorbing the blow from the brute. It seemed just as shocked as I was. I didn't have the Stone anymore, so why was I able to conjure a shield? I quickly tried to make the blade that I had used on Rayna, but it wouldn't work. Perhaps only some powers remained?

Another question, I thought to myself as I regained some of my composure and looked to the sword for answers.

The sword had been imbued with the power of the Ruby, but didn't need the Stone itself. It was possible that the power would run out eventually; it had to. All power is finite. Perhaps by having the Onyx, I was left with some residual power. And much like the sword can only be set aflame, it made sense to me that the shield was the only residual power I was left with—the shield that I had used against the roaming helcat on the way to the Cathedral.

I had no time to ponder the powers given, making a move for the sword. I was able to grab the hilt and tuck into a roll just as the brute's forearm collided with the trunk of the tree where the sword had landed. The sound of the impact left me surprised that the tree still stood, though it wore a mighty dent for the rest of its days.

I returned to my footing and locked eyes with the brute. We shared another hate-filled pause and, as if called for by some unseen voice, we began our collision-course. I called for the fire of my blade, and when I saw that it was striking low, I leaped, thinking to go over it and land safely behind. Much to my chagrin, I was plucked out of the air by the tentacles, failing to jump as high as I needed to. I felt one grab my leg, just above the ankle, and my momentum stopped. I slammed into the brute's back and felt the other tentacles grabbing for me. I tried to keep my arms up and away from them, as I was sure I would need them to get myself free.

The brute stood upright, leaving me to hang upside down on its back. When it noticed that it had captured me—it didn't seem too bright—I felt it tugging on my legs as if to lift me. When I saw one of the tentacles arch outwards, away from the body in order to get the leverage to toss me, I swung and cut clean.

The brute spun, letting go of me in the middle of the turn and sending me flying. My shoulders slammed into the trunk of a tree that lined our makeshift arena, and I fell to the ground below. I looked up and saw the brute had eyes on me, a fire burning in each and every one of them.

I had to forget the pain as I pushed myself up and weakly readied my sword. It looked to pin me against the tree with a clenched fist, I could see. So I waited. I would bide my time as it closed the distance—considerable as it was—and wait for my moment. I was surprised merely to be standing. When the brute was close, and it began to strike, I cleared my mind. In a flash, I summoned the black shield, knocking away the blow much as it had knocked away my sword before, and I dropped low, rising with my blade and stabbing it through the chest. The tentacles began to flail wildly, but I was out of reach as I had buried myself in its midsection as the creature curled around me like a cocoon, twisting the sword and holding on for dear life as it tried to pull itself off. Every time I felt my blade coming loose, or a hand coming towards me, I would jerk it up or down to discourage it. If it tried to walk, I went with it. The purple-black blood oozed down my blade, over the guard, and down my hand as I waited.

And then the brute moved no more.

It took all of my strength to keep the lifeless beast from crushing me as it fell dead; but I was able to push it to the side, though doing so tore the wound considerably. I was covered in the thing's blood as it tumbled to the ground next to me. I took a deep breath and found a clean piece of my cloak that I wiped the blade of my sword with before sheathing it. I looked over to the academy shield, resting against a tree as though calling out to me, and walked over to it. I slung it to my back, thinking it would be good to have in case the Onyx powers would run out. And with how quickly these things seemed to move, having protection on my back might prove useful as well.

But none of it helped me escape the damned forest.

"Are you still with me, Py?" I asked the woods around me.

"For a time," she said. "I just wanted you to see what awaited you."

"Where?"

"Everywhere."

With that, the dark line of trees ahead of me seemed to part, and I saw a hill running down, the Alduin Academy standing in the distance. The sky was as red as ever, and I could see farther than before. And as I stood on the precipice of the forest, I could see the shadow spreading out from the Cathedral of Woe in the center of the Necropolis in all directions, like a swarm spreading out, seeking food.

The State of Things

When I emerged from the forest, and began my trek back into the heart of Alduin, I had intended to cross the city, and try to cut through as much of the Necropolis as I could on my way to Castleford. I looked back to see that the woods I had come from were large, yes; but there was no way that they were large enough for me to get lost in, unless I was traveling in circles. It even seemed as though the village the Faeries lived in could not have been housed there, for the trees were smaller now than they had been on the inside.

More illusions, I thought to myself.

The undead had seemingly retreated, leaving behind mostly barren lands. Though the closer I got to the center of the realm, the thicker with *other* creatures it got. As I reached the southern border of Alduin, I saw another creature: its form was feminine, slender, and tall. Her arms were stick-thin and stretched down below where I imagined her knees would be, as her legs were concealed by a tight gown that ran all the way down to the ground. It clung to her like another skin. Her fingers were proportionally long and skinny, and she seemed to *glide* across the ground more than walk. Her face was quaint and small, unimpressive on a normal looking—though bald and sheen—head. Her mouth was closed, thin lips pressed tightly together, and it sounded as though she were humming a tune. And while there was something alluring about the tune, I steered clear.

I was just about out of the city, having remained mostly unseen by the creatures that were filtering in. It was as though they were waves of new tenants, moving for the ruins that us people had left behind.

And then I made an error in judgment.

There was a home that was still mostly standing by the southern border, a farmhouse, the wood burnt a deep black on the wall that was facing the center of the city. I did not check before rounding the corner and found myself standing in front of one of the women I had begun to see. She stood as tall as I was, possibly taller, and looked down on me. Her song stopped, and as I stared into her eyes, the features on her face vanished; in their place, a small hole appeared in the center. The skin around it began to peel back, and suddenly the face opened like a mouth, rimmed with fangs. She screamed at me and lunged, and I worried that she might be able to swallow me whole.

I jumped back and watched as she returned to an upright position, her face closing and her eyes and mouth reappearing. Her song continued as she rounded the corner, and continued on her path, now that I had removed myself from it.

My heart was racing, but only for a moment. Her shriek would surely call the attention of more aggressive monsters, so I continued to move south with haste, not wishing to see what other horrors it would bring.

As I got close to the Necropolis, I saw the swirling vortex of colors that surrounded the Cathedral, like a tornado of paint that only went as high as the building. And as I got closer, I could see the shadow take form, many forms, as it exited the base of the tornado, rushing onward looking to reclaim the world that once belonged to it, and I wondered if they were governed all by the same thought, the same purpose; whether they were aware of it or not.

Were we, as people, so different?

My thoughts once again found Kat, wondering where she had gone after everything that had happened. I was beginning to feel that I had let her down, as well as myself, though I had considered myself productive on a quest I had, at one time and another, wanted no part of. It should have been noted how far both of us had made it without an inkling of heroism in our blood, despite what we knew in our hearts we were doing. We were guided by strings we couldn't feel; guided by hands we couldn't see and a master we couldn't talk to or reason with or plead with.

Fate was a cruel and stubborn mistress.

I wet my blade several times on my travels and each time, each creature I encountered seemed easier than the last. By the time I had reached the Necropolis, I veered more towards the center than I had initially planned to, feeling emboldened by my success in the encounters to that point. It was there that I saw the light of a Wisp—not that *that* would normally concern me, having seen so many already—moving erratically through the stacks of graves.

It didn't look like Kat; it was small like the others, nothing but a soul trying to carry out one last selfless act before passing on. There was something about the way it moved, though, that gave me pause.

It forced me to watch and follow it as it danced about the darkened sky, washed out by the red if it ever soared too high.

I lost it for a second behind one of the stacks but moved quickly to see around the caskets. From there on, I didn't take my eyes from it, moving with it, ensuring that it wasn't drawing me to the center or any other danger that may have been waiting. The Necropolis was crawling with monsters, and although I had entered brimming with confidence, I was feeling outnumbered already.

A large slug-like creature slithered through the stacks down one of the main through-ways, wider than most of the winding paths through the Necropolis as it would eventually end at the Cathedral, so cart traffic had to be afforded.

The creature was about as tall as I, and twice as long. I saw no features save for a relatively small mouth at the front and the light black speckling amongst the deep purple and slimy skin. There was a frill that ran along the whole thing, almost like a moist skirt that was leaving a trail of mud, but I couldn't help but notice thousands of little imprints in the trail like footprints.

When it was past, I made a break for the other side. The Wisp had, strangely, *waited* for me on the other side. I dashed across, trying my best to step over the mud trail that the slug had left, but it was wider than a full step, and it was too late to jump. There was a thin membrane of some sort of slime still on the ground, viscous but transparent, that my boot found purchase in. I tried to avoid vocalizing my disgust, and pushed forward, having to use some effort to pull my foot free.

The dark is full of wretched creatures, I thought to myself. Everything I had seen since emerging from the forest had been *wrong* somehow. They were difficult to describe, and many of them I outright avoided because of this. Just thinking about the things that I saw as I moved through the Necropolis and beyond sends a chill running all the way up and down my back, even though the sight of them is still blurry and unfinished. I couldn't—and still can't—think of the words to describe them, even to myself, and that scared me enough that I avoided them entirely if I could.

If I could.

I continued to follow the Wisp's light as it took me through the infested Necropolis. I was beginning to regret my choice to follow the thing, as I was beginning to see more monsters beyond my imagination, though I couldn't be sure that I wasn't seeing the same species many times—they were far too strange for me to paint a full picture of them, the closer I got to the vortex in the center. I felt my mind slipping away from me and I began considering abandoning the pursuit.

But curiosity proved stronger than will, and I pressed on.

I had to squeeze between two stacks, though there was barely enough room to get through with the shield on my back, so I had to remove it to make sure I didn't get stuck. On the other side was a small clearing, hidden among the stacked caskets that seemed to be threatening to tumble in on us. The Wisp floated up into the sky and vanished, and I watched it go with disappointment. Most of them had brought my attention to items that had been discarded or dropped by the people that had been there before—this one seemed to have brought me to a dead end in a graveyard full of monsters.

I scanned the ground once more, trying to abate my anger and frustration. It was dark in there, the lean inwards on the stacks doing well to block out most of the sky. The ground sunk a few steps closer to the middle, and I wondered if it may have been the surface of one of the collapsed tunnels below. Most of them were unmapped, weakened by years of desperate digging, while looking for unused space.

And there in the center, I saw a familiar woman sitting, cross-legged, facing away from me. It was Kat; but she no longer carried with her the blue glow of the Wisp that she had before. I stepped around, to see her from the front, and there was no longer any doubt in my mind; it was her. She sat there in front of me, eyes closed and head bowed, but it was her.

"Kat?" I whispered, leaning down in front of her.

She did not answer.

"Kat, we have to go. These monsters are beyond me, I fear." I looked up to the opening I had slid through, thinking I saw a shadow pass and not wanting to be heard. When I was sure there was no more movement, I looked back to her. "Can you stand?"

She looked up at me, smiling. "I can," she said softly, "but I wont. This is where I'll stay."

I shook my head. "It's too dangerous to stay, let's go. We do not know what these monsters can do." I reached out to grab her hand, but she pulled it away.

"I have done what I can," she said, looking at my withdrawing hand and then to me. "I cannot come with you any longer. I am of no use to you in this new world; I'd just slow you down. This is where I must stay—this is where I belong."

I stood back up, looking down at her. She wasn't wrong. I needed every advantage I could get, and while she had proven indispensable to a point, we both knew that as long as she traveled with me, keeping an eye on her would always be on my mind. It was a distraction; one that neither of us could afford in such trying times.

"The Ones Who Came Before did this without blood," Kat said as she let her head hang, almost to herself. "They sparked the fire once more to drive out the darkness. Darkness knows no other language than carnage and viscera and *death*." She almost sounded pleased. "Cut down the night, and make it bleed; is that what you'll do?"

"What are you talking about?"

She shook her head. "There's no time for questions; too many questions. You have to go, you said it yourself." I reached out to her again and she swatted my hand away. "You haven't failed yet," she barked. "But if you continue to pause, we both will."

I took a step back.

"*I* can't die again," she said as if realizing what she was. "I can't *live* again, either." She looked up at me, and there was no pain in her eyes; there was only anger. "But *you* can stop the Wizard. He rests to the South. Opening the gate has tired him, and the Stones. You still have time to retrieve them, but you must leave now."

I sighed. "I will." I started to head towards the crawl space that would lead out of the clearing, but Kat stopped me. I turned to face her.

"*End this.*"

Return to Castleford

I learned two things upon my return to Castleford: One was the Spires *were* important, without question; the other was that the Castleford Spire—the one to match those I had seen in the other cities—truly did stand in the center of the city, in the market square, shrouded in haze. It dawned on me how easy it must have been for Azazel, a master of illusions, to hide it from me.

I also saw the halo around the head of each and every blank-faced person that walked the streets of Castleford, indifferent to my presence. They, too, were in a haze; and much like the Spire, I knew that the only way to break them free from it was to destroy the one that summoned it.

The climb to the cliff was a quiet one, silent determination driving me. I was alone in the world, even among the rest of man. Maybe that was for the best, considering what had happened to the others I had encountered. Even before I came above ground, I set the wheels in motion for many things; how had I become so lucky? There I was, climbing up a cliff. A cliff that held a castle. A castle that had suddenly appeared, after just as suddenly *disappearing* so very long ago; home to a wizard who called himself the Lord of Dragons. And I was doing all of it so that I might feel the Sun on my face once more, as I had in the vision.

I had no illusions about it; I yearned for that feeling far more than I desired it for others. I knew that the world was ours, and I knew then at least some of what we had to do to *make* it ours, more than I had ever known before. I was walking on the surface of the world that could be, and it wasn't one that I wanted to live in. Castleford was still safe from the monsters pouring out of the pit to the North; but they were far from free from the Darkness.

More of Azazel's magic, no doubt, was keeping the monsters at bay. It was either that or the monsters—Azazel included—had an understanding about themselves, and they were steering clear out of re-spect for the one that freed them.

I had finished my climb, and stood to face the massive black castle ahead of me, before my gaze was drawn just beyond it, to the sky. Azazel's bloody Sun was gone, no longer needed. The sky above Castleford was the same dark red that it was everywhere else. Behind the filter that had been drawn over our sky, I saw the Moon, blacker than ever, standing strong above the pit in the center of the Necropo-lis. It was like a vacuum; I couldn't look away. It seemed as though nothing would escape the darkness of the Moon, larger somehow than I ever remembered, as if it were closer. I found myself being drawn to it just as well.

Until I heard a cough.

"The Lord awaits," a disembodied voice said. "He has an impor-tant errand he must attend to, although, I am happy to report he has found time, to *deal* with you before he is needed elsewhere."

I looked around for the source of the voice, but it only seemed to be coming from the castle itself. I looked at the large double doors and wondered, for just a second, if the castle was speaking to me. I shook the thought from my mind and stole one more glance at the Black Moon hanging in the sky before looking back to the castle. "It would be rude to keep the Lord waiting," I muttered to myself as I entered, the doors opening for me.

The Castle foyer was bright and massive. It almost didn't translate to me how big just the foyer was compared to the size of the Castle when viewed from the outside, let alone whatever else must have been waiting behind the large doors set into the walls. There was a chandelier hanging, red flames dancing on the empty candle holders. The room, which was two floors, though the ceilings were quite high and almost enough for another floor between them, was bisected by a deep red carpet that split diagonally up the large staircases that ran up to the second-floor landing. The walls were a reddish-brown and fa-vored the many shadows cast by the dancing magic flames that lit the room. There were also the doors: there was the set of double doors on the wall between the stairs as well as one each to my left and right on the second floor landing, each almost twice as tall as I. The walls to my left and right were adorned with portraits of Azazel, clad in different armors and robes.

"The waiting is so hard, Traveler," Azazel's disembodied voice said, "I've invited a great many friends to keep me company, while I waited for you; I fear they have grown tired of the *usual* festivities, much as I."

"Why did you help me?" I asked.

"It wasn't supposed to make you stronger," the voice said. "Without my urging, you would have surely failed, and I would not have retrieved all the stones. Make no mistake, I hold no fire for the hollow shells you've struck down. They are returned by my hand, *not* any stolen light. But enough talk! I have become accustomed to sitting here in silence while I wait; both for the pit to empty, as well as for my power to return to me. So! There are three keys, hidden deep—some deeper than others—in the... more *fun*... parts of the Castle. All of these keys will be needed to open the door to where I wait. *Then* and *only* then can we discuss what it is we're about to do."

"I've no time for your games—"

"But I do," he said, interrupting me. "So, as I said; enough talk. Let the game begin."

He had me. I had no other choice in the matter but to play his game. I needed to stop him from opening the door in the mountain, from waking the Black Dragon. I would have to figure out the pit later. But for now, I had to play Azazel's game and find the keys that he had no doubt defended well. I couldn't see them, but I could feel the halls beyond each of the doors, filled with the armies of the dead, in the various forms they came in, just waiting for me. I drew my sword and took a deep breath. I was becoming intrigued by what I might find, a feeling that surprised me. I looked to the first door, then to the giant portrait of Azazel that hung between the second floor landings, gaudy and rote.

"As you wish, *Lord*."

The First Key

Seeing three doors, and being told that there were only three keys, I wasted no time in moving forward, towards the doors between the stairs. As I looked around the foyer, I saw spaces between the portraits and imagined a different layout must have once existed. Perhaps the Castle shifted to fit its master's will? Was this only one possible construct?

I pushed open the double doors, with some effort, and they gave with mighty creak. They were heavy wooden doors, as thick as I was and almost twice as tall. I opened them just wide enough that I could squeeze through, and stepped into the hallway beyond.

The floor was checkered, black and white squares neatly placed all the way down. The wall on the left was stone and bare, dark grey and unimpressive save for the mirrors that were set upon it, spaced evenly apart and facing the tall windows to the right. They almost seemed to be the same dimensions as the mirrors, tall enough and positioned high enough that one could be seen from the waist up if they stood in front of them. Beneath the mirrors were small tables with candelabras on them, each brightly shining with red fire.

And scraping along the checkered floor, creating a screeching sound that I felt, more than I heard, was the pole-arm of an Undead soldier shambling towards me. Behind him, there was another one, with a longsword and a small wooden shield. The hallway was barely wide enough for two, so they moved single-file towards me.

The one in the front, with the pole-arm, swung the weapon upwards. I knocked it away with my sword, and the metal tip of the soldier's weapon skittered fruitlessly up the stone wall. I leaned forward, throwing my shoulder into the chest of the front soldier in order to send him tumbling into his friend. While they were both stunned, I raised my sword and cut through the first, the magic bursting out as it had before, only when I absorbed it into me, my eyes began to burn.

I recoiled, covering my face with the back of my hand. When I brought it down everything was brighter than it had been before. My eyes took a moment to focus, and in that time the longsword soldier had climbed over the pieces that were left of his compatriot. He lazily swung his sword at me, but it still caught me off guard. I narrowly dodged the blade tip, and felt it graze my cloak as I jumped back. I brought my sword up quick, and cut the arm from the soldier, his longsword making a loud clatter as it fell to the ground, his hand still gripping the hilt. Without thinking I brought the sword back down, cutting diagonally from the neck to the armpit of swordsman.

I was blinded again.

The trick of Azazel's game was clear to me now. Instead of needing to kill his army to bolster my sight, he meant to use it to harm me. Every one of his that I killed would increase my susceptibility to light, which he had made sure there was plenty of in his home. I had to be careful about how I went on, but even as I stood there piecing these things together, my sight returned to normal. The effect, while painful, did not seem to last particularly long. The problem would come if I face more enemies in groups, I imagined; striking down too many in a row would have surely left me blind or worse.

I moved to the end of the hall, this new wrinkle in mind, and stepped through another set of double doors, not unlike the ones leading to the foyer.

The room I entered was a library. It was large, much like the foyer, and was two floors with a landing up above. It reminded me of the library in Dewpond though the stacks here did not stretch from floor to ceiling. The walls and the stacks were the reddish-brown color that had adorned the foyer, and the books seemed far more sequential, most of which with matching dust jackets and spines; volumes of massive texts. Instead of ladders, there were spiral staircases, on alternating sides, every other row. The bookshelves themselves didn't reach as high as Dewpond, though they were still high enough that even someone as tall as I would have difficulty reaching the tops. The landing wrapped around three of the four walls, standing open above the door where I had entered. I could only see one other door in the room, and it was on the second floor landing across from me.

There were also several enemies between me and the only other door in the room.

Between the stacks, moving towards me were two undead soldiers, garden variety. Both held longswords, and the one in the front had a wooden kite shield. On the closest two shelves, standing one per shelf, were archers. The two archers on the first floor were holding crossbows, and taking aim at me. There were two archers on the second floor landing as well, wielding longbows. At the back of the room, in front of the door, where the second floor landing was the widest and longest, stood something I hadn't seen before. I could barely make it out at that distance, but it looked tall and lithe, like the faceless women I had seen in Alduin, only this one was more masculine; though still wearing a long, tight robe. A hood was pulled up over the tall and narrow head, but I couldn't see a face. He wore a mask, metal and uncolored, though it did have human-like facial features. In his hands, he held a staff.

I spun my sword to prepare myself, and took a step into the room. The soldiers broke into a speedy shamble, coming at me as fast as they could without falling apart. As I ran to meet them, I heard the *click* of a crossbow, raising my left arm and using the Onyx shield to block the bolt. I parried the first swordsman's attack and countered with one of my own. It was able to get the shield across in time to block, the blade of my sword getting stuck in the wood of his shield. I tried to pull it free, but the soldier yanked. I was glad he did, as I used the momentum to dodge the swing from the second swordsman. I heard another click and brought my arm up on instinct, blocking another bolt. I lowered it just in time to hear a longbow arrow whiz by, crunching and bouncing off the tile floor.

I planted my boot on the shield, and while gripping my sword with both hands, pushed off, jumping backwards. I slid on the ground, and narrowly avoided an arrow and a crossbow bolt in the process. Once I found my footing, I charged forward, calling the shield to cover as much of my front as it could. I plowed through with the shield and my shoulder down, and took at least one soldier to the ground with me. I rolled through to my feet and got close to the bookshelf on the left, far too close for the archers on that side to have a shot at me, cutting my long range worries in half.

The soldier I hadn't knocked down stepped in closer and swung upwards, but his blade barely left the ground before I had kicked it away, plunging my own sword into his chest. I ripped my sword and let the body fall to the ground, and I was blinded once again, but just for a second.

While recoiling from the sudden spike in brightness, the room going from dark muted browns to bright and colorful reds, I narrowly avoided the thrusting attack from an undead soldier with a dagger that had been hiding between the stacks in silence. In surprise, I swung my sword around, cutting through just below the ribs of my attacker, cleaving them in half horizontally. As its top tumbled to the ground, the room got brighter, and the pain in my eyes was suddenly everywhere, the low hum replaced with a high shriek.

The library was smaller than the one in the Dewpond, or at least not as deep. There were only six stacks, three a side, and it appeared that only the ones closest to the doors had archers on them. It was possible that more attackers were hiding in the shadows between the stacks, but I wasn't prepared to move from where I was until I regained at least some of my sight. Fighting in the dark, it turned out, was much more comfortable than fighting while blinded by light.

I heard, instead of saw, an arrowhead finding purchase in the wood of the shelves just to my left, and I slunk back deeper into what I had hoped and recalled to be shadows. I waited for the pain to subside—it only took a few more seconds—but when it did, the swordsman I had knocked down earlier had rounded the corner and was moving towards me. The archers across the way, I determined, were without line of sight due to the overhang of the second floor landing.

But still I heard a *click!* I quickly looked up to see the bolt leaving the weapon, aimed directly at me. I fell back, and brought my left arm close across my chest. When I brought forth the Onyx shield, it caught the bolt, rather than deflected it.

At the same time, the swordsman was on me, both hands on the hilt of his blade, holding it above his head. He swung downwards, and I parried to the left, albeit weakly. I kicked out, hitting him in the chest and sending him stumbling. I scrambled to my feet as I heard the archer above reloading his weapon.

And what have you got? I asked myself as I felt the wall coming up, and my space running out. I nearly cursed out loud when I remembered the small crossbow I had obtained earlier. It would be useless against the monsters outside, but it had proven quite the opposite against the common undead. I reached for it, and as it was ready to fire I took quick aim at the archer above. I let the bolt fly, and watched is it tore through the wrist of the hand that was holding the crossbow. The archer dropped its weapon, but didn't seem immediately aware of it.

My sight had just returned, and I didn't want to experience that pain again. I knew I had to get to the door on the second floor. I wouldn't be able to do so with the still six—or more possibly hiding in the shadows—of Azazel's 'friends' left in the room. The tall man at the end had yet to do anything, and that scared me.

One at a time, I told myself. I could handle the pain after killing one. It was only a moment or so that the effect lasted—mercy, perhaps? Some part of Rayna's Sunsight still with me and countering?

Either way, it was nothing that I couldn't get used to, and learn to fight through. I would have to, I was already sure of that. Even in that moment, while I was scrambling up the bookshelf like a ladder. The archer fumbled, trying to draw his sword with no hand.

I knew that as soon as I reached the top, the archer on the stack opposite would have a clear shot. I clambered up onto the wide plank of wood that was the top of the bookshelf, the undead closest to me still trying to draw its sword. Behind him, the crossbow archer on the shelf across seemed to howl in excitement when it saw me again, taking aim.

I sheathed my sword and ran forward, directly into the fumbling corpse standing before me. I reached out and grabbed it by the upper arms and pushed. I heard the click of the crossbow from across the way, and felt the ripple of the impact as it landed in the back of the soldier I was carrying. I used the thing as a shield until I reached the end of the shelf, and without thinking I tossed him behind me. I jumped down to the floor below, a fair enough drop. I was on the move so quick I cannot recall if I even felt pain from it, pushing forward instead of allowing it to slow me down. I dashed into the space between the first and second shelves, and began to climb.

I scrambled to the top, quicker than I had on the other side, and drew my sword. The archer let his crossbow fall and reached for his own sword, but I was quicker. I relieved him of his head, and stepped back to where the second floor archer opposite me could no longer have a clear shot. I took a knee and waited for the sting to subside. I thought about climbing down from where I had come up, but there was another hidden soldier beginning to climb, and the archer from the other side—still without his hand, of course—was attempting—and failing—to climb as well.

The spiral staircase, between the shelves I stood on and the second row, presented an interesting idea. I climbed down the other side to save my legs from another jump, hoping that I would still be in the second floor archer's blind spot. I reached the ground, and moved to the end of the stack quickly, peering around the corner just as I saw the Tall Man waving his staff around, his head lolling from side to side. It was almost hypnotizing until I heard a morbid rustling.

From behind the bookshelves on either side of the Tall Man rolled a skeletal orb. They were slightly smaller than the ones I had faced before, but they seemed quicker as a result. I took a deep breath and thoughtlessly blocked an arrow with the Onyx shield as the orbs rolled up and over the railing of the second floor landing, hitting the ground with a crunch but not losing any speed or momentum as they barreled down on me, each struggling to expose a blade or anything to do more than just knock me down.

I dove between them as they tried to close in, both veering slightly to hit me, not concerned about colliding with one another. I turned as I slid on my knee, and stole a glance to my left to see one undead had made it to the top of the shelf, but stood up there, appearing to be lost now that I had come back down; and the armless archer still had yet to notice that I was no longer on top of the shelf.

The orbs skittered to a stop, and I could hear them shuffling around, crunching whatever was necessary to free arms. The one on the left had two, one holding a scimitar, the other a basic longsword; the one on the right had twice as many, each holding a dagger, at least two of which seemed to be dripping with poison.

They rolled at me once more, and I tried to block each of them. I lowered my stance and tried to draw the shield off my back on my right side, but only got as far as my shoulder. The Onyx shield took the full blow from the sword-wielding orb; the Academy shield took the first dagger well, but left my side open for the second.

The cut was shallow across my right shoulder, but it still stung. I could only hope it wasn't one of the poison daggers, but I hadn't the time to check. I rose to my feet and tried to shake the academy shield back to where it was. I grabbed the hilt of my sword with both hands and took a deep breath, garnering focus.

When the orbs began to roll, I ran forward, the dagger orb on my left now, the sword orb on my right. I saw the sword orb aiming for my head, while the daggers were lower, so I dropped and slid on my knees. I slashed downward, and took both arms—and both weapons —from that side of the orb to my left; barely sliding under the sword of the right one.

I jumped to my feet again, and ran around the shelf to steal a moment to catch my breath. I look down at my hands and saw they were shaking. I gripped my sword tight in my right, but just kept staring at my left; the nugget of an idea was beginning to come to me. I heard the skittering of bone on the floor, even on the carpet, and rounded the corner.

The orbs came at me once more, alternating sides in a bid to confuse me, it seemed. I caught a quick glance at the Tall Man, still waving his staff, and it was apparent that he was in control. I blocked arrows from the left and right, one right after the other, and continued walking towards the approaching orbs.

When they reached me, the sword one was on my left again. I parried its attack, and spun around, slashing across to tear a large hole in the side of the dagger-wielding orb to the right. My arms screamed from the force it took, but splinters of bone littered the ground as the orb awkwardly rolled away, and tried to turn.

I ran to it while it tried to regain balance, and ducked under a slash with one of the poison-tipped daggers. I drove my left hand into the 'wound' that I had made, and summoned the Onyx shield, as large as I could; the force of the magic ripped outwards, and the orb burst into a rain of broken bone fragments. I remained, a black stone in my fist, crumbling to dust before I could really look at it to determine what it was. I didn't recall grabbing it when I reached inside, not thinking to look. But even in the times since I could never see it well enough before the thing fell away to ash; I just understood at once that it was their 'core'. And without it, there was no reforming.

I turned around, more due to the sound I heard than anything else. Bones crunched and churned as the other orb began to morph. I watched as the Tall Man moved his free hand about as though he were drawing the desired form for the mass of bones to take. It flattened itself into a disk once more, only it seemed to find more blades—including the ones dropped by its former ally—as they were all around the outside of the now skeletal wheel.

It rolled towards me with great speed, skipping as the longer swords came into contact with the ground. I jumped to the left to avoid it, and it rolled past, turning very quickly. I almost didn't have time to recover and it was on me again. An arrow from above found the shield on my back, and bounced off; though I barely registered that it had happened at all, and wondered how many arrows I had mindlessly and fortunately blocked. I dove right from my still-crouched position, though it was a hair too early; I felt the wheel break the air just beneath my foot, having been afforded time to course-correct, albeit slightly.

I landed on my shoulder and rolled through, but slammed into a bookshelf. My arm screamed in agony from the bump, but I still managed to rise, to avoid a third pass by the wheel, dodging almost too late—

And without time to correct, the wheel crashed into the bookshelf, and fell onto its side. I took the opportunity, and ran to it, attempting to find footing on the mess of bones beneath me, hearing them crunch as I walked towards the center of the wheel, only a few steps in. I sliced with my sword to break free an opening, and grabbed for the core with my left hand, once again using the Onyx to break the whole thing apart.

I had wished I could revel in my victory, but the archers were still firing arrows from above; though their aim wasn't the best. Unlike the orbs I had faced before, these didn't seem to alter my vision, and I was unharmed after striking them down. I made for one of the staircases quickly, and heard the sound of heavy doors opening and closing at the back of the room. The Tall Man must have escaped.

When I reached the second floor, I moved to the archer closest to me. The door was to my left, and as I came out from behind the shelves, I could see that the Tall Man had, in fact, fled. I pulled up the Onyx shield to block a close-range shot from the archer nearest, the one on the other side seemingly out of arrows, shambling towards us the long way around and drawing his sword.

The archer closest swung at me with its bow, which I easily deflected. I was growing tired already of the fight, and brought my sword up, blade first, running it up below the ribs of the archer, the blade emerging between the top of his shoulders. My eyes burned, but I was starting to grow numb to it already. I withdrew my blade and brought it up to block the other soldier.

He was a worse swordsman than he was an archer, so it was not hard to break through his guard and land a killing blow. I stopped to take a breath and let the pain in my eyes subside, and looked down to see the other two were still where I had left them. They were both watching me, but neither of them could seem to figure out how to get to me. Their master's weakness must have weakened them as well, as they possessed almost no cunning anymore.

I moved to the door, trying to catch my breath but knowing that there was little time to do so. With each moment that passed, Azazel was regaining power, and the beasts of old were reinfecting the realm. Worse still, once Azazel recollected the stones, he would be able to awake the Black Dragon, the 'mother' of all dragons, if the stories were to be believed. I only hoped that not all of the rooms were like the library had been.

They were.

The Tall Man's Trail

As I entered the next room—an Observatory—I took notice of the figure across from me: it was the Tall Man, just finishing a spell and turning to the only other doors, stepping through and out of sight. Before he left, I saw something hanging from around his neck; a key.

The Observatory was large and cavernous, the roof open, allowing the red sky to pour through like a smog, filling the chamber with an ominous glow. There was a telescope in the center of the room, larger than any I had ever seen before—not that I could recall seeing many. Along one wall, there were tables, angled, with drawings on them; constellations that I might have heard of when I was young, but I likely had not laid eyes on knowingly since then. The other wall had a window running the entire length that looked out onto Castleford, the city appearing asleep. I crossed the room, reaching for the door. My hand was met with resistance; a wall, invisible to my eye until I touched it when it shimmered a light blue, barring my path through.

My attention was drawn upwards by a loud sound, coming from the roof above, like giant, plodding footsteps moving towards the opening. They stopped, albeit only for a second before the thing made its appearance in the gap, jumping down to the floor just on the other side of the telescope, and mostly out of view, before I could get a clear picture of it, though it was *large*.

There was a mechanical whir, winding up for a second as a shadow seemed to pass over. Then, a *clack*, and suddenly everything went dark. The skylight had closed. There was the sound of another mechanism—another part of the first, no doubt—and then I heard several panels sliding open along the walls.

While my eyes adjusted to yet another lighting change, I heard the familiar sounds of the undead, coming towards me from where the panels had opened. I couldn't hear the footsteps—or *any* movement, for that matter—of the giant, which concerned me greatly.

I felt a hand on my arm, spindly and cold, and brushed it off before pushing its owner back with a shoulder bump. I drew my sword, and the flames lit some of the area around me. Much like the fight with Rayna, the darkness was strong here, oppressive and almost a blinding force. Present, more than ambient.

Without thinking, I cut down the undead closest to me. Like a flash of lightning, I could see everything in the room, including a blur, something big coming at me. There was a mouth—large, protruding fangs, at least two of them—that was agape and screaming. There was a pair of meaty arms, hands clenched together in one massive fist and raised above its head. There was armor plating strapped to various parts, and a relatively small circlet around its bald head.

I managed to get my Onyx shield up in time to absorb most of the blow—had I used the Alduin shield, it not doubt would have broke—and tried to side-step the beast. I had to shake free of the pain, but by the time my vision had once again begun to fade, the giant was nowhere to be seen. I stopped and listened; it wasn't the giant I was looking for anymore, no; this *was* a game that Azazel was playing. I wondered if he meant to kill me at all, or just toy with me and see what I could do.

Or merely he meant to waste my time.

I heard the shambling coming closer, though while trying to pinpoint it, another sound began to rise: the muted shuffling of something larger. I quickly decided between jumping forward or back, and chose forward, feeling the wind as the giant passed behind me, catching a glimpse in the limited light of the sword in my hand, weaker than ever. I was beginning to wonder how much longer the magic within it would last.

As I rose, I was grabbed from behind by an undead. None of them seemed to have weapons, fortunately enough; but that didn't mean they weren't deadly. Their bites and scratches add up over time, and they often carry with them illnesses that could only lead to joining their ranks, from years of festering in the ground. These ones, I surmised, were left unarmed to act as a nuisance more than a threat; slowing me down so that the big beast could strike me down while I was distracted. The one that had grabbed me was clinging to my back, and I threw myself backwards, hoping that we were close to a wall. There was a crunching sound, and I was released.

I could see again, and I tried my best to ignore the pain and focus on the giant armored *thing* that was barreling towards me. I dove right, and it crashed into the wall. I heard it stumble—though its feet were quiet, and I wondered if they weren't padded with some sort of dampening magic as part of this 'game'—and then fall.

When I spun, I could see that it had knocked itself out for the moment. My vision was already beginning to fade, but I wasted no time, pushing off the ground and closing the short distance. I quickly lifted my sword, high above my head, with the blade facing downwards. I plunged it into the throat of the giant. I swear, as I did, it opened its eyes, and for a brief second it seemed scared.

The thing kept trying to move, but every time it did the sword seemed to cut a little more this way, a little more that way, and it would stop struggling. There was a gurgling sound and I felt wetness in my boot from the blood that was draining out of the ever-widening wound. I tried to close my eyes, urging the thing to stop struggling, but it didn't want to listen. I just wanted it to end, taking no joy in the struggle, so I pushed the sword hard right, then pulled left, opening a massive gash that ran across the entire neck. The gurgling stopped, and so did all of the sounds it was making. I stepped back and pushed an undead to the ground, and waited for the bloody sight to go away.

The lights came back on, and I was alone in the room. I looked down, and there was still blood on my boot from the pool I had been standing in—but that was the only sign of the conflict. I saw no panels in the walls, nor bodies—standing or otherwise—in the room. I looked to the door where the Tall Man had left, and saw the magic fade away. I ran to it, and then through it.

The other side of the door was sleeping quarters. It was a smaller room, though there were now two doors instead of only one, and they were single doors, standing just a head taller than I. The room was dark and smelled of sweat and something else that turned my stomach. There were a few undead soldiers in this room, some with longswords, one with a halberd, and another with a mace. I was able to take them out relatively quick, though I could not be sure which of the doors the Tall Man went through. The layout of the Castle wasn't making much sense to me at all, and I couldn't help but entertain the thought once more that the layout of the Castle was not set.

I worried that once I went through one of the doors, I would not be able to return. I opened the one on the West wall, and tried to peer through. There was only darkness on the other side, but I could feel a chill in the air there. I heard a whooshing sound as though something was cutting through the blackness, growing louder, coming towards me. It was almost too late that I saw the shadowy arm reaching for me, and I threw myself to the ground as it grabbed for the empty air where I had been. I kicked at the door in an attempt to shut it, and when the arm retreated—briefly, for it was knocking again in no time—the door finally closed.

Not that one, I told myself as I crawled away, watching the door to make sure it would stay shut.

I moved through the other door and found myself in a fountain room. It was almost like a bath: everything was white, or off-white; there were columns, carefully placed and ornate unlike anything I had seen in the Castle to that point. The floor was split into two levels, a square in the center that was cut into the floor. It was only a couple steps down to where the fountain itself lived, a woman with great wings. Her arms were spread outwards, and on each rested a minia-ture dragon. Wrapped around her waist was a larger dragon, its head peeking out from beside her hip. All three dragons were spouting wa-ter into the wide basin below, enough that a half dozen people could comfortably bathe in there. The floor was white, but something was different about it. It was more ivory than eggshell, and seemed *lumpy.* Because there were so many my mind didn't seem to want to compre-hend it, it took me a second to realize that the floor *was* bones. From a few steps ahead of me, surrounding the fountain were countless skele-tons, broken apart and littered with no concern as to who or what they once were, not unlike the twisted priest's Church in Brakas; only these were spread out and much more fragmented.

And behind the fountain stood the Tall Man, staring at me. Beside him, a black rock floated in the air, shoulder-level. It glowed as the Tall Man waved his staff around, and I heard the skittering of bone on bone as the fragments began to rise up, forming around the rock.

The shape they formed was not an orb, but seemed more human in appearance: two hulking arms, long enough that the knuckles dragged along the ground as it walked, kicking up more bones as it went. It stood two of me high, and as it looked at me, it leaned back. It lifted the club that was its right arm, and I heard the sound of bones crunching as they shifted inside, swords and spears and axes emerg-ing from within, erratically dotting the arm and turning it into some-thing of a spike-ball.

It wasn't the fastest, which I tried to use to my advantage. I broke right, and tried to get a column between me and the skeleton creature. It swung its massive arm and it took but one blow from the spiked-club that was its right arm to destroy the column. I looked up at the ceiling, to make sure it wouldn't collapse, before returning all of my attention to the lumbering monster in front of me.

I ran for it, and tried to close the distance; I didn't think that it would be able to hurt me up close. I had hoped that it would have to shift forms, and that would give me the time needed to get to the core.

Instead, as I went to slash at the chest, a half-formed skeleton burst from just above its belly, and quickly slashed at me with a dagger. Caught off-guard, I narrowly avoided the strike, though the blade did cut along my cheek. The cut burned, but I ducked away, under the left arm of the monster and behind it, running to the other side of the room to reconsider strategy.

I tried to catch my breath and looked around for something that I could use to my advantage. The fountain room was empty, save for the fountain—which was no longer working, the basin only filled with a small amount of water and mostly bones—and the countless skeleton fragments that littered the ground.

I reached for the crossbow, and loaded it. I was running out of bolts, and cursed myself for not picking some up in the library before leaving, though I couldn't be sure of its usefulness against such a collection of bone. I had to reach the core of the thing, one way or another; I needed everything I could get. When I looked at the beast, the skeleton that had risen from its abdomen still writhed, ready to defend the core. I wondered how many more would emerge.

As if on cue, two more skeleton torsos formed out of the thing's shoulders, each with two curved swords. The thing was lumbering towards me again, and just as it passed the fountain, I noticed the gap between its legs that it left when taking its wide steps.

I ran forward and took aim with the crossbow. I took my shot, and nearly exclaimed when I saw the bolt break apart the hand of the skeleton holding the dagger that had cut my face. The dagger fell to the ground and I dove for it, rolling through the monster's legs and struggling slightly to regain my footing on the unsure floor of bone. I jumped onto its back and, using the dagger, began to madly swipe at it, until I could make a hole to get my hand through. All the while, the skeletons on the shoulders were taking swipes at me, getting close enough that I would have to stop my attacks to dodge.

I started to see a way in, pulling my left hand back so that I could hit with enough force—and suddenly I was on the ground. The monster had exploded outwards in a mess of bones and weapons, sending me flying. All that was left was the core, which floated lazily back over to the Tall Man, where it collected more bones.

It was a different configuration this time; smaller, and quicker. The arms were almost twice as long as the legs, and the body was made of the familiar orb shape. There were two shorter arms higher up on the orb, each with hands holding daggers. The thing jumped up, and I lost it in the dark of the high ceiling. I could hear it swinging around, grabbing unseen rafters and moving under the cover of darkness, demanding all of my attention; though I kept stealing glances at the Tall Man, wondering if he was in control of all the skeletal orbs I had faced, or just these ones. The ones in the Castle seemed different, somehow; as though they were smarter and more versatile in the forms that they used. They were smarter in the way they attacked as well, and that all but confirmed to me in my mind that he was the one controlling this thing. Without him, there would be no thing.

There needed to be no Tall Man.

I moved with renewed focus, feeling the weight of my sword in my hand. I reached across and gripped it with both, my anger building steadily inside, a frustration that had been left unchecked since entering the castle, simmering just beneath the surface the whole while. I wanted to be done with it all, but I no longer wanted to go home; I wanted to win, and quick.

It was that desire, that drive, that made me act so carelessly, missing the falling dust just above where the Tall Man stood, as if to warn of the impending attack from above; unheeded as I reached back to strike at the Tall Man with everything I had.

The creature dropped from above almost too early, but it caught me with enough of its attack that it knocked me to the ground. I was dazed and my left shoulder screamed in pain—the arm was caught under me when I was pinned—but I had no time to dwell on it. I rolled to my right, and tried to plant my feet. I only managed to get to a knee before being struck by the back of the long but lithe arms of the thing's current form.

I landed on my front hard, driving the wind from my lungs. I gasped for air and looked to see the creature jumping back up into the shadows and out of sight. I scrambled to my feet, kicking up bones as I did, and readied my sword, scanning the ceiling once more. I followed the shuffling around in the shadows, straining my eyes to try and focus on movement in the dark, but only seeing flashes of it. I also tried to keep an eye on the Tall Man, hoping I could find an opportunity to strike, wishing I had time to reload the crossbow. I knew as soon as I reached for it, the thing would attack. It was in control of the situation, and he was in control of it; I had no more illusions about the order of things.

It hit me like a flash. I swapped my sword from my right hand to my left, and reached over my shoulder to grab the Academy shield. I stole a glance at the Tall Man once more, taking aim. I flung the shield at him, hoping that my plan would work. The thing dropped down, not on me, but in the path of the shield. It was still facing the Tall Man, obviously having to backtrack from where it was, which was just above me, it seemed, in order to defend him; the Tall Man seemed incapable of moving or defending himself while controlling the golem.

I ran to attack, jumping on the back of the golem, avoiding the small arms on the back as they contorted to reach for me. I swapped my sword again and reached in with my left hand, finding a space between the mess of bones that allowed me to get in far enough that when the shield came, it shattered the golem to pieces. The stone floated harmlessly between me and the Tall Man, and I could have sworn I saw the brows of the mask turn upward as if to plea with me.

It did not work, and I cut him down.

I had the First Key.

Door Two

The door on the other side of the fountain—somehow—returned me to the foyer. I stood, perplexed, staring up at the chandelier in disbelief. It was the strangest feeling of disorientation that I had ever experienced, as if my internal compass had lost its bearings.

I looked up, back and forth between the two doors on the second floor. I opted to go to the door on the West first, though I couldn't be sure what guided the choice, or whether it would have mattered. If this entire castle was constructed just to be reformed time and again, what was to say that Azazel hadn't laid out the order well in advance. Would the Eastern door have even opened, I wondered. And if it did, would it open to the same path; the same configuration, regardless of which door I chose?

The large double doors, which looked the same as the ones I had passed through on the first floor, opened with ease, closing on their own after I passed through. I paid it no mind to their autonomous movement as I took in my surroundings.

In front of me were steps leading down onto a dirt path through a grassy balcony, overlooking the town. There was another fountain here, though more abstract in shape, and did not seem to function. There was a stone railing to my right, articulate and ornate. At the far right end there stood a watchtower, the door set into the stone in the corner of the small garden. To the left, the castle continued. There were small porthole windows, amber light shining through; though the windows were too high to see through. There was a door at the far end leading back inside.

Seeing no connecting rooms, I opted to check the watchtower first, and moved slowly across the grass, ignoring the path. I heard the flapping of wings, coming from all around me, though I saw no birds; only the red sky was above me.

The door to the watchtower opened without resistance, and I

stepped inside. It was narrow, the stairs winding upward around the central column, made of hard stone bricks. I followed the stairs all the way up until I reached the nest above, open on all sides save for four support pillars for the canopy cover. I could see a great deal more from up there, and looked ahead on the path.

I followed the roof of the hallway section that the other door led to. It was only wide enough to be a tunnel, and seemed to lead down into a wider room. The roof of the low room was flat, though it looked as though there were four skylights spaced evenly apart. The room beneath the glass looked dark; much darker than the connecting tunnel. Beyond the large chamber, there was another set of stairs leading up, only they were uncovered, as was a stone maze, laid out at the end of them. There was an iron gate at this end of the maze, which opened to a path leading to a large tower, round and wide.

Behind the gate stood one of the Twins, though I could not tell which from where I was. They were waving at me. After they were done, they turned and walked into the tower, light blooming from behind the open windows, and I knew where the second key would be.

I climbed back down the tower, feeling unease, the likes of which I hadn't felt in quite some time. Of all the things I had faced since emerging from under the ground, nothing filled me with fear quite like a dragon. I had heard they were invincible, though it seemed very few remained. And two was *more* than enough, so if I had to face one to keep Azazel from waking up *the* dragon—so be it. By the time I had reached the bottom of the tower, I had swallowed my fear. I stepped out into the garden, sword in hand, and began to walk across the grass to the only other door available.

The flapping of wings returned, smaller than the dragons but larger than any birds I knew. I looked around again, but saw nothing. Suddenly there was a blur—that's all I could see, as though I was looking through a dirty window, and only for a second; then it was gone. The flapping was moving around me in circles and I turned to follow it. I took a deep breath and held it, closing my eyes and focusing on the sound.

Left!

I ducked right and spun left, swinging my blade and catching something, the flapping of wings suddenly drowned out by the screeching of some creature, briefly seen before it cloaked itself again. What it was that I had seen, I knew I had not seen before; it was pink all over, with an elongated head. It didn't have any eyes, but the beak was large and rimmed with tiny jagged teeth. It had scrawny arms and legs, held together by a scrawny little body, but its wings were large and strong looking, webbed like a bat's. It bled from the shallow wound left by my sword, purple in color like the creatures outside, the ones from the pit. When it cloaked again, it was mostly invisible; even the blood couldn't be seen until it dripped from the monster and fell to the ground.

I followed the trail of blood drips, as well as the sounds of the wings, slower than before, until it finally came to a stop. Blood began to pool, just a few quick strides from where I stood. I hunched as if to pounce, but hesitated. Why had it stopped? It had to know that I was tracking it, so why did it wait for me to strike? I assumed a level of intelligence—the thing had snuck up on me, after all—so it wasn't an outside possibility that it had some sort of trick planned.

With caution, I reached for the crossbow hanging at my side. I pulled back the string of the bow, sliding it into the lock with a click. As soon as I did, there was a shriek, and the flapping grew more intense, the blood trail on the move once again.

Of course, I thought to myself. *It doesn't have eyes, but it must have ears.*

While it was alerted, I finished reloading the crossbow and quickly moved across the grass, crossing the dirt path with a crunch and stopping, an idea striking me. I crossed the dirt to the other side, and then turned back. I stretched over the loud dirt, and stepped into the quiet grass on the opposite side of the path, and there I waited; one hand holding the crossbow at the ready, sword in the other.

There was a cutting of the air across from me, where I had stood only seconds before, as the thing attacked—with what, I do not know —but I took the opportunity, while I knew where it was—the blood droplets had also given it away—and struck out with my sword. The piercing shriek of the creature was all that I needed to know that I had made contact, but the ripple sent up my arms as my blade was met with resistance meant everything so much more.

The thud of the creature's body hitting the ground sounded before its cloaking would fade away, leaving the sad and crumpled corpse of the flying creature on the grass below. My sword had caught it just below the left armpit, cutting nearly to the neck. Blood pooled beneath it, and I waited for the pain of light; only none came. It did not appear as though this creature were powered by Azazel's magic, or the stolen light, or whatever it was that truly gave them life; this creature appeared to be closer to the Old Ones, the ones that poured from the pit in the center of the Necropolis.

I gave my head a shake, regaining focus. I didn't have time to marvel or question the existence of demons and monsters; I had seen plenty of them, and I knew that I would see plenty more while I lived. Azazel was regaining power every second that I wasted, and the monsters and demons were infecting every corner of Alghast. I moved to the door, and stepped through.

It was, as I had perceived outside, a hallway. There were flames dancing within lanterns hanging from chains along the center of the hallway; the arch was made of deep brown wood while the walls were made of cold grey stone. Often I wonder if that was the warmest I felt during my journey, something about the quiet nature of the hallway putting me at ease after spending so much thought on the path ahead and behind. I wanted to stay in that hallway, with that feeling; I was running out of reasons *not* to every second I stood there.

But something was itchy.

I didn't care anymore about the Stones or the dragons; the world was dead already, so they could have it. I just wanted to rest. When was the last time I had slept? I couldn't face a *dragon*, I knew that much; would it be so bad for me to be at ease before my death?

But my neck was so very itchy.

I wanted to reach back to scratch it, but the urge only lasted for a second and then it was gone. Something about the way it kept repeating—over and over again every couple seconds—made me take hold of it, best that I could, and I pulled my head to the right quickly. I felt something tug on the nape of my neck, and my eyes flew open. I reached behind, and was able to grab something that felt sharp. I pulled it free from my neck and turned to see what it was, but it pulled free from my hands and disappeared into the shadows above.

I again felt my neck, a small puncture left behind by the wicked vine. To this day, I swear I felt thorns when I grabbed it, threatening to punch through the leather of my gloves. I only hoped it hadn't left behind any poison. I looked up and down the hall, but I could see no sign of where the vine had come from—or where it had gone. On my left, the hall was a dead end. There was a bookshelf there—odd placement, I thought—and a small reading desk. The other end had stairs leading down, and though I couldn't see from where I stood I knew from looking upon it from the watchtower that there was a door there.

While I looked, I thought I saw movement in the shadows, right at the apex of the arch of the roof. Something was slithering down the beam, just out of sight, down the stairs.

What manner of horrors did this man keep? I wondered to myself as I tried—and failed—to picture what that vine was attached to. The next room, which was wide and flat from what I saw outside, would likely play host to it; I could feel it in my bones. I readied my sword and part of me wished I had just let the vine keep at it, for it would have been such a peaceful death; though I told myself that was just some kind of venom, left-over from the sting.

I pushed through the hesitation and fear and stepped towards the stairs slowly, fearing a quick strike. They were sharp enough to pierce skin without me knowing, even when all was quiet; they had no reason not to attack at full force—and full speed—now that they had been discovered. And if there were more than just the one vine, they could have surely skewered me and torn me to pieces. It was a grisly thought that I focused on for such a short time, though I was still disappointed with how long I allowed it to take hold.

The stairs were steep but few. They led down to a small landing, where the roof met a stone wall. There was a single door, red against the grey. Above the door was a tall window, a narrow slit cut into the stone that ran up to nearly the tip of the ceiling. There was no glass, and the slit was so narrow that it was hard to truly see anything beyond it, even when I stopped walking; the dark room on the other side seemed to be in contrast to the hall I was in.

I pushed open the door, and stepped into the other room. The question of whether or not there were more vines was one that I felt foolish for. The number of them I saw when I walked through that door was beyond memory, even. They lined the floor, thick and thin, some moving around and others seemingly planted in the ground. They also ran across the ceiling, thicker than they were on the floor, blocking out the windows and the sky above. The base of the plant was in the center of the room, which was a stone garden of some kind. The plant was almost as tall as the room; the bulb taking a good portion of that. It was closed when I entered, a dark purple color, and while closed, it was about the size that I was. The stalk was thick and covered with thorns, and spread out above and below the bulb, breaking apart into the vines that filled the room like a legion of deadly snakes.

I was filled with terror as I looked upon the plant. It was like nothing I had seen or heard of before. I wasn't sure if it was nature or magic that gave birth to the foul creature; it was an abomination nonetheless, offering no respite for my tired perception of the new world and its denizens.

The room was, as I had thought, a stone garden. Beneath the glass skylights there were squares of grass, rimmed by deep running moats of water that fed into the soil beneath them. There was a stone brick path that ran between the patches of grass, the plant growing in the center on its own small patch of grass, hidden beneath its mass. There was one door, on the other side of the room, though it was barred shut by vines.

I took a step forward, igniting the fading light on my sword, and prepared myself for the onslaught of vines. I was sure I could block many with the Shadow shield—though that would consume a large amount of whatever magic I had remaining, I was sure—and I could cut down many with the sword, and hope that the fire travels quick. Either way would consume what remained of the Stones' magic in me, though I was so close to the end that I hoped it would be enough.

Then I heard the flapping of wings; at least three sets of them, and my use of the magic was validated ever more.

I broke into a run, heading for the stalk of the plant. As I approached, I saw movement all over the room, and the cacophony that resulted drowned out the flapping sound of the cloaked creatures with the oblong heads. I tried to clear my mind and kept my left arm at my side, as though I were wielding an invisible shield, praying that the power within would have a little of its own instinct remaining as well. The shield on my back would help cover a second of three sides, the last guarded by my sword, which I held out from me so I could maneuver it quickly.

But the vines came quicker and harder than I was prepared for. I blocked one, then two to the left. I was able to cut through one on the right as another slapped my back, sending me stumbling forward. Another came from the right, and whipped me hard into the air, and I crashed into the thick of a root that was running *through* the stone in the floor to one of the moats, rather than on top of it.

I rolled onto my front and turtled beneath the shield on my back, and felt a cluster of vines hit the metal, the force enough to knock some of the wind from me. They retracted and I did the opposite. I got to my feet and turned to see how far I was from the stalk. Before I could surmise, there was a spindly hand on my throat, lift me from the ground and taking me away from the center of the room.

It dropped me—whether it meant to, or my weight was too much for its scrawny arms, I do not know—a few strides from where I had landed. I noticed then that all four moats of water had roots running to them, actively drinking from the self-replenishing water source. I had never seen a plant feed so hungrily before, but the movement in the water suggested it was almost constantly drawing water.

I tried to block out the sounds of the room and listen for the flapping wings. I would have liked to have been afforded the opportunity to deal with them first, but I did not know to what degree the plant would interfere, should I leave to its own devices for a short while. Part of me wanted to cut the plant down first, but it seemed to be at peace when I entered—the whole room did, mind you—but the plant only grew agitated when I lashed out at it; when I got too close.

Losing myself in thought somehow allowed me to drown out the sounds around me, and I heard the rhythmic flapping of wings; though to me it sounded not unlike the beating of a heart. I grabbed for the crossbow at my hip, and took aim at the source of the sound. I aimed with my ears, more than my eyes, and squeezed the trigger. The bolt found home in the chest of the Oblong, causing it to appear almost at once as it fell to the ground and writhed in pain until falling still and dead.

I reloaded quickly, but just as I finished I was knocked off my feet. I fell to the ground in one of the grass patches, my fall broken on a bed of dead flowers and tangled vines. I rose to see what struck me, as I was unsure if it was a vine or another Oblong. I couldn't hear any flapping, but wondered if maybe they had wisened to my methods of tracking them, and ceased to fly. I remembered that they needed sound to find me, and chuckled to myself; if we *all* stood still, we would be lost to each other in the ambience.

Though the option of doing nothing was appealing, living life as a statue along with the other occupants of the room, wondering who would give in to the madness first and give themselves away; I couldn't let it end that way. There was a confidence building in me, though I wasn't sure why I was thinking it then, as I looked back on where I had come from.

I had learned to fight in the underground, with the remnants of humanity; a desperate people, surviving not by skill, but mostly by luck. And even the luck of our people was driven by a fear that they would not ignore, that only grew as it spread. From there I have faced all manner of creature, small to large, and still I live. It was a marvel to me that still holds true to this day. It filled me with such vigor that I felt no weariness from battle or dread from what lay ahead; I only felt powerful. I felt powerful enough to finish what I started. I wasn't forced to do this, any of this; I *chose* this destiny, I *chose* this fate.

My story wasn't ending here.

Vines appeared to float through the air, listlessly waiting for their moment to strike, coiling back so that they may lash out quicker and deadlier. I stood, quiet as a I could, listening to my surroundings for any signs of the Oblongs. There were two left, by my estimation, and the plant was still pulsating in the center of the room.

To my right, feet on grass—the Oblongs, naturally, were not wearing boots, so grass rather than stone was their biggest tell—amidst the rising and falling sounds of nature around us. I fired the crossbow and while the bolt didn't hit, it did make the Oblong leave the ground, the quick movement briefly revealing it. I struck down hard with my sword, catching it between the neck and shoulder, sending it crashing back to the ground in a crumpled heap.

I withdrew the sword, swinging instinctually behind me, without thinking. I connected with something, the third and final Oblong becoming briefly visible as the tip of my sword slashed across its chest. It zipped away from me, and went clear once more. I stole a glance at the plant and the vines to once again make sure that they were calm; though it was clear it was still prepared to defend itself.

A problem for later, I gathered.

There was quick movement, ahead of me, and the monster gave itself away not by sight, but by sound; shrieking loudly as it barreled down on me. It caught me by surprise. Enough that I barely got my left arm up to block it with the Onyx's Shadow shield, being hit with enough force to stagger backwards a step.

I felt the air cutting behind me, and the sound of a cracking whip. I turned my head just enough to see a vine retracting from a quick strike. There was another one coming, at least from where I was looking—I didn't dare imagine what was looming on the other side—and I realized that the attack wasn't to harm, but to knock me back out of the plant's space.

I pushed back and to the left after finding my footing. The Oblong didn't give much at first, but I was able to push past it. I heard the whip-like crack of one of the vines I hadn't seen readying to strike, and spun as I fell to the ground to see it had grabbed something. Something that I couldn't see.

The vine wrapped around the invisible creature, until it found the wound from my sword. I saw the vine disappear into nothingness, and I knew that it had entered its chest. I heard the shrieking cries of the beast as the vine appeared to suck the life out of it, and I realized how close I had come to the same fate.

It also appeared this plant had a temper, and was no longer in the mood for playing games.

I broke out of the trance of watching the—now visible—ghost being drained of its essence, and made a quick move for the closest root. I raised my sword above my head and brought it down in a chopping motion as hard as I could, screaming out with effort, knowing that I was seconds away from being struck.

Or worse.

My sword cut through with ease—largely in thanks to the fire, waning still—and both ends of the cut withered faster than the fire could spread. The end in the water never stopped shriveling, until there was almost nothing left but a speck floating on the calming surface of the now resting water; the end still attached the plant retreated into bulb, the stalk closing over the wound. It—and I—moved so quickly after the root was cut that I couldn't quite be sure *what* I saw; I just knew that I needed to get to one of the other roots before it recovered from whatever pain I had caused it.

As I was running to the root in northwestern corner of the room, I heard a sound that should not have been as loud as it was. It was a beautiful sound, one that I couldn't actively remember; but rather, it was a memory that could be recalled if triggered. Only this sound—this sound I heard, as I was praying that the plant would grant me a more pleasant death than the Oblong it had just fed on, or that it were full and would feed no more; this sound was *too loud* to have been that sound. The sound I heard filled the room, and my heart, with a palpable dread. I looked to my right to see that the flower of the plant had opened, and like a horrible mouth, the petals were lined with jagged teeth—thousands of them—and at the heart of the flower there was an opening rimmed with much larger—and much sharper—fangs. And each of the teeth, in the opening and along the petals; each of them was *oozing* with something much thicker than water.

I couldn't break my stride to stare, no matter how badly I wanted to. But in that brief glance that I stole the plant appeared to hiss at me, as if it were aware of my plan, crying out in protest and warning.

I swung down to cut the root, lighter than before to conserve the energy, hoping that the quick cut was the same. Before my blade could connect I was knocked off my feet; not by a vine but by the empty corpse of the Oblong, drained of all its fluids, its skin already beginning to turn to dust. I pushed the body off me and tried to get up, but a vine wrapped around my leg and began to tug. I was able to cut myself free, blocking another attack with my shield before scrambling back to my feet. I turned and cut the root, and began my run to the next one before even seeing the one I had just cut start to wither.

I slid under a sweeping vine and rose to a run once more, chopping down another as it came across to stop my forward progress. I was focused on getting to the final two roots, hoping that would be enough to kill the plant, which was far more alive than I ever thought possible. I almost didn't see something hit the ground in front of me as I was running past.

Whatever it was, it was fast, wide, and pierced the ground with ease. It had to be sharp. I was given more opportunities to see them, as they were beginning to litter the ground in batches—two or three at a time—though they were always quite close.

They were coming from the petals.

It seemed to me the plant had only freshly flowered, the wavering of its petals still unfamiliar to it, so its aim was not the best; which was in my favor, of course.

Still, it was shooting its *teeth* at me.

I dove for the root, and sliced through it. The plant *screamed* in agony as the pieces pulled back, slower than before. The flames from my sword were able to reach almost to the bulb, and that seemed to agitate the plant even more.

One more to go, I thought to myself with hope, the task almost done. I scrambled into a dash for the last lifeline of the deadly flower, and all of the vines seemed to encircle me at once. I was covered in shadow—everything went dark—but I could feel something closing in around me until I couldn't move anymore. I felt hundreds of thousands of tiny needles, poking and prodding at me, trying to pierce through. I tried to scream but there was no room.

The first pain was in my arm. It was beyond anything I had felt before, and it felt like something was ripping *out* of me, rather than in. The second pain was in my head; a throbbing that would not go away for some time afterwards, strong enough to force my eyes closed while the cacophony of sound around finally ceased. When I opened my eyes, I had fallen to my knees. The room was not silent; I just couldn't hear it anymore. The plant was writhing around as though it had been set ablaze, only I saw no fire. In fact, I saw nothing but the plant's roots. The vines had all gone.

I pushed through the pain in my head—and my arm—and ran to the last root, cutting through it and falling to the ground with exhaustion as I watched it retract halfway to the plant and then stop, the whole thing falling silent.

I looked down at my left arm, and saw a mix of black and red, and felt somewhere deep within that the shield—and the power of the Onyx—was gone from me.

As was more than some of my blood.

The Maze

I bandaged my arm, wrapping cloth torn from my cloak tightly around it from elbow to wrist, rested for a moment, and made my way through the door that had been barred by the vines of the plant. The hallway on the other side was dimly lit, and open on top; I mounted the stairs there that led up to the iron gate, which in turn opened to the stone maze I had seen from the watchtower.

When I was young, in the catacombs, my friends and I would do mazes to pass the time. We were only so useful when we were young; only so much energy and attention to be spent on work. Though even our play was not without purpose, with the mazes and other puzzles being used to strengthen our minds, just as the other work strengthened our bodies. I got quite good at the mazes before I became old enough to carry a sword.

Still, I was not eager to face a maze that size. They were much less formidable on paper than they were in person, and the pathways were far more narrow than they had appeared, when I had looked on from the watchtower. It was my hope that, at the very least, I would be afforded some time to rest my arm. I would need to start using the Academy Shield once more, now that the power of the Onyx had left me. My only hope was the fire of the Ruby, still in my blade after all this time, would last. The end was in sight.

When I entered, the stone I felt weighing down my stomach descended into a pit. I wasn't sure why, but I was filled with a sense of fear, the hairs on my arms and neck standing on end and I felt as though I was covered in bugs; tiny little legs crawling all over my—

I heard a clicking sound, something hard on stone, heading towards me at the entrance. The tops of the walls were too far for me to reach, even when jumping, the walls so smooth that there was nary a foothold to find. The hallways were so narrow that I would have very little room to swing a sword anything more than up and down strikes.

While thinking about my limitations, combat-wise, as if by some cosmic attempt at humor, the *click-click* sound came to an end, just above me. I looked up at saw a shiny black point, planted on the top of the wall. And as the rest of the thing came into view. I saw that it was a leg; one of eight, all leading to the biggest spider I had ever seen.

It was hairless; its shell hard and black, reflecting the red glow of the sky, giving it an almost ghastly appearance; ethereal, as though it were moving somewhere between this world and the next. It stared down at me with its cluster of eyes, like jewels set into a head as large as mine, cocked to the side; its mandibles twitched hungrily. The legs were long and narrow, ending in points that—I wasn't too interested in confirming—seemed as though they would be able to pierce what armor I had; I tried to dress light to allow for easier movement, at the cost of piercing defense. I deeply regretted the choice as I pictured the spider leg shooting through me, dangling me like meat on a stick.

I tried to shake the thought from my head and watched the monster closely. I was waiting for signs of movement; a twitch of a leg, or a shifting of the abdomen—but there was nothing. I felt a tinge of aggression in the pit of my belly, that stone trying to climb back out as though in defiance of whatever fear put it there in the first place. I called forth the flames on my blade, though I knew they were growing weaker each time. I saw them reflecting in the eyes of the spider, its attention turned from me to the sword, and I heard it shriek before turning and departing. When it was out of sight, I thought I heard it tumble, falling down into the maze, and realized that it would be too wide to fit, horizontally; it was restricted to the top.

While that was better for me, it still wasn't ideal, as I would have to avoid the spider while navigating the maze—it would take advantage of any careless moments on my part to skewer me—as well as after I exited; the bridge on the other side of the gate at the end was wide and open. The spider could easily confront me there, and although a part of me was excited about the idea of, once again, facing a creature of that size in open combat, for I had acquired a taste for victory against odds, it seemed; I knew that it would be easier if I could somehow deal with the spider while we both were limited.

I put out the fire on my sword, hoping that it would keep the spider at bay for at least a few moments. I could easily scare it away, it seemed, if it caught me at an inopportune time, or if it were to happen to overwhelm me; though I still was hesitant to face it.

I never did like spiders.

Stepping back into the more open area at the entrance of the maze, I pulled the Academy shield off my back, and equipped it to my left forearm. I only had slight clearance on either side of the shield when holding it up, but it would serve as good protection held over my head, should the spider want to exchange blows with me.

I pushed forward, keeping my left shoulder as close to the wall as I could while looking upwards, watching and listening for any movement coming closer. I used the shoulder to guide me, always having success following the left wall when I was first starting with mazes; it may not have been the quickest method, but it was sure to lead to the exit.

Briefly—only a second—I was able to see the image of the maze from overhead; the one that I saw when I stood at the top of the watchtower and looked ahead on the path. I tried to remember as much as I could from the image, but it was gone as quick as it had arrived. In my focus, I nearly ignored an incoming strike from the spider, a swipe scraping the floor of the maze, coming from behind me.

It was as though it were trying to flick me away, much the same I would to a bothersome fly. I was able to block with my shield, keeping my footing though sliding back a bit from the force. I tried to drop my shield and bring my sword around, over my head, but by the time the blade clanged off the ground, the spider had already retracted its leg and scurried away.

Moving forward through the maze, I tried to keep my head on a swivel; at all times, I was looking up—behind then ahead, ahead then behind—while keeping my shoulder against the wall to navigate the turns. I was still trying to recall what the maze had looked like from above, though it was proving difficult to concentrate, while also focusing on the spider that was lurking above.

It appeared again, quickly slashing at me with both its front legs. I was able to withstand the blow with my shield, and pinned one of the legs to the wall—the other slipped free just in time. I tried to raise my sword to strike, but the blade caught the wall behind me. The spider swung again, with a free leg, and I had to press up against the wall— and the pinned spider leg—in order to avoid it. I took a deep breath, and let the leg go. I swung upwards—

And was overjoyed and then disgusted when the remaining stump that the spider pulled back sprayed its blue-black blood all over my face; the severed leg falling to the floor in front of me. I wiped the blood, quick as I could, and looked up at the spider, which was vibrating with fury; it almost looked to be casting its own light: fire and venom, the black of the spider's shell and the red of the sky sending me into a trance. It was a trance that lasted only for a moment, as the spider bellowed out a piercing scream, keeping what was left of its leg

—just below the 'knee' I'd suppose—close to its body.

"Come at me, you—" I ducked a sudden strike from the spider, taking a few steps back and getting my shield in front of me. *Yes,* I thought; *like that.*

The spider kept its distance, staring down at me before slowly disappearing to my left. I listened for the sound of its legs on the stone walls, but after a moment it was gone; there was only silence remaining.

Cautiously, I moved forward. I resumed the position I had before: my left shoulder pressed against the wall with my shield angled up in front of me. My sword I held down, in the hopes the I could either swing upwards, or windmill into a downward strike—at the cost of some strength, however.

I rounded several more corners before reaching my first dead end. I kept following the wall back around, trying to keep as quiet as I could; though I knew that the spider would be able to find me with ease should it truly wish to.

It may have also feared me. I took away one of its legs, and it didn't seem to be growing back. Even spiders have only so many they can spare, and surely this one didn't hate me enough to risk losing all of them by keeping me ready. Perhaps it was smart enough to think: the more time it gave me, the more I would let my guard down. To some degree, the beast was right.

There was another dead end, then another. The next one doubled back quite a bit. All the while, the spider stayed away. I rounded a corner, and to my right I could see the top of the iron gate that was leading away from the maze. I was getting close to the exit, at least in proximity if not progress, though I gathered there were still two rows to go.

How I wished I could just climb the walls.

The sight of the gate had distracted me, and I was caught looking. The spider struck, flicking once more with its leg; the strike hitting me hard, up the length of my back, sending me flying forward like a rag doll. I landed, coughing and clutching at my chest; trying to keep the breath from leaving me. I scrambled to my feet just in time to see the spider leg jam into the stone where I had just been laid out.

I also saw my shield lying on the ground, on the other side of the still-planted spider leg.

And I watched as the spider took notice of the shield as well; its abdomen lowering, turning inward. I had seen spiders spin web before, though seeing it at that size was terrifying—a solid strand of web shot out, and covered my shield. I heard it. It didn't strike as something that should have a sound.

But my trepidation turned to opportunity when I saw that the spider's leg had gotten stuck in the stone, striking hard enough to pierce not only meme; but the heavy stone I had been laying on only seconds before, as well. I lifted my sword and the spider screamed in protest, pulling harder on the stuck leg. I cut on a steep angle down, right through the outer shell and the flesh below, and the spider pulled away and disappeared once more. Only this time, I could hear its wails as it fled. I also heard the clang of metal, fading over time.

It took my shield.

I caught my breath and went back to the wall. I had to hurry, and get to the end of the maze. I felt naked without my shield, but my only hope was to make it to the end.

I rounded another corner, followed the wall all the way around, and then another twist and…

I was out of the maze, staring at the iron gate; which now stood open. I passed through, taking a deep breath. I heard a loud metallic sound behind me, light and high, just as my shield had sounded when the spider fled previous. The sound had come from somewhere beyond the precipice of the maze, and I scanned the top of the walls for any signs of movement. I thought I saw a shadow pass overhead— large but fast—though I saw nothing in or even on the maze behind me.

When I turned to face the bridge once more, I saw that the shadow had landed.

The spider still had six of its legs; the front two that I had cut were drawn in close and still bleeding. It stared at me, and I stared right back. I could feel the fury behind its eyes, burning hot. It was clouding, *blinding*, even; that rage. The spider had proven to be cunning, yes; but did it *hate* the same way that we do?

I raised my sword, and smiled at the creature standing before me. "Well?" I said, mockingly.

The spider shrieked and moved forward. *Fast.*

I started backing away, but that didn't prove to be fast enough. I turned and *ran* back to the maze, beyond the gate. I heard the spider closing in on me as I passed the narrow entrance back into the labyrinth. Then I heard the spider stop, yelping in pain rather than anger. It had gotten stuck; wedged between the walls, between its first —the ones I severed—and second set of legs. I watched as it struggled to pull itself free, but wasted no time; I brought my sword down hard on the spider's head, and it fell lifeless to the ground at my feet.

I took a deep breath, then climbed over the body of the spider.

When I reached the other end, I looked for my shield, but the web looked to have torn off. My shield was lost somewhere in the maze behind me, though I did not know where.

The thought of proceeding without a shield was not one that I wanted to entertain; but neither was the thought of going through the maze once more to retrieve it. I just didn't have the time for it. Azazel would regain his strength soon, and return to the Cathedral to retrieve the Stones. I couldn't let him open that door; couldn't let him awaken the Black Dragon.

So I proceeded without a shield.

GAME OVER

What manner of place was I in? It seemed like something out of a dream; not at all what I had pictured the great Castle of Azazel to be. It seemed made to be *played* instead of lived in. It was a thought that began to take hold in my mind as I approached the doors on the tower that I had watched one of the Twins—I was too far away to see which —enter earlier.

I stared down at the ground for a moment, collecting my thoughts. There was likely a dragon waiting for me, and I wasn't sure how I would face it. I wasn't sure I was even *ready* to face it. I had proven myself a competent fighter, yes; but none had killed a dragon before.

Or had they?

If dragons could not be killed, why then were only three remaining? Where had all the others gone? If we were just food for them, how did we win, if even for a short while? Everything I had seen; the visions of the time before the Light and the piercing and subsequent Emergence of the Old Ones, the dragons, *and* us—they only left me with more questions as my thoughts lingered over them.

I was stalling. I could hear myself; a voice, somewhere in the back of my mind, screaming out to get my attention, calling me back to the task at hand. I didn't want to listen to it, but I knew that I had to; I was just surprised that the voice had been *mine* for once.

I caught my breath and pushed on the door, slowly, with my free hand; my sword held tight by my side, my knuckles white beneath the brown leather gloves.

The chamber inside was open, round, and brightly lit. There were windows evenly spaced around the perimeter of the room, and the floor was designed with a dark ring around the center, where a podium stood. On the podium, there was a key.

"Sorry to disappoint," a voice said, echoing through the chamber. It was the male twin. "The other matters we had to attend to required our attention sooner than we had intended. We'll have to finish *our* game another day; but you might as well finish his and join us for the unveiling."

What did he mean by that? Was Azazel at full power? Were they preparing to open the door, and release the Black Dragon? Had I taken too long?

Panic struck and I ran for the key. There was a set of wooden double doors on the other side of the chamber, which I ran to. As I expected, they returned me to the foyer. I came crashing through the door so quickly that I almost fell over the railing.

As I regained my balance, I noticed that the three doors—two of the three, I had already entered and returned from, as part of Azazel's game. As I surveyed the foyer, I saw that the three doors were the only doors remaining in the hall; the door that I had entered the castle from was gone, though by what manner of trick, I couldn't be sure. Azazel seemed to be a master of illusions; far more than I could have given him credit for before.

The words of the dragon still burning in my mind, I went to the only door I hadn't entered yet. On the other side was a hallway, long and dark, that seemed to go on forever.

I took a few steps into the hallway and felt a chill wash over me. There was a cool draft coming from somewhere down the tunnel, but it was too dark; I couldn't see very far. There was the sound of a door closing, somewhere far off, and I turned around to see that the door I had came through was gone; there was only more hall in its place. And just as the door vanished, I felt a weight lifting from my satchel— the keys were gone as well, disappeared as though they were never really there to begin with.

I pressed on, away from where the door had been, knowing that even if it *were* an illusion, I would have to continue in order to finish the game, and hopefully find Azazel at the other end. At the very least, I hoped it would allow me to finally leave this Castle, though I mostly worried that I had wasted too much time in the other paths, and I would be too late. The disappearing keys were far too concerning for me to waste any more time going anywhere but forwards.

Though it was the weight of concern, not fear, that slowed me. My walk down that hallway was slow and methodical; with each step, each *breath* meaning to free me from the shackles of that doubt. If I was too late, I would figure it out; that part didn't matter. Ending this game, stopping the door in the mountain from opening; *those* were the things that mattered.

If the apocalypse was happening, I couldn't stop it from inside the

Castle.

"The Faeries trusted you, I see," said a voice from every dark corner of the hall. It was Azazel. "The Old Eyes are a gift, indeed; to see the world for what it was *meant* to be is not something to take lightly. Was it Py that treated your wounds? I hope she is still well; it's been so long since I've visited."

I kept walking, my mouth shut.

"Don't feel like talking?" Azazel chuckled, the laugh echoing up and down the hall, driving my anger higher. I was through with his playfulness. "That's quite all right, because I could talk for ages. Do you know how lonely it has been, hiding all this time? The Twins, great as they are, are not the best company; they're dragons, after all.

"I bet you didn't know dragons could do that! They can't, really; not all of them could, anyway. The Twins—Tal and Declan, by the way, if I haven't properly introduced them yet—they were taught the skills to hide among us, after we turned on them. We didn't have to, you know? Turn on them, that is." Azazel sighed, his voice turning solemn. "We were capable of being so much more than what we are," he said, taking a deep breath. "Instead we let our anger and our thirst for vengeance against nature herself guide us, and even still, we stood divided as time marched on. We were wrong. *You* were wrong."

"I have done nothing," I finally said, unable to take anymore.

"You have done *everything!* It wasn't enough to drive them away? It wasn't enough to see them spend eternity in an endless abyss for all we knew, with the other creatures we deemed unsavory? They could have taught us to be more, if we had let them."

"You're starting to sound like a madman," I said quietly, my walk gaining purpose.

"No," his voice gained an edge. "I'm starting to sound like a *dragon*. And you, my dear friend; are a fool. For as Py has stripped the layers of illusions away from your eyes, so that you may see the world as it is—She *taught* me my illusions. Though I fear I have far surpassed what even she thought possible."

The air grew colder, fast. The wind picked up, howling as though it were passing through a cavern. I turned to face the hall behind, and it had gone, replaced with the mouth of a cave.

No, I thought. I turned and walked deeper into the cave, until I stood at the entrance to the cavern where Azazel stood at the door, the four gemstones entered, and his arms held out at his side as though he were waiting for me to enter.

"I do appreciate you giving me that time," he said. "I was just so tired, and I knew Mother would want things a little more like the way she left them." There was a sarcastic lunacy to his voice, as though he knew I expected it. I took a step towards him, but something stopped me in my tracks. Azazel was waving a finger. "She might be a little groggy when she wakes up, so you stay right there."

Before I was worried about fighting *a* dragon. Now I was going to have to worry about fighting *the* dragon, if the legends are to be believed.

"You were stalling," I said, working it out in my head. "Stalling while you returned to the Necropolis, collected the stones?"

"We were not expecting your return," he said with a smile. "We weren't expecting you to leave the Cathedral alive. No, I was expecting to see you next as but one of my walking corpses, milling about the new world. It will be much more kind to dead men than living men, I assure you—at least for a time. There's only so much I can do to quell their anger, you see. But there will be a time where man and dragon will watch over all; that, I promise you."

There was still so much I didn't understand, but I knew that it wasn't the time to think about it. I did not consider my chances very high of me escaping that room, so I didn't see the point in dwelling on something that I couldn't be sure I would need to. I thought to turn and run, maybe live to fight another day; but didn't see any reason to wait. Things would only get worse from here; if I had any chance, it would be when the Black Dragon was, as Azazel put it, 'groggy'.

The door appeared to brighten, silver instead of gray; it gave off its own light that filled the room. It was enough that Azazel blocked his eyes, though I could not tear mine away. The light subsided, and the door set back into the rock, and then slowly slid out of the way. For as large as it was, it moved in silence.

As I stared at the opening, it seemed as though it were smaller than the Black Dragon I saw in my vision. Perhaps it was a different one that rested there? Or perhaps the fear of the beast warped the Faeries' perspective, presenting her as larger than she was. It didn't help to stomp out the fear very much, but it was a thought that I grasped to keep the panic from rising too high.

There was a growl, coming from deep within the darkness on the other side of the door. Azazel approached with caution, which did not go unnoticed. "It is time to awaken; time to take back the world. Your children await you outside, where darkness once again persists. For you, I have done it all; for you I—"

There was a loud *whoosh* and Azazel suddenly stopped talking. In fact, Azazel was *gone*. I heard the crash of something into the cave wall, to the right of where I was standing. I moved out of the way, and found that Azazel's hold on me was gone. I stumbled and fell to the ground, scrambling to find a rock to hide behind.

The dust settled, and standing within it was the Black Dragon. It was a smaller version of the dragon in my vision, but something was off about the way it was moving. It seemed as though it were gaining mass with every passing moment, as though the darkness in the cavern was feeding it. I looked back at the door, and remembered the light, releasing from it as though being sent out into nothingness, leaving only dark.

They had imprisoned her, *weakened* her in light.

Beneath one of her clawed feet was Azazel's head, his face bloodied. I thought I saw him try to speak. His body was a mangled mess; twisted and contorted by sudden attack, and the impact into the rock wall. The Black Dragon pressed down onto the rock effortlessly and Azazel moved no more. The dragon looked down at her foot, and the mess beneath it.

"Yes, you are done," she hissed before leaping back, and flying out of the cave that she was rapidly outgrowing.

I stood, and looked to Azazel, his body broken all over and without a head, and I almost pitied him. I don't know what made me look, but I looked to the door and saw that the Stones were still slotted there. I heard the cries of dragons outside, but I'm glad I looked. I ran to the door, and popped each Stone out, the Onyx almost excited to return to its spot in my palm.

There was no ignoring the cries outside. They were still close, the reunion just beyond the cave mouth still ongoing. I made my way to the precipice slowly, and found a shadow in which to hide. The Black Dragon had grown to nearly twice the size of the others, returned to their true forms, and hovered in the air between them. Flames brewed in the mouths of all three dragons as they bounced, excited to be together again.

I froze. Ice ran through my blood like a helcat, and I became paralyzed at the sight of them. To go out there, to try and stop them now would be suicide; though I did now have the Stones. I wondered how much power they would have left, though I knew how to use the Onyx and—through osmosis—the Ruby. I didn't have time to figure out what the Sapphire and Emerald *really* did.

Before I could think, the dragons departed. The twins, Tal and Declan, though I couldn't tell which was which when they were in their dragon forms, let alone their human disguises, flew north, setting fire to Castleford below as they passed, branching out east and west, their fires never seeming to cease as they vanished into the distance, only their fires remaining in view.

The Black Dragon flew north on her own, stopping over the Cathedral of Woe in the center of the Necropolis. The storm had stopped, and while there were a great many creatures still moving away from the pit, it looked as though they had finished their emergence.

The dragon hovered above, flapping her wings and staring down. She seemed to be drawing in air, the fire in her mouth growing more intense with each passing second, so much so that I tricked myself into thinking I could feel it from where I stood, still on the mountain, far enough away to barely make out what was happening.

But I could not mistake the fire shooting downwards, burning the Cathedral away, as if to dust. And it didn't stop there; the fire spread outwards into the Necropolis, black tinged with white, the likes of which I had never seen before, leaving nothing in its wake. All things, living, dead, and neither: all were reduced to ashes in the blink of an eye.

And just as fast, the fire was gone. The red sky returned as it was, and the Black Dragon lowered. Above her, drawing my gaze was the Moon, black as it had ever been, and my heart felt as though it were about to leap from my chest. I struggled to breathe as I reluctantly looked up at it, and was suddenly blinded by flashes of white light. Amidst them, I saw movement; thousands of creatures slithering amongst one another like a pit of snakes, only these snakes had wings; these snakes had arms and legs.

These snakes were dragons.

I took a deep breath and forced my eyes back down to the Black Dragon, the feeling in my gut telling me more than anyone ever could. I didn't know if these visions were to be trusted but it had never been more clear to me than it was in that moment.

The Black Dragon straddled the pit, and a bulb of light began to form in her neck. She wretched it up, and dropped it into the hole before flying up above it, looking down and patiently waiting. The pit exploded with the beam that I had seem in my vision before, shooting up into the sky and reaching the moon, and all at once I heard the cry of a thousand dragons, waiting to be born.

BOOK FOUR: BLACK MOON

Fields of Glass

The surface was gone. Whatever had been done at the beginning of the Long Night paled in comparison to what came *that* night; I knew all at once that my Long Night would be coming to an end, and soon.

Castleford had been finally reduced to rubble, care of the Twins on their way outwards, continuing to burn the villages on their way. The ones untouched by the fires before, largely for the reason of needlessness, were reduced to ashes. Now, the need was to return things to the way they were; to when the dragons ruled the sky *and* the land, which meant eliminating all traces of the humans.

But the land that was ours as much as it was theirs. Neither of our species was born here, if what the Faeries showed me was to be believed. Where we came from, I did not know and I did not care; we had beaten the dragons *and* the Darkness back once before. We had fought for the soil that we built those villages—those *homes* on.

We would do it once again.

Only this time, there would be blood. There would *have* to be blood. There already was so much blood. I knew as I looked over the wasteland left from the Black Dragon's black fire that there would be no room for sympathy or mercy for dragons; they felt none for us or even the creatures that had once again emerged from the pit. All burned the same.

Kat.

I wondered if she would have even felt the fires; if she were even capable of dying again, as she had lamented before. Was she truly stuck here, bound to me by some unseen destiny? If so, why had she left me?

Why had I left her?

In the distance, I could see the fires spread far beyond Dewpond and Brakas as well. I could only surmise that it had reached Alduin, and this, the hot death of the realm we knew as Alghast would be the last light that anyone would see.

Then it dawned on me that there may not be anyone left alive *but* me to see it. A sobering thought, and one that kept me frozen in place as I watched from the cliffside. The Stones were too weak for me to use them, especially the Onyx for information. It seemed as though I could still use the shield and the fire, but the Emerald and the Sapphire just would not respond to me, as though having no previous connection to them rendered them useless to me. I hoped it was only for the time being, as I was sure I would need all the help that I could get.

As I stared out into Alghast from where I stood, on the cliffside by Azazel's castle, I noticed a few things. First, the energy that was coming from the pit, and engulfing the Moon in the sky—it was no longer the bright light I had seen in the vision, but rather a dark energy that seemed to be sapping what little light out of the air that the still-burning fires were creating; the Black Dragon floated, suspended in the beam, cocooned by her own wings. Second, thanks to the waning firelight, I was able to see monolithic shapes persisting in the places I *could* see; that included Castleford, whose Spire stood tall in what *used* to be the center of town, revealed fully now that Azazel—and his illusions—were no more.

It was then that I began to wonder what Azazel meant about Py, and how much of what I had seen were illusions crafted by either of them. Had Azazel said that Py taught him those illusions? And did the Faeries *help* the dragons? If they had, did that mean I was deceived again; put on a path to complete a task that ran away from the goal I had hoped to achieve, instead of towards it?

I wondered if there would ever be any time to ask these questions, let alone listen for the answers; yet still I stood, in stunned silence, as the world I knew—like the one I knew before it—burned around me. What was even *left* to save? And where would I go next?

The heart—the one I had seen in my visions; the same visions that left me feeling uneasy as I looked at the Black Moon, hanging in the sky, feeding on the darkness oozing from the core of the planet hungrily. I kept picturing it, the sea of scales that I had seen, slithering around like serpents biding their time—and they had waited so long already that they were growing restless, hungry in their own rights.

My thought was to return to the Faeries in the Forest to the north of Alduin. Py and Zig—and whoever else may have been left but hiding—would hopefully be of some help to me; though I had seen very little of them once the veil had been pulled from my eyes, and I could see things as they truly were. I remembered fondly the luminescent leaves that had adorned the trees when I had first awoken in the Forest. The trees had not looked that way for long, but there was something about them that seemed so real that I questioned whether or not they had been purely the creation of Py's illusion; or if they were based on a memory, happy but distant. And after the memory had faded, the Faeries seemed to retreat as well.

I only hoped the fires wouldn't reach them.

But I was getting distracted. My mind was trying to focus on everything but the moment. The Faerie forest was a long ways away, through many destroyed—some twice and even three times over—towns and villages. And with the dragons patrolling the skies...

I knew not how to face a dragon, and there were three out in the world—including the one that was so feared that she didn't seem to be given a name. My hope was that I could gain some insight into what I might do in order to see my quest through to the end. Py may also have been able to explain why the Black Dragon turned on Azazel so rapidly after being released, crushing the life from him as though she were excited to do so.

Her hatred for humans ran deeper than respect for loyalty, it seems.

The surface was out of the question. Not only were the fires still burning, but I didn't want to risk being found by the dragons. It was only a matter of time before they began to wonder where I went, if they even wondered at all. Perhaps they knew that one man against three dragons were impossible odds, and left me alone. The Stones were all but sapped of their power, and aside from the residual powers I had before—the shield and the flame—there didn't seem to be much that they could do to help. Maybe they were right and all of this was moot; though there was nowhere left for me to go. Nowhere left for me to wait for the world to end, once and for all. I could return to the Catacombs, where I—

That was it!

I could take the network of Catacombs. I could enter through Castleford and hope the way was open to the North, either directly beneath the Necropolis—though it was not ideal—or around it. I would be able to make it as far as Alduin, and at least then I would be able to see how bad things were there.

I also knew there were survivors in Alduin, still underground. I hoped that the dragon's fire wasn't enough to get through the surface, as fire has an interesting way of traveling, as though looking for every nook and cranny that it can find its way into. They had not been warm to me before, though I could imagine things might be different once they knew what was happening above ground.

The Catacombs weren't going to be safe for much longer, either.

I wasn't sure if there was anyone still living beneath the ground in Castleford, though Azazel had inferred that not all of them made it to the surface when he called them. There was only one way to find out, and looking out into the chaos that filled the world ahead of me, I knew that it was the best course of action. I descended from the hill, and as I did, I nearly jumped out of my skin when I saw a brute, not unlike Brok—I thought for a second it may have *been* him—sitting on a rock.

He was a Dawnflayer, looking almost the same as Brok in terms of the build; though it was his face that was different, and the most telling. His face was a wreck. Blood pooled in his left eye, whether from the eye itself or the large, now closed, wound on his forehead. His face was stained with blood, which had dried to the point of almost being black. When he looked at me, it flaked and flew off, disappearing into the breeze like a part of him becoming snow caught on a winter breeze. It looked as though part of him wished that he would fade away entirely. He paid me no mind at first, though I stood unmoving before him, one hand on the hilt of my sword.

"You'll get no fight here," he said. He was much more well-spoken than Brok. "Not much use, is there?" The Dawnflayer looked up at the Moon, taking in the ominous force surrounding it, freezing it in place.

"Did you come from—?" I trailed off, nodding towards the Necropolis.

The Dawnflayer turned to follow my gaze before looking back at me and nodding. "We'd been down there a while," his voice turned grave and sullen. "The whole time thinking about what we were going to do when we got free. 'The world will be ours again!' some said. 'The humans will pay!' said others. I just wanted to stop *her* from waking. Now I see that she cannot be stopped. The Gestation has begun. In time, this world will finish feeding the Moon; then you will see what future we do not have."

I listened intently.

The Dawnflayer looked back to the Moon. "I never did like them, you know? Dragons, that is." He drew a deep breath and held it, before sighing heavily. "Their reign was because they knew that they alone held power over all others—living or dead—in the realm. That is not leadership. It was borne of fear, not respect—demanded instead of earned. Some grew to accept that fear, to follow it without question; while others like myself, we asked questions and paid in blood for the answers." He shifted, coughing. He spat, and I thought I saw blood in it. He looked back to me, shaking his head, but still the corner of his mouth curled up into a smirk.

"You know, long ago, we shared this world. You humans were mostly just food for the dragons, but there were those of us that sympathized, seeing the potential in you to be something more than just cattle." The Dawnflayer scoffed. "You all have voices, you learned to speak from us; but you did not learn to speak so loudly from anyone but yourselves. It was that trait, none other, that found your species the folly of the dragons. You grew beyond our teachings, and we were punished for setting you on the path. The Dawnflayers were made the enemies of the dragons—worse than food, as they killed us only for sport."

He raised a finger, as if to stop me from interrupting his story. I had no words. "But it was also that trait that finally let man take hold of the world. The dragons were all but killed, and everything else that ever harmed one of you, or gave someone nightmares; all were sent to live in the Dark Abyss, in the black pit where all the world's darkness is borne." He looked down at his hands, bloodied; his arms resting on his thighs. "Even the ones who helped you grow to what you had become, save for the Faeries. Some Dawnflayers remained loyal to the dragons, and that was enough for our kind to be all but banished as well. We waited there for so long, and now we are dead; the Black Moon far too powerful to be stopped now. We were let loose too late."

I looked out and saw the glow of the fires. There was a small forest between me and Castleford proper, but I could still see the signs of the inferno over the mess of branches and trunks that lay before me. The trees were dead—years without the light of the Sun will do that—but they still stood as a reminder of the world before, sobering but strong, almost in spite of the dying light.

I could also see the Spire poking out in the center of town, and thought it deserved some investigating as well. The dragons were far enough away and I trusted I would be able to navigate the remaining fires well enough.

But first…

"You still live," I finally said quietly, almost in a whisper.

He just shook his head. He looked up at the Moon one last time. "With the sight I see, I do not wish to be. These are truly dark times." he said wistfully; the last words he would speak to me.

The Spires' Secret

The center of Castleford was one of the many things in the world that I did not get to experience, given my youth when the Long Night began. Seeing it then, as it remained, still held weight; even to my virginal eyes.

It was more than just burned away—the courtyard had been decimated, as though an explosion had happened. I wondered if it might have been an impact crater, but it looked as though it were from several concentrated blasts; there were some holes in the ground, almost deep as I was tall; and the area itself had sunk about a foot below the rest the surrounding town.

Though in the center, the Spire stood. Black, straight, and narrow as the other three; it shot up into the Red Sky, unmoved by the fires of dragons. It did not fear them, for it was beyond them; how and why, I would soon discover.

I walked around the Spire, still convinced that there must be somewhere for the stone to be set, though I could not find anything; the surface was smooth all the way around. Peculiarly, I noticed that there was no reflection in the face of the Spire. I stepped towards it, hoping to catch some glimpse of my movement but it was black as shadow; impenetrable. I almost didn't see the hole at the base of it, quickly pulling my foot back and catching my balance after I stepped and found nothing.

I looked down, the hole following the wall of the Spire down, down, down; it seemed to go deeper than the rest, and the ground around it looked caved in, more than anything. With how deep it was, I thought there was a good chance it would run to the Catacombs below. I thought about exploring the rest of the town—in case I found survivors, hopefully having been freed from Azazel's spell. That would mean that whatever spell was keeping the monsters out of Castleford would be lifted as well, and if the Dawnflayer was any indication that more might be heading for Azazel; I didn't want to be there when they arrived. And I knew, deep in my heart, that there were likely no survivors left above ground, after the fires blanketed the city. If anyone had managed to hide, they deserved to remain unfound; at least until all this was over.

The ceiling *had* caved in on a chamber of some kind. I was able to climb down a stone wall that had been constructed alongside the Spire, much like in the Alduin Academy. When I reached the bottom, I saw that the masonry was very similar to chambers found in the Catacombs—it was evident that they had all been built at the same time, by the same people; who that was, I did not know. But it was there, in that chamber, that I found what I was looking for: the Ruby's home.

Set against the shadow-black of the Spire was a plate made of something very similar to the door in the cave where the Black Dragon slept. Its look resembled metal, but not entirely; something was off about it, I just couldn't quite explain. The touch was off, too. It wasn't cold and uninviting like most metals I had felt, rather it seemed warm to the touch; I could feel it radiating through my fingertips as I ran them over the face of the placard. There were strange markings to the left and right of the Stone's slot, running vertically. They looked very similar to my memory of the markings on the cave door as well.

I suddenly *felt* the stone reacting. I held it out, and it faintly glowed. It seemed as though there was some power left still within it, and I could see something in the glow that caught my attention, drawing me in. I was lost in a trance, and I thought I heard voices in the back of my head urging me to slot the Stone. I closed my eyes as if to quiet the voices, and opened them when I felt my hand extend.

Whether I meant to or not, I had inserted the Stone. It clicked home, feeling as though it jumped from my hand. Once it had gone, I stood back, looking at the Spire, waiting for something to happen.

Nothing did.

I took a step forward and reached out for the stone with my left hand.

"Don't!" A weak, raspy voice shrieked at me as if from all around —as was the custom in these times, it seemed. "The stone must remain here," it said.

"Why?" My hand started to hurt. I turned it to look at the Onyx, its black tendrils reaching out from the Stone buried just beneath the skin.

"We must go home," it said. "It is home."

I tried to ask more questions, but the Onyx wouldn't respond. It must have used what strength it had to warn me from retaking the depleted Ruby. Perhaps the Spires would recharge them, being their 'homes'? The powers would prove most useful, especially for facing *three* dragons. I just wished I knew for sure what would happen if I returned the Stones, assuming that each of them had chambers like this; hoping that they connected to the Catacombs.

I waited for a moment, to see if anything would happen to the Ruby; but nothing did. It sat in its slot, the faint glow having faded, the deep red stone all that remained. It almost disappeared into the black of the Spire.

The thought of leaving it there was not something I wanted to think about. It was one of only *two* of the four Stones that I might have had some idea of the use for; I didn't want to leave it behind, in the chance that it might regain a charge shortly after my leaving.

Worse still was the thought of all four Stones needing to be set in order for them to charge, which had entered my mind as I waited for some activity in the Ruby, looking at the others in my hand with much thought. I could ill afford the time to travel to each city's Catacombs to find the Spire Chamber, let alone time to backtrack and retrieve them all if it worked.

So I thought of a compromise: I would leave the Ruby and travel to Dewpond. The Catacombs there were the most familiar to me, and the Stone was the least. On my way to Brakas, I would return through Castleford, and check on the Ruby. If it was active again, I would retrieve it and double back for the Sapphire before continuing, probably north and finishing in Brakas. If not, I would end in Alduin.

Thought it wasn't a vision, I saw the Moon in my mind's eye, and what I knew in my heart what was within. I wondered in silence what would happen if the dragons came down. Surely they would own these lands once more; what's left of humankind bred like cattle for slaughter. I saw it all in the blink of an eye, and I felt the fear that had always been there—though I had gotten quite adept at pushing it to the back of my mind.

There was no way that I would be able to fight the dragons without the Stones. Legends told of them being immortal—though they *did* fall to something—and if I were to die, I wanted it to be with the best possible odds, so I decided to leave the Ruby and make for Dewpond, scanning my mind for any chambers like the one I had been standing in and finding nothing.

There was also the matter of potential survivors. I could not be sure that Azazel had lured everyone up to the surface. Though the thought of some being able to resist his spell, while I had fallen for his mere words, made me feel ever more foolish.

The rest of the chamber was, for the most part, empty; there were a few placards on the wall: signs bearing the crest of Castleford. It was the silhouette of the Castle on the Mountain, standing before a beautiful sunrise. The wall opposite the Spire had a single iron door set against the stone, heavy rivets holding it in place. I pulled the door, which opened to a small hallway; only a few paces long.

At the end of the hallway was another door, smaller this time, and of lighter construction. I pushed it open, and found that I was standing in a kitchen of some kind. I looked behind me as the door fell shut and saw that it was a part of the wood paneling, where the cooks could hang what tools they had, as well as pots and pans. It was far more elaborate than the mess hall we had to the Northwest. Most of our food was prepared in batches, by whoever was on kitchen detail. This appeared set to be used by many, and all at once.

The hallway was hidden, I could tell as the door fell closed. Now that I knew it was there, I could see the seams; though it would be easy to mistake them for natural breaks in construction, looking at the rest of the wall. It also only opened *out* into the kitchen, so unless it was pulled on in just the right manner, there would be no noticeable movement from the door. I couldn't help but admire the design and wonder where such craftsmanship might exist in Dewpond.

It would be easy to guess, knowing where the Spire stands—they are hard to miss—though it would be easy to lose track underground, should the hallways wind enough. I would also need to go to the surface in order to get my bearings, and that could prove dangerous; though it was likely that there were more enemies below ground than above, thanks to the dragon's fire. But even once I found the location of the Spire, I would have to figure out which side the chamber was on, and search rooms adjacent. I was currently on the Western side of the Southern Spire, so reason did not seem to play into the placement, perhaps on purpose.

Though now that I had seen what manner of hiding they employed, it might help me locate something similar in the other Catacombs.

There was an eerie calm over the room, and the same calm permeated the others I checked while I was down below. I was able to find a great deal of evidence that the people of Castleford were known for their crafts. There was a familiarity to the designs of the weapons and armor that I found, though it seemed to me very common.

Nothing of use to me was found, nor did it seem that there was anyone remaining, though I did not take the time to check thoroughly. There may yet have been people hiding there, smartly avoiding any exposure that might lead them to harm.

I didn't blame them. Part of me wished that I could have remained down below, ignorant and unawares of the world as it was, and as it ought to be—which seemed to vary, depending on who you asked. It was a quest that I did not undertake lightly, nor with great enthusiasm; yet there I was, cutting down the ever-dwindling numbers of undead soldiers (which was where I recognized the armor from, confirming my suspicions that Azazel had been arming them as well; his control over the people of Castleford running deep), traveling to restore hidden power to Stones so that I might stop the race of dragons from returning to claim their Dark Throne.

It was madness; but I was thriving in it. Chosen by fate, I may have been. But I am no longer chosen; rather, I am *choosing*. Every step I took from the moment Azazel was killed was my own, and for once I felt in control of my own destiny. And even though it was presumably the Onyx that told me the Stones needed to be returned, the choice remained mine. Of the paths before me—confront the dragons, or hide —the one I chose required the Stones.

And so it was that I went onward to Dewpond, where I briefly looked above ground to locate the Spire. I saw it amidst the ashes of the Library, and remembered my first meeting with Rayna, as well as the fight with Brok in the courtyard outside. It was gone now, only the memory remains. Had they only trusted me, would things be different? Would they be traveling with me?

There was no time for regrets, and no time to reminisce. I returned below ground and navigated the maze of hallways until I was sure I was by the Spire. I could not know how the deep the Spire went, but to my knowledge the Dewpond Catacombs had only one level, unlike Alduin's, which had two.

When I found the door to the Spire Chamber in Dewpond, it was where the laundry was usually kept. There were wooden shelves that ran the length of the long closet, set against heavy wooden backing board. There was a seam in the board that I noticed did not run all the way up to the ceiling. The shelves were easy to remove, and I found behind one of them a latch which made the door spring free from the wall. I pulled it open and entered. It was difficult by design.

Beyond that was the same as Castleford: the same hallway; the same heavy iron door; the same small chamber adorned with the crests of the city above—an open book with the Sun on one page, the Moon on the other; and finally the Spire itself between. The placard was the same, dark and made of whatever it was made of. I pulled out the Sapphire, which glowed similarly to the Ruby, only blue, and slotted it into the Spire wall. It returned home with a click and I took a step backwards.

After I was satisfied that nothing would happen, I made my way back to Castleford. Part of me wanted to return to the surface, to see what was happening above; I had already spent a considerable amount of time on my journey, and while I was fast on my feet, I still needed breaks. I just kept telling myself that it didn't matter how long it took; the Stones having power was my only chance of defeating *any* dragons, whether it was three or three thousand.

It was as I feared when I returned to Castleford: the Ruby remained dormant, locked within the Spire. I tried to remove it, to see if I could will it to life in the palm of my hand, but some force kept it from me. Its glow had returned, but remained faint. I thought better of waiting any longer, and continued to Brakas, briefly searching the East side of the Castleford Catacombs on my way out, finding nothing.

Brakas was largely the same, although the tunnels leading to it were much more crowded with the undead. It also appeared as though several of the creatures from the pit had made it down below, including one of the six eyed monsters I had encountered south of the Faerie's Forest. I was able to cut through most of them with relative ease, but they slowed my journey down considerably. I was beginning to grow anxious about time, and hurried my trek, pushing myself to the brink before taking slowing. I had managed to keep my strength up using some herbs and tonic that I had found in Dewpond, having known where such things would be.

The actual Catacombs in Brakas were largely bereft of movement, save for me desperately searching for a way into the secret chamber. I found it on the South side of the Spire, behind a large painting of Father Paxton; though it did not appear as though that painting was the one originally there, and I began to wonder who the Father had replaced.

The Chamber itself was different as well, though still adorned with the crest of Brakas; a woman's silhouette with two wings: one beautiful and feathered, like a bird; the other webbed and sharp, not unlike a dragon. It was meant to represent the duality of the town, renowned for its liberal nature just as much as its conservative. On either side of the crests were elaborate candelabras, the same as those I saw in the Church above. Beside the Spire there was a pedestal with a book on each side. The one on the right was open to a blank page, save for one signature toward the top. The other was printed, symbols not unlike the ones around the stone's slot on the Spire. I flipped through each book, but was unable to find anything of use to me. I quickly placed the Emerald into the slot, and as soon as I heard the click I turned; though I thought I saw a green light begin to glow as I was turning.

It was when I turned North to Alduin, the only place I had not been below ground yet, that I finally began to learn the true purpose of the Spires, bittersweet as it may be.

The Four Before

When I reached the doors of the Alduin Catacombs, they were sealed tight. Though I tried to move them, my strength proved not enough to break them free from their holds. And when I heard the voice calling out to me from the other side of the door, I knew why the door remained closed.

"The soldiers of the dead aren't so persistent," the voice said. "Who goes there?" It wasn't the same voice as before, when I visited the door above; though it was the same words. I had hoped the fires hadn't broken through, and infected the halls below.

"I seek to end the Night," I said, feeling emboldened as I said it. "I have in my possession the Onyx; the precious gem of your city. I seek to return it to where it belongs, and in order to do so I need you to open this door."

There was a small laugh from the other side of the door. "You must be someone to be still alive out there; the world of man is over beyond these doors, far as we could tell. How do you plan on ending the cursed Night?"

I thought hard about what I could try to convince him, but honesty seemed like the best course of action. "As I said, I have the Onyx; though it is spent, and I very much hope that returning it to the Spire will recharge it, so that I might use it against the dragons."

"*Dragons?*" the voice stumbled over the word. There was a silence. "So it *is* as we feared," he said to himself. After a second, there was the click of a latch, and a viewport in the door opened, large enough to see the entire man's face—it was dirty, the hair long and matted down by oils and sweat; he wore a long beard, though it, too, was unkempt. He looked me over with what seemed like one good eye, and then balked. "Where's the Stone?"

I held out my left hand, and flipped it over so that the palm was facing upwards, so that he might see the stone lodged into my skin.

"With me the same as it has been," I said. "It is a Stone that values closeness above all else."

"Quite," the Doorman nodded, and stepped out of view. There was another loud sound of a latch, and the whole door began to move, opening outwards into the hall.

The Doorman gestured for me to enter the chamber that he had been standing guard in. I wasn't sure of the original purpose, but it seemed to me that it had been outfitted as a guard chamber. There was a weapon rack on the wall to the right of the door, a small wooden chair and a large flask with some kind of liquid in it was sitting next to that. There was another door on the other end of the room, just as heavy as the one I had passed through. I tried to wonder if the Northern Catacombs were always this way, or if they used their cunning to convert it, after the fighting began down here.

I thought to say that I was from the Western Catacombs, hoping that the sting of the battle, and all those lost, was long gone by then; but it then dawn on me that I had largely been responsible for those fights beginning as well. It was I that brought to light the invader, come from the North to pilfer our supplies; though with things going the way that they were, it was only a matter of time before humanity resolved to open conflict, as they had so many times before.

I walked towards the door on the other side of the makeshift Guard's Room when the guard himself stepped between me and the door. Now that I could see more than his face, I could see that he was a shorter man—his eyes stared directly into my chest, and I wondered for but a second if he might be a tall Halfling, another creature of legend—though he was attired with iron plate, tunics and trousers with thick leather hides stitched to them under the plate. I understood why he was sweating almost at once when I saw how he was dressed. He probably hasn't seen a sword in months, since the fighting moved topside; but still he wears the armor. It was noble, if not questionably foolish.

"Where are the others?" He stood between me and the second door. He crossed his arms and I could hear his foot tapping on the ground. "The other Stones, do you have them as well?"

"I did," I nodded, "but I do not have them with me now. That is why I must find a chamber hidden within your tunnels here: within it is access to the base of to Spire above, and the slot in which the stones seem *made* to fit—or they were made to fit these Stones," I shook my head, losing myself in the thoughts. "Either way, I must return the Onyx to the Spire, in the hopes that I can regain the powers. It is the only hope I have in facing the dragons."

The guard paused, looking off to the side pensively before turning back to me with a nod. "Maybe if it were a better secret, the woman at the school wouldn't have been able to take the damned thing from where it was." I saw no movement, but I heard the latch on the door behind the guard release. "My name is Horace, by the way," he said coldly, continuing: "And if you so much as reach for that blade of yours, we *will* cut you down." He moved in close to me, saying under his breath: "We've gotten quite used to living in the dark, Mr. Hero."

He took me through hallways littered with people, some walking while others were just sitting against the walls. The halls were wide here, made of stone bricks, though they seemed to be just as sweaty as the people down here. I was beginning to notice the heat as well. It then occurred to me: as the ground above cooked under the dragon's flame, the tunnels below the ground would heat up. It was surely the only reason the flames still stayed; not to mention why they razed everything above ground, and not just the cities. Were the flames still burning in Alduin? Why would they focus their fire here?

They were trying to smoke out survivors.

"I can't take you all the way to where you want to go," Horace said as we walked. We passed a woman with a small child, though the child was eerily quiet, and the woman was beside herself with grief. "Though I don't mean to delay you, if you plan to do what you say; as you can see, things have reached almost bottom here. We long for the surface once more, though most of us remaining have never seen it."

I let out a sigh. Part of me wanted to hold my tongue, to maintain some level of hope in these people; but alas, I spoke. "The surface is gone, Horace; burned away by the dragons. I fear things down here, by my eyes, are far more hopeful than things above. Even if I am able to complete my mission, and restore the light, there is much work for us to do in order to restore things as they once were. Were you born before the Night?"

Horace shook his head. "I was born down here, first year of the Long Night," he said as we rounded a corner into a much more narrow hallway, forcing us to walk single-file with Horace at the head. "I had pulled guard duty on the surface door a few times, but have never seen it in the light. Is it as beautiful as all of the elders say?"

I thought for a second, wistful. There was a feeling there, or a memory of a feeling; but there was no image, at least no clear one. All I could see was light, filling the picture until it was white. The warmth I felt, touching my skin like a soft cloth that had been sitting in front of a roaring fire, warm but dry. I felt the hot rays of the sun pushing on my forehead, threatening to burn it if I weren't careful. I thought about the sweat, not from activity but just from ambience, pooling on my lower back and brow. I felt all of it, all at once, and for a moment I felt as though it was a fool's errand to want to feel all of those things once more.

I had no doubt in my quest; I felt as though I was far from finished. And while I had hoped that the Stones would even the odds against the dragons, I held no illusions about my chances. These beasts managed to enslave our entire race, and use them as food and playthings for countless ages; how could just one of us hope to stop three of them, including the Mother of all Dragons?

The doubt kept repeating itself, but it was growing weaker each time. Something inside of me was pushing through it in a way that I had never quite experienced before. There was a resolve, unspoken, that simmered just beneath the surface of that doubt, beginning to shine through. As I looked upon the people in the Alduin Catacombs—quite possibly the last survivors of the human race—I felt that I *had* to succeed, no matter what the cost, so that these people might have a chance at life and light once more. We weren't out of chances yet, dammit.

"Where are you taking me?" I asked, after a few moments of quiet walking.

"The Master of Records, Iowyn," Horace said, looking over his shoulder at me. "She might be the only one down here that still knows where that chamber is, other than myself. And I'm not supposed to know where it is, so to avoid getting a tongue lashing, I will let her show you. Used to be Lady Artemis' apprentice, so she knows almost as much as the headmistress when it comes to these lands. She might be able to answer some questions for you as well, should you have any."

He took me to a room filled with desks. There were seven rows of five desks each, though they looked to be the desks of young students, not taking up much room. The chairs by them were not attached, but appeared to be part of a set, following the same rudimentary construction. They were made to be built fast, not sturdy. At the head of the room was a larger desk, with legs of iron and a table made of thick, heavy wood. Atop it were several books, some open, most stacked to the side. There were books on the ground next to the desk as well, and the stone wall was covered by a large placard of wood, which was covered with pages removed from books. I saw the marking that I had seen in Py's hut, and the library, and so many other places on my journey; the seven-pointed rune, the cross with a diamond around the middle. Behind the desk sat a woman, reading hurriedly.

Iowyn looked young, though she was older than I. She seemed learned, and the serious expression that she wore on her face was intimidating. Her eyes were piercing beneath furrowed, dark eyebrows. Her hair was black, and tied back tightly. She wore a white shirt, fitted but the material was thick, and looked warm. She seemed small in stature, even from a seated position, and I wondered if her feet were even touching the ground under the desk; though I thought better of asking.

"This here's Iowyn," Horace said before departing with a nod to both of us. He closed the door behind him.

"How long have you been up there?" Iowyn asked without looking up from the desk. "And where all have you been?"

I shook my head. "Not sure how long—hard to tell the days from the nights when I could only see the Moon; beyond that I can't say I ever tried to count." I shifted in place, crossing my arms across my chest. "Long enough," I said.

"As for where I've been: I've been to each of the four major cities, and passed through several villages in between; I have been to the Necropolis; I have been to Azazel's Castle and the Mountain to the South; and now I can say that I have been to the Catacombs beneath each of the cities." I drew a deep breath, and exhaled, shrugging my shoulders. "I haven't decided where I will go next."

Iowyn just nodded, dumbstruck by my story. She caught herself, shaking off the shock and clearing her throat. "Was it just you?"

I shook my head. "There was a Wisp with me—at least, that's what we think she was—that remained in the Necropolis. I'm not sure if she survived the Black Dragon's Fire or not."

Iowyn was taken aback by something I said, but the surprise quickly changed to fear. "The Black Dragon is free?" She stood up from her chair—there was a small, almost imperceptible hop down—and pressed her fingers to her temples. She looked up at me, moving from behind the desk, as though she had a thousand questions and didn't know where to begin. I watched her as she stepped towards me, then away; all the while trying to pluck something—*anything*—out of the air. After a moment she stopped pacing, just before I began to lose patience, considering what was happening outside.

"If you fear her then you know there is little time for talk," I said, taking a step towards Iowyn. She backed up a step. "I do have questions for you, but the first and most pressing is where the Spire Chamber is; I have a Stone to return." I held up the Onyx, and Iowyn took three large steps away, cowering in fear at the sight of it.

"If not for our need of it, I'd wish that thing destroyed," she said

from behind her arms. "If you have it then surely you must have witnessed what the Academy looks like now!" She paused for a second,
lowering her arms and giving me a perplexing glance. "*You* were the
one knocking, all that time ago!" She raised her arms once more when
she saw I still held out my hand with the Onyx showing. "It will take
you as it took Artemis—though she took it first."

I lowered my hand. "What do you mean?"

"That Wizard from the South promised her knowledge of all
things; then, now and forever," Iowyn said, catching my attention.
"All she had to do was remove the Stone from the Spire."

"Artemis removed the Stone?"

Iowyn nodded. "She pretended to debate it, as though she hadn't
already succumbed to his tempting promise; she always sought
knowledge, often talking at length to students who had traveled from
lands she was unfamiliar with. She wanted to know everything that
there was to know about Alghast, from beginning to end." Iowyn
bowed her head. "When I last saw her, she was being cocooned by the
very knowledge she sought, in what used to be the cafeteria. And
now?"

"Artemis is dead," I said.

"She died long before now," she said softly, nodding. "And what
of the Wizard?"

"Azazel?" I said, and with images flashing in my mind of his mu-
tilated corpse; "he is also dead."

Iowyn started walking to the door of her chamber. "I will show
you to the Spire," she said. "Where are the other Stones?"

"Returned to their Spires," I said. "I only hope that this returns
their power to them, so that I might use it to fight the dragons."

She stopped. Turning back to me, she said: "That is not what will
happen." She looked me in the eyes, searching for something before
turning back to the door, walking through. I followed. "Returning the
stones will reactivate the Spires—hopefully."

"What do they do?" I asked while trying to keep pace.

"We're not sure," she said after a moment. "Some think they keep
the Sun in the sky; while others wonder if that may be what made the
dragons mortal in the first place. There is much we do not know about
the quest of those four; the ones who ended the dragons' reign and
brought about the First Day."

"Who were these four?"

"Four who stood up to the dragons, and it is said the Heart of
Darkness itself. When they returned, they had with them four stones,
each said to possess one of the strengths of the dragons; in a bid to

activate whatever ancient machine they had built."

"The Spires," I said aloud, but only to myself.

"Yes, and there was something else; the Gate over the Pit."

"So they set the stones and, what?" She rounded corners so quickly that I almost had to jog to keep up. "Did that banish the monsters to the Pit; make the dragons mortal; or did it bring about the Day? Was it all three?"

"It's difficult to say. And if the Stones are drained of their power, as you say, it's likely that we won't find out today. In their weakened state they may not do much." She pushed through a door, and we were in a dormitory. There was no one there, only four cots set against the right wall. There were three beds and a dresser on the left. Iowyn walked to the dresser and stopped. "Though we may be able to set the balance in our favor." She pulled on the dresser, revealing the path to the Chamber.

The Alduin Chamber was like the Dewpond and Castleford ones; though the banner here was a three-pointed star, a white circle in the center. Besides that, there was little to the room other than the Spire itself, and the indent where the Onyx would reside. I stopped as we entered. "And how would we do that?"

She turned to face me and then gestured to the Spire. "Let's see if we need to, first."

I stepped to the Spire after some hesitation, and looked down at the palm of my hand. The Onyx made no move to release itself from my palm, so I held it, outward towards the Spire, moving towards it. I pictured the Spire pulling the Onyx, ripping it from my skin and taking it back, as though I was the one that stole it in the first place.

But it wasn't violent; it wasn't even unpleasant. I didn't feel the Onyx transfer from my hand to the Spire, because as soon as I placed my hand on the placard, I felt not the stone leaving me—I only heard the *click* to indicate that it had returned home—but rather the sting of a light; a light so vibrant and bright that I thought for a second that I had gone blind.

And when I could see again, I was no longer in the secret Chamber of the Spire in the Northern Catacombs.

Guided by the Past

The white light gave way to many images, filing in rapidly and overlapping one another in my mind. I could see the picture behind, though it was just out of reach. But I saw so many things. Things that I wish I could go back and see again, if only that I might remember them correctly.

I do remember seeing the Black Dragon, floating calmly in the Dark Energy emerging from the Pit, its wings wrapped around itself as though it were resting—if it hadn't already rested enough. I saw the Moon cracking, like an egg starting to hatch, which only served to confirm suspicions I had before, as ludicrous as they may have sounded to me. Then I saw flashes of the land, in various states from the beginning, when nothing existed and before the first Emergence; then I saw the world of Man begin to take hold, and the Spires were erected; then the Darkness went away. The Sun rose on the horizon and my eyes once again filled with white until it was not the light that left, but shadows that came to me; four of them, to be exact.

There was a Man, young and idealistic looking. His hair was long —just below the shoulders—and straight. There was a short beard on the hardened face, even though the bright eyes and shining hair seemed to betray the toughness. He was clad in leathers, crude armor at best; though he was still the most protected of the four that I saw.

Next to him was a Woman; older by almost a lifetime though not showing many of the usual wear that comes with such an age. She wore not armor, but her clothes fit tight and seemed to favor movement; quick and nimble, although you might not expect it by looking at her aged face.

Third, there was a Faerie. I could see its true form, standing about half as tall as the others on feet made of many tentacles, writhing along the ground as if constantly searching for something. I could not tell if it was man or woman, though when it finally spoke I heard a man's voice coming from it. The face was more narrow and long than the ones I had seen before were, yet the hair was still alive like snakes, and it was hard to not get lost in the eyes, as they seemed the type to stare into one's soul. It did not seem to have the same vertical mouth as Py, though it is possible that it did not need to open it to speak, his voice entering my ears by way of my mind.

The final figure, I couldn't quite see. As the others stepped forward, out of the light and to where I could see them, the fourth—a man—remained shrouded in the light. I kept looking to him, past the others as they stood before me, confusion mounting on top of confusion; I was getting used to these visions, mind you. They proved to be quite common in relation to the strange magic I had found myself entangled in.

"The Stones have been returned," the Man said, stepping towards me. The white light all around us cast a heavenly aura around him. There was a sense of wonder that washed over me as he spoke. He did not move his mouth; instead, it was as if his voice was coming from everywhere, but I knew it was him talking.

"Though I fear they are far too weak to end the Night," said the Faerie.

"Humankind had enjoyed the fruits of our efforts far too much, it seems," said the Woman. "Though the perseverance of this one shows what I have always said: there must be something to balance the True Dark, awaiting outside."

"If he is the proof of the best of man, then should we not look within ourselves to see the balance to that?" asked the Faerie.

The Man, as though offended, scoffed. "Had we listened to counsel, this might have been avoided. But our desire to *end* the dragons, rather than return them to the True Dark with all of the other monsters it spawned, it seems, has truly betrayed us."

"It's because they were smarter than us," the shrouded man said. "We saw that as something to be feared, rather than respected. When we did what we did, and activated our machine; we showed that we could be stronger, *together*. They could have taught us so much, if we only shared the world with them—" he stepped forward, his face becoming clearer—"rather than try to take it from them. All in pursuit of revenge!" *It couldn't be.* I could see his whole face now. "But would a farmer not question cattle, should it try to revolt? I have been both savior and destroyer of my own race, all for something that was never within my grasp; my vision was clouded by promises, and so I clouded the vision of others. There is no balance between human and dragon; I know now that as long as there is dragon, there is *only* dragon," said Azazel.

They continued to speak as though I wasn't there, including Azazel; the one who, as far as I had learned, played a part in starting the Long Night. It was the same Azazel that had used me to retrieve the Stones for him, so that he might release the Black Dragon. Was I to take his presence here to mean he was one of the four who secured the Stones in the legends?

I realized I had gotten lost in thought, losing some of their conversation, though I returned my attention just as it was turning to address me.

"—there is not enough strength left in the stones for that," the Woman was saying. "It is clear to me that we must ask a favor of the poor Traveler. Which favor that may be, I do not know."

"Either way, he must go to the North," said the Man.

"The Stones are not completely without power," said the Faerie. "There may be enough to partially activate the machine."

"What do you mean?" asked Azazel. He looked at me with heavy eyes, as though there was some element of embarrassment in him.

I just kept seeing his body in the cave.

"We might not be able to break through the fog of the Mountain; but we could try to return the monsters and close the Gate." The Faerie brought a hand to his chin, deep in thought. "Activating the Spires, though, trying to close the Pit, the magic is imprecise; it would include all things living above ground—that's why the Catacombs were built in secret—*except* the dragons. We could also make the dragons mortal." Azazel gasped at this. The Faerie continued: "That would still prove to be a difficult task for one who faces a dragon in combat, for we are still designed to be their prey, you and I. No matter which one we try, someone will still need to go to the North, to the Mountain, where the Heart of Darkness and the Crystals from which these Stones were gathered lie. We used the Crystals to subdue the Heart, and the power of the Black Dragon. We chose mercy over reason on that day. If you wish to stop the flow of Darkness, feeding the thing you *know* is in the Moon above; you must travel north to the Mountain and drive your sword deep into the Heart of Darkness. Then, and only then, can Day return, to keep the Dark below."

The Faerie spoke and I tried to listen, though my attention was caught by Azazel, standing just off to the side, separate from the other three. I finally broke my silence. "Why is he here?"

The Faerie stopped and all three of them turned to face the Wizard, then back to me. "His soul has finally returned," the Faerie said.

"Though we haven't seen our friend in some time," said the Man.

"I gather there is much to talk about, given how our last meeting went."

Azazel merely nodded in silence. The Woman stepped forward. "Our souls were bound to the stones, as here is where we are meant to spend eternity, should our counsel ever be needed again. It came as much of a shock to the three of us when Azazel failed to arrive, even after so long."

"Was that a gift from my kind, or theirs?" the Faerie stroked his chin once more. "I wonder."

I began to wonder myself. Azazel always spoke as though he wasn't human—although I knew now that he thought himself *more* than human—but legends of his long life were abundant. It was clear, just by his presence there in that world of light, that he was older than even *I* had guessed. No one ever quite knew how long ago the Spires were first built; let alone what they could do. I began to wonder if time was passing in the Chamber at the same length as it was in my vision, if it even *was* a vision. Then my thoughts returned to the Wizard, one of the Four that brought about the First Day; but also the one that set in motion a plot that would bring about the Long Night and, eventually, the awakening of the Black Dragon.

How could he turn his back on us? And what was the cost to him after such a long life?

"There is much we must discuss with our compatriot," said the Faerie, nodding to me in farewell.

"This is where we part ways, I fear," said the Man.

"You can end the Darkness, Traveler. Once and for all," said the Woman.

Azazel stood silent as the lights dimmed around us all, the walls of the Chamber slipping into view as though it were a shadow itself. I felt uneasy as I got used to seeing the floor beneath me, not realizing that I had felt like I was floating. I tried to steady myself, but I could hear a sound somewhere in the distance, repeating itself. It was Iowyn, calling out to me.

"How long was I gone?" I asked, gasping for air as though I hadn't drawn any in some time.

"You didn't *go* anywhere," she said. "You froze here, with your hand on the Spire, unmoving."

My breath sped up as I tried to remember where I was. "I must go to the Mountain," I finally said. I was determined that it was the right choice; my journey had no other place to end. I thought about staying in the Catacombs, with the people of Alduin; but underground was no way for us to live.

I heard no objections, although they were given. I could not afford to allow doubt to enter my mind.

And as I stood in the Chamber, I heard a voice call out:

"What do you choose?" she asked.

I took a deep breath, in through the nose.

"Make them mortal," I said.

Resurfacing

Iowyn had lead me through the Catacombs, and up to the second level where the bulk of the actual dormitories seemed to be. As we passed by them, I saw people lying in cots with arms draped over their eyes, and others still who were sitting against the wall with their face buried between their knees. There was a low rumbling coming from above that seemed to permeate everything on this level, and I wondered how much all of these people had to heard as they tried to sleep.

If they could even sleep at all.

I exited through the door that I had knocked at earlier, when I first came to Alduin. I had been below ground long enough that the dragon's fire had waned, low embers still burning on the ground but the towering flames all but gone; as was everything else in the town.

I felt a snowflake land on my face, big and heavier than I remembered snow being, even as a youth. It also seemed far too warm for snow, so I curiously wiped at the flake that had landed on my face, bringing back fingers colored black with ash.

I looked up to the sky around me and I saw ash falling as though it were coming from the sky. But I knew where it was coming from; I had seen Alduin before and it was not the flat and barren land that was before me as I emerged from the Catacombs there. The ash on my face could have been just a remnant—one piece of thousands upon thousands, floating listlessly through the air, serving as just a memory for those who saw what *used* to be.

Though I was getting tired of thinking about what *used* to be.

I began to wonder how much of everything Py knew. It was as I was having that thought that another found its way into my mind: how much of this was *real?*

Azazel and Py—the Faeries at large, it seemed—had a knack for illusions; what's to say there wasn't still some kind of veil being pulled over my eyes? Perhaps there was yet more to be revealed, as fate seemed to be far from done with pulling the rug out from under me. It was baffling how ingrained into all of this Azazel was, being both the savior and destructor of the human race; and it was all for nothing. He doesn't even get to witness the death and destruction he has wrought on the world he once set out to reclaim.

My journey to the North, to the Heart of the Mountain—which seemed to be where the Red Sky I saw was bleeding from—would take me through the Faerie Forest again, as there was only one path. I would be remiss if I didn't pause to at least speak to the ones that took such good care of me after the Necropolis, where Azazel's betrayal had first been revealed to me.

And where was Kat? She had seemed so... *odd* when I saw her at the Necropolis as I headed south, almost as if she wasn't herself. Not that I knew the woman well to begin with, given our interactions largely limited to shift changes on guard duty, prior to my getting her exiled from the Catacombs.

Iowyn's interest in my traveling companion being a Wisp was not lost on me, either; I was already out of the Catacombs and heading on my way north through the open fields of ash before the thought occurred to me, and by then it was too late to go back.

I did not walk without fear or trepidation, either. The dragon's Fire had leveled everything—no structures remained as far as the eye could see, save for the sturdy outpost that lead down below. It was only a matter of time before one of the twins made their way down there, I thought, and put an end to humans once and for all.

Or perhaps they meant to leave the survivors below. They would need us, once again, for food. If they could keep us underground and breeding, then smoke us out when they get too hungry, I imagined that they would be able to keep what's left of mankind from getting too comfortable. We would be forced to stay on the move, to keep them guessing. But if the Moon 'hatched' and all of those dragons came down to the surface?

I wondered if maybe eliminating the food supply might be the only option, but what would keep them from moving on to another world? Was that even within their power?

There was still so much I didn't understand: magic, the Spires, and the large beating Heart with the four Crystals in the Mountain to the North; where did it all come from?

I knew I didn't have time to get the answers. There was no time for answers at all anymore; hardly even any time for conversation. As I stole a glance to the South, I saw the Dark Energy pulsing from the

Pit, the silhouette of the Black Dragon resting within the beam, waiting for her children to return to her.

The Moon itself was vacuous. I meant only to steal a glance before continuing on my way, but the black at its core had become so powerful that it pulled my gaze to it and wouldn't let it go. It was as though I could hear the screams of the people; I could feel the fire of the flames; I could smell the death and destruction and the burning flesh and forests. Then I could see the dragons; smaller and younger than even the Twins, impatiently waiting to be free and have a world to call their own—which is really all *we* wanted, too.

I began to piece some things together in my head as I passed through the Northern border of Alduin, into the Woods, hoping that Py would guide me through once she detected that I had returned.

The dragons in the Moon, I gathered, were still young. There was a reason why Azazel waited as long as he did, I suppose, to tempt the others into removing their stones and deactivating the Spires. It seemed to me that not only did Azazel need to regain strength—his castle was hidden from view for quite a long time though he was never truly gone—but as did the Black Dragon, deep within the prison that was created for her in the South Mountain. The Moon also needed time, I gathered, to gestate so many dragons; though the vision Py showed me seemed to imply this had been attempted before, so I couldn't be sure. Perhaps he just needed to wait for history to become legend, so that he could operate under the nose of mankind's infamous ignorance.

Then I remembered the Black Dragon after she had left the cave, and killed Azazel. She almost seemed to *feed* on the Darkness around us, giving her mass and strength. Perhaps the Darkness from the pit was feeding the Moon, giving the dragons within strength and life.

I had made it fairly deep into the woods without much incident—only a few monsters still remained that had wandered further north from the town, into the forest where the Fires hadn't yet spread. I had made the right choice, if it had worked at all; I couldn't imagine that the trek could have gone much easier, had I decided to reseal the Pit yet leave the dragons invulnerable. I could only hope that they were left unaware to their new weakness, so that I might use *their* arrogance to my advantage.

As I feared, I began to lose my way in the woods, much as I had when leaving them all that time ago. I waited for Py to intervene and guide me, at least back to the Faerie Forest; but I felt as though I was on an island, unreachable. I entered a clearing and saw signs of a battle. There were pieces of armor—marked with the crest of Alghast that the Undead had been wearing—as well as weapons scattered among the ground; longswords, maces, shields, bows, arrows, and a few spears—most broken, some not.

There were no signs to indicate it as such, but part of me began to think that I might have been looking upon Brok and Rayna's handiwork, and I lamented our final meeting, wishing that they had been around to help in the tasks at hand.

There was a rustle in the leaves of the trees, like a strong gust of wind traveling overtop and through them, though it seemed to be traveling in a path instead of a line. The sound twisted and turned, until it surrounded me, and I was enveloped by a cacophony of noises both soft and booming as the gusts began to grow into a howl, and the flapping of mighty wings broke through the steady hum with their percussive beats. I looked up through a break in the trees and saw above me a dragon, descending slowly, silhouetted by the red sky behind it.

It landed softly on the ground across the clearing from me, looking into my eyes. Its own eyes were hot, like fire, burning as they stared at me—through me. They glowed yellow in the dark, and even at a distance I could see the large black slits of its pupils locked to mine. It brewed fire in its maw, the flames escaping the side of its closed mouth as it stared. And then, without so much as moving its mouth, it spoke to me.

"Azazel is no longer around to protect you," She said. I knew at once that it was Tal, the female of the Twins that had been at Azazel's side, all the while they must have known that he would be killed. "I never was sure why he wanted to keep you alive."

Maybe he hadn't given up on people entirely; he hoped that someone would rise up as the Four had before. I thought this, but I stayed silent, staring down the beast that had landed across the clearing from me, though her size made the distance smaller than I would have liked. It didn't matter anymore why. He was dead. We were not.

"Hide with the Faeries," Tal said. "It might be the only place safe from our Fire." She was taunting me. I wasn't going to let it work. "There is no stopping what Mother has started. Soon we will take back our home, and our fires will find the tunnels that they missed so many times before, and the parasite that is humankind can be returned to its one—and only—purpose—"

I drew my sword quickly, all the while staring Tal down. My movement seemed to stop her in her tracks, as though she expected me to listen to her inane ramblings. "You talk too much," I said, breaking into a run.

Tal reacted late, caught off guard by my sudden attack; she barely made it off the ground before I had brought my sword up, narrowly missing her on the downswing. She flew above, and I heard the fires churning in her mouth. The stream she shot was narrow and fast, concentrated and designed to turn me to ash in an instant. I dove to my right and felt the heat at the bottom of my foot as the beam of fire cut into the soft ground below, and even through some of the armor and weapons left on the ground.

"Our self-proclaimed *lord*," she said with much animosity, "he let you get away with far too much. I will not grant you a quick death, do not worry; you have been a thorn in our side for too long for me to want to do anything but *rip* you to shreds and *tear* you limb from limb." She quickly descended, slamming into the ground with a loud thud. I could feel the tremor from where I stood, amidst one of the larger piles of armor, seemingly collected before whoever was doing it gave up and moved on.

We stood off for a second, and I looked very quickly for a strategy. She had a long head, flattening off at the bridge into a narrow plate that split into two horns, which curled upwards. Her neck was as long, seven or eight feet, and was covered with spiky scales, black; the underside of the neck seemed to be softer, lighter scales. She was on all fours, and at the end of each lean leg was a hand, not unlike my own with the addition of sharp talons on each finger, instead of feet. Her wings were pulled back behind her, pointing mostly up as though she were ready to lift off at any moment. Her tail reached out behind, and at the end was a club of spikes.

I had a sword.

I looked around me for something I could use, grabbing a wooden shield first, finding nothing immediately around me that I thought better than my sword. I wished for the power of the Ruby, hoping that the fire would be of some help.

I didn't even know if the Spires worked. Tal did not seem to fear harm, going so far as to threaten to toy with me rather than kill me outright. My only hope was to use that to my advantage, and strike true before she realized her new vulnerability.

Tal dashed forward, pushing off with her back legs and slashing at me with both front. She slashed a second time with each set of claws, alternating this time, and I could do nothing but dodge and deflect what I could. It was an intricate dance; one that relied more on instinct than anything, reacting to things I couldn't even comprehend: feelings that swelled up inside me and moved my body for me, as if taking me on a ride.

I slashed with my sword high, but the blade only bounced off the hard scales of Tal's neck; though me getting in close enough to attack seemed to spook her and she jumped back, away from me. She reached up to where the blade had hit—just above the shoulders—and stared at me, almost impressed.

She leapt forward once more, and I anticipated another strike with her front claws. Instead, she barreled through; it was all I could do to dive out of the way of her charge. I felt a shockwave by my head and spun in time to see the end of her tail scraping out of the impact crater it left right beside me. By the time I had returned to my feet, Tal had turned around, and was on me once more with a flurry of claw strikes. I got in close again, but she was ready; deflecting my sword with the back of one arm, she knocked me away with the back of the other. I was sent flying into a pile of armor pieces—which did not exactly break my fall.

I realized quickly that I was separated from my sword; feeling but not seeing it at the feet of Tal. At least, at where Tal's feet *had* been, for she was already on the move towards me. I fumbled around the ground, looking for something to defend myself with. When Tal realized I had not gotten up, she slowed down, and reared up on her hind legs. She seemed to extend the claws on her front legs, and I could have sworn she was smiling as she prepared to bring them down on me. As soon as she moved, I brought around what I had found—

And the spear found purchase between the soft scales, just above her breast at the base of the neck. Her confident eyes turned to shock, and the fire drained from behind them as she felt something she hadn't expected to feel: pain.

"What—" she stammered, "what did you do to me?" She looked down to see the spear, being driven deeper into her chest just by her weight; she was using all she could to paw at it, but in her desperation she only broke the wooden handle. She backed away from me, gasping for breath and clawing at the splintered handle until there was nothing left for her to grab. She collapsed onto her side and I watched as her breath slowed, and she stopped clawing herself, and her wings fell down the ground, and she was finally still.

I had killed a dragon.

The Omission

Somewhere off in the distance there was a bellowing roar, mournful; as if he knew that his sister had perished.

The cry had come from further to the North.

I was resting after my fight with Tal, though the break I took was quick, considering what I had done. I left the wooden shield, as it had fallen mostly to tatters deflecting her blows. It had served me well, but it had nothing left to offer. I began to think about my desire for a shield when I felt a tingle in my left arm. I held it up, and to my surprise the Shadow shield once formed by the Onyx appeared.

Had I regained the power?

I held up my sword, surprised and thankful that it had not broken in the fight, and called up the Ruby's flame.

Nothing.

I tried once more, but to no avail. It seemed that only one of the powers had returned to me, as if by the death of one of the dragons. Unless of course the power of one of the other stones that I had not used had come. I became frustrated at the thought until I remembered where I was.

I only hoped Py would be willing to help. And Tal had made it sound as though the Faeries were still protected somehow, which allowed that hope to drive me forward, ending the much needed break early.

The deeper I went into the Forest, the more the thick fog seemed to encircle me and close in. I began to lose track of direction, and could barely see the ground before me as I walked, the fog was becoming so thick. When I could not see things an arm's length away, I started to feel as though I was becoming consumed by it; that I would be lost in it forever. It was irrational, I knew even at the time; but I still could not shake the paranoia and fear that I would be lost in it forever.

"Stop," I commanded to the air around me.

"You failed," a voice called out from the trees. "You failed and she is awake."

"Why didn't you tell me he was one of the four? That *you* taught him his magic?" There was only silence. The fog seemed to lift slightly. "And the Twins?" I continued, paying no heed to the fog that seemed to be weakly retreating around me. "Their tricks of shapes and forms; who did they learn those from? Who were you protecting?"

There was a long silence as the question was pondered. Just when I was convinced that the conversation had ended—I could see *a* way even if it wasn't *the* way—the voice finally returned.

"Ourselves," it said. I had known all along it was Py speaking to me, but that was the first time I heard her voice, and not a collection of voices blended together to sound like something different, something powerful and haunting.

There was a cracking of wood and my eyes seemed to fail me for a second. There was movement all around me, but I couldn't place where it was coming from or where it was going. It sounded as though the trees around me had uprooted and begun to shift on their own, but my eyes couldn't confirm anything other than blurs of shapes and colors. Even as I try to recall what I saw in the forest that day, I feel my stomach turning and my head begins to spin.

When I could see again—when things started to make *sense* again —I was in the Faerie Forest, dark and concealed as it had been before. I had hoped to return to see the luminescent forest that I had seen before Py ripped from me the last of the illusions. The illusions that the Faeries had seemingly ingrained into us. But the Forest I returned to was not the one I saw in my dreams, rather the one that still left me feeling a certain sadness for the creatures. Even after I saw them as they were, their true forms, I still preferred to think of them as the woodland creatures I had laid eyes on before. It was a much more pleasant image.

I found Py standing in the center of the Faerie settlement, over a wide metal basin that was filled with ashes, atop a stand of spiraling pieces of metal rods. She seemed to be staring into the ashes, her arms hanging at her sides. She looked as though she had been trying to make sense of something, or at least was trying to find some solution; though whether it was to solve the Faerie problem of being found, or the world's problem of the dragons at large, I could never know. My faith in the Faeries had shaken.

"Why did you not tell me you helped them?" I stepped towards Py, calling my question out to her before she even turned to greet me.

"I also helped to bring about the First Day," she said slowly; "but I don't hear you asking me about *that*."

"If you knew Azazel was in league with the dragons—"

"I knew that Azazel was one of the heroes of our entire realm—when he came to me to learn his magics he was planning to use it *against* the dragons." I could hear frustration seeping into the occasional word as she spoke, trying to maintain her composure as she explained. "And once the time came," she continued, "for the Spires to be activated and the Day to begin, the dragons began to flee; unaffected by the spells that sealed the others back whence they came.

"But that wasn't enough for man," Py finally turned to me, and I could see a fresh wound running down her face, from her forehead all the way to her chin, across a now blank, white eye. "It's never enough for man."

I stayed where I was, still a few paces from Py, taking careful notice of the fresh wound. It was a deep gouge. It looked as though it were left by a claw, and I was more surprised that Py still had an eye at all on that side. I wondered if whichever one did it meant to kill, or simply maim. "Is that thanks to one of their tricks?"

Py reached up for her face. "Declan was unhappy with me for helping you, much as you are unhappy for me helping them." She looked upwards, at nothing in particular. "You can't help anyone without harming someone else, it seems."

"Perhaps I could try an easier question, since we are short on time," I said with a lower voice. My eyes met Py's one remaining, and she seemed relieved at the subject change. "There is little time for debate, but I must know at least one thing, and I am hoping that you can help me. When I ended Tal, just south of here, the power of the Onyx was returned to me. Why?"

Py started tapping on her chin with a finger. "Curious," she said. "Though the dragons' hearts are tied to Darkness; it gives them strength just as they give strength to it. The Stones, after they were used, were depleted of energy. But I have felt an overwhelming Darkness blanketing everything, as though all that has accumulated here, through days and nights and endless fights—it's as if all of it has begun to pour out to the surface. I cannot feel any light anymore, save for in you.

"If you've killed one of them then you've returned the Stones to the Spires," she continued, the doubt and fear draining from her voice. "But the Night remains, and the monsters out there remain as well; it seems as though the Stones are weak as well as blocked by the encroaching Darkness. The emergence of your power from touching the Stones, even though that was a while ago, is only stronger proof that the Darkness means to impede your progress. Was it only the Onyx that awoke?"

I shrugged my shoulders. "Out of the four, I have only held some power of the Onyx and the Ruby; I am not sure what the other two do and therefore could not know if I have obtained powers from either of them. Though surely the Onyx could be used for more than just a shield and quick attacks?"

"You do not possess the Stones themselves," Py said. "You only possess whatever you were able to absorb during your possession of the Stones. The power will be finite. As for *what* the powers are, I cannot say. Each stone is capable of many great things, but tends to gear itself towards the user.

"The Onyx, for example, is the stone that is meant to represent the knowledge of the dragons, yet you use it for protection and even self-defense." She sighed. "I do not wish to deceive you, or leave you asking questions when answers are needed so much more right now; but I cannot help you discover what you—and only you—can discover for yourself. If you discover it at all," she trailed off and turned her back to me once more.

Her doubt became mine as I looked down at my empty hands. My mind was racing, and it seemed as though I was trying to engage something within me; I just didn't know what. "Could you at least tell me what each stone was meant to represent—if such correlations exist—so that I might at least have some frame of reference on where to begin searching myself for these powers?"

Py explained to me that the stones were merely chips off the larger crystals I had seen in my visions. Each one had been extracted from the Mountain to the North, where the Heart of the invading Darkness took refuge, thousands of years ago. It blocked out the sun, and brought about endless night so that the dragons and monsters it had spawned could thrive. When the humans rose, they were able to extract from the Heart of Darkness the wisdom, power, speed, and life of the evil itself; in the form of four crystals: Onyx, Ruby, Emerald, and Sapphire.

I only wished the story had helped.

Py urged me to continue onwards, and not to wait. There were few Faeries remaining, and she feared that they would not be strong enough to hold back the dragons on their own, should the Black Dragon complete her plot to release the rest of her kind.

"Though I wonder if it isn't someone else's time," Py said quietly. "Man has done little but feed the Darkness for centuries with their hate and want for what they do not have. There is no 'good enough' for man."

I couldn't correct her.

We bid one another farewell, and I continued north towards the Mountain. The woods there were thick as well, though there was no fog to speak of. The trunks of the trees around me stood incredibly tall and naked, save for their bark, before exploding into a tapestry of branches that blocked out the sky above almost entirely—just small flecks of red were piercing through. There was a wide path cut into the woods, although it looked less cut as I went on, and more as though the trees took caution to grow around, so they might watch fools such as myself, making the journey north.

I continued walking on the path for some time before I came to a stop. There was a blue glowing light on the path ahead of me, coming closer. I took a cautious step towards it; then another. It was almost touching me before the light finally faded, and Kat stood before me. Her eyes were glassy with tears, and her face wrought with worry.

"Why do you go on?" she pleaded. "We have already failed, so why do you continue to an early death?"

"If death will come for me it will be on my terms," I said, surprised at how immediate and stoic I was more than Kat's sudden arrival. "Why do *you* return?"

She looked up at me, into my eyes, as though she was looking for some kind of answer to my question. "You don't have to do this!"

I grabbed for her shoulders, half-expecting my hands to go through, confirming this was illusion. When they found purchase I did not hesitate, and pulled her close. "Why do you mean to stop me?"

"Do you not think there is another way, now that the beasts are mortal? You could still have your day!"

I let her go and took a few steps back. "My day has come," I said defiantly. "If you were bound to see my—*our*, as you called it—quest through to the end and you now stand before me in opposition, it means your duty is done."

She shook her head, her demeanor hardening. "My duty is not done so long as you are still marching, it has merely altered."

Her tone was ominous. Something was tugging at my arm, drawing my hand towards the hilt of my sword. I fought it as I stared at her, watching her eyes. They never stopped searching. It was like they were watching everything all at once.

"I only wish I had the strength to restrain you; take you back to the Faeries and you can tell each other stories while you wait for the perfect moment to return to the world," she said, taking a step towards me. I stepped back. "But alas," she was holding her hands out, palms up, "I am not yet strong enough. I've learned so much; I just need you to not do what it is you plan to do." She seemed to surprise herself with an idea. "Actually, let me. I can end the night, and let the day return. I will go on alone; you return to Py."

"Who are you?"

Kat—or whoever stood before me—simply laughed. "Your trusty companion, of course! And we did so well!" She leaned forward. "But I didn't do well enough, and for that I am sorry." There was a disingenuous tone to her voice that didn't sit well with me, a bite that filled me with an anger that I couldn't quite understand at first.

As it blossomed I saw it more for what it was: I was tired of being misled. I stared at the Wisp on the path ahead of me, and while I wondered who she was—who she *had* been—I felt that anger spread out from my chest into my arms and legs. I felt it tugging at my muscles, wanting me to attack.

But I held back. I stared her down and I watched as she stared back. She smiled at me and sighed. "You won't turn back?"

I shook my head.

"Please don't do this," she cried. "It will be a death most terrible and you will suffer long for it. You still have a chance at life! Underground, like you had before! I could come with you, and we could stay there together!"

I pulled away from her, and though she continued to grab for me, I walked past her. "Like we had before," I repeated. "That wasn't life."

Path of Vengeance

Kat did not try to follow me, nor did I look back to confirm that she hadn't. When I broke through the tree-line, and found myself outside the forest, I was too taken aback by the sight to think about what stood behind me.

Before me was a long mountain path, winding through a rocky field that crested on either side with small peaks. There were collections of everything from rocks to boulders piled on either side of the path leading up the slight but steady inclines before the smaller mountains seemed to shoot up out of the ground. The peaks continued to the left and right, and I knew from my travels and from my lessons growing up that they encircled all of Alghast, breaking only for the Great Sea in Brakas. As the path went on, the ground grew darker, and the air around it was waving with the increasing heat as you got closer to the Mountain.

The path lead slightly up to the right before turning back on itself and up to a small cliff with an opening leading inside. I began walking, checking either side of the path, waiting for something to jump out from behind a pile of rocks; but nothing ever did.

Instead, I heard the familiar flapping of wings overhead.

It was almost as though a shock went through my whole body, an image in my brain of an attack coming from behind, and quick. All at once, something happened, and I recall moving to the right to avoid the attack—I just don't know how I moved so far, so fast. I was looking back on where I was and although I could recall moving, it seemed to happen all at once, even in my mind. I watched as Declan's talons scraped the ground below, where I stood only seconds ago, and he flew back up.

He hovered in the air, looking down on me as I stood, trying to hide my still nagging confusion about how I'd moved so fast before it finally dawned on me.

"You," Declan snarled at me, "you are a *festering wound* on this world; one that will not heal until you are erased!"

I stared back up at the dragon in the sky, looking fairly similar to Tal; though his brow was wider than it was long, and the end of his tail seemed more akin to an axe than a club. He also seemed to favor walking upright on his hind legs, which made me wish I had brought another spear with me, unless I could figure out how to—

Before I could finish thinking, Declan was screaming down at me, cutting through the air like an arrow. He made a sweeping slash, his arm running perfectly parallel with the ground and just hairs above it, sending small rocks and dirt flying upwards by the sheer velocity of it.

But I stood on the other side of the arm, watching as the rest of the dragon flew past me, unharmed. I turned to see it fly away, and re-called leaping over the strike; but it again happened in an instant, con-firming my suspicions: I had obtained the warping powers from the Emerald that Rayna and Father Paxton had used.

I was relieved; it would be a most useful power, indeed—I just needed to get it under control so that I did not use all of it.

Just enough to survive, I told myself.

Declan rose up into the sky again, churning fire inside of his maw. He faced me, pushing out his chest and pulling in more air to fuel the fire. "Your tricks and magic only rob me of the satisfaction of killing you with my hands!" He reared back and then threw his head for-ward, launching a stream of fire that blanketed the ground I was standing on, burning everything.

He held the stream for quite some time, and I could swear, some-where amidst the deafening scream of the fire was an impassioned wail of a brother in mourning.

When the fires stopped, and Declan floated weakly above, trying to catch his breath; I lowered my arm, the black tendrils of the Onyx retreating. I didn't let on how much of a toll the force of the fire had still taken on me; standing instead defiant, with an equally defiant smile upon my face.

Declan lowered to the ground, his breathing calming, and he stared at me. There was no surprise in his eyes; even the fires of anger had waned. He looked at me with sadness and desperate hatred. If he could cry, simply out of frustration, I was sure at that moment that he would.

"I wish nothing more than to grind you into a fine paste," Declan said at me, with a hiss like a snake, his voice dripping with hate. "You, and your entire species, all for the slaughter! I never even cared for the taste of you! I just enjoyed the sounds that you made; the screams of pain and agony; the *crunching* of bone; the *rending* of flesh: it was all *music* to my ears."

I stepped forward, towards the dragon. I held my sword down at my side, ready for him to strike at any time. "Perhaps you—"

"*You do not speak!*" Declan's voice seemed to echo all around me, booming and commanding. "You were an ill choice for the *gift* of speech; it should be reserved for only the *survivors!*" He began to run at me, pulling back both hands to prepare for a pincer strike.

I lifted my sword, and dropped into stance. *I've survived so far,* I thought to myself, and waited.

Declan closed the gap quickly, and when he brought his claws across in a sweeping motion, I warped back; away from the strike. I didn't wait for him to reset—he had leaned forward, as he waited only until he was sure he could reach me, even if it meant stretching out forward, a desperation to his strike that I knew all too well.

I warped back to him, and quickly planted my sword into the soft scales underneath. I heard a surprised yelp coming from above me, and just as I felt him try to pull away, I warped once more; this time it was on to the dragon's shoulders, making sure to not lose my grip on the sword. The speed at which I moved made the blade *rip* under the hard scales on its way around to the back, and the blade had pierced deep enough on the initial stab that it cut through everything *but* the hard scales, and the dragon's head and neck from the shoulders up fell limp to the ground; followed soon after by the body.

I nestled into a natural perch in the dragon's scales, and saw a vision of Azazel in the sky; the Rider, the Wizard, the Hero, the Villain, and now what was he?

Just a memory.

Using the Emerald was exhausting, not just to the supply of power that I had—I couldn't be sure the limits anymore, of anything, for that matter—but also to me physically. Though as the final twitches of the dragon below me ceased, I felt as though I was at my peak.

I climbed down from the dragon, and walked a few steps to get a feel for myself again. It was as though all the fatigue went away; even that which I had merely gotten used to. I ran at full speed for a distance—I was faster than I recalled, as well—and when I stopped I still needed to catch my breath.

I just caught it quicker.

I wiped Declan's purple-black blood from my blade. It was thick like tar. While I was looking at the sword, I pulled back my left hand, and tried to call the fires of the Ruby.

Although I was not entirely shocked, I was mildly amused when the blaze took hold of the blade, and burned the dragon's blood away in an instant, as though it were flammable itself; an interesting thought to say the least.

There I stood, in the center of the path. I looked to the Mountain and it looked back at me, as though it were waiting for me—as if it knew that we were reaching the end. I could feel a tension in the air between us I looked back, unmoving. Almost as if in response to my defiance, the Darkness seemed to offer another desperate attempt to dissuade me.

The piles of rocks, varying in size, that were littered on either side of the path, all the way to where the incline began, some hundred or more paces away from where I stood; they began to stir as tendrils of purple-black energy seeped from the ground around them and slid into the cracks between the rocks. One by one, the piles began to rise, taking the shape of something almost human-like; arms, legs, and usually proportioned not unlike a person—some even had appropriately shaped rocks for heads.

I was taken aback by their quickness. Either that, or I was so mesmerized by the Golems forming that I didn't notice two closing the distance fast. They weren't even the two closest ones; though they were also moving towards me quickly.

Part of me thought to stay and fight, but there was a desperation building within me as well—a tiredness; not physical, thanks to the power of the Sapphire: it was exhaustion. I had been all over the world to that point; I had seen everything that there was to see both real and legend. The only thing I wished to see again, more than the cities as they were when I was oblivious to their fragile nature; more than the people and the wildlife and the farms; and certainly more than daily grind that would likely return with them…I wanted to see the sun, breaking on the horizon like I remembered. We took it for granted, much the same way we seem to do everything; we counted on it being there until we never even thought about it, we just accepted that it would be there.

In that moment, it was *all* I could think about. I felt everything all at once: I felt the anger and the rage; I felt the overwhelming sadness at all that we lost; but most of all I felt determined. I was determined to reach the end of the path, and I did. There was only one dragon remaining, and she appeared to be in dire need of Darkness; if I pierced the Heart, was it possible that she could die too? As I ran, I began to use the warp a little bit more to dodge the Golems, who were throwing themselves at me, swinging at me with their arms at times and trying to tackle me others.

I reached the base of the Mountain, and began to climb. My heart was racing. I wasn't sure what I would expect inside. The higher I climbed, the hotter the air got. I was sweating so much that my hair was matting to my face, faster than the air could dry it. I wasn't sure if the Sapphire kept me hydrated as well, and I was too busy to question it. The Golems were crashing into the mountain side below me, combining and forming a large Golem that only grew in size as more rocks crashed into it; the purple-black core of Darkness swirling within, revealed in the cracks between the rocks orbiting it. I could almost hear its desperate scream as I outpaced its growth, and made it to the cliff as a rock hand came crashing down behind me.

The hand seemed to stay on cliff, though the arm retracted. The rocks in the hand rolled forward, forming two Golems, each with dark energy cores. They both looked to me, and I drew my sword, pausing for just a second before exhaling and turning abruptly, making a mad dash for the cave entrance, the golems in hot pursuit.

HEART OF DARKNESS

The inside of the cave was hot. It hit me almost immediately as I ran through the opening, across the wide stone bridge that was overhanging a pool of molten hot lava. The air was wavy from the heat, obscuring anything more than a few paces away.

My run slowed as the heat tore away at me. It felt as though my clothes should be melting away, but they remained. Even the power of the Sapphire could not keep me from feeling the effects of the heat as I pushed forward. I was screaming out, but the pain was louder, and I couldn't hear myself.

The Golems behind me were slowing as well; whatever energy that controlled them seemed ill-fitted for the climate, and began to fizzle out the farther in we got, until the rocks fell to the ground. Some even rolled into the lava below.

I struggled to breathe after a while and my vision became so blurry that I thought my eyes were melting. After several shaky attempts, I sheathed my sword in the fear the I would drop it if I continued to hold it.

In the distance I saw shapes appearing: there were four close to me, each of a different color; Red, Blue, Green, and Black. They were floating in the air about a foot or so off the ground, though they each were bound by chains attached to steel rings that ensnared each crystal around the middle. The closer I got to them, the less I felt the heat.

I heard something through the roar of the cavern; something rhythmic and without looking up or focusing my ears drowned out all other sounds except for it:

The heartbeat.

The visions started replaying in my head of the massive heart and the four crystals and I felt it all around me like a presence. I stopped ten or so paces from where the crystals floated in a line, and looked up. There, beating to a terrible rhythm, was the Heart.

It was massive—taller than me easily, and nearly twice as wide. I could see all of it, and reminded me of a cattle's heart. It was suspended by two sets of large veins and arteries: one going down, into the lava below, and the other leading up, breaking off and each disappearing into the rock walls on either side, which glowed red with the heat. I watched it beat, hypnotized by the sound. So much so that I didn't hear her voice at first.

"Please," she said, and I looked down to see Kat standing in front of me; only now the blue glow was gone. "I was wrong! Light *needs* Dark! There has to be another way!"

I shook my head at her. "We already tried the other way."

Kat's eyes, frantic at first, calmed. She stared me down, and her lips curled up into a twisted smile. "You weren't supposed to make it this far. I figured you would have died and joined me at the Cathedral. You would have made a good little knight."

I took a step forward, and she held out a hand. "Who are you?" I asked. "You are not the girl, Kat, are you?"

She shook her head. "Do not come closer, or I will destroy the crystals. The Spires will be useless then. At least now the Black Dragon is still mortal. Turn around and slay her, and you may fight what remains of my kin—*your* kin—for the surface. I will even return your precious Sun."

Behind her, all at once, the crystals gave off a sudden but noticeable glow. She didn't notice.

I looked up at the Heart, and then back to the thing pretending to be Kat. I was starting to piece things together. It was just a specter; a mouth from which the Darkness could speak. It was a manifestation based on memories. It was a manipulator, helping to push me on the path that would lead to Azazel retrieving the stones. Hell, it even helped convince me that I could be the one to return light to the world. It learned from me as I went; what it would need to do to push me forward, whether it was some hero complex or my own repressed guilt over the things that I had done.

"There *is* no other way," I said and the stones came to life, shining so bright that the already well lit cave was white. I trusted in a feeling, and it paid off. The crystals were somehow connecting to the powers in me, strengthening them. I used the warp, quickly dashing past the thing pretending to be Kat and, jumping off one of the rings holding the crystals, soared high into the air. I drew my sword, the fires of the Ruby burning brightly on them, and raised it above my head with the blade down. While time was still slow for me I brought the sword down, and drove it deep into the Heart.

It began to spasm wildly, but I held on the best I could. Blood poured out of it—at least, what I thought was blood until some landed on my boot and melted the tip, as well as some of my toe, away. The pain from the lava-blood was excruciating, but the Sapphire closed the wound quickly, and I didn't feel anymore pain after that. The black shield of the Onyx emerged from my arm, but didn't stop until it encased all of the pulsating heart as it began to ooze the red-hot liquid from every pore, protecting me from anything more.

There was a loud and piercing shriek, muffled by the shield around the heart, as though it were the one screaming. I could only imagine how deafening the wail would have been without the shadow encasing it. The cavern began to rumble, rocks falling from the overhang above me. I couldn't help but feel as though the cave itself was trying to knock me loose from the source of the Darkness—the same that had taken the Light. The Onyx splintered off from the case it had created around the heart and blocked as many rocks as it could from hitting me, but I had no worries about brushing off pain. My thoughts were singular by that point. The rest of the shield had closed around the hilt of the sword, and ran up the blade, protecting me from the heat of the bleeding heart while I held on during its death throes. The Onyx had mixed with fires of the Ruby as it traveled up the sword and around the heart. The red-hot blood was replaced by the bright flames of the Ruby, though they did not harm me.

The shriek, the one that had come from all around before, seemed to centralize below and I looked down as the Heart had fallen still. Kat —or whoever it was—had been looking up at me, face distorted in terror and mouth opened wide, and it seemed as though she had been controlling at least the tremors. Suddenly she transformed into a black smoke, and flew up at me. I'm not sure if it was the Onyx, the Ruby, or my own instincts that made me move, but I detached from the heart, sword and all, and pushed away from the still and shriveling organ. The smoke blew past, and the Mountain grew dark once more, save only for the colorful glow of the Crystals. Something took hold of me, some otherworldly force, and carried me back down to the ground below, back far enough that I could see all four Crystals shining brilliantly before me.

Before the Crystals, silhouettes stood—though it wasn't of the four I had talked to in Alduin. I could not make out distinct shapes; I could just see that they were all people. I couldn't even tell if they were male or female; the only distinguishing feature was the Crystal they chose to stand before.

"There is much for you to celebrate," the Ruby said.

"Though there is also much that must change," said the Onyx.

The Sapphire spoke up, "And much for *all* to learn."

"But first," said the Emerald, holding up a shadowy hand. "You should go outside." It gestured with the hand for me to turn around and I did. The opening to the cave was suddenly right there, and I stepped through it and out onto the cliffside.

I looked down and saw that all of the Golems had fallen back into piles of rocks. I then looked up at the sky, and saw the red that had covered everything was beginning to peel away like dead skin, disappearing into the ether as though it were never there in the first place. I felt a rumble beneath my feet, deep enough to almost cost me my footing, but I was able to steady myself. It rolled outwards, and down the Mountain side. I could see the piles of rocks vibrating as the tremor moved, picking up speed. The trees of the forests to the South shook with the quake.

I moved to the edge of the cliff and took a seat, following the tremor as it moved farther south until I couldn't see it anymore. I took a deep breath, the air feeling clearer than it ever had before, and I felt a snap, just behind my eyes. In a flash, I saw the cold, dark eyes of the Black Dragon, staring back at me, enraged. I quickly rose to my feet and looked out to the Necropolis. I felt something overtake me, and my eyes rolled back in my head, and all of a sudden my sight was careening towards the center of the world where the beam of dark energy was beginning to falter, and the Black Dragon began to stir.

And just like that, my vision was back to me. I dropped to my hands and knees, and struggled to catch my breath, the new sensation alarming me. I looked back to the cave, and saw that the glow of the crystals was dimming. I was losing their power quick.

I looked back to the South, and thought I could hear the sound of the wings—*her* wings—before I could even see the dragon coming. The shadow which began as an obscure black shape quickly grew and took on form, and I could feel her rage before I could see it in her eyes. She was already churning fire in her mouth, and I knew that she would unleash as soon as she was in range. When she did, I could run back into the caves, and that was about it; there was no quick way down, and I couldn't rely on the Onyx to keep me safe, even if she were also weakened.

There was a crack, loud and immediate that overtook all other sounds. Behind the dragon, from the Necropolis, there was a flash of light, pure white, that radiating outwards with enough force to move trees. It knocked over all of the rocks at the base of the mountain in the instant that it passed by, overtaking the dragon speeding towards me as well. And with the ring of light came a wall of sound, the thunder to go with the lightning, and it brought me to my knees. I covered my ears and looked up to see the wall, distorting the air much the same as heat does, retreating back from whence it came.

And when the retreating wall reached the speeding dragon, she suddenly stopped. She screamed out in confusion and panic, and seemed to be fighting a force that was pulling her backwards. I watched with just as much confusion as she was yanked away from me quickly. Other shapes and forms, pulled up from the woods below as the dome closed in, joined her. I watched until all of the shapes faded in the distance, but I knew where they all were going.

Though they had stopped to help me make it to the Heart, and deal the killing blow; the Crystals had dispersed their powers out once more to activate the Spires fully. The monsters—somehow this time including the Black Dragon—had been pulled back into the Pit, which was once again sealed, something I would confirm myself at the earliest opportunity.

The beam of energy, feeding the Moon, had also ceased. I spent a fair amount of time on the cliff, watching as the Moon continued to drift west as it had before. And I continued to sit, and I continued to watch, until the Moon had disappeared once more, behind the cliffs of Dewpond.

While I was still on the cliff, and was sure that the Moon had gone for now, I let my head hang. There was a feeling of relief that was washing over me. I had done what I never set out to do; I had finished the quest I never intended to undertake. Fate may have set me on the path, but I chose to finish it and the realization of that was washing over me. I resisted the urge to cry, though the tears came anyway when I felt a comforting warmth on my left, and a familiar tinge of pain in the corner of my eye. I knew what it was at once, and took a deep breath to prepare myself. I closed my eyes tight, and the tears fell freely to the dirt below me. I turned my head Eastward, and opened my eyes.

ACKNOWLEDGEMENTS

Thank you, for reading the book I never intended to write, that is blossoming in my mind into something that I cannot stop thinking about and building upon. It has been a journey from frustration to excitement as I write this, my first read-through of the novel complete and as I prepare to submit it for printing.

Black Moon started as nothing more than a writing exercise for me, a way to keep the muscles fresh for when I finally found whatever story it was that I had wanted to tell since I was in High School (I am 31 now), spurned on by two words on my whiteboard: "Black Moon".

The reason the words were up there was not related to anything in the book, either. It was merely a reminder that, should I record an album in 2018—as was the plan from the onset of the year—I would include a cover of the song, released by the group Emerson, Lake and Palmer in 2006. It was one of my favorite tunes by them, and I had always admired the underlying triumph I felt when I listened to their music.

I began with a prologue about the nature of being a hero. That prologue is no longer in the book, but would serve as a jumping off point. Between the title and the theme, I knew where I wanted to begin. And if not for my good friend Colin Anderson (on Google Play/ iTunes/Spotify, by the way) reading along as I wrote, sharing his enthusiasm for the story with me, there is still a chance that I would not have finished this, and thus wouldn't even be typing the story of how and why it came to be.

Then there's Courtney. I can't even begin to explain how important she is to all of this—even to her—so I won't even try. Without her to help keep my feet on the ground, I would have been lost to the clouds, without a doubt; a prisoner of my own mind if she wasn't around to listen to the ranting and raving, just to get it out, to unleash. She's been encouraging and supportive from "Go,," and I can't thank her enough for that.

But they weren't the only ones that kept me going. The 'Street Team' as I like to call them, inspired by the enthusiastic youth that represented up and coming bands, back in the day, is critical. Els, Alex, Christina, Cheryl, Britt, Will; brighter days are ahead—and as of this revision, for many of us, they're already here. April, Chris, Jason, Jen, Lou, Leah, and everyone else who ever listened to my ramblings or entertained my eccentricities: I thank you from the bottom of my heart.

It's an incredible feeling, to be able to look back and see the story that I told; to read the words that I wrote and get lost in them. I had wanted to do something creative with my life since I was young, dreaming of being a filmmaker or a video game designer or a musician...

But above all else, I wanted to be a writer. That was the constant throughout all of the dreams, and the visions of my future: I wanted to tell stories.

I had just convinced myself I wasn't very good at it.

I think differently now.

I'm excited to tell more stories.

With love,
Howard Scarrow

Patch Notes

Version 1.0 - December 13th, 2018:
- First released version. Edited by Howard Scarrow; contributing editor Colin Anderson.

Version 1.1 - March 2019:
- Acknowledgements 2.0
- Added "Edited by:" credit to the copyright page
- Fixed Book One's title placement
- Various stability and spelling fixes
- Added Author Bio and Alghast symbol to back cover.
- Updated cover
- Added social media
- Fixed alignment issues with chapters and titles
- Updated title to reflect additional volumes
- Adjust headers to include Author and Title

About the Author

Howard Scarrow lives in Sarnia, Ontario, Canada. Originally from the small town of Simcoe, Ontario, he has been dabbling in the creative and art for as long as he can remember. As well as this book, he also writes music, has developed at least one working card game, and many other projects that, for one reason or another, have yet to see the light of the day.